THE
FREEDOM
PLANT

Publisher's Note:

This book is fiction and all persons and incidents are fictitious. However, in addition to the pleasure of reading a good mystery and appreciation of the excellent writing, the reader will learn a great deal about the fishing industry on the U.S. East Coast in the last part of the 20th Century.

The story is set during the Cold War, a time of military and political stand-offs between the U.S. and the Soviet Union and it reflects the tensions of those times.

During the 1960s and 1970s, foreign fishing fleets, often doubling as intelligence-gatherers, hauled vast catches of fish from the North Atlantic, just off the North American coasts. Deeply and angrily resented by U.S. fishermen, who considered them both spies and poachers, Soviets, Japanese, and others ruthlessly fished and depleted the resources, leaving vast areas of pollution in their wake. Hostile confrontations and "incidents" were frequent: an American boat fishing off Pt. Judith, Rhode Island actually snared a submarine in its net; a (then-communist) East German ship rammed a Gloucester boat, leaving the crew for dead …

These "fishing wars," coupled with the lack of strong federal fisheries policies, constantly-changing regulations, weak or non-existent enforcements of the existing laws, and the resulting social and environmental damage form the real-life background of this novel.

THE FREEDOM PLANT

by
Capt. Kevin M. McCormick

THE GLENCANNON PRESS

Palo Alto
2007

Published by The Glencannon Press
P.O. Box 341, Palo Alto, CA 94302
Tel. 800-711-8985, Fax. 510-528-3194
www.glencannon.com

First Edition, first printing.

ISBN   978-1-889901-40-4
       1-889901-40-7

Library of Congress Cataloging-in-Publication Data

McCormick, Kevin M., 1953-
    The freedom plant / by Kevin M. McCormick.-- 1st ed.
        p. cm.
    ISBN-13: 978-1-889901-40-4 (alk. paper)
    ISBN-10: 1-889901-40-7 (alk. paper)
    1. Fishers--North Atlantic Ocean--Fiction. I. Title.
    PS3613.C3827F74 2007
    813'.6--dc22

                                                    2007027010

Dedication

For Dad,
whose overwhelming horse sense
was connected to a great sense of humor,

For Keith,
whose hands were connected to his brain
by a conduit of genius,

And for Nan,
Whose heart connected us all.

They that go down to the sea in ships,
    that do business in great waters;
    these see the works of the Lord
    and his wonders in the deep.

Psalms 107:23-24

Fishermen are chiefly to be cherished,
    for they bring in much wealth
    and ask nothing in return.

Sir Dudley Diggs
Addressing the English Parliament in the 1600s

CONTENTS

PROLOGUE:..xiii
1 — BOOTHBAY HARBOR..1
2 — DAMARISCOVE ISLAND HARBOR......................9
3 — DAMARISCOVE STATION...................................17
4 — THE CORNER ROOM..29
5 — THE WORKSHOP..37
6 — POOR SHOAL...43
7 — "RISE AGAIN!"...61
8 — THE POINT..87
9 — NANTUCKET LIGHTSHIP.................................101
10 — THE BRIDGE..121
11 — MAIL CALL...131
12 — THE RIGHT WHALE..143
13 — THE CORNER..161
14 — MUSKEGET CAN...175
15 — EDGARTOWN..197
16 — NOMANS...207
17 — NEWPORT...219
18 — NORTH OF VEATCH'S..225
19 — ON THE HEAP...237
20 — SID 'N' EVA'S CHAIR..245
21 — ABOARD THE ZVEZDA RYBAKA............................251
22 — IN THE LEE...261
23 — RULES OF THE ROAD...269
24 — THE ICE DOCK..281
25 — THROUGH THE SOUND.......................................291
26 — THE SEA WITCH..303
27 — RESERVED CHANNEL...313
28 — BOSTON..325
29 — SEBAGO...331
EPILOGUE...341
ABOUT THE AUTHOR...347

THE
FREEDOM
PLANT

PROLOGUE:
THE *ROWLEY KNIGHT*

"Try these on for size, Mr. Hitler."

Shop foreman Perling Hamalainen muttered under his breath as he closed the drawer to the munitions filing cabinet. He took the final brass shell casing, sealed it in waxed shipping paper, then loaded it into a wooden shipping crate alongside its sisters.

On the floor beside him was the output of the shift's twelve-hour grind at C.N. Grove Machine Works: Crates of 105mm howitzer shells destined for a munitions facility and, after loading with explosives, to be shipped to the troops across the big pond.

Over the last year, Ham had developed a ritual for the final shell of the day. Hardly perceptible in battle, but certainly noticeable to the eye, was a small engraving on the shell, running the length of the casing. The Finnish message, *Yhdysvallat isa*, literally meaning 'United States father,' went with each shipment. It was a personal code that Ham hoped would say hello to his son who was serving Uncle Sam in the infantry of the European theater. Holding spare nails in his mouth, he pounded the wooden crate shut.

Outside, snow lightly drifted to the ground as a cold breeze began to stir the flakes into small drifts, collecting against the factory doors. The streets were in total darkness — wartime conditions — save for the two splashes of light that escaped from the headlights of the truck that was backing into the loading dock. Ham passed the shipping order to the driver and limped into the darkness, making his way cautiously along the fifteen slippery blocks to home.

At the top of the front stoop, Ham's wife met him at the door, a steaming cup of tea in her hand. He kicked off his boots, took his tea and followed her into the kitchen, where he came face to face with an Army Chaplain.

The tea splashed on the floor.

"I'm very sorry, but on behalf of a grateful nation …"

~~~

FEBRUARY 1944
PORTLAND, MAINE

"Lord Jaysus, bye, I was yellin' t' the gang. Haul hard, she'll come easy! But you know what? You know what? More cussed numb than a bunch of pounded thumbs they were!"

Capt. Albert Helliott was holding court at Greene's Portside Bar, the waterfront tavern that served as his impromptu office between winter fishing trips. Bert Helliott was strong, stocky, gray-bearded and bushy-eyebrowed. He was best described by his own inimitable declaration, "tougher than a boiled boot and twice as smart."

"Let me guess, Bert, let me see if I can get this on my own," Mary Greene chided, as she waved her hands to stop the flow of the story. She winked across the bar to the other patrons, then offered, "I'll go way out on a limb here and take a wild guess that you pulled him aboard by yourself."

"Garr-en-teed ain't nobody got bigger mitts than these, bye, nobody!" Bert bellowed. He slammed his two paws down on the bar as he pontificated, "I yanked 'im aboard with one hand and lit me a cigarette with the other!"

As gales of laughter erupted, he promptly stole a cigarette from the man next to him, bent a match and lit it, oddly enough, with one hand. "You byes from the west'ard don't know nuthin' 'bout one-handin' anythin', but let me tell ya, back home in Newfoundland you learn some mighty quick tricks when you're freezin' and you gotta get a bag o' fish aboard. Which reminds me ... have I ever told ya aboot th' biggest codfish I ever saw?" Smoke rings curled from his mouth as he looked at the ceiling, waiting for someone to pick up the cue.

"No Cap, how big was it?" came the inevitable request from the end of the bar.

"Wellsuh, I'll tell ya. The biggest codfish I ever saw filled the whole of an eighteen foot dory." His large hand drew out the length in cigarette smoke along the bar. "Head hung over one end, tail hung oot the other." Speaking very slowly and softly he added, "But ya know, I never really told anyone this part before now ..."

Mary rolled her eyes, continued wiping her bar glasses and jumped into the discourse, asking, "What's that, Bert?"

"She filled a dory all right ... yessuh she did ... but that was just the liver!"

As laughter permeated the dockside retreat, two uniformed Coast Guardsmen observed the show from a corner table.

"That's your answer to our problem?" one whispered to the other. "Him?"

"Do you know anyone else with master's papers for more than a rowboat that isn't already taking a Liberty Ship across?" came the curt reply of the chief petty officer.

"Okay, Okay, but I joined the Coast Guard to save lives. Whose side are you on?"

"Look son, all he has to do is steam that old slab from Portland to Boston. Twelve hours on the water ... that old dog should know that route blindfolded. We get that ship to Boston, we help the front lines and that's how we save lives, get it?"

"Yup, you're right, Chief ... I guess. But how are we going to get him to take it? The last entry we have for him as master of a ship was a coastal oil lighter in 1935. He's been running his own fishing boat since then," said the bosun's mate suspiciously.

"Simple. With anything on the water the pointed end always goes first. You ever heard of Newfoundland Screech, son?" He detected the rise in curiosity and smugly answered his own question. "Finest gut-rot rum that man ever built. Now go to the end of the bar and

I'll show you what I mean." He looked straight into the face of his young charge. "Make sure you follow my lead or you'll be scraping barnacles off the dock pilings with your own backside."

CPO Lee Chambers strode to the bar. He raised his hand and, with a fingersnap, got Mary's attention over the raucous proceedings. Noticing who it was, she grimaced, but came and leaned over the bar, putting herself in close earshot.

"Darlin', you got any Screech back there?" the chief inquired.

"Lee, just what is it that you're up to now?" she asked in a low but very direct voice. "This can't be good."

"Mary, do I need to remind you there's a war on? I've got my orders, same as anyone else who wears a uniform, you know that."

"What I know is, if that Screech comes out, the world war makes Hitler look like a choirboy compared to Bert with a couple shots in him. Can you get the Marines back from the Pacific, or are you and that stilt-legged kid down the other end of the bar going to handle him?" she said, a deep frown creasing her brow.

"Mary, don't you have a boy over in Europe?"

She closed her eyes, exhaled loudly and shook her head in disgust. "I hope you know what you're doing. I want my boy home more than anything, but let's make sure there's something to come home to!" She frowned again and looked in his eyes, burning with the frustration of someone who knows when they are on the bad end of a deal. "I'm sure you aren't at liberty to discuss this, but it better be a wartime situation. It sure will be wartime to me!"

Mary reached down behind the bar, slammed the bottle down, then dealt out three shot glasses beside it.

"And what will the commander of the maritime press gang be drinking tonight?" she asked caustically. "And by the way, the bottle comes with a fifty dollar deposit."

The chief slapped down a one hundred dollar bill. "Keep the change. I'll have the usual," he replied.

Mary deftly turned to the tricks of the bartender's trade and poured two shots of the amber colored Screech, then in the third shot glass, mixed a small amount of brandy, cut with water, to perfectly match the color of the other two.

"Bombs away," she muttered, sliding the last glass to Chambers. "I'll just call the police now so they can stop in. Hopefully they'll get here at the first hundred dollars' worth of damage."

As Mary headed for the phone, the chief stood and gave a loud two-fingered whistle to get everyone's attention.

"Gentlemen, and … my dearest lady!" he announced, addressing the crowd, glancing at Mary Greene as his hand swept the air. "My young bosun's mate down there says he learned to drink rum when he earned the Order of the Dragon crossing the Dateline last summer. I say the only rum worth a real seaman's salt is that which is made in God's own country by the devil's own people!" He raised his watered down mixture, as he continued trolling for his catch. "Be there a real man among us who can educate this scrod about what is fair and good in this world?" His facial expression turned from that of genial town crier to that of the cocky hunter, showing he meant business in this challenge. "Real sea dogs drink Screech, am I right?"

"Garr-en-teed … garr-en-teed there's only one man here got that qualification, and if that kid only met the dragon once, I've still squeezed more water oot of my socks than that spawn ever sailed on!" Bert took the bait hook, line and shot glass and motioned for the concoction to be passed down the bar. Looking at his new student, he charged, "Old Son, them long legs of yours built of hackmatack or oak? Walk 'em down here and get yourself an ed-u-cation, Lanky."

"Lanky" smiled, enjoying his newfound nickname, until the burning glare of his commanding officer settled upon him. Chief Chambers motioned his head, silently ordering the lad to take his place on the battle line.

The rowdy crowd settled into a hush, some with jaws dropped open in surprise, some with eyes squinting in anticipation. Three men left hurriedly with the door still swinging, one watched Mary to see if she made contact with the police, the rest pulled their stools closer to watch the show.

"An appropriate toast, if you please, my dear sir," Lee asked.

As he raised his glass, Bert intoned Tennyson's immortal words, "'… there'll be no moanin' for me when I cross the bar'"

At the calculated moment of shared glances, all three hoisted and downed the screech. Chambers, of course, had no problem with his, while his mate came up coughing and blowing. The old Newfoundlander shook it off, like a slight chill, then, after catching his breath and wiping his eyes, managed to rasp out, "smoo-oooo--ooth!"

The tavern erupted into cheers as Mary grit her teeth and mixed the next round, same as the first. Her eyes constantly swept from her work as a chemist to survey the scene, looking anxiously for the arrival of the police and watching the participants in the time-honored show of manhood. No toasting this time, no pleasantries, no show; it was all business. She set 'em up, they sent 'em down, to the delight of the patrons who were viewing the ultimate clientele-provided entertainment.

Chief Chambers' plan was reaching a crisis in timing. His eyes were constantly moving, too. He had to work fast before the police arrived. Needing to speed up the process, he sweetened the deal with a twenty dollar bill … the first to toss back five rounds would get this prize. All the while, he was watching the street outside the window and watching Bert. *Watch those eyebrows, watch those eyebrows*, he thought.

At round number four, the bite of the Screech began to harden. Lanky's legs went from oak to rubber, his eyes went from saucers to slits, his arms from props to anchors. Reeling and swaying, the crowd steered him chairbound as he succumbed to the cumulative effects of alcohol and gravity and fell over backwards. Chambers nodded silently.

Bert staggered to his feet to declare victory as he downed the fifth round, As he rose, he noticed that Chambers was also standing. Rocking back and forth from heel to toe, the full effect of the cocktail kicked in. His last semi-clear thought was that he had been taken for a one-way ride.

Bert's eyebrows were a solid line of bushy rage. "Chammmmm-bers, you scurrrrr-vy dog, ain't no way you can hannn-dle that load. To the bottom is where you belong, and that's … where … you'll go!" he screamed.

Helliott reeled back on his heels, preparing to launch a barrel-house swing as his fists closed together. The cheering section rushed back as Mary Greene crossed herself and slid behind the bar, waiting for Armageddon to commence. Chambers saw those notorious eyebrows coming towards him and deftly side-stepped the sucker punch as the Newfoundlander's fist grazed past him. The missed shot only angered the old sea dog further. He tried to cut his losses by swinging a bar stool. Breaking glass was the only sound heard over the roar of Chambers as he grinned and egged his opponent on.

"You couldn't hit the broadside of a barn, you useless redfish picker!" Chambers yelled through a laugh of abandon. "My grandmother can fight better than that!"

The chief danced through the crowd to escape the onslaught, taunting his opponent as he went. As Bert's bar stool split the air like a tree limb cut loose in a hurricane, Chambers began to wonder whether he would actually have to defend himself for real. As the situation looked like it might become an all-out bar fight, he grabbed a chair and turned to challenge the enraged captain, hoping to buy some time. *Where are they, where are they?* he desperately thought. Like a streetfighter, he screamed, "Como on, come get me! You haven't got the guts, you hopeless piece of hookbait!"

As Chambers adopted the stance of a lion tamer and began to back away, he forgot one key development in his earlier strategy. He fell over backwards, tripping on the fallen hulk of his young bosun.

Bert yelled with a savage scream, then staggered over to his intended victim and readied himself to drive the stool into the Chief's skull. As if in slow motion, the wooden weapon was raised and began to swing in its arc of terror as Chambers covered his face with his arms, tightened his body and expected the worst. The whoosh of wood cutting air was all that was heard until, at the moment before impact, the stool's deadly mission was stopped short, grabbed within inches of Chambers' skull.

"Rearranging the furniture Bert?" The voice was that of Sergeant Mike Neal of the Portland Police. Neal swiftly knocked his free elbow into Bert's chest to incapacitate him, then brought the drunken sea dog's arm around behind his back, exerting enough pressure to create a sobering amount of pain.

"Bert, we've talked about this before, haven't we?" As the Sergeant lectured, he continued to twist Bert's arm further, accentuating every syllable with more pain. "Let-those-fists-go-and I'll let you go, but not — until!" he commanded. "Bert! For the love of Pete, knock it off!" he shouted.

Sergeant Neal's trained eyes carefully surveyed the battleground. Never releasing his grip, he was relieved as he caught sight of Mary Greene as she re-emerged from the safe haven behind the bar. He looked around, then down ... then groaned in disgust, shaking his head.

"Chambers! I might have known! ... Boys, put the cuffs on Bert, here."

He relinquished his arm hold, passing the babbling Newfoundlander off. Bert's handcuffed, defeated form was poured into a chair, with a careful guard kept over him.

"I hate to say this, but I think we arrived just one minute too quick, what do you think, Chambers?" Sgt. Neal asked as he extended his hand to help the chief off the floor. "One more minute would have taught you something, I think, but it never quite works out that way does it? On the one hand, I witnessed a dream come true, but on the other hand, the legal one, that is, we stopped an assault and battery with a dangerous weapon." Turning to the crowd he inquired in a sarcastic tone, "I need to ask who saw this and who started it. Now you all know the answer, so instead of arresting the whole bunch of you and sorting it out at the station house, I'll turn my back and someone tell us what we need to know."

For the second time that evening, the bar stood at a dead quiet, no one wanted to be the one who broke the silence. Everyone looked at the floor, everyone except Chambers, who was waiting for someone to complete his plan. Sensing that he might actually lose this stalemate, and the opportunity he sought to orchestrate, he kicked the sleeping bosun's mate's shins, hoping to arouse the only person who would turn the events his way. No response to the first kick, but on the second, the guttural moan gave way to a drunken exclamation, "I feel like I'm gonna die and its all that Newfie's fault …"

As Lanky's voice trailed off into a drunken slumber, Chambers seized the moment. "You heard it … you heard it! If I didn't jump in, Helliott would have killed that kid, pure and simple! Now Sergeant, you and I are both brothers in uniform and I'm sure you can understand what a uniformed man must do in times of attack. I'm really not sure what provoked this fine gentleman into this homicidal rage, but I won't press charges if you'll release him to me. I'm sure that this unfortunate incident can be rectified if I take him home and care for him. After all, aren't we all brothers of the sea?" Chambers lawyered at his finest rhetorical best, leaving the police officer an easy out.

"I don't know what you're up to here, but if I can get home before midnight, that sounds fine to me," the police Sergeant relented. "Okay, Chambers, we'll give you guys a lift and let Mary get back to business. Where are you staying?"

"Thank you kind sir, and may I add …"

"Can it, Coastie! I'm doing myself a favor, not you. Where do you want to go, and don't say Scowhegan, either."

"The three of us need only be delivered right down the bottom of the bulkhead, at Widgell's wharf, if you please." Chambers said.

"Widgell's wharf? The only thing there is that old hulk of the *Rowley Knight*. Is that where you're staying?" the policeman asked suspiciously.

"Shhhh. Loose lips sink ships, sergeant."

Chief Petty Officer Lee Chambers, a man who looked like W.C. Fields but employed the philosophy of P.T. Barnum, had once again proven why his superior officers always gave him the dirty work. Chambers was a master of manipulation via human nature, but it was his cynical use of Stalinist tactics that got the best results ... the front line troops are always expendable.

Dawn broke cold and clear over Portland harbor as a strong northwest breeze brought the Montreal express gusting over the water. The relative warmth of the thirty-four degree seawater showed in the rising vapor that water folk call seasmoke, making an eerie glow against the orange strains of the rising winter sun.

From up on the hill that makes the city of Portland, the eastward view was no different from many zero degree winter mornings, but surveying the seascape, one particular sight caught the eye of the many early risers of this blue collar town. Out of the seasmoke, rising above the white and orange creamsicle sky, a plume of thick black smoke curled skyward, then was caught by the wind and blown out to sea in a piercing horizontal spiral.

"Coffee's on, boys ... time to rise and shine! Got some of my mother's best biscuits here, got some beans goin' and got some snapper haddock fryin' up."

The voice of the ship's cook awoke Chambers as he squinted one eye open to greet the friendly gesture. "Looks like you folks survived a cannon fight, but just barely," the cook added, chuckling. "Is that our new skipper over there, cuffed to his bunk?"

"Yep, that's your boatdriver to Boston," Chambers rasped through the morning-after cobwebs. "Only he don't know it yet. Jeez, that coffee sure smells good. Will you give me a hand wakin' up the gang, Hoofie?"

"Sure thing, sure thing, I've got just the right touch to get this crew on its feet, by godfrey mighty, do I ever. This is an old ship's cook trick, Lee, so don't go stealin' it, now, will ya," Hoof Scott joked as he took a large pot and slid it over the sleeping bosun's mate's head. "You think this is easy, don't you, Lee ... well ... it takes a lot of classical music training to do this right, ya know."

For the second time in less than twelve hours, Lee Chambers was on his back, covering his head, awaiting disaster. He pulled the pillow over his head to cover his ears ...

BOING! BOING! BOING! went the sound of ladle against pot as the ship's cook used his time honored technique to raise the rumsick. BOING! BOING! Hoof hesitated for a few seconds, smiled a big wide grin, then raised the ladle again, but cut his swing short when he detected life within his victim and the sound of a weak and shaken bosun's mate pleading for mercy.

"Stop shooting, I surrender," came the muffled echo from within the pot. "On second thought, please kill me, please shoot me ... anything to stop this headache!"

"Whatdya think of that, Lee? Shall we try it on the corpse over here?" Hoof asked with a mischievous zeal in his voice, the ladle swinging like a drum major's baton. But before he could strike up the band, the next victim shook his head awake.

"Lord Jaysus ... Lord Jaysus, Hoof, I've eaten some of your mug-ups, ya know ... that's not the first time you stewed up someone's head and passed it off for a meal. You get that thing near me and I'll teach you how to eat it!" But as he tried to move his hands, Bert realized he was handcuffed to the bunk. "Where the hell am I and what's goin' on here, and how come I'm chained to the rack and what the hell are you doin' here, Hoof?" Bert bellowed as he rattled the bunk with his body, attempting to break free.

"Well, as I live and breathe, the Old Dog 'imself has come back to the merchant fleet. Welcome back, Bert, it's been a few years since we've been shipmates ... if I knew that was you over there under the feathers I would've gone a little easier. By godfrey mighty," Hoof exclaimed incredulously, "the Old Dog, me and Dick Spring together for one last haul down the coast. You weren't kiddin' were you, Lee? How in the name of godfrey did you talk 'im into it?"

"Before you get any ideas, he ain't talked me into anything short of a Screech rumsquall, and you and me and especially Dick Spring ain't goin' nowheres!" Bert interrupted forcefully. "The last I heard of Dick he'd lost both legs from a torpedo and was damned lucky to be alive. He's up in Bangor living with his daughter, and that's a good place for 'im, away from here! Lord Jaysus, Hoofie, where in hell are we? … you'd better give me a straight answer and for the luvva Pete, take off these cussed fool handcuffs!"

"Bert, look around ya, look around ya … the last time we were here was fifteen years ago, before we tied up the old girl at Searsport. Good thing they never scrapped her, huh? The three of us are back on the *Knight* again! Just like the good ol' days, by godfrey!"

Bert struggled to sit up as best as he could and gazed around him. The cramped bunks did look vaguely familiar. He craned his head around and looked down the companionway where the smell of coffee and biscuits filled the air. He turned the other way, and by straining at the handcuffs, managed to hike himself up to peek out of the portlight. When he got the view, he could see the funnels bellowing black smoke. It was the *Rowley Knight*, alright, and she was building steam. He laid back down in his rack, shook his head and closed his eyes with a loudly, exhaled "phew."

"Garr-en-teed ain't no way there's a man alive who can stoke those boilers like Dick. No one could run this engineroom like Dick, but like I say, he's up in Bangor at his daughter's, with no legs, for Pete's sake. Who the hell is down below in this sled, anyway, but besides that, I ain't goin' nowhere in this rig and neither are you! If these cuffs don't come offen me, I'll chew my arms off like a trapped muskrat before I sail on this slab again! Hoof, it's been nice to see ya, but now, Chambers, it's time to let me on my way. I'll go see Mary and settle up with her if I did anything, God knows I can't remember."

Chambers had been waiting silently, letting the cook do his welcome and break the news. He could see that the old boy network wasn't enough to complete the plan, so he started with plan B.

"Bert, we'll get those cuffs off you real soon, but first we've got to talk a little business. First off, I owe you a twenty spot for the fifth round of Screech, you won that fair and square." He stuffed a twenty dollar bill into Bert's shirt pocket and buttoned the flap. "Have you ever heard of the *Mount Washington*, Cap?" Chambers asked with his squinted eyes trained on the Newfoundlander.

"Yup, big hill in New Hampshire, but what's that got to do …"

"Not the mountain, the cruise boat … the excursion boat, on Lake Winnepesaukee," Chambers interrupted. "The boat the tourists take around the lake in the summer, you ever heard of that?"

"Sure, I've heard of it, but …"

"But this, Cap! The *Mount Washington* was cut in two and hauled overland to Portsmouth. They conscripted it, took it like a lot of other boats. They put it back together to use in the war effort along the coast. Do you have your war risk insurance paid up on that dragger you own, what's the name of it, the *Renegade*?"

A great wave of fear settled in Bert Helliott's stomach. Nothing was more precious to him than the boat that encompassed his entire savings and his livelihood. The *Renegade* was the culmination of his life's work, his identity, his escape, his wife, mistress and daughter.

"You can't take her for the war, you can't, Chambers," Bert pleaded with his eyes closed. "For God's sake, man, she's only sixty-eight feet overall, that's not big enough to mount a gun in the hold, not like some of the other draggers on the sub patrol like the *Saint Nicholas* or the *Riptide*. She's no good to you … you can't take her … you just can't. Please! … isn't there some other way?"

"Relax, Bert, I don't want your boat, but the papers are right here in my shirt pocket, see?" Chambers unbuttoned his pocket and held out the papers for the downtrodden fisherman to view. "I told 'em the same thing, but you know those desk commanders at the First District in Boston. My orders are to get this ship to Boston. Any ideas, Cap?"

The Newfoundlander was at checkmate, handcuffed to a bunk in a ship that was to be scrapped fifteen years ago, fighting for his life's work and losing the battle with a screeching Screech hangover. He closed his eyes, then muttered, "If I take this heap of scrap to Boston, can I keep the *Renegade*?"

"You do your part, I'll do mine, Old Dog."

"How can I trust you to leave my boat out of it?"

"That's why your old drinking buddy, Lanky, is going to sail with you. He'll have the papers with him and will give you all three copies as soon as you pass Graves Light. He's also instructed to get you guys up to the Old Howard Theatre once you hit the wharf at the Army Base in Reserved Channel."

"The Old Howard? Lord Jaysus, where they have certain shows …?"

"Certain shows that everyone knows," Chambers jumped in. "It's a twelve-hour run from here to there, how hard can it be?"

"I can do it, I guess, but garr-en-teed you still need someone in the engine room who knows this old sled. Dick was the only guy who could keep her goin' but he can't do this cussed stuff anymore, bye."

Chambers smiled a broad grin and threw the handcuff keys to the ship's cook. Hoof caught them one-handed and unlocked the cuffs. "C'mon, Bert, you've got to see this to believe it!" the cook exclaimed as Bert sat up and rubbed his wrists to relieve the stiffness. "By godfrey, you won't believe it!"

Hoof grabbed his cane with his good hand and shuffled off down the companionway to the galley, his five-foot-five frame making a beckoning gesture as he stopped at the end. Bert followed hesitantly. As Hoof basked in the delight of seeing his old shipmate, he loped along, then turned the corner. It was the galley of the *Knight*, alright. The same table running down the middle of the deckhouse sole, the same oil-fired stove over in the corner, the same beans on the top, and that same great smell of Hoof's mother's biscuits in the oven. A crackling of frying emanated from the huge skillet that was cooking up small fillets of haddock. He paused at the stove long enough to prop up the cane under his arm and move the mug-up's pans to the warming rack on the back of the stove.

"By godfrey, I am an artist in the galley, ain't I? C'mon, Bert, don't stop there, not just yet, you've still got to see the best part!" Hoof exclaimed, like a kid on Christmas morning.

He motioned for Bert to follow him to the end of the companionway, where he stood at a haphazardly constructed rail and looked down ... way down. Hoof gathered up a rope leading into the abyss below and pulled on it three times, making a signal to the bowels of the ship. Pretty soon, the rope tugged back at Hoof's hand and he turned to face the Newfoundlander with a big cheshire cat grin.

"Okay, Bert, how's it go, haul hard, she'll come easy?" the cook quipped. "Take this line and throw it over that snatchblock there and then we haul hard, by godfrey. Let's get the rest of the boys to help."

Chambers and his shaking mate soon joined in on the rope and all hands began to haul away, chanting the familiar "yup" as they pulled in unison. "Yup," pull, "yup," pull, went the hand-over-hand rotation as the line slowly inched its way to the top. "Yup," pull, "yup," pull, until a panting crew saw the four-way bridle of the hoist come into view. "Yup," pull, and the next thing to come into view was two burly forearms, holding on to the hoisting bridles. "Yup," pull ... the next view was a wheelchair, and sitting in it was a man of slight frame, almost too slight for the size of the arms clutching the hoisting bridle.

"Cleat that line off. Swing him over here, now, and we'll get some breakfast underway, by godfrey."

Bert Helliott was beside himself with wonder, his chin about to hit the deck, his mind working in total disbelief. Staring back at him, swinging from a makeshift elevator, was the mirror image of another person who was having trouble comprehending what he was seeing.

"Oh gawwwd ... I don't believe it ... the Old Dawwwg 'imself. Well, Lee, you did it, but dammed if I know how! So how's things with you, Bert?"

Bert cleared his eyes and took another look.

"Dicky, Lord Jaysus! What in the luvva Pete you doin' here?"

"Makin' steam, Old Dawwwg, nuthin' new 'sides that," Dick Spring drawled matter-of-factly with his slow Maine accent.

Bert's eyes were uncontrollably drawn to the seat of the wheelchair. It was true what he had heard, Dick Spring had lost both legs. As he stared at the sight of his old friend in such a state, Dick saw the Old Dog's gaze and broke the awkward silence.

"Bert, you've gotta remember, a guy my age only keeps things below his belt for old time's sake, anyway. I was one of the lucky ones, ya know. Rest of the gang went down."

"What ... how ... how are you doin', Dicky?" Bert stammered out in disbelief, not able to tear his gaze away from where his old shipmate's limbs once were.

"Better than ..."

"Better than ... what?" Bert asked confusedly, looking up, forgetting this ritualistic greeting.

"Better than sittin' on a sharp stick, Old Dawwwg, ayuh." Spring felt his stomach rumble. "Hoofie, I hope you got me up here for a mug-up. Should we tell the boys?"

"By godfrey, its getting cold, c'mon, times-a-wastin!" Hoof grabbed his cane, limped up the companionway to the galley and starting rustling dishes.

Chambers turned to his young mate. "Son, find your way to the engine room and send up the gang so's they can eat. You stay there and watch things until they get back. Hoof'll keep yours on the back of the stove."

"You can have mine, anyway," Lanky mumbled as he stumbled for the ladder.

The crew sat down at the galley table to partake in the old seaman's tradition of a great meal spiced with conversation. The cook served up steaming platters of food. As soon as Spring wheeled into position alongside the table, the men filled their plates and set to the business at hand.

"Who've you got down there with you, Dicky?" Bert inquired between bites.

"The best damn crew on the coast ... my two nephews, ayuh. Oh ... here they are now ... say hello to the Old Dawwwg, boys." The two youngsters smiled, nodded and sat down, piling their plates high.

"Lord Jaysus, they was just a twinkle to a dime, last we were together ... they old enough for this?"

"Same age as when we started, Old Dawwwg, fifteen and fourteen, just like us. I got 'em trained as to what to do. All the valves and controls are marked — they're just doin' what my legs and hands can't. Doin' real good, too, good kids, ayuh."

"Just like us ... God help us." The Newfoundlander shook his head. "This rig gonna run?"

"Bert, it's the same as what I told them jerks up in Searsport years ago. Those are Hodge boilers down there ... you'll never kill 'em. We cleaned out a few clinkers, fired 'em up, Danny towed us down and we tied her here while we finished. You were out fishin' so you missed the whole thing. I can tell you this, Old Dawwwg, she's makin' steam for us, ayuh, you just find us the way to the Old Howard!"

"Alright, I guess," Bert relented, turning his head. "Chambers, what are they gonna do with this sled, anyway? She won't make it to Europe, especially in the winter. Boston, sure, then what? My deal's to Boston, nothing farther."

"Well, Cap, there's a couple of reasons why. First off, they want it for a floating storage barn right there at Boston Harbor. She probably won't leave there, except for target practice someday. You know, Peddocks Island is bustin' at the seams with German POWs. They figure that the storage building can house another five hundred, and the *Knight* will take its place. I figure that any German soldier that's stuck on Peddocks won't be shooting at our guys, so let's open up another hotel for them."

"Okay, that's simple, what's the second reason all aboot?"

"This came a few days later. Out at Selkirk, New York, there's a big railyard ... a huge rail switchyard. Anything coming from the

Midwest goes through there. Well, a train of fifteen cars got diverted to Portland during that last ice storm that hit Boston and the Cape around the first of the year. The signals got screwed up so they sent them here to get to Boston on the B&M line. Since that storm, the swing bridge across the Merrimack River at Newburyport is stuck open, too, so the railcars were finally sent down here to Widgell's and the cargo was loaded onto the *Knight* during the last four nights."

"I remember that bridge well. Used to run oil up there in one of Socony's lighters. It never worked right, even in summer. So what's aboard this rig?"

"Got the bill of lading right here. Let's see, forward hold ... engine parts ... GM engines for PT boats built in Ipswich ... reels of copper wire ... howitzer shells ..."

"Garr-en-teed ain't no way I'm taking ammo anywhere! Keep the *Renegade*, I ain't haulin' no shells nowheres!" Bert stood up, threw his fork in his plate in defiance and started to storm out, eyebrows clenched. As Hoof raised his hands and stood to quell the mutiny, Chambers blocked the way and turned to the cook for reassurance. "Hoofie, tell him what's in those shells, will ya?"

"Nothin', Bert, nothin', I swear. They're brand new shells from a machine shop in Wisconsin. They ain't primed, loaded or nothin', just hollow brass tubes. We checked 'em ourselves, every crate. I know where you're comin' from, but there's nothin' in 'em, and I'll swear that on Beulah's grave, by godfrey mighty!"

Bert stopped short when his eye caught sight of Dick Spring, sitting quietly, eating his mug-up flanked by his two nephews.

"Whatta you think, Dicky?"

"Ayuh, I'm goin', Bert, that's all there is to it. Since we lost Richard on the *Arizona* I've had no choice but to do what I can. I can't mount a rifle on this wheelchair ya know." Dick took a long breath and swung his head from side to side, exchanging knowing glances with his young engine room crew. "The boys and I have already discussed it. If you don't take it, they'll carry me up to the wheelhouse. License or not, I'll get us down to Boston, or close enough for a tug to grab us."

"Lord Jaysus, what's in the aft hold, rattlesnakes?"

"The bill of lading lists farm products, that's it. The hatches are all battened now, but look if you want to," Chambers offered.

Bert took another look at his old shipmates and shook his head in disgust. "You byes can't hog all the fun, I guess. When are we going to …"

The *Rowley Knight* took a lurch toward the dock, while a noticeable thud hit the hull outboard of the galley. The crew looked at each other with alarm, but Chambers just nodded and looked at his watch.

"Yup, there's the *Winslett*, right on time a half-hour late at the crack of eight. You gents know Danny, 'Half-Hour' Hall, don't you?"

Before anyone could answer, a knock came on the outboard porthole. A black watch cap on top of a grinning face appeared in the glass, his wintered cheeks nearly swallowing his eyes. Hoof ambled over, loosened the dogs that held the porthole closed, and swung it open. The skipper of the tugboat *Winslett*, Danny Hall, pushed his face through the porthole and sniffed the pleasant aromas coming from the galley. He was standing on the rail of his tug, while his mate made their lines fast to the *Knight's* bitts.

"I knew it! Hoofie, I could smell those biscuits from the dock at Peak's Island! Let's have a few of those for the road, eh? Dick, is she gonna go under her own power?" Half-Hour Hall asked in his energetic, raspy, high voice.

"Ayuh"

"Gotta hand it to you, Lee, you got the Old Dog to take her, though I don't know how. Good to see you, Bert, you ready to roll? I've got an oil barge to take back to Chebeague by noon. Gotta get rollin'."

"You're full a-speed in a tight circle, as usual, Danny," Bert countered. "How far can you tow us?"

"You should be fine if I get you between the Head light and Cushing Island, shouldn't you?"

Bert shifted his gaze to Spring, looking for a confirmation. Spring looked up from his plate and nodded an assuring yes, took a last sip on his coffee, then started down the companionway in his wheelchair, his two nephews following.

"All right, then. I'll make-up to pull you off the wharf, then come around and get on a head tow. This nor'west wind is going to set us, so we've got to look sharp!" To Danny Hall, this was just another ship in another day's work. To the crew aboard, it was anything but. "You bound out, Lee, or are you going to jump ship now?"

Chambers quickly answered, knowing Hall was always in a rush to be late somewhere else. "Give me a second, Danny! Just let me shore up my mate when he gets up top here. I'm going ashore! Just give me a second!"

Bo'sun's Mate Lanky Anderson appeared in the companionway as Dick Spring was being lowered to the engine room by his nephews and the ship's cook. He helped man the human winch, then reported to his commanding officer. Chambers passed the papers for the *Renegade* and the bill of lading to him, then gave his final instructions.

"Stay on the wheel with Helliott and get that ship to Boston. Give him these papers when you get to Graves Light … you know where that is, don't you?"

"At the entrance to Boston Harbor, Chief."

"Take this fifty dollar bill to get yourself a truck from the motor pool. For that fifty, that'll get you guys on the road and will get you directions to the Old Howard, if you play your cards right. Any questions?" Before Lanky could answer, Chambers gave his final order: "Remember, this is wartime. The Old Dog'll know this, but anyway … radio silence, got it?"

"C'mon, Lanky!" Bert yelled from partway up the stairway. "Danny's got half the lines offen us. Let's get up to the idiot box of this sled and steer her oot of the harbor."

Chambers bolted for the outside and just made the leap to the dock before the ship began to pull away. A long, loud blast from the horn, signalling the *Knight* was entering the channel, rattled him.

Well, he remembered where the horn was, anyway, Chambers thought as he composed himself. With hands on hips, he turned and watched the ship as the tug *Winslett* came around to attach a towline to the bow. Black smoke poured from its funnels. "Give 'em some steam, Dicky," he mumbled.

Chambers stood on the pier and watched until the hull of the old coastal freighter was swallowed by seasmoke. As she left the harbor, all that could be seen above the rising vapor was the masts, the wheelhouse, and the smoke of the boilers, jogging eerily above the winter mist. With this job behind him, and more to go, he pulled up the collar of his pea coat, bent his shoulder into the wind and made his way towards town.

The trip through the inner harbor was uneventful, the *Winslett* chugging away, towing the *Knight* at a manageable headway speed. On the bridge of the ship, Capt. Bert and Mate Lanky were settling in, the Old Dog laying out compass courses for the next leg of the journey and Lanky steering the ship so as to keep step with the towboat ahead.

"See here, now, Lanky, pay attention. Now, we're going to go south of the Jordan Reef buoy, south of Pine Tree Ledge buoy, then make off for the buoy south of West Cod. From there we'll go to the Lightship, then lay in a course for just outside of Boon Island Ledge, then outside Dry Salvages, outside Thatcher's Island, then straight on to Graves, through President Roads, and then to the Old Howard, by the Lord Jaysus! We can go by sight as long as the sun cooperates and keeps this mist burned off enough to see the buoys."

As Bert's massive fingers traced the route on the chart, he began to emanate a confidence that the trip would go well. Lanky, standing at the wheel, began to lose his queasy night-before feeling. *How bad can it be?* he thought, *I'm clear of Chambers for a couple days, and I'll be at the Old Howard in twelve hours.*

One thing the *Knight* always had was steam, good steam. The radiators in the wheelhouse banged and clattered as they circulated heat to the steering station and the two men occupying it. The sounds brought a reassuring familiarity to the Old Dog, even though he wasn't conscious of it. He took a second to look around him, then smiled. *On the* Knight *again with Dicky and Hoofie, with Half-Hour towing us off ... Lord Jaysus, what next?* he thought.

"We should be able to see from Thatcher's to Graves if it's clear, Lanky," he announced. "Now I'm figurin' the course from the Lightship to Boon is sou'west by west. See, she's a little touchy on her east-west deviation, and I'm leavin' a little leeway for the nor'west to set us off a little, how's that sound to you, Lanky?" Bert asked.

"Great. What's that in degrees?"

"De ... what? ... Degrees? ... Degrees! I thought you were a bosun's mate? Ain't you guys s'posed to be boat handlers?"

Lanky's confidence was short lived. "I'm ... I'm ... kinda used to using numbers to steer by, Cap," he answered sheepishly. "That's the way they taught us."

"Well, I'll teach you how to lay off a course from the school of H-N."

"H-N?"

"That's right, bye, Hard Knocks. Now go down on deck and stand by that forward bitt. Listen for my signal when we're clear of Danny."

The *Knight* and the *Winslett* rounded the point and headed for the open ocean. Some long rollers left over from the previous night's storm greeted them, and against the northwest wind, shot some white caps that bounced off the sterns of both vessels. Bert folded his hands over the spokes of the wheel and looked at Cushing Island buoy coming up on the port bow. Out the starboard window, Portland Head light was standing guard. *This is it*, he thought.

Up ahead, the *Winslett* gave two quick toots from her whistle, then began to slow her speed. Lanky made his way to the bow and stood by the towing bitt, ready to release the line on command. Bert grimaced and gave one long blast on the *Knight*'s horn, then rang the ship's telegraph for slow ahead. *I'd rather know now if she doesn't make way*, Bert thought. *C'mon, old girl. Trot, trot to Boston.*

Lanky looked to the wheelhouse for a signal as Danny Hall looked to his vessel's stern and turned off to the northward, keeping just clear of his tow. He watched cautiously to see if he was going to be bringing the ship back home or scrambling to get out of its way. His deckhand stood by the bitt, ready to retrieve the towing hawser, or if necessary, cut it with the fire axe.

"I don't know how you're going to do it, but give us some power, Dicky," Bert nervously said to himself, drumming his fingers on the helm. "You didn't fail us on the first trial, so don't start now."

More seconds passed … and passed, but this time, the Old Dog smiled as he pulled on the horn lanyard to sound the "all clear" long blast. With a jolt, the *Rowley Knight*, once a proud denizen of the eastern seaboard, once a derelict sold for scrap, was under her own power, heading for Boston once again. Lanky let the hawser slip free, and as fast as it was retrieved aboard the *Winslett*, the *Knight* slipped past the tug's stern and headed for the open sea.

"Sweet Love of Jesus," Danny "Half-Hour" Hall whispered, his hands on his hips. "I guess the Almighty does love drunks and fools." Looking to the southwestern sky, he asked aloud, "Keep an eye on 'em, will ya?"

Lanky stumbled aft to get his breakfast and the Old Dog stayed on the wheel, guiding the old sled out to the Lightship, then made the turn for Boon Island. The northwest wind beat against the broadside of the hull making some spray freeze on the deck as the ship lunged and rolled on its course. After about twenty minutes, the smell of coffee filled the warmth of the wheelhouse as Lanky and Hoof climbed the stairs to the idiot box.

The ship's cook gave a mug of coffee to the Old Dog and said, "By godfrey, she feels good, don't she, Bert?"

"I'll have to admit, she feels pretty cussed good, yessuh she does ... Lanky, see this course I'm on right here ... just steer that, okay? Hey Hoofie, have I ever told you aboot the biggest codfish I ever saw?"

The smiling cook winked to Lanky, who was standing at the wheel, then answered with his cheshire grin, "No, Bert, how big was it?"

The next few hours went along like clockwork. The sounds of the wheelhouse alternated between laughter, lies and memories, all punctuated with the ever-present banging and clanging of the heating system. Spray hit the deck and wheelhouse, instantly freezing into a slick surface. The seas stayed at six to eight feet, the sky was clear and so was the coast.

At half-past noon, the *Knight* eased outside of Boon Island Ledge and was making good time for Dry Salvages buoy outside of Cape Ann. Below, Dick Spring and his crew of recruits were basking in the warmth of the boiler's glow. Spring himself felt a proud glow from within for making the mission succeed and an even warmer inner feeling watching his two nephews make it happen.

In the wheelhouse, Lanky, Hoof and the Old Dog were enjoying the ride, when Bert suddenly raised his hand abruptly in mid-sentence. "Did you hear that, Hoof?"

"What?"

"That bang!"

"What, the radiator? By godfrey that's been ..."

"There it is, again! That's not the radiator, Hoofie!"

Bert went over to the lee side window and lowered it, then craned his neck outside to hear. All three wheelhouse partners stood motionless to listen but heard nothing. After a while, Bert pulled his head back in and pulled up the window, but still wasn't convinced. Silence pervaded the once jovial steering station as all three exchanged glances.

"There ... you must've heard it that time!" the Old Dog exclaimed, looking for someone to agree with him, though deep down, he hoped he was wrong.

"By godfrey Bert, how much Screech did you get into last night? I don't hear anything but that damn fool radiator," Hoof said through a hint of fear.

Eyebrows closing, Bert turned to Lanky. Uncharacteristically calm, speaking from intuition, he said, "You still got them papers on you?"

"Sure, but you know Chief Chambers said to wait until ..."

"Never mind the papers on the *Renegade*, son. I mean the bill of lading ... the cargo ... what's in the aft hold?"

Lanky fished inside his shirt and unfolded the paper. "Farm products, that's it ... just farm products."

The Old Dog thought for a second, then sprung into action. "Hoofie! Get on that wheel! C'mon, Lanky, let's go see what's in the aft hold! Move!"

The two scrambled to the deck below, made their way across the rolling icy deck and undogged the access hatch to the after hold. Spray shot over the rail as the northwest wind slapped the sea against the starboard side.

"Get down the ladder and tell me what's in there!" Bert yelled over the sound of the wind as salt spray pelted him in sheets, freezing to his shirt.

The Bosun's Mate climbed down the ladder and looked around, then echoed back to the deck above, "It's burlap bags ... they're marked grain ... that's farm products, right?" he yelled above. *As long as it's not ammo!* he thought. Once again, the haunting "bang" sounded, only this time, Lanky heard it too.

"Son, throw some of those bags aside. Work your way into the pile a little bit! See if that stuff is dry or not!" Bert ordered.

The young mate did as ordered, then yelled back to the Old Dog, "You're right, once you get in a little bit, the bags are wet ... below that, it's just all grain ... they must have just dumped 'em in when they off-loaded the train. So what? Are you planning on baking bread?"

"Get up here quick, son! NOW!"

Lanky looked puzzled as he scrambled up the ladder, heeding the urgency in Bert's voice.

"Now listen, son, get up in that wheelhouse and tell Hoofie to change course to nor'west by nor'd three-quarter nor'd, got it? If we're lucky, we can make it to the beach at Plum Island ... that's the best stretch of sand inside of us; good clear run, better than Wingaersheek. After that, go tell Dicky to give it all she can handle and start all the pumps, then hook him up on that cussed lift line and get him and those kids up on deck!"

"But ... but ... what's going on?"

"Lord Jaysus, bye, a flatlander like you should know what happens to wet grain ... it expands ... just like when water freezes! It can part iron in two! It's prob'ly got a seam of rivets loose, which is givin' it more water. Get your long legs to do their duty, Lanky, or our next port is Fiddler's Green!"

~~~

Two Coast Guardsmen were on patrol on the outer beach of Plum Island.

"I think I see something over there."

"Where?"

"Over there in the surf. My God, it looks like a body!"

Splashing chest deep into the winter surf, they grabbed the bobbing, lifeless body of a teenage boy. With frostbitten limbs, they carried the boy across the wind-whipped dunes to the Knobbs Coast Guard Station, but it was no use. He was long gone.

The flotsam and jetsam tossed ashore gave a positive ID that the wreckage was from the old coastal freighter *Rowley Knight*. War was war, and the ever-present German submarine threat gave a ready explanation as to the poor lad's demise. But why was he clutching the handle of a wheelchair?

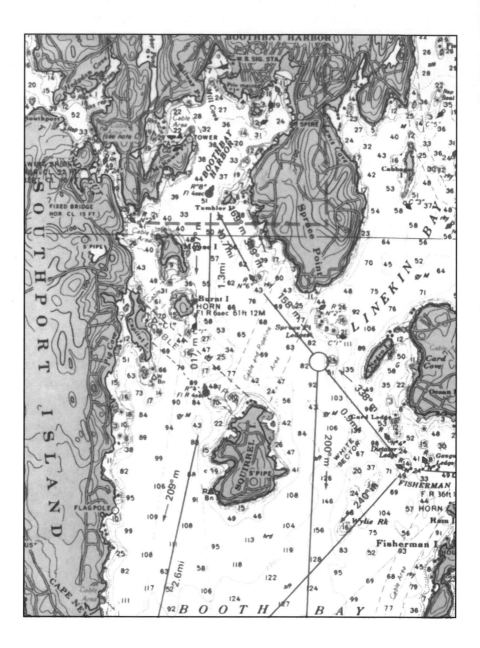

1

BOOTHBAY HARBOR

LAT. 43 DEG. 51.1 MIN. N.
69 DEG. 37.7 MIN. W.

Boothbay Harbor, Maine
June, 1995.

"Yuh, that's right, two and a half miles southeast of th' Cuckolds Light, yuh, there's a gong buoy they-uh. You'll prob'ly hear it, bein' that close to th' water, I 'spect. You sure you know what you're doin' in that damned contraption?"

"I've been all the way from Eastport in this, but that's nothing, really. Some cultures used these boats for centuries. This is the same design, it's just made of modern materials. History repeating itself, if you will."

"Yuh, well ... there's a lotta guys off haulin' lobster gear out they-uh ... they won't see ya in this pea-soup fog, ya know. You don't want to repeat Howard Blackburn's hist'ry."

"I'll be just fine, I always carry my good luck charm, even if it takes up room that food could fit into. This fog should burn off by mid-morning, anyway."

"Tell me again, so's ever'one up t' th' coffee shop will hear it right. You're doin' this boat trip so's you can be a doctor ... of what ... for Gawd's sake?"

"Well, it's called cultural fisheries anthropology. I'm a Ph.D candidate at Harvard University. You see, the people involved in the fishing industry are the last hunter/gatherers on the planet. They run counter to most of society; in fact, the hunter/gatherers were around before people devised basic agriculture."

"So lemme get this straight ... all of us guys that go fishin' are really just a bunch of cavemen in boots?"

"Don't take it the wrong way. You're a very resourceful group of individuals. You have to play the cards you're dealt, for lack of a better way to describe it. It's a great way to study the past, if you believe that history repeats itself, as I do. Technology changes, but people really don't."

"Yuh ... if you say so, Doc ... What've you got for good luck, a dinosaur bone?"

"No ... it's a plant that came from my Mother. It's all I have of hers, but so far, it's done the trick. You sure James Mackenzie still lives out there?"

"James who? Oh, Spice, ya mean. Yuh, he's they-uh ... been they-uh for ten years, now, I guess. He caretakes the old Coast Guard station and does a lotta work with the school out they-uh. Lives on a boat moored in the far end of the hah-bah. Whatdya want with him?"

"Spice?"

"Yuh, that's him. So, whatdya want with him, annaways?"

"I ... I just want to see if history repeats itself. Thanks, Mr. Lester ... you've been a lot of help."

"I'll get on th' radio and tell the boys out lobsterin' that some damned nut in a kayak is goin' to paddle to Dam'iscove Island. Hopefully, they won't run ya down. I thought you Hah-vid guys were s'posed to have some brains packed in they-uh ... seems like a damn fool thing to do, goin' off in th' fog like that. Why don'tcha have Spice call us on the radio when you meet up with him, just so's we know you made it, and all."

"No, no, don't worry about me. I've spent plenty of time on the water. I'd rather keep things on the quiet side. It makes a better study in the long run. Please don't bother anyone with the radio."

"Suit yourself. I'll let your painter go. Be caff-ul, Doc!"

As fast as Chappy Lester untied the bowline holding the kayak to the Boothbay Fishermen's Co-op Dock, he lost sight of the small craft paddling away in the fog. The old-timers claim that Maine has its own fog factory, it's just that no one ever figured out how to make a living from it. Today, the factory was working overtime, making a wet blanket from the confluence of warm summer air flowing over the Atlantic cold delivered by the Labrador current. The sun's rays penetrated at various times, making a glare on the water that illuminated the fog, but even the June sun didn't dry up the soup at seven in the morning. The sea was calm, with a long, low swell that leisurely rolled into outer Boothbay harbor.

Christian Brown was a Ph.D candidate at Harvard University, working on the prestigious Meade fellowship provided to exceptional students who study the socioeconomics of failing fishing communities. At the age of twenty-five, the little orphan who started life as Kristiian Brueen already had enough experience for many lifetimes. Before he was five, Chris had witnessed his parents' murder, been to sea on a large factory trawler and lost his only sister in suspicious circumstances. At age six he was adopted from behind the Iron Curtain and brought to America to live with his great aunt in Wisconsin. By sixteen, he had mastered the English language so fluently his accent from the old country had all but disappeared. At seventeen, he was valedictorian of his high school class. He earned his Bachelor of Science degree in biological oceanography at North Carolina State in three years, then a master's degree in anthropology at Princeton.

Chris' Scandinavian heritage showed in his features: light brown hair, blue eyes, strong build with wide shoulders, an engaging smile, a hearty laugh and a sworn duty for living every moment to its fullest. He was a student of primitive life in modern surroundings. He was also serving a dark, personal agenda.

Chris's project proposal to the Meade fellowship was unanimously endorsed by the board of trustees. He would tour the coast of New England by sea kayak, interviewing members of the fishing industry and inhabitants of the commercial fishing communities along the way. The object of his proposal was to document the demise of the New England fisheries through the eyes of the people who were affected most — the hunter/gatherers, otherwise known as the fishermen. "The point of view of the scientists of the day are well documented," he told the committee, "but they are not representative of an ancient culture under duress, they merely represent the change of technology."

Chris wanted to tour the coast in an ancient vessel, propelled only by his two arms, thereby insuring that he would get no farther from the sea and its people than sea level itself.

Growing up in Wisconsin, one of the first books written in English that he read was Edward Rowe Snow's *Strange Tales from Nova Scotia to Cape Hatteras*. In this 1949 book, the well-known maritime author hiked 1158 miles from Canada to Cape Hatteras and investigated the coast's strange tales, ghost stories, shipwrecks and legends.

It was young Chris's dream to retrace those steps by sea. This was his second summer following Rowe's travelogue. Last year, he paddled his kayak to Grand Manan, Canada and climbed the 300-foot cliff that James Lawson, intrepid survivor of the wrecked schooner *Ashburnham*, scaled in the dead of the 1857 winter. Next, he visited the Acadian section of the Canadian Maritimes, later immortalized in Longfellow's tragic poem, "Evangeline."

This summer, he had continued Snow's seaborne tour of Maine during the first three weeks of June. Working his way southwest from Eastport, he visited Anemone Cave on Mount Desert Island, stood on top of Trask's rock in Castine, viewed the site of the Castine treasure and stopped at Fort William Henry at Pemaquid. After a quick layover in Boothbay Harbor, he was pressing on to his summer teaching duties at the Damariscove Island Marine Research Center, on the island that lies outside of Boothbay. His working plan was to assist in the undergraduate programs that the research center offered, and on free days, paddle to other ports to continue his doctoral research.

That was the public story. But there was another one. The previous winter, Chris began to piece together traces of his past and took on a personal quest that he would pursue with a silent vengeance. That his parents were murdered while the family was attempting to escape their Communist homeland was fact — he was there and witnessed them gunned down at the border stop. It was the death of his sister that still raised many questions. They had been inseparable; even sharing the same bunk aboard that floating factory. He knew she would never leave him voluntarily. He would never believe that she was caught up in some international intelligence incident and he never believed she jumped overboard from the Russian factory trawler fishing twenty miles east of Cape Cod in 1975.

The Freedom of Information Act, passed in 1975, provided avenues of information for Chris to use in his quest. Many formerly classified incidents between American fishing boats and Soviet bloc trawlers were documented; these were very useful in his doctoral anthropology study. The Act also opened up a world of information on intelligence gathered on the distant water fleets that systematically devastated the New England coast's fisheries through the '60s and '70s. Did the Soviet bloc factory ships track U.S. Navy subs and ships and Air Force planes? Why was there such a rash of unexplained sinkings in the domestic fleet? Why did references to the name Spice keep coming up?

Chris Brown found that his research on the New England fleet might yield the answer to the burning questions that infused every day of his life: What really happened to his sister? Was there any chance that she was alive?

Chris left the dock and paddled south, guided by his compass, intuition and prior planning. An astute seat-of-the-pants navigator, he had laid out the courses for this leg of the journey on a plastic-coated chartlet which he bungee-corded in front of his cockpit, next to the compass. In a little over three-tenths of a mile, the shore of Spruce Point came into view. By combining the little visibility he had with the smell of the seaweed on the rocks, he followed Spruce Point around until red nun buoy number "6" came into view. He then shifted course to 213 degrees, which shortly brought him to the shore of Squirrel Island. Following the shore of Squirrel Island to the westward, the sound of Cuckolds Light foghorn could be heard in the distance, a little over two miles away. Chris kept the foghorn in his left ear and shot across to the shore of Southport Island, the peninsula that makes the western reach of Booth Bay.

Now, all I have to do is keep the sound of the swells breaking on shore in my right ear and the sound of Cuckolds foghorn straight ahead, Chris thought. *It feels like the tide is on my stern. I'd better remember to adjust my course from Cuckolds to the Damariscove Island gong buoy, otherwise, I'll be set out to sea.*

As he paddled up and down over the long summer swells, he occasionally heard engines and the banging of lobster traps against the hulls of the lobster boats. He felt safe enough, though, staying in tight to the Southport shore.

Chris made good time with the fair tide and eventually got to Cuckolds Light, with its foghorn now blaring in his right ear. He stopped paddling. "Is that the sun, or the lighthouse?" he asked himself. Checking his watch, he timed the murky flashes ... "One, two flashes ... one, two, three, four, five, six seconds ... two more flashes ... that's it! Here we go ... let's try 150 degrees, that should compensate for the tide and bring me across ... I hope."

The years of canoeing on Lake Michigan as a youth came into play now, as he began to sprint-paddle across the seaward end of Booth Bay. This was where he was most vulnerable. A wrong guess on the tide, and he would be pushed too far into the ocean, or set too far back into Boothbay. In addition, any number of boats could be traversing this area, or working their lobster gear; some of the larger offshore fishing boats could be steaming through.

Chris picked up his pace and kept the sound of Cuckolds foghorn squarely to his stern by balancing the sound at the back of each ear. Occasionally, he turned his head from side to side to check on the foghorn's bearing. He knew that the pace he kept was roughly five knots, so after fifteen minutes, he figured he was at the half-way point of the crossing. *C'mon, you can do it,* he thought.

Paddle right … paddle left, alternating strokes … paddle right, paddle left … As his blades alternately dipped into the Atlantic, Chris began to notice the fog was lifting, ever so slowly. The muffled sunlight glinted off the paddle blades with every stroke, as ripples followed the kayak's movement tracing his progress in an ever widening "V." Seagulls swooped overhead as the tiny boat's path disturbed a passing school of tinker mackerel, bringing the water to a boil. *Paddle right … paddle left … paddle … paddle … inhale … exhale …*

Up and over the grey, syrupy swells he paddled, straining his hearing to pick up the sound of the gong buoy. *It should be coming up on my right ear, a little off the starboard bow,* he thought. The sound of Cuckolds foghorn was fading off the stern. *It's been twenty-eight minutes. I'm either right next to this thing or I've overshot it somehow. Wait! Maybe there isn't enough wave action to make the gong clappers strike the gong. Now what?* He squinted his eyes trying to see … anything … nothing. In fact, the little bit of sun filtering through the fog just made more glare on the water, but it wasn't burning off the fog.

He stopped paddling and listened intently, swinging his head from side to side. "It's got to be here, it's got to be!" he said aloud. Suddenly, he began to hear the sound of a boat in the distance. "I'll be all right, that's far enough away," he consoled himself. But as he listened the sound of the boat's engine kept getting louder and louder ... closer and closer. *Calm down now, just stay put. Keep on your compass course and listen. It sounds like he's crossing ahead.* Chris clenched his hands on the paddle grips and waited, his heart pounding. The sound of the engine was in his right ear ... then straight ahead ... then in his left ear ... then, "Gong! Gong!"

A great sigh of relief and a large smile came over him. The passing boat had gone close enough to the gong buoy for its wake to rock the buoy and cause the clappers to strike the gong. He made it ... the buoy was dead ahead and the course into Damariscove Island harbor from here was 25 degrees. "*Kaunis*," Chris muttered as he chuckled to himself. "Beautiful."

2

Damariscove Island Harbor

Lat. 43 deg. 45.5 min. N.
Long. 69 deg. 36.85 min. W.

A s James Mackenzie steered his lobster boat, the *Susan G*, homeward past the Damariscove Island gong buoy marking the rocks called the "Motions," he noticed an odd flashing coming from the westward of his position. *That can't be the Cuckolds,* he thought. *Wrong number of flashes ... Maybe it's just the sun reflecting off someone's windows while they're hauling gear.* Squinting his eyes at the next glance, he noticed that the odd flashing had stopped. *Must be someone hauling gear that turned around.* He continued on into Damariscove Island harbor, following his compass and watching the outline of the rocky shores in the radar. "That's strange ... never seen that before," he whispered to himself, still thinking about the odd flashing through the fog.

He slowed the boat's engine as he entered the harbor, and like piercing a wet veil, the vessel burst through the fog to a misty warm sun. The island's rocks had absorbed enough sun-driven heat to burn off the fog in the harbor. The old Coast Guard Station, now the Damariscove Island Marine Research Center, came into view on his port side. Straight ahead at the northern end of the harbor lay his homeboat, the *Elizabeth Gale*, bobbing up and down on her mooring. Seagulls cackled and swooped in the sun overhead as they followed the *Susan G*, hoping to grab a scrap of something edible that may be tossed overboard.

Mackenzie maneuvered the *Susan G* alongside the floating dock next to his homeboat, put the engine in reverse for braking, then neutral. Once the boat's forward motion stopped, he reached over the side and tied a line from beside his steering station to a cleat on the float. Putting the engine in high idle speed, he began spraying with the wash-down hose to clean off the vessel's deck and stern rails. Looking back towards the harbor mouth, the fog bank that he had just broken through was still eerily in place; only the sky directly above was blue.

Something caught his eye again ... the same strange flashing as before was now in the mouth of the harbor, just beyond the clear air into the fog. Flash ... flash ... flash ... He watched again. It seemed to be getting closer. Flash. Flash. Flash. Now the strains of light didn't line up ... they were flashing left, right, left, right ... not like the sun's reflection off of boat windows, at least not on such a calm day. Mackenzie threw the hose over the rail and studied this development intently. "Is it a signal mirror? Is someone in trouble out there?" he asked himself. He stood at the stern of his boat and shaded his eyes with cupped hands, trying to concentrate on the shape that was coming into view. The odd flashes were coming from a dark shape on the water which quickly changed to bright red as it burst through the fog bank.

Mackenzie smiled, shook his head in amusement and folded his arms across his chest as he finally realized what the mysterious phenomenon was. "You gotta be kiddin' me. That's one for the books," he laughed softly.

Chris Brown paddled into the sunny harbor, his red kayak gleaming and his wet paddles flashing the sunlight's reflection with every stroke. Without missing a beat, he paddled up to the stern of the *Susan G*, coming to a stop by deftly turning the small craft sideways to the transom. He looked up at the man who peered from under the visor of his hat, chuckling through his beard.

"You had me goin', there, Old Scout ... you must be Chris Brown."

"Mr. Mackenzie?"

"Nope ... mister was my father ... I'm Mack. They told me to keep an eye out for you, but I didn't think I'd see you for a couple more days. How was your trip?"

"Great, no problems at all." Chris craned his neck around to take a quick look at the granite island rising above him on three sides. "It sure is beautiful here."

Before Mackenzie could answer, the radio at the helm of the *Susan G* crackled to life.

"*Amanda May* callin' the *Susan G*."

Mackenzie raised his finger to indicate 'what a minute,' then walked forward to answer the radio.

"Go ahead, Chappy," he answered into the microphone.

"Top of the mornin' to ya, Spice man, how's the buggin'?"

"I just set out the fish traps, no lobsterin' this morning ... what's goin' on, you out?"

"Nope, chafing the dock ... yuh. Just thought I should tell you, some kid in a kayak is headed your way. He said not to call you, but, annaways, once I got up t' th' coffee shop and told the wife he was out there, she gave me hell for lettin' him leave."

Mackenzie looked out at Chris, who was bobbing off the stern of the boat, taking in the scenery. "He's here already, Chappy, I'm looking right at him."

"Yuh, well ... he is? How in hell did he do that, magic?"

"Damned if I know, Chap. We're all set here though ... thanks for the call."

"Yuh, Okay ... *Amanda May* by."

"*Susan G* standing by." Mackenzie put the microphone back in its holder on the overhead, shut off the engine, then walked back to the stern of his boat. "Chris, did you happen to meet Chappy Lester back in Boothbay harbor?" he asked.

"Yes ... Nice old gentleman."

"That was him on the radio. He wanted to make sure you got here in one piece."

"Was that all he said?" Chris asked.

"That's about it. C'mon, why don't you get out of that thing and I'll take you over to the school so you can get settled in. Do you want to go by water, or would you like to walk?"

"At this point, I'd rather walk."

"Good. C'mon, tie your rig up to the float here and we'll take my peapod over to shore. We can walk over to the old station and grab a coffee. Some of the other staff members are here already; the troops should be here in a couple of days. Chappy runs the mail boat out here every third day, so they'll probably come with him the day after tomorrow. Nothing as dramatic as your arrival, to be sure."

Chris brought his kayak alongside the float, tied it up, and, with experienced finesse, slid his body out of the cockpit and up onto the deck of the float. He stood to full height, slipped off his waterproof kayak skirt, stretched his arms, then went to shake hands with Mackenzie. "It's nice to meet you," he said, his arm extended.

"Glad to know you, Old Scout," Mackenzie offered. The two shook hands and shuffled down to the end of Mackenzie's float and got aboard his rowboat. Chris couldn't help but admire the shapely hull and varnished brightwork of the peapod. "Have a seat in the stern, there ... you've done enough struggling-stick-motoring today, haven't you?"

"This is a gorgeous little rowboat, Mr. Mackenzie. Did you build it?"

"Mack ... forget the mister crap ... yup, this comes from an old set of loftings that my grandfather had. Makes a good winter hobby, but this is all the varnish I care to do every spring." Mackenzie fit the oars between the thole pins, two dowels jutting out of the rail, used for oarlocks, then untied the boat and started to row for shore. Chris silently sat in the stern, looking around in fascination at the island and its raw beauty as the sun finally felt warm and summer like.

I feel connected to this place somehow. I don't know why, Chris thought. He'd been on many islands along the Maine coast during his kayak excursions, and even some of the islands in the great lakes were similar, but this felt different.

As Chris sat in the stern his gaze turned to the man rowing. Jim Mackenzie was a man of slight build and height, with a salt and pepper beard. He looked rather young for what Chris knew his age to be, even though what skin that could be seen on his face revealed that he had spent his life outdoors. A white hat with "Maine Maritime Academy" emblazoned on the front topped his head with the visor pulled low to shade his eyes. *It's hard to believe this guy is connected to the word "spice,"* he questioned himself silently. *But ... Mr. Lester did say ...*

Before Chris could finish his thought, the peapod lurched onto shore at a small stretch of sand between the jutting rocks. Mackenzie hopped over the bow and tied the boat's line to a ring that was drilled into the granite a few steps away.

They started walking along the shoreside trail cut through the beach plums and poison ivy.

"Did you get that hat at Maine Maritime, Mack?"

"Nope, my two nephews are there. I went to Oregon State for Oceanography."

"Oh ... when they told me you were a fisherman, I naturally assumed," he said, trying to draw him out.

"I get that a lot. Most times I don't admit having a couple degrees. People think you're something that you're not. Everybody's got the same amount of knowledge, sooner or later, anyway, and generally, all the answers you want are tucked in someone's head, and that's usually someone's head who had to learn it the hard way. You know that, you're an anthropologist, right? One of my old shipmates said his grandfather called it the school of H-N."

"H-N?" Chris asked, perplexed.

"Yup ... hard knocks."

They both chuckled as they walked over the rocky landscape.

"Well said. That's what I'm here for, to unlock some of that caged up knowledge and document it."

"Well, the fishing folks could use some of that, especially from someone who's objective. Go easy on letting them know you're from Harvard, though, know what I mean? If you say you're from Harvard and are here to help, you'll hear one of two sounds ...running feet or a shotgun being cocked."

"Why?"

"Simple. Fishing went along just fine since before colonial times until the foreign distant water fleets got over here. They did a tremendous amount of damage which caused the inception of the 200-mile limit, which brought in all the degreed experts with very good intentions, God love 'em, who alienated the fishing folks with their regulations, which ultimately put many people out of business. Every time something was done *for* the fishing fleet, it ended up doing something *to* the fleet."

"I understand, believe me, I do. Forgive me, but it's an anthropologist's dream come true! You know, Mr. Lester already let me in on that, in his own way." He mocked Chappy Lester with his voice, pointing his finger at Mackenzie, "you Hah-vid guys!"

"Don't let him bother you." Mackenzie laughed, pointing the way where two paths forked. He took a deep breath, then exhaled. "I read your resume' when the school director said you were coming over ... read your project proposal, too. I pleaded with her to be involved ... I hope you don't mind.

You've got to educate the public about the fisheries mess. It's got to be done ... God knows I've tried. The final answer rests with you, of course, but if I can help in any way ..."

"Mind, are you kidding me? Welcome aboard!"

They stopped and shook hands, sealing the deal. *If he knows anything about the foreign fleets, I certainly want to pick his brain, Chris thought.* Vaieta ... *be quiet,* he reminded himself. *He doesn't know I asked to be assigned to him.*

They walked on, up over a rise and down into a grassy spot where startled grasshoppers took to flight. The old Coast Guard Station, now the Marine Lab, came into view again.

"You ever done any real fishing, Chris?" Mackenzie asked.

"I had a job on a fishing boat once," Chris replied with great understatement.

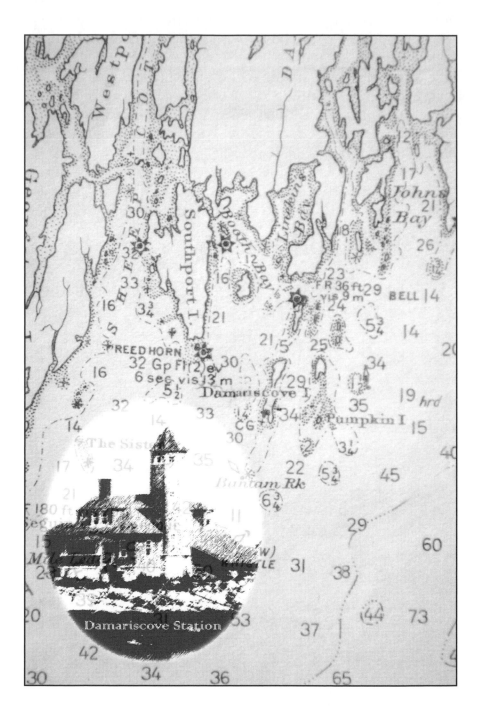

3
DAMARISCOVE STATION

LAT. 43 DEG. 45.2 MIN. N.
LONG. 69 DEG. 36.95 MIN W.

The two men trekked on through the scrubby bushes, toward some of the old houses left from when Damariscove was a bustling fishing community. A light west breeze began to stir the vegetation, bringing more summer from the mainland.

"My grandmother lived out here on Dam'iscove when she was a little girl, you know," Mackenzie announced proudly. "She, her mother, three sisters and two brothers lived right over here when their father was assigned to the station." He stopped and pointed out an old foundation. "That was where the barn was … that's the house, there, minus the ell that was off to the right side. The ell was blown off in the …" he thought for a moment, stroking his beard. "… the '54 hurricane, I think it was. 'Course she was my grandmother at that point, living on the mainland. There was a one-room schoolhouse over there … a meeting house over there,"

17

he explained. "Poole's dairy farm was up there where you can see a little bit of pastureland left." His hand swept the landscape, then he turned towards the harbor. "The wharf's been in excellent shape since they built it down there all those years ago. Quite a place!"

They moved forward, past a few "mainland looking" trees with birds merrily chirping within, then walked on to the Marine Research Center. The center still looked very much like the old Coast Guard station that it proudly was in its former life. As they passed a few raspberry and wild rose bushes, they entered a clearing and stopped. Both pairs of eyes went skyward to take in the view of the old watchtower, the focal point of the station. Mackenzie looked over at Chris and nodded to himself as he saw the look of awe on the young man's face.

"Nice, huh? C'mon," Jim beckoned. They walked around the outside of the boathouse and he pulled open the heavy varnished mahogany door that led up into the main entrance to the mess hall and galley. The aroma of fresh paint and varnish coupled with coffee drifted out to greet them in the salt air.

"Wow!" exclaimed Chris. "This is something!"

The view he was treated to was a spectacular vision of a bygone era. Ahead lay a panorama of gleaming hardwood floors, pure white walls and varnished brightwork trim. As the sun entered the windows from behind them, it reflected off of the mess hall's impressive woodwork, lighting up the room. Chris entered and strolled around, shaking his head in disbelief.

"I've never seen anything like this … the varnish must be a quarter of an inch thick," his voice echoed. "This is incredible; I've been in churches that didn't have woodwork like this!"

"The old Coast Guard motto, 'if it doesn't move, paint it', applies, huh?" Mackenzie joked. "The guys that were stationed out here really loved this place … you can tell, can't you? 'Course they also had some time to kill."

"Yes, but this hasn't been a working station for awhile. Someone had to keep all of this up."

"Yup, well, I had a little spare time, myself. Let's go into the galley and find the coffee machine. Right through here."

Chris followed his tour guide into the adjoining kitchen, which was a modern contrast of stainless steel appliances and formica countertops.

"Have a seat." As Chris sat down at the cook's table, Mackenzie walked over to one of the many cupboards that lined the walls and retrieved two mugs. "How do you want yours?" he asked, pouring coffee into the mugs.

"Black is fine, thanks."

"I like it that way, too. Here you go." He slid the mug to him, then went to the refrigerator. "I think there's some danish left from yesterday," Jim said, rummaging around inside. "I'll nuke us a couple of pieces." He cut two pieces and put them in the microwave.

Mackenzie looked outside and smiled. "Here come the boys. I don't know how they do it, but when that refrigerator door opens, they hear it every time."

He got up, opened the screen door to the back of the galley and two cats bounded in. They went right to Mack, rubbed on his legs, then went over to Chris with the same greeting.

"They like you," Mack remarked. "Usually they won't come near anyone until they've seen them around for awhile."

Chris bent down to stroke the two cats as they enjoyed his attention.

"And who do we have here? You're good boys, yes, you are." He smiled and continued caressing the animals, as they purred with delight.

"The orange one is Ezekial. We found him a few years ago clinging to a piece of driftwood when he washed up into the cove. He'd been hit by birdshot ... man was he full of holes! He needed a biblical name because he was so 'holy,' so my wife named him Ezekial." Mack looked at the cat ... "Huh, Zeke?"

"There's always a story behind a cat's name. So what's this guy's name?"

"He's Rogers. Grand old man of the cat world, he is. Interesting story about him, too. He jumped ship on June the second, in 1983. There was a sailboat that laid-to for the night out here on the wharf. The next day they left, but ole' Rog, here, found the mouse hunting just too good to leave behind. We contacted the owners on the radio, but they said if he really wanted to stay, then just keep him, so ... we did."

"They just left this beautiful Siamese cat? Incredible! So ... were the people's name Rogers?" Chris asked, putting his mug down, looking puzzled.

"No, here's where the name comes in." Mackenzie took a sip from his mug and swallowed. "That's good coffee if you can drink it without using a knife and fork ... anyway, the day he jumped ship was the day that Stan Rogers died."

"I'm sorry ... was he a shipmate of yours, or something?"

"You might say that. Stan Rogers was one of the greatest, if not the greatest, maritime folk singers to ever come along. He was from Canada ... died that day in some freak plane accident ... it didn't crash. I think there was a fire aboard. I'll tell ya, his songs can keep you going through some pretty hard times. You've never heard that song, the 'Mary Ellen Carter,' where the refrain goes ... 'Rise Again!' ... C'mon, you must've heard that?"

"I'm afraid not. I was only thirteen in 1983," Chris answered sheepishly, sipping on his coffee

"Yeah, that's right ... I am dating myself, aren't I? Well, you'll hear it, to be sure; it's on the hit list at all the campfires we have out here. When everyone gets rounded up and settled in on Saturday, we'll have a big singalong and campfire. Actually, every Saturday night we have one, weather permitting, of course."

"Can I sit in? I play a little guitar."

"Sure, by all means, love to have you play, but you don't have a guitar stashed in that kayak, do you?" Mackenzie asked.

"No. I mailed a lot of things to myself. Clothes, books, laptop, stuff like that. I had room for the guitar, so that's in there, too."

"How did you pack it up? Here's your pastry." Mack slid the plate to him.

"I put everything in one big crate, it seemed like the easiest way at the time."

Mackenzie smiled and nodded. "Well, you know ... Chappy runs the mail out here. That one big crate will get him back for busting your chops!"

"Oh ... I never gave a thought as to how it was going to be delivered."

"Trust me, Old Scout ... it'll build character, and you and I both know, Chappy's a character!" Mackenzie chuckled. "You got him on that one, Hah-vid!"

Both men sat for a moment and ate their pastry while the cats fed from their dishes on the floor, nearby.

"Hey ... where is everybody, anyway?" Chris asked, the realization just dawning on him that he'd only met one person and two cats since arriving.

"Greg handles the galley out here, but he's out tending to his gang of lobster traps. His wife and family are up at Sebago running their summer camp for special ed and disabled kids. Doctor Dave and his wife, Sandy are up on Wood End doing core samples, that's the north part of the island beyond the causeway. They're geologists doing work on the glacial period. Dr. Grayson, the school director, is in her office, typing away. She's trying to get a new curriculum ready for Monday. Paul took the research boat over to Staple's yard in Boothbay to clean and paint the bottom, change the zincs, stuff like that. He should be back Saturday, if they get off the ways," Jim explained, counting off his fingers as he named names. "My wife is staying with our daughters in Boston ... she plays cello with the Pops. One daughter's at the Conservatory of Music in the gifted youth summer program, the other is doing her first year nursing school clinical course at Mass General ... Brains and beauty!

"The main offices for the directors are in the old workshop, that's the building that's farthest away from us," he continued. "Dr. G should be there, or not far away. The old service building is their living quarters, that's the next building beyond the door where we came in.

"The old crew's barracks are upstairs here ... that's where they'll have you stay, along with the students. It's kind of nice. We did it all up in single or double staterooms, like on old ships ... comfy, but not spacious. You, being part of the staff, will get first come, first serve, so, seeing how you're here first, you'd better claim your room today," Mackenzie advised, then took the last bite of his pastry.

Chris finished his snack and cleared the table, washed everything in the sink quickly and left the cups and plates in the strainer to dry. "Thanks for the breakfast. I know I should get over to meet Dr. Grayson, but I would really love to get up in that tower," Chris said, looking up at the ceiling. "Is it okay to go up there?"

"Sure. Tell you what ... I've got some things to do. Why don't you go ahead up. I'm sure you can find your way. I'll go tell Dr. G. that you're up there and then I'm going back to the boat and take care of a couple things. I'll tow your kayak over to the wharf out front and tie it off for you."

"Are you sure? Don't you need help getting your peapod off the sand?"

"Naah. I've got an outhaul and tay-kle all rigged up over there. I do it all the time ... you can never count on help being around out here. Nope, you go ahead up ... in fact," Mackenzie reached in the cupboard above his head, "take these binoculars."

"You sure you don't need the help?" Chris asked again as he took the binoculars and put them around his neck.

"I'll catch up to you later," Mack said, waving his hand to indicate "no." "Go ahead up while the west wind has things half-way clear. You never know when your next chance on good visibility will be!" He excused himself and headed for the door. "See ya a little later."

Chris went back down the hallway and saw a door with a polished brass sign that read "watchtower." He opened the door and peered in. A spiral staircase led to the top of the tower where shafts of sunlight streamed in, illuminating the stairwell. He grabbed the handrail and began to climb, his feet walking on polished brass stair treads that had depressions worn in them from the thousands of times they were walked and scuffed on. He kept his gaze skyward, imagining as he climbed what life must have been like for the crew that kept the watch from above. *This place is almost magical,* he thought.

Finally, he reached the last step and came to the top of the watchtower. The view took his breath away. Looking north, he could see the whole expanse of the island stretching out before him. The deep green landscape was punctuated with rock outcroppings, remains of old dwellings, wild rose bushes, beach plums and places that were once pastureland. Old footpaths were still evident; one leading to the community well, one going north to the pond where ice was cut, a path from there to the bridge across the causeway to Wood End, paths to and from old house foundations, to the wharves ...

Across the harbor, looking east, the second watchtower stood guard on the eastern shore, with a well worn path leading to it. He could imagine someone on foot patrol in the early 1900's, walking to that tower in a blinding snowstorm, making sure the clock inside was punched to verify that his watch was kept. He swung around and looked to the west, and sure enough, there was the other clock station, standing guard on the high point, and beyond that, he could make out two lobster boats bobbing back and forth, working their gear about a mile off of the western shore. To the south, he saw a bright blue boat steaming through the harbor mouth, chased by noisy seagulls. He trained the binoculars on the bow ... the name was the *Hayley and Blair*. The boat went to the north end of the harbor, then tied up behind Mackenzie's 'homeboat' across from the *Susan G* and his red kayak. He watched as the skipper of the *Hayley and Blair* tied up, then got out on the float and put his hands on his hips, looking at the kayak. A moment later, he got back aboard the boat and went to the same wash-down ritual that all workboats subscribe to when they arrive in port.

Chris was so enthralled with the view that he didn't hear someone climbing the steps behind him.

"Beautiful view, isn't it?" Dr. Felicia Grayson asked, startling Chris back to reality.

"Oh ..." he reeled around, surprised. "I'm Chris Brown. You must be Dr. Grayson. I'm very honored to meet you." They smiled at each other and shook hands. "I should apologize for making you climb these steps. I hope that I didn't inconvenience you."

"Don't be silly ... I love it up here. I didn't even realize you'd arrived until Mack told me you were topside. The apology should be mine," she replied, smiling through her winded speech.

Chris studied the elderly woman's face and instantly felt at ease with her. *She looks the same as her picture on the book jacket from 1980,* he thought.

"One of the first books that really brought me into marine science was your *One Sea, One Life United*. When I read that, I never dreamed I could be here meeting you in person one day. It truly is an honor to be able to work with you," Chris said.

"It is I who have the pleasure ... I've never seen a resume' like yours," she replied craning her neck to see up into his blue eyes. I'm glad you're here a little early ... we could use some help getting the curriculum together."

"My pleasure ... whatever I can do."

Dr. Grayson took a deep breath. "Well ... I must assume that you have chatted with Mack for a little bit. Do you still want to work with him?"

"Yes, most definitely. It was funny ... he said he pleaded with you so he could work with me. I found that odd, but it was a nice gesture. I didn't mention my request to be assigned to him, though," Chris replied, looking down at this sprite dynamo while he reminded himself, *Vaieta*!

"I need some clarification, young man," Dr. Grayson inquired. "Why did you want to spend so much time with him?"

"Well, to get to the bottom of my thesis, I need someone who's been around the fishing scene for a long time ... different ports, different boats, types of fishing, etc. He seems to be one of the few men left around that experienced the distant water fleets firsthand and has the unique ability to articulate himself well. My investigations turned him up in a variety of situations, and he's one of a kind; who else is equally at home in books or boots? That project he wrote on the creation of the fishing boat/research partnership ... he was five years ahead of everyone in that, alone! I need the knowledge he has ... it's all firsthand," Chris asserted.

"I understand, but he can be quite a handful, you know."

"In what way?"

"To answer that, I have to turn a long story into an excruciatingly long story." She smiled and shook her head. "Well, not really, but it would make more sense to you if I related a couple of things," she said. "He can be a royal pain in the neck."

"C'mon, he can't be that bad."

"Well ... the first time I ran into James Mackenzie was at a public hearing in 1979. At that time, the fisheries management was using quotas to try to limit landings of codfish. What the boats were doing was throwing over thousands of pounds of codfish, staying within the quotas, so they could take what few flatfish came up in the nets with them. The Feds said that they had no statistics that the codfish existed, so they couldn't be out there in the first place, so they can't possibly be landed," she started.

"So they were discarded dead, thereby staying within the landing quotas. I recall reading about this. They were still doing that last spring, sixteen years later, as I remember," Chris countered. "They still don't get it!"

"Okay then, hearing you say that makes this an easier story," Dr. Grayson continued. "It was a big hearing in Boston

... the place is packed to the rafters with angry fishermen. The Feds had a panel of fisheries scientists, managers, all kinds of honchos to explain to the guys that there was no fish out there, so don't land any."

"And these same guys were throwing the phantom fish overboard, dead," Chris interrupted, "Right?"

"Right. Mackenzie got up and took the scientists, one of which was the acting director from Washington, to task. Do you remember statistics 101 ... a multiple regression equation?"

"Sure ... A plus B plus C plus D equals the end result. In other words, granite, plus labor, plus mortar, plus vision, plus need ... equals this tower. Right?" Chris asked, puzzled.

"You're right, for the purposes of this exercise. Now, do you remember the f-test?" Dr. Grayson asked, sounding just like the demanding professor that she was. "The factorial review ... remember that?"

"The factorial review. Sure ... you pit all the variables against each other to find which one, or ones are significant, if at all. It gives you a percentage of how much you can trust your figures, to put it in layman's terms." Chris looked to his interrogator for reassurance that his answer was correct.

"Very good. Now ... is five percent a good number for a factorial review?"

"Five percent? ... No! Five tenths of one percent would be good, but not five. Five isn't even in the ballpark!"

Dr. Grayson looked at her new student, pleased. "Great, now for the 'rest of the story,'" she continued, paraphrasing newscaster Paul Harvey. "Mackenzie had the statistics from the study on the codfish ... a five percent factorial review ... he was livid! He was the only one sitting in that room that knew what it meant, besides the panel up front, of course. Well ... he listened to about all he could take, then went storming up front to where the acting head honcho was showing charts and graphs on an overhead projector. He grabbed the marker out of the guy's hand and proceeded to explain the regression equation to the audience."

"That must have been something to watch," Chris said, eager to hear more. "So ... what happened next?" he asked, smiling in pure enjoyment, motioning his hands in a 'tell me more' gesture.

"He exposed the whole thing. The statistics were extremely flawed. This whole industry of people were having their livelihoods decided upon with faulty data. Behind him, the panelists began to get eye contact with each other, looking like, 'uh-oh, he knows this stuff.' He then explained the f-test, and ended with something like, 'five percent looks great, but it's the difference between Texas and Timbuktu!' Then he threw the marker across the room."

"Wow."

"Yes, wow ... but it didn't turn out like you think."

"What do you mean? That should have been the silver bullet!"

"If bullets were flying, they would have been meant for him. The whole room erupted and booed him down. Every fisherman sitting in that room thought he was nuts ... five percent error, no big deal, right? Leave well enough alone. He barely got out of there with his life." Dr. Grayson took the binoculars and watched in the distance as she saw Mackenzie climbing over the rocks to kedge off his peapod. She shook her head as she watched him row out to his float. "He's a cross between deMontaigne and Sonny Bono."

Chris looked bewildered. "A cross between who and who?"

"deMontaigne was the French writer who popularized the word essay. In French, it means attempt. He was the original essayist, and he was quoted as saying, 'I am, myself, the manner of my book'."

"And Sonny Bono, where does he come in?" Chris was thoroughly intrigued with this learned woman and her view of humanity.

"Very simply, Mr. Brown, Sonny Bono, like him or not, has been a success at everything he does, even though no one takes him seriously. When Jim Mackenzie thinks he's right, he is a royal pain in the rump. When he knows he's right, he's like a bulldog chewing on a tire! But it's hard to take him seriously, that's why he asked me to get his message out through you. You've got the credibility ... he's got the knowledge and contacts." Dr. Grayson's voice became dark and stern. She turned, stood on her tip-toes, and put her finger in Chris's face. "I caution you, I am your advisor here. If your findings match his ruminations, I'll back you to the hilt ... if not, make sure you have enough spare fingers to take a tire away from a bulldog chewing on it."

She looked through the binoculars again, watching Mackenzie chatting with his dockmate from the *Hayley and Blair*. "There were Graysons on these waters before the mainland was a colony, but that is no longer the case ... good intentions coupled with twisted science and outside agendas got the whole fisheries situation into the mess it is now. Make sure you maintain the highest standards!"

Chris was stunned. He'd verbally gone from the watchtower to the proverbial woodshed, all in seconds. Not being one to shy away, though, he reached within for resolve and asserted himself. "Dr. Grayson ... is he right ... or ... does he just think that he's right?"

Dr. Felicia Grayson took in a long inhale, then slowly let it out, tightening her lower lip. Her view through the binoculars was that of two old friends standing next to their boats, having a great time laughing about something. She peeled her eyes away and looked up into Chris Brown's face. "He's right."

If he was anywhere near Cape Cod in 1975, he'll be more than right, Chris thought. He smiled at Dr. Grayson. "Then I came to the right place." he said.

4

THE CORNER ROOM

LAT. 43 DEG. 45.2 MIN. N.
LONG. 69 DEG. 36.95 MIN. W.

Chris was deep in thought as he left the tower to look for his room. It took a few minutes to grasp what Dr. Grayson had said, and what she meant by it. *I know that effectively nothing has changed since she published her groundbreaking book in 1980. I probably should have told her I've held her in the same regard as Rachel Carson ... her book really was the* Silent Spring *of the fisheries. And no one took Dr. Grayson seriously when they really should have.* Chris smiled and nodded his head ...

He followed the second floor hallway to the room at the northeast end, opened the door, walked in. The same white walls and varnished trim as the rest of the building made this room very appealing. There was one bed, a desk, a bureau, a nightstand, two chairs, a fairly large closet and a big window that provided a panoramic view of the harbor. The room was sunny, bright and cheerful, which redeemed its small size. Chris nodded. *This is perfect,* he thought. He turned to open the window, but realized the position of the bed bothered him. He surveyed the room, mentally making the best arrangement, then dragged the bed alongside the wall. "That's better," he said, opening the window, letting the fresh ocean air rustle through the curtains.

Chris flopped on the bed, propped his head up with his hands, took a deep breath and relaxed. So far, it was only noontime and he was already having quite a day for himself. He closed his eyes and tried to fit some of the pieces of his puzzle together. *Spice? Don't get your hopes up, it could be a dead end, but maybe he can give you some information. I'll have to go very gently ... and not make it obvious. Besides that, though, he'll be a great resource in my research.* He closed his eyes, kicked off his sneakers, and drifted off to sleep.

"Help! Help!" came a desperate cry from outside the window.

Chris bounded off the bed and thrust his head out the window. Someone was in trouble at the end of the wharf. "Oh no!" he said, "Hold on! Don't panic, I'm coming!" he screamed. He fumbled for his sneakers and made a vain attempt to tie them.

"Help! Somebody's got to help me! Help!"

Chris bounded down the stairs, nearly tripping over his shoelaces and ran out the door.

"Just take it easy, I'll help you ... don't try to move!" he yelled as he rapidly stumbled his way to the wharf. "I'm coming!"

He ran to the shore then down the aluminum rampway to the floating dock that bobbed outside the granite wharf. The man was holding a paddle in one hand, slapping the water with it, his other arm flailing helplessly. "Give me your hand ... quick ...!" he shouted.

Chris lay down on the deck of the float and made a vain arm's-length-attempt to grab a hold of the distressed man's hand. "Try again ... before the tide takes you!"

He watched anxiously as the hapless stranger tried to paddle back alongside the float. "Stick out the paddle ...

I can grab that … just stick out the paddle!" he shouted. Lying on the float again and stretching, Chris managed to grab the blade of the paddle, pulled, and brought the victim alongside the wharf.

"I was doin' okay until it came time to get back out of this thing … how do you get out without tippin' over?" gasped the stranger leaning his head alongside the wharf as he caught his breath.

Chris shook his head. "It's real easy … just let me talk you through it …" Chris assured him.

"Okay … put your left hand up on the cleat here … that'll make a good hand hold. Now … I'll grab the collar of your shirt and you slide yourself ever … so … gent … ly up … out of the seat … and sit on the float. Don't try to push much with your legs, and don't, whatever you do, try to stand up! Straighten your upper body and I'll get my arm around you … you ready?"

"Awright," came the not-so-sure reply.

"Here we go," Chris said with as much reassurance as he could muster. *This guy is as big as me … we'll either make it or we're both going for a swim,* he thought.

"Ready … grab a hold of the cleat … good. Now, tighten up and start to slide out … I've got you here … just slide … don't stand." Chris instructed.

Slowly, the two men began to move as the seagulls swooped and cackled overhead, seemingly enjoying the show.

"You're almost there … just slide your butt up on the float … I've got a hold of you … just a couple more inches." Both men were now perspiring in the heat and breathing heavily. "On three. One … two … threeeee!" Chris grabbed the stranger and dragged him aboard the float, both of them collapsing in a panting heap.

"You can keep that thing," came the muffled assessment from the bottom of the pigpile. "I thought I was doin' Mack a favor, bringin' this thing over, but I don't know …"

Both men collected themselves and stood, shaking off the fall.

"The name's Carleton Gregory, but call me Greg like everyone else does. You've gotta be Chris Brown." Greg extended his hand in friendship. "Glad to know ya, Slimey."

Never one to be too upset by anything, Chris chuckled and shook hands with Greg. "Slimey?" he asked.

"Yup ... anybody who can slither out of that thing must have some eel in him!"

"Slimey. Okay. Well, how did you like your first kayak trip? It is the first ... right?"

Greg laughed. "And last! It's great once you get in and get moving, but it takes an act of Congress to get back out. Mack says you paddled out from Boothbay Harbor in this morning's fog. You're a better man than me, I'll tell ya that!"

"It's like anything that takes a little practice ... just like riding a bike. There's nothing to it, really."

"If you say so, Slimey. Hey, you ready for a mug-up?"

"Starved. I'm not even going to be polite ... I'm starved," Chris replied.

"Good ... let's go get us a sangwich," Greg said. "I usually don't put out a big meal during the noontime. Breakfast and dinner, yup, but at noon, there's always a big spread of coldcuts, cheeses, breads, stuff like that. You can always help yourself, too. The best guest is one that takes care of himself, ya know," he said. Greg's eyes smiled even when his gray mustache didn't.

"Thank you. I'll remember that," Chris offered. *I've known this guy for two minutes and he already treats me like I've known him for years,* he thought.

"Hey!" Greg stopped. "Should we carry your rig up to the station, or do ya wanna leave it here?" he asked as he cocked his hat on the back of his gray hair and rested his rugged hands on his hips.

"That would be great, if you don't mind. Then I can unpack and officially move in after," he said.

They untied the kayak, turned it perpendicular and slid it up on the float. Each grabbed an end and started walking up the rampway, heading for the station. "Let's head west," Greg said. "It never hurt Custer!

"Mack's been real excited you were coming, I am too," Greg called back over his shoulder as they walked. "If there's anything I can do, please let me know. I'm from Casco Bay … there's plenty of guys up there that would like to vent their spleens! Ya know, Mack and I were shipmates back in the early days, 'course that was after OSU … we were roommates out there. I was from Maine, he was from Massachusetts and that's where we met up. Howdya figure? We were together on the *Elizabeth Gale* back at the Point, too."

"The Point … you mean Point Judith, in Rhode Island?"

"Yup. It's his homeboat now … when it was still fishing back in the 70s, I mean," he answered. "We went through plenty on that sled, I'll tell ya!"

"I'd love to hear anything you can tell me, Greg, that's what I'm here for."

"Slimey, some one of these days, I'll fill your head with all kinds of sea stories. There's one difference, though … these are all true. Ya know, Mack wants to bend your ear about politics, regulations, quotas, trickle-down economics, pollution and all kinds of technical stuff, but he'll probably never open up on anything personal. I told him the Berlin wall fell six years ago, but he won't take down his wall, I don't think," Greg proffered as they trudged along.

Chris was puzzled, but felt like an old buddy with this man he had just met, who, very uncharacteristic for a Maine fisherman, was very chatty and open. "Why do you say that?" he shouted.

"Aaah, it's like my father … he was in the Battle of the Bulge in World War II but never said anything about it. Same thing."

Lunchtime conversation was a role-reversal for Chris. Instead of being the inquisitor, he was the main subject of conversation. He kept Greg entertained with stories of Harvard and Boston's nightlife, his kayak excursions along the coast and about his dealings with the characters he met researching the anthropological aspects of fishing communities.

"Chappy said what?" Greg asked, laughing at one story. "That old coot! 'Cavemen in boots.' He's a piece of work, isn't he?"

Chris did not reveal his innermost research project. There was a better chance of finding out more indirectly, since he just became aware of the added bonus of striking up a friendship with Jim Mackenzie's shipmate on the *Elizabeth Gale*. He saw an opportunity, however, when he got Greg laughing about Chappy Lester.

"Greg, when I left the dock over there at Boothbay, he called Jim Mackenzie 'Spice'," Chris asked, trying to not sound too curious. "Is that a regular nickname for him?"

"Hoo boy, I dunno ... Chappy's the only one who can get away with that."

"Oh, well ... forget it."

"Well ... can you keep this to yourself?" Greg asked, after thinking it over for a second.

Chris's heart was pounding. *Calm down ...* vaieta! he thought. "Sure," he replied.

"This is pure Chappy, all the way; a 'Lesterism' if there ever was one. Well, you know by now that Chappy is a little bit larger than life, right?"

"That's one way of putting it." Chris responded.

"It was back, oh, in 1991, I think ... yup, '91. We had a hurricane coming up the coast. I piled all my lobster traps up on the wharf, Paul brought the *Eva Maker*, the research boat, into Boothbay with all the students, we tied everything down, ya know, getting ready for the storm, then we went into Boothbay with our boats. Mack took the *Elizabeth Gale* and towed his other boat in with him. We evacuated the place, just in case ... you can't be too careful with students, and Dr. G. is no spring chicken, either. So ... there we were in town, one big flotilla of the Dam'iscove pirates, all tied up at the co-op."

"Did the storm ever hit?"

"Oh, my, yes. It blew about eighty for a few hours. It didn't pan out to be the huge killer storm they thought, though, not that anyone found a complaint with that. So, anyway, here we were all huddled in town ... the students and Dr. G. went to a hotel; us guys stayed with the boats." Greg thought for a second. "Did you get into the Booth Baygull coffee shop when you stopped in there?"

"As a matter of fact, I did," Chris answered.

"Well, then, you met Chappy's wife, Esther. That's her shop. She's a peach of a lady, isn't she?" Greg continued.

"Yes, she was very nice to me."

"She's the best. Anyway, she took pity on all of us guys stuck on our boats, so she put on a huge turkey dinner for us. There wasn't anyone in town ... no business at the shop ... I mean the whole coast was like a ghost town with the weather. So, Chappy gets into the rum, hard, and decides to help out in the kitchen. Esther made a big bowl of mashed potatoes ... she told him to serve them on each plate, give them a little salt and pepper; you know, something easy to keep him busy that he couldn't screw up. Chappy got into the pantry and brought out white pepper and proceeded to mix it into everyone's mashed potatoes. Some got a little, some got a lot ... Mack got a half a bushel in his. So, now the meal's going on and Esther serves this lovely dinner ... she is the dearest, sweetest person, don't you think?"

"She sure is. So ...?" Chris asked.

"Here we are, all enjoying this meal, complimenting Esther on her great generosity and wonderful cooking," Greg rolled back in his chair as he continued talking while beginning to laugh. "Mack is choking down his potatoes with rivers of tears running down his cheeks." Greg burst into a fit of laughter, laboring to get the rest of the story out. "He never flinched! He told her how great everything was, meanwhile, he's got a ten alarm fire going off in his mouth!"

They both sat and laughed like old buddies. "Mack still doesn't want to hear about it," Greg said, "and that's exactly why Chappy keeps it going. See, what Mack forgets sometimes is that Chappy lost his son in Vietnam. He and Esther look at us as some kind of a way to fill that hole."

"I see ..." Chris said, disappointed in a story that closed with two sad endings ... Chappy's son, and ... a dead end for him. The pair of new/old buddies sat and finished their lunch, Greg still chuckling and Chris quietly fighting off his chagrin over false hopes. They both looked up to greet Dr. Grayson entering the galley.

"I'm going to make a quick bite ... Mr. Brown, could I see you in my office at two o'clock to discuss the curriculum?" she asked, in a very businesslike tone.

"Yes, by all means, I'll be there, Dr. Grayson," he answered.

With lunch finished, Greg went to his duties as galley chef and Chris began moving his belongings from his kayak to his room. From the stern compartment, he carried up his duffle bag containing three changes of clothes that he washed in the laundry in Boothbay. From the front compartment he took his charts, his Edward Rowe Snow and Dr. Felicia Grayson books and his good luck charm, an offshoot of his mother's original porcelain plant, growing in a small ceramic pot.

Before doing anything else in his room, he put the plant on the windowsill and carefully hung the offshoot over the curtainrod so that the plant would grow like a vine along the window casing. Small, star-like flowers, just beginning to show, hung in suspended pink clusters — delicate, fragrant star-like flowers that, although living, resembled flowers that were crafted of porcelain.

Looking at the timeless flowers, he remembered the last time he saw his mother alive, when she gave him and his sister each a cutting of the plant:

"The *vaaran vuodet* [years of danger] will be over for us shortly, she reassured them. "When we get to the *Yhdysvallat* [United States], we each will start our own *kasui* [plant] in our new *koti* [home]."

One hour after hearing these hopeful words, he and his older sister, Mari, were orphaned.

5
THE WORKSHOP

LAT. 43 DEG. 45.2 MIN. N.
LONG. 69 DEG. 36.95 MIN. W.

Chris found his way to the shower, and after changing clothes, headed for Dr. Grayson's office, ready to begin work. As he walked through the sea breeze between the two buildings, the two cats, Zeke and Rogers, bounded along behind him in the shadow of the watchtower. He reached the building that still had its brass sign of old that read "workshop," knocked on the slightly ajar door and pushed it open.

"Come in, Mr. Brown ... come in," Dr. Grayson offered from behind her desk. "Have a seat, please." She motioned for him to sit down. "How are you finding things so far? Did you get settled in all right?"

"Yes, I moved into the corner room upstairs."

"That's the best room, in my opinion. The sunrise is spectacular from that room ... you can't sleep late even if you wanted to."

"I would never want to, Dr. Grayson. That's the best part of the day," he replied.

"I just got off the phone from Cambridge. I had a very informative conversation with an old colleague, Dr. Lawrence Frederick. He told me a couple of things that weren't in your resume."

Chris felt a little jolt of adrenaline in the pit of his stomach. "How is Fred doing?" he asked with a little apprehension.

"Great, as usual … he said to say hello to you. I checked with him to see which class would be best for you to teach, but he completely shattered my plans. An introductory class in oceanography would be a great waste of your talent.

"He feels that it is time for you to go public with your activities of last spring, and thought that the perfect place to start would be right here. His office faxed me the transcripts of your presentation in New York." She sat back in her chair and folded her arms, watching him keenly, awaiting a response.

Chris' face showed his displeasure. "That was supposed to be kept in confidence, Dr. Grayson. Some of my best friends could be very hurt by that. Which transcripts did you receive?"

"First of all, I know that you and Fred had an understanding. He explained the fine print … he agreed to keep this quiet unless it was absolutely necessary. I'm not going to be around much longer and the year 2000 isn't far away … if your money is where your mouth is, you can't deny the seriousness of the situation. Fred said he'd handle damage control on the other end … they'll understand … And the transcript? The one translated from Finnish to English? That was a masterstroke, addressing the United Nations Conference on Ending World Hunger in the language of Finland. As the kids say, 'what's up with that'?"

"I can't believe this," Chris whispered, in a daze.

Dr. Grayson came out from behind her desk and perched herself on the corner, closer to Chris. She put her hand on his shoulder in a motherly gesture. "Look, Chris, you've trusted him all these years ... when you needed a push, he gave it to you. Now he's pushing you out of the nest ... not to fall, but to fly! It's time for you to get out there and take up where the rest of us leave off. Mack Mackenzie, Me, Fred, we're like the dinosaurs. We've had our shot and now we're just lumbering around, hoping the asteroid misses us. We're good at what we do, sure, but what good is being a good dinosaur? Good or bad, they all met the same fate."

"I understand. But what about the guys on the team?"

"If you really meant what you said at the U.N., the guys on the team will thank you — eventually. They can't share your sense of purpose and vision ... but it might just be that you save one of their kid's lives in some way, someday. Oh, vision is a blessing and a curse, and, by the way, thanks for the plug in your speech!" She looked into his blue eyes and smiled reassuringly as if she were his own mother. "It's up to you. The problem won't go away, you know that."

"What do you have in mind?" Chris was adjusting to this unexpected development.

"It's all right here in these paragraphs." Dr. Grayson held out the transcript and pointed to a section she had highlighted in yellow. "Read this — aloud — because this, believe it or not, is your mission statement."

Chris exhaled, rattling his lips. He took the paper and began to read ...

"'In 1980, Dr. Felicia Grayson warned us that the protein sources in the oceans of the earth were in danger of collapse due to the cumulative effects of pollution, bungled opportunities and mismanagement of fisheries. Two-thirds of the commercial species of fish depend on the estuaries for some part of their life cycle ... the very estuaries that cling to survival in the shadow of man's development. The population of the earth will be over six billion by the year 2000 ... the estimates are that by the year 2050, the population will be at least nine billion, possibly much more ... Consider, my friends, that the world can only indefinitely sustain the needs of two billion people at the living standard of present day Europeans. Right now, the fishing interests of the United States throw tons of fish back into the sea to satisfy the management schemes of people who have never stepped aboard a fishing boat, unlike myself.'

"'Speaking as an oceanographer, I find this reprehensible. Right now, the fertile farmland near the banks of the Mississippi River is being systematically washed into the Gulf of Mexico, along with its cargo of excess fertilizer, creating what has been termed the Dead Zone, where nothing lives. Farmland, the bastion of food production, is killing the other bastion of food production — the ocean! Speaking as an anthropologist, I warn you, and all citizens of this fragile sphere ... history has a way of rearing its ugly head when you least expect it. The next great war will not be fought over gold or strategic territory by industrialized armies, it will be fought in every street, jungle, house, and corner of the globe ... it will be hand-to-hand fighting for the scraps of food that will be in such short supply. Supply and demand? Supply and demand? If we do not address the supply, the demand will be addressed by horrific means.'"

Chris paused, then went on, reading more slowly as the impact of his own words sank in.

"'Speaking once again as an anthropologist, and also an oceanographer, I feel that one of the best ways to help stabilize the food shortage is to definitively realize what makes the mighty oceans tick. Aquaculture is a wonderful, alternative, futuristic means of providing food, and all available means should be afforded to its continued inception, however, it is still unlikely to replace the wild harvest's rate of protein production by the year 2000. It is highly unlikely that it, or any food production scheme on its own, will keep pace with the population growth. Simply put, we still can't beat Mother Nature's protein production from the seas. I propose we ascertain, beyond the shadow of a doubt, what the level of prudent sustainable yield of the wild populations of the oceans are, and employ a common sense methodology that has as its mission statement the pledge of zero waste. We should stop harrassing, and rather partner with, the food producers that learned their trade in antiquity. Fishermen are hunter/gatherers ... they came before farmers, before computers, before all of us. To use the words of Sir Dudley Diggs when he addressed the English Parliament in the 1600's, 'They are chiefly to be cherished, for they bring in much wealth and ask nothing in return.' I go rambling on, but I guess that's it ..." He stopped.

Dr. Grayson looked at him. Her eyes blazed. "That's your curriculum, right there ... that's your class ... that's what I want you to teach the next round of kids coming through ... and keep hammering it into them! I wish I was there to hear that, but actually, this was better ... and you did that whole talk in Finnish? How come?" There wasn't much that got to Felicia Grayson at this stage in her career, but this certainly did.

Chris stood up and went over to the window, looking out at the afternoon sky closing in with fog again. "I had to make a hard choice when I went there ... I couldn't tell my teammates where I went. I thought if I made the address in Finnish, the news media wouldn't bother to broadcast any sound bites of my speech. I told the team coach I broke my shoulder and went to Mass General to get patched up. Then I took off the sling, hopped a train and went to New York."

"I know about your whitewater kayaking ambition. It must have torn you apart not to try out for the Olympic team. Do you think you would have made it?"

He continued staring out the window, watching the afternoon southeast air flow turn on the fog factory. "The qualifying times weren't even close to my worst runs ... yeah ... I could have made it. All the other guys I trained with made it, and I could beat any one of them."

"Why, then, Chris, why?" Dr. Felicia Grayson, as stern a taskmaster as she was, felt her heart going out to the earnest young man.

"I figured that if I went to the Olympics, I could represent the country, but if I went to the U.N., I could represent the world. My sister told me once that this thing we call life is the real thing, not a dress rehearsal ... you're always in the show. A lot of her dreams rubbed off on me, I guess. It sounds like a great sacrifice, but, really, I did it for one person," he said in a choking voice. "That's what she would have done, if it came down to the choice and that's all I needed to know."

Outside, the fog rolled in, cool, wet and heavy. The sun was swallowed up. In the distance, the sound of Cuckolds Light foghorn could just barely be heard. Damariscove and its denizens were isolated unto themselves once again.

The evening mug-up was quiet and contemplative for Chris. He did meet and chat with Dr. Dave Burkette and his wife, Sandy, both very nice folk, glaciologists working on an ice-age project up at Wood End. Mack stayed on his homeboat, missing the meal entirely; Greg said that was normal, "... if he's wrapped up in something, which, a lot of times, he is."

Later that evening, cup of tea in hand, Carleton Gregory took his nightly walk down to the wharf and noticed a light glowing through the fog from the corner room upstairs in the station. *That kid don't give up,* he thought. *He needs a day out of the barrel, and the best way to do that is in a bait barrel!*

6
POOR SHOAL

LAT. 43 DEG. 43.4 MIN. N.
LONG. 69 DEG. 36.5 MIN. W.

"Slimey ... hey, you awake?" It was 5:30 A.M. on Friday, the next day. Greg stood outside Chris's door and spoke in a low volume. "Hey Slimey, breakfast is on ... I didn't know if you wanted to help me haul the lobster gear after mug-up."

Greg knocked on the door. It came unlatched and swung open slightly as a bright summer sun illuminated the room. "Hey Slimey ... Chris ... you gettin' up or what?" Greg called quietly.

Gee, I wonder if he's all right, Greg thought.

He creaked the door open just enough to get his head in. On the desk was a stack of papers. What he saw next made him stop and look in wide-eyed puzzlement. The bed was drawn tight along the wall and Chris was asleep on his side, lying as straight as an arrow. His back was literally riding up the wall, leaving most of the bed unused. The pillows weren't under his head, but jammed alongside his body.

43

That's really strange, Greg thought.

"Hey Slimey, you're burnin' daylight," Greg said in a loud voice.

"*Pozhalujsta! Pozhalujsta! Ya nye ponimayu! Pozhalujsta, Starpom Fedorovich!*" [In Russian: "Please! Please! I do not understand! Please, Deputy Captain Fedorovich!"]

Greg pulled the door shut very gently and crept away shaking his head. *He's probably been up all night working on something. Either that, or he got captured by aliens and he's trying to tell me Elvis's address. I'd better leave him alone,* he thought and crept back downstairs to the galley.

In ten minutes, Chris appeared at the breakfast table, yawning and stretching. "Did I hear someone calling for me a few minutes ago?"

"I did, Slimey ... I'm sorry if I disturbed you," Greg answered, still bewildered. "Here ... I'll pour you a coffee."

"Oh ... no problem, actually, thanks for getting me up. Coffee smells good ... I guess I went back to sleep after I heard someone steaming out of the harbor," he answered through a half-awake yawn.

"Yeah, Mack's got a fish trap experiment going in the deep water outside Poor Shoal. He's got a bunch of those collapsible fish traps from the west coast out there. He's even got an underwater camera on one of them. Wanna ride along when I haul my lobster gear? Maybe we can catch him out there ... we'll be back somewhere around early afternoon. Whatd'ya say? Fresh air, lively conversation and no pay, how can you beat that?"

Chris thought for a moment, fighting off his dutiful instincts. *All I have to do is put that curriculum on Dr. Grayson's desk. It's all done, but I can't type it until my laptop gets here on the mail boat.*

"Hey ... why not," he answered. "We don't start class until Monday, right?"

"That's the ticket, Slimey!"

"I want to help if I go, Greg. No freebies here ... I want to help," Chris said, enthusiastically.

"Well, the state doesn't let you do much without a sternman license. I'll be doing most of the work, but you can ask me about your thesis, how's that?"

Chris looked out at the crystal clear bluebird day. "Deal!"

"Good, get yourself fed, I'll make us a couple of sangwiches and we'll head for the boat. We'll leave this grub under the heat lamps for the rest of the gang. The kitchen is all cleaned up; I'll get the plates when we get back. I wanna get my traps baited to the doors so we can take the weekend off for the students comin' on. You can't haul on Sundays in the summer, anyway."

Chris bounded up the stairs to his room, gathered up his night's work, ran back down and tacked a manila envelope marked, "Fisheries Anthropology 212. Aspects, ramifications and historical comparisons of ancient vs. modern coastal cultures," on Dr. Grayson's door. The two new/old friends finished their breakfast, made their lunch, and went down the dew-laden path to the wharf. Seagulls floated overhead on a slight west breeze, which brought just enough air movement to make the water sparkle and glimmer in the best summer sea fashion.

Greg looked up and took a deep breath of warm salty air. "We won't get many days like this one, Slimey! Look out there ... flatass calm all the way to Portugal! We'll prob'ly be able to see Monhegan Island today ... you lucked out, that's for sure! My punt is over here on the end of the float. Wanna take her? She'll start first pull."

At the inside end of the float lay a blue, ten-foot long, wooden flatiron skiff. The name *H&B Too* was on either side of the bow, next to the Maine registration numbers. Chris crawled over the seats to the outboard motor hanging off the stern and gave the recoil cord a hearty yank, bringing the motor to smokey life.

"I told ya," Greg semi-yelled over the noise, with a smile. "She's like an old horse ...knows her way! Let me get the grub in, and we'll flemish down in Bristol fashion."

The *H&B Too* cut a watery path to the north end of the harbor where Greg's pretty lobsterboat, the *Hayley and Blair* was riding next to the float. They loaded their lunch bag onto the bigger boat. Chris couldn't stop smiling ... that little ride was pure enjoyment.

"I'll get the engine going, Slimey," Greg said as he lifted the hatch to the engine compartment and propped it open. He put his head in and began checking the engine, viewing the oil and coolant levels, opening the seacock, taking a quick look at the belts and pumps; all the things that become second nature to a waterman at the start of the day. While waiting, Chris strolled the float and was amazed at what he hadn't really paid attention to on landing the day before.

At the far end of the floats was a mast, about ten feet high. On top was a small windmill generator, cycling away in quiet motion. A bank of solar cells was mounted off one side of the yardarms, and a solar heating panel was mounted off the other. At eye level was a plastic battery box with cables leading to it from the float deck and upwards to the electrical components mounted above. A pair of plastic pipes led from the heating panel to floor fittings which led below the deck of the float. Chris put his ear down to the deck of the float and could make out a very faint whirring sound. *This is interesting,* he thought.

Above him loomed the side of Mack Mackenzie's homeboat, the *Elizabeth Gale*. Her sixty-eight foot length took up the opposite side of the float system, and more. The bow extended a good twenty feet beyond, tethered to a substantial mooring chain that led to the harbor floor.

The *Elizabeth Gale* was one of the few members left of what was once a proud seafaring sorority. She was a wooden eastern rig, built in Maine and refined by evolution from the days of sail. Every line of the vessel was a graceful curve: strong, beautiful and functional. The eastern rig fishing vessels were the ultimate blend of form following function; of art imitating life; of rare beauty in man's most dangerous industry. Like their ancestors, the fishing schooners, every view from every angle commanded respect for the craftsmen who assembled them, and further commanded respect for the people who depended on them for their lifeblood and living.

The "Lizgale" was built at the Newbert and Wallace Shipyard in Thomaston, Maine in 1968. She was sixty-eight feet overall, drew just shy of nine feet of water and was twenty-one feet wide. From her ancestors, the fishing schooners, the steering station evolved to the wheelhouse, located on the stern. Under the wheelhouse was the engine room, which was the most practical place to install an engine when the first sailing vessels were powered. Ahead of the curved fore-section of the wheelhouse lay the winch, used when she was fishing. Ahead of that, the deck, with its fish hold underneath. At the forward end of the vessel, the doghouse made a curved shelter for the ladder leading below to the fo'c'sle which housed the crew's accommodations and galley. There were two masts, again a holdover from the early days, but they now were used to handle fish and gear rather than sails. The high main mast was located just aft of the doghouse, the other, just ahead of the wheelhouse. Rigging stretched and criss-crossed between the two.

Three things showed that she no longer was an active fishing vessel. The hatch cover for the fish hold was very obvious. Where once was a small opening only large enough for a two-bushel basket to be hoisted through, was now a curved arch of windows, revealing that the hold was now part of Mack's living arrangements. Second, on the foremast was the same arrangement of solar panels and windmill as on the float. Third, was the total lack of any netting or fishing gear stowed anywhere on deck. Every square inch of the boat was painted to perfection … neat as a pin. She looked imposing and mighty, yet cheerful and cozy.

Chris looked aloft with his mouth open wide, taking in the view. He remembered these boats well ... they were etched in his memory from his boyhood. The eastern rigs from New Bedford, Newport, Pt. Judith, Gloucester, Boston and Provincetown all, at one time or other, plied the same offshore waters where he had spent his early years on the *Zvezda Rybaka*, also known as Soviet factory ship no. 610, the *Fisherman's Star*. In his boyish memory, all the eastern rigs looked the same, and all had foreign names ... this one looked as familiar, or as remote, as they all had. His memory shifted back to *Starshi Pomoshchnik*, *Starpom* Fedorovich, who was his father figure aboard the *Fisherman's Star*. In his thoughts, he was back aboard no. 610, the deputy captain holding young Kristiian's hand at the rail and pointing out at the Americans ...

"See how they all fish so independent of each other. *Konkurentsiya*! ... I tell you, young one, *we* fish together, for the good of all ... *khozraschet*, we support each other! But ... the Americans fish for themselves, from their own little ships ... who will win that contest, my young friend, eh?"

"Hey, Slimey!" Greg called, interrupting Chris's memories. He hadn't heard the engine start, or noticed that Greg was standing on the float holding onto his boat after removing all the docklines. "Let's go fishin!"

Chris shook off the old haunts and bounded aboard the *Hayley and Blair*.

"Why don't you take the wheel and head on out ... I'm going to stretch things a little bit and fill some bait bags on the way out. You can run this rig, can't you?" Greg asked.

Chris felt like a kid with a new toy, rejuvenated in spirit and free of the adult world of constraint. "You mean it?" he asked, smiling broadly, his eyes like saucers. "You want me to take it out?"

"Sure ... throttle's the left lever, shift's the right, the pointed end goes first. Just put her in gear, rev her up to about twelve hundred, stay in the center of the harbor and head for the gong buoy outside the Motions," Greg instructed in a voice loud enough to be heard over the engine. "There's so many lobsters they're bustin' the doors out of my traps ... let's go get 'em!"

The bright blue hull of the *Hayley and Blair* eased away from the float and began to make its way out of the harbor. Onboard were five barrels of salted herring for bait, three hundred gallons of diesel fuel, assorted tools and spare parts of the trap fishery trade and ... two big kids wearing broad smiles. Chris looked around with joy as he piloted the boat through the harbor. The sun glinted off the water for as far as he could see; up ahead, lobster buoys began to come into view, their differing colors bobbing merrily on the low swells. On the deck behind him, Chris saw Greg filling small mesh bags with the salted herring from the barrels, which later would be hung inside his lobster traps when they were hauled and checked. The activity aboard aroused the interest of a few seagulls who followed along behind, cackling and flying low, hoping for a handout as the engine sang out its low, powerful presence. The fine lines of the hull cut through the water, leaving a wake that other sea birds resting in the harbor rode up and over, coming to rest in the same position, never noticing or caring about their displacement.

Chris began to examine the vessel he was piloting as the pair motored along past the Marine Science Center. The *Hayley and Blair* was thirty-six feet long and as pretty a Maine lobsterboat as was ever built. She was the product of the hands of master boatbuilder Ralph Stanley from Southwest Harbor, on Mt. Desert Island. The lines of the hull were unmistakeably Ralph's — smooth, fair, just a slight angle-off of the bow and the trademark angling-in of the top of the transom; a tumblehome stern, the coasters called it. Her mahogany hull was painted bright blue, with a white waterline, or bootstripe, running all around at the water's edge. The cabin was painted white with a two-portlight trunk forward.

The steering station was nestled under the cabin roof, on the starboard side. Above the wheel, mounted on the overhead, was a GPS unit for satellite navigation, a LORAN unit, for navigation from shore-based signals, two VHF radios for contact with other boats and emergency hailing to the Coast Guard, and a radar display unit, to view the surroundings in times of reduced visibility. In front of him, mounted next to the compass, was the color video depth sounder, a paper recording depth sounder and the control handle to the hydraulic system that powered the hauler. Hanging out over the rail next to the steering wheel was a structure of welded stainless steel pipe called the davit, which had a snatchblock, an open sided pulley, hanging from its upper extremity. On the bottom of the davit, next to the rail, was mounted the hydraulic hauler, which resembled two pie plates bolted together backwards. Once spinning, these plates gripped the buoy rope between them and pulled the traps to the surface.

"This is a beautiful boat, Greg," Chris yelled back at his shipmate, who pulled his head out of a bait barrel to answer.

"Yeah ... she sure is, if I do say so. Mack and I went together and ordered a pair of sisters ... his is just painted black and cream color, that's all. We figured that if we standardized a lot of things, it would make it easier for the both of us. The boats are a little different, but the engines, pumps, electronics, hydraulics ... all that stuff is the same," Greg semi-yelled back. "We keep spare parts, filters, hoses, all that sorta thing in the Lizgale engineroom ... that way, we can keep going more and help ourselves out even when we're living out here for the summer. He put that longer house on his; that's about the only difference besides the paint! Yup, Ralph builds a fine boat, don't he?"

"He sure does. We're at the gong buoy, where do you want to go?" Chris asked.

Before Greg could answer, the radio on the overhead came to life, startling the new skipper.

"*Susan G.* callin' the *Haley and Blair* ... you on, Greg?" It was Mackenzie.

Chris turned to Greg to see what he should do. "Why don't you answer him, I'm up to my ears in baitjuice," Greg said with a hand gesture to the microphone.

"*Haley and Blair* here ... good morning, Jim," Chris spoke into the microphone.

"Hey ... did that pirate shanghai you, or what, Old Scout?" Mackenzie radioed back. "Where are you guys, on your way?"

"Right now we're at the gong buoy outside of the harbor ... Greg's right here ... hang on a sec." Even though Chris could comfortably address the United Nations in a foreign language, he felt a little awkward talking into the radio. He motioned for Greg to come take over. Greg smiled and took the microphone while Chris kept steering the boat straight ahead.

"What's up, Mack, you killin' the breed or what?" Greg transmitted.

"Hey, Cap ... are you going to haul your gear down here at Poor Shoal today?"

"Well, I was going there last ... why?"

"If you can break your routine, you might want to come see this ... I think we've solved the problem. I'm watching this big old soaker codfish on the underwater camera trying to make up his mind whether to come into this trap. You've got to see this, that is ... if you've got a few minutes."

Greg smiled and looked at Chris, who looked back with an eager expression on his face. Greg nodded and pointed out the front window to a boat off in the distance. "See that boat? That's Mack over there about a mile-and-a-half away. Why don't you shove the throttle up to eighteen hundred and head for him." Greg grabbed the microphone again. "We'll be right there!"

Chris pushed the throttle ahead and the boat picked up speed, spritely skipping over the swells to Mack's position. Once they were close, Greg came forward and took over at the controls. "Chris ... get a couple fenders off the starboard side, will ya, please?" Greg asked. Chris found two rubber fenders, then tied them hanging over the side to prevent the boats from hitting each other. Greg deftly brought the *Hayley and Blair* alongside Mack's boat. Once the two boats were tied together, Greg and Chris hopped aboard the *Susan G.*

"Take a look in the tank … you won't believe it!" Mack exclaimed. "Look!" he beckoned as he held up the cover of his circulating tank, normally reserved for the preservation and transport of live lobsters.

Greg and Chris walked over and peered in — the tank was half full of live codfish, flapping their fins in the water flow to hold their position. Mack was jubilant. He looked up with his eyebrows raised, waiting for a reaction.

"How'ja do it?" Greg asked, cocking his hat on the back of his head.

"Took a lesson from Einstein, Cap. Until we put the camera on the gear I didn't know … relativity! It's so common sensical, I forgot!" Mack explained from under his hat's visor, his hands held out, palms up, accentuating every syllable. "Just make everything move relative, and things won't go haywire!"

Greg got eye contact with Chris and winked, conveying a 'wait for more information' message.

"C'mon down in the foc'sle here … take a look in the video monitor," Mack urged.

They crowded down the ladder leading to the foc'sle and sat at the galley table, where a video monitor was fastened with bungee cords. Greg and Chris were wide-eyed and silent. Ahead of them was a picture of fish swimming in a fish trap lying on the bottom of the ocean, some 235 feet below. Mack pointed up to the screen showing a few fish in the trap.

"See this one, right here?" he said, his finger chasing a video image around the screen. "This one came in about a half hour ago … he's already tried the escape vent and won't fit through … too big. See this one?" He shifted his finger to another fish. "This guy has only been in here a minute … watch! … see? There he goes … out the vent … too small! We'll catch him next year," he said, smiling.

"Now ... let me shift the camera over to the entrance ..." Mack took the joystick control and the view of the lens changed. "See this big old soaker? ... he's been around ... knows the ropes ... but I think we're wearing down his resistance. Watch him ... c'mon ... c'mon!" Mack tried to encourage the fish with his hand movements.

They watched the video monitor as the two boats gently rose and settled on the swells in unison. "How big is that trap?" Chris asked.

"I got 'em from the west coast ... they're black cod traps. They're big ... about four-and-a-half feet square, but they collapse on deck to move them around." Mack answered.

"They heavy?" Chris asked.

"Heavy for one guy, but it isn't like I'm handling a lot of them," Mack replied, his eyes still glued to the screen, making hand motions to the fish below.

"Here he comes ... he's coming in!" Greg exclaimed. "C'mon in ... you can do it!"

Mack, Chris and Greg were on the edge of their seats in anticipation. Slowly, the large codfish swam around then made a charge for the opening and attacked the bag of bait hanging inside, his head swinging back and forth in a feeding motion. Cheers of joy erupted, sounding like a one-second-to-go touchdown at the Superbowl. The three clenched their fists and hooted out in unison ... "Yeah! Alright! ... We got 'im! ... Wa-hoo!"

Mack put his hands up, palms down, getting serious. "Okay ... here's where we go real gentle. See ... Einstein. As long as I haul this thing nice and slow, the fish inside move relative to the trap and they make it to the surface alive. I was yanking these up too fast and it smashed the fish into the sides of the trap and each other ... I didn't know until I put the camera on there! I'll go rig this up ... keep an eye on the screen and let me know if I'm going too fast." He bounded up the ladder, stood at the rail and fed the buoy line over the snatchblock and between the two plates of the hauler. Ever so slightly, he moved the control handle to start the hauler in rotary motion, the line singing as it became taut under the strain.

Chris looked at Greg, who was peering intently at the screen, waiting for the trap to begin its ascent. "What's he up to, anyway, Greg?" he asked.

Not moving his gaze, Greg answered. "Well, he wants to be able to catch fish without any small fish discarded dead, Okay? Then he wants to bring them ashore ... alive, no less ... and sell 'em for a premium price. So far, he's got the catching part down to a T, but now it looks like he's got the live part working. Oh ... here she goes!" Greg shifted his voice up to the foc'sle companionway, his eyes still glued to the screen. "Here she comes, Mack ... take it easy ... okay, they're settled down, just keep it easy ... beautiful!"

Chris maneuvered himself around Greg and scurried to the deck above as Mack stood by the hauler, his left hand on the control lever and his right retrieving the camera cable, letting it fall to the deck. Chris went to the rail and took over on the cable, watching down into the water with anticipation. Soon, the trap broke free of the surface and inched its way to the top of the davit. Inside, it was teeming with fish ... ten codfish ... five cusk ... two ocean pout ... a flipping mass of sea life.

"Quick, here, Old Scout, let's get this thing opened and get the codfish into the tank!" Mack spoke over the engine to Chris. They speedily opened the top of the trap and grabbed for the wriggling fish inside. With strong hands and determination, what looked like a greased pig chase eventually had all the codfish, even the old soaker, safely deposited in the live tank. Greg stood at the top of the foc'sle companionway, his arms folded, laughing through his moustache. Mack and Chris looked at each other with an unspoken, phew!

"I'm going to have to head for town and unload," Mack said, leaning against the side of the tank. "I think there's about five hundred pounds in here, and with all the other stuff, the cusk and whatnot, I think I've got close to eight hundred on board. I really want to see how long these guys will live in the co-op tanks ... I don't dare take any more. I was going to haul some lobster gear, but I guess it'll have to wait until Monday," he reasoned.

"Well, congratulations, Cap!" Greg offered. "You need any help, or should we head along?"

"Naah." Mack waved his hand, no. "You've played with me long enough ... thanks for coming over ... Hey! What do you think of this operation, Old Scout?" Mack asked with a touch of victory in his voice.

Chris had only been away from the dock for an hour, but his answer was a question of characteristic understatement. "Do you guys always have this much fun?"

After a few chuckles, the two boats parted company. The *Susan G* steamed for Boothbay Harbor to unload, Greg and Chris took a short jaunt back over the top of Poor Shoal and laid-to beside Greg's lobster buoys. He had his traps arranged in ten-trap trawls; ten lobster traps tethered together off a long groundline with a buoy at either end of the system. His boat was now at the southeast end of one of the trawls.

Through many years of experimentation and refinement, Greg had settled on wire mesh traps, four foot long, eighteen inches high and two feet wide. He called them double-parlor, meaning there were two entrances, one on either side of each end, called the kitchen, then two parlor sections where the lobsters would remain beyond two one-way ramps of netting. Every lobsterman had his own preferences for his gear; no two ever used the same exact configuration.

Greg maneuvered the boat alongside a bobbing flourescent green and orange buoy, then gaffed it with his boathook. He threaded the line through the snatchblock and then to the plates of the hauler. Turning the control lever, he said over his shoulder, "Sorry you can't get more involved, but this is where you need a state sternman license, Slimey." The rope spun through the hauler and fed its way to deck in a haphazard coil. "Sure is a beautiful day, huh?"

Chris sat on top of the lobster tank and watched the goings-on at the rail with heavy anticipation. One by one, the traps of the trawl made their way to the surface. Greg took the groundline out of the snatchblock, popped the trap on the rail, opened the access door on top and re-fed the line to the hauler in one deft, synchronous motion. Then he put in a fresh bait bag, threw over any lobsters that were obviously too short to be legal, checked the ones that were close and stored the keepers on a tray for later. As the next trap was winding its way to the surface, he slid the previous trap along the boat's rail and stacked it on the stern with the others. The deck became a mass of seemingly tangled line, but with one kick, the excess line was under the rail, out of harm's way.

Chris folded his arms and marveled at how well the boat, gear and man blended together to make an efficient operation. By the end of the first trawl, Greg had eleven keepers to which he applied rubber bands to keep their claws immobile. He handed them to Chris, who slid them into the live tank below him.

"A little over a pound to the trap ... that's okay, but I think we can do better," Greg said. "I'm just trying this area out ... the stuff over by Pumpkin Island is in the hot spot. But these guys will be shedding shortly. Once they change their pants, they don't come out for a while. Those shells all feel hard to you?" Greg asked. Chris nodded a scrunched-mouth, yes.

Greg turned the boat and put the throttle up to a fast clip. He threw the end buoy and the first trap overboard, then steamed on a southeasterly course. The groundline raced off the stern, became taut, then lurched the next trap overboard, then the next ... and the next ... in breathtaking speed.

"You sure don't want to step in the wrong place do you, Greg?" Chris asked loudly over the sound of whistling rope and engine.

"You definitely want to be careful, that's for sure, Slimey! Every now and then somebody goes over in a tangle ... they usually find the boat going around in a circle. I always remind myself that I have to be smarter than a piece of line, but even the best of us can get ganged up on by inanimate objects!" he quipped, making light of a somber topic. "You just can't be in too much of a hurry, that's all." Greg steered the boat to the next trawl and gaffed the buoy.

"So Greg," Chris asked over the sound of engine, hydraulics and tight line. "Tell me about some of the old adventures you and Jim had in Pt. Judith."

"Well," Greg yelled back over his shoulder as he worked at the rail. "We were roommates at OSU ... this was the early seventies, okay?" Without waiting for a reply, he continued. "One day, my father wrote me a letter. He had put in a couple newspaper clippings and a patch from my scuba diving course that I took in the summer. He was a hot spud ... told me to sew the patch to my tank!

"Anyway," he continued, "one of the clippings he put in was for Mack. See, Mack is from the North Shore of Massachusetts ... that's north of Boston." Greg paused while he slid a trap down the rail to the stern. "So," he went on, "the article was about how the East Germans were fishing outside of where Mack lived ... on Jeffreys Ledge. Jeffreys isn't too far from shore, you know ... it runs all the way from Cape Ann to up off of Kennebunk. It's about thirty miles off at the most, but heck, that isn't far. The East German factory ships had set up shop there and they were just running all over the ledge, left, right and crooked. Some of the Gloucester and Newburyport guys had gillnets set there, ya know ... monofilament nets that sit on the bottom to entangle the fish. They came back the next morning and found half the iron curtain had wrecked all their gear and they were pushed out of the area. With all their gear gone, there was no sense to hang around, and anyways, what's a couple forty foot Novi boats gonna do against a fleet of factory ships? So ... off they went, tail between their legs."

"Now ... one of the Gloucester draggers, an eastern rig called the ... um ..." Greg thought for a minute while he rebaited a trap. "The *Maria and Rose*, I think ... yup, I think that was the name ... she was steaming past the area at night and noticed all the lights, so they figured there must be some decent fishin' there. Well ... they laid-to and were going to wait for daylight to set the net in. They stopped right over a wreck, ya know, so's to be out of the way, and damned if one of the East German ships didn't haul back and come over to them. I don't know what happened next, but that ship's skipper didn't want them around there, that's for sure, so they rammed 'em! They cut the Gloucester boat in two and left the gang for dead." Greg slid another trap down the rail to the stern, then returned to the helm.

"Wow ... they just left those guys out there floating around?" Chris asked increduously.

"Yeah ... funny how it went. I mean there's s'posed to be some code to all seafolks isn't there? Thank God they all survived, but you don't just leave someone, even if it is your fault. 'Course, we didn't know then what we found out later; when we read the article we were sittin' out in Oregon, three thousand miles away." Greg recollected.

"How could that have possibly affected you two, being all the way across the country?" Chris inquired.

"Well ... that's another strange part, Slimey. The article had the lat and long of where the Coast Guard picked these guys up. Mack recognized the bearings and looked it up on the chart he had hanging on our dormroom wall ... the Gloucester boat had laid-to right over the wreck of an old freighter that went down in World War II," Greg continued. "See, Mack had fished out there on a boat from New Hampshire during summers, so he knew the area a little," he said as he took another trap back to the stern. "You know, those big factory ships were towing some big nets across the bottom of the ocean, but there isn't a net or ship strong enough to tow a net through the wreck of a freighter and come out in one piece. Why would they want that piece of bottom? They couldn't tow a net across it and come out with any fish," he explained. "It was years before all the pieces of that puzzle were put together."

"Did you ever find out the name of the ship?" Chris asked between lobster traps being pulled over the rail.

"Oh yeah ... we found out, that wasn't hard. Every fisherman that worked around Jeffreys knew where the *Rowley Knight* was ... it even showed up on the depth sounder if you got close to it. There's probably enough torn-up nets on that wreck to start your own twine shop."

"I'm confused ... you were going to tell me about Point Judith, Rhode Island. How does this incident off northern Massachusetts tie in when you guys weren't even there?" Chris asked over the sound of the engine and hauler.

Greg looked off in the distance and took a deep breath, shut off the hauler and turned to face his young shipmate. He'd lost his chatty demeanor and was looking down at the deck. "It's a long story, Slimey," he said seriously, resuming eye contact. "I guess I mentioned it because one of our shipmates at the Point was the grandson of the captain of the *Rowley Knight*," he explained. To deflect more questioning, he added, "I thought you'd find it interesting that the East Germans were in that area, that's all."

Chris sensed he was in an awkward position so he decided not to push the issue. "I don't think many people knew about the distant water fleets being within eye contact of shore ... that is an interesting fact to add to my research," he said.

I wonder what's got him upset? Chris thought. To change the subject, he asked, "How many traps are you planning to haul today?"

Greg came back from the past and brightened up to his usual friendly luster, shaking his head as if he was recovering from a bad fall. "Oh yeah ... well, I figure this way, Slimey ... we're doin' good here, but that hot spot over at Pumpkin Island," he explained, talking animatedly and pointing to the east, "that has a hundred and eighty traps in it. We've got ten more trawls here, but what I'd like to know is about the Great Lakes … Boy, can you believe how nice this day is? … You lived out there, right?"

7

"Rise Again!"

LAT. 43 DEG. 45.19 MIN. N.
LONG. 69 DEG. 36.9 MIN. W.

Saturday morning's sunrise was hazy and orange as it broke over the Atlantic's horizon and drifted into Chris's room. He got out of bed, went to the window and knelt on the floor, folding his arms on the window sill. The ocean beyond looked serene and inviting. He smiled as he remembered the previous day, one of the most pleasant and fun days he'd had in his entire life. Fishing to him was always a calculated business, an assembly-line, a factory. It always seemed like work; noble work, but work nonetheless. Yesterday was different ... it was fishing, but it also was just pure fun, from piloting Greg's boat to watching Mackenzie to catching lobsters. The giddy anticipation of what was coming up next — he had never felt that on a factory trawler. Fishing was all drudgery until he saw the different side of it yesterday. *Those guys have got it made*, he thought as he looked to the north end of the harbor where the lobster boats rode next to the floats. *I can understand why they love it so much out there, but I can't help but wonder what happened to those guys down at Point Judith, though ...*

He arrived at the galley a little after 6:00 A.M. Taped to the cupboard door over the coffee machine was a notice from Dr. Grayson: "Staff meeting 9:00 A.M. in mess hall. Agenda includes class schedules and assignments. Students arriving today on 3:00 P.M. mailboat. Thank you. Dr. G."

Chris poured a cup of coffee, already made by Dr. Grayson or, perhaps, Greg, who both were up before him.

The two cats meowed at the back door. Setting his cup down, he let them in before he sat at the galley table. The cats instinctively and affectionately rubbed their bodies against his legs and purred for attention. "How are you boys today?" he asked, looking down. "You're good boys, yes, you are," he said in half baby-talk while extending his hand to pat them.

"They've got a friend with you, that's for sure," Mackenzie said as he strolled into the room. "They'll have you trained to feed them within a day or so," he said, as he put his hat on the back of his head and reached into the cupboard for a mug. "Seagulls in cat costumes, that's what you are, huh?

"So how you doing today, Old Scout?" he asked as he sat down.

"Oh ... fine. How did you make out with your fish yesterday? Did they all make it?" he asked, patting the cats.

"Yup ... as far as I know, they're all still swimming in the tank at the co-op. Now, if they don't need the space for lobsters, the next step is to see how long they'll live and still be a top-quality product. I tell ya, I'm pleased with what we did yesterday. Even if we lose them after a few days, we can still play the market with the freshest catch available. Fresh off the boat is old hat now."

Chris smiled and nodded. He was amused listening to Mackenzie. The fact that his experiment was going well was a pleasure to hear, but it was Mack's use of the word "we" that he found interesting. No matter where or when he talked to fishermen, they frequently used the word "we" even if they were completely alone in their waterborne efforts. Perhaps the word was more of a comfort to them than the lonely I, or perhaps it revealed the fact that many waterpeople find the ocean a spiritual place where you never are truly alone. Understandably, they'd never admit to that, other than using the word "we," of course.

"That's excellent, Mack," Chris said. "It sure looks like you and Greg have a fine time out there. I can't remember when I've had more fun ... it makes me want to go buy a boat and join in!" he added.

"I know how you feel, Chris, believe me I do. The problem is ... the more time you spend out there and the more you enjoy it, the more you won't fit into anything else." Mackenzie tucked his chin down as if to look over an imaginary set of glasses. "Isn't that the basis of your research?" he countered.

Chris looked up from patting the cats and shook his head, smiling in the realization that he forgot why he was even there. He sipped his coffee then admitted, "You got me there ... Fishing sure gets a hold of you, though, doesn't it?" he answered, looking for assurance.

"It sure does ... but not every day is a bluebird day in the summer, you know," Mackenzie countered, looking over his imaginary glasses again. "But, yeah, once you get into the lifestyle, it's hard to adapt to shoreside again. I mean, look at it this way ... are we all eternal optimists, like the sociologists say, or are we gambling addicts at a floating crap game? That's up to you to figure out, Hah-vidd!"

They both laughed. *That's why I wanted to pick this guy's brain,* Chris thought. *He's got a firm grasp on the obvious. But ... that was still a lot of fun yesterday.*

At 9:00, the staff gathered in the mess hall. Dr. Grayson called the meeting to order and passed out the school's schedules and assignments. Present were Mackenzie, Greg, Chris, and the Burkettes. Dr. G. said that the rest of the staff would be here on the mailboat, or as in the case of Paul and Jack, the research boat, captain and mate, they would be back, hopefully, after launching their boat on the evening high tide.

"Good morning everyone, thank you for coming. In front of you is the final version of our schedule and class rotations. As usual, I have arranged to have the students meet with me, Dave, and Sandy in the mornings to allow you fellows," she motioned to Greg and Mackenzie, "to work your fishing gear when it is best for you. Chris," she said, turning to face him, "excellent job on your preparation of the course ... thank you very much for the manuscript you left on my door. I've put you in for three mornings a week ... Monday, Wednesday and Friday from 10:30 to noon. That should give you quality time with all students and still give you four days out of the seven to conduct your doctoral research in whatever way you deem most fruitful. Is that good with you?" she asked.

"That's great, Dr. Grayson," he answered. "That's very generous. I have a question," he said, as he raised his finger.

"Yes?"

"I'd like to assist in some of the oceanography projects ... specifically, some of the aquaculture projects with Jim Mackenzie," he said, establishing eye contact with Mackenzie. "Would it be possible to help out some afternoons, schedule permitting?"

Mackenzie nodded a firm 'yes' and looked to Dr. Grayson with the same unspoken reply.

"As long as you two keep your emphasis on the students and the course while you are engaged in that course," she replied. "In other words, while engaged in oceanography, think oceanography ... while engaged in aquaculture, think along those lines. I want a firm blend of all the inter-disciplinary courses, but not a blurring. The students come first ... am I clear?" she lectured, maintaining control. "I am wholeheartedly in favor of your research and the combining of your talents, just make sure that your talents are combined on doctoral research outside of the class time."

"Deal," Mackenzie said.

"Yes ... your thoughts are well-taken, thank you," Chris answered.

"Mornings, I will take the introductory ecology classes, as usual ... 9:00 to 10:30, Monday, Wednesday and Friday." She continued, "10:30 to noon will be the new, and excellent-sounding, I might add, Fisheries Anthropology course from Chris. Dave and Sandy, your two rotations will be Tuesday and Thursday mornings, as you requested. I put in some extra time so that you can walk up to Wood End to your research site. If fifteen minutes is enough, that will put your two classes from 8:15 to 9:45 and 10:00 to 11:30. That means that there is fifteen minutes walk time after breakfast is over at 8:00. We all aboard?" Dr. Grayson asked.

Both geologists nodded an approval.

"Paul will make the research boat available for all twelve students together on Tuesday and Thursday afternoons ... his activities will be to reinforce what I cover in the previous class," she explained. "Greg ... you and Mack will have your boats available for special projects that Paul can't fit into his schedule, correct?"

They exchanged glances with each other and nodded. "Just let us know, Dr. G.," Greg answered. "We've always managed to fit a couple research projects in somewhere."

"Good," she said firmly. "On Monday-Wednesday-Friday afternoons all twelve students will be with Mack, myself, and now, Chris from two to five. I've called it 'Special Problems in Marine Ecology.' In March, the students were instructed by mail to develop a research project to work on. This year will be a little different ... they gave us no notice of their intentions. We'll see what they have for ideas, then group them and guide them accordingly. I thought it would get the old adrenaline going if we had to develop a few projects off the cuff ... make a good example of resourcefulness, too. What do you think?"

Mackenzie rocked his chair to the two back legs and hung his hat on the back of his head, exhaling while he thought to himself, smiling. "I like it ... it will definitely keep things interesting." He put the chair back on all four legs and crossed his arms. "Yup ... I think that's a great idea. It'll teach them that you can't always orchestrate what you'd like for conditions or funding," he said approvingly. "Yup, that's a winner ... you up to the challenge, Old Scout?" he asked, turning his head.

"I can't wait," Chris replied. "I wish this program was available to me when I was an undergrad."

Dr. Grayson folded her arms and nodded in sly approval, knowing full well what the outcome of the discussion would be before she even broached the subject. "Any questions, then?"

Dave Burkette, the geologist, raised his hand. "Enough of the trivial stuff about work ... I have a couple of important questions. First, is the mailboat still on schedule for a three o'clock landing, and ... more importantly, will we be having lobsters and clams tonight at the campfire?"

Everyone laughed and looked at each other.

"I haven't heard any problems with the boat, Dave," she responded. "What do our two fishermen think about the last request?"

"I've got about five hundred pounds of bugs crated up under the float. Thirty pounds or so wouldn't kill me. What do you think, Mack?" Greg asked.

"I'll match that on bugs," Mack chimed in. "I haven't checked the upweller in a week or so, but there should be close to twenty bushels of clams in there at legal size. Sure ... let's have a blowout!" he added exuberantly, sweeping his hands through the air.

"All right, then, thank you for coming, and ... thank you for your generosity, gentlemen," Grayson said, nodding to Greg and Mack. "And we'll all look forward to a great summer," she concluded, adding, "I'm going to tidy up a few loose ends ... it will be three before we know it!"

The group dispersed with all members going off to various tasks before the arrival of the students. Mack and Greg went to work on their boats; the Burkettes went north to Wood End. Chris was left with time on his hands so he packed a lunch from the galley and strolled off with a map of the island from one of the student handbooks. Shortly, Zeke and Rogers, the two cats, came following along behind. "I'd better know my way around a little, if I'm on the staff," he said to the two felines. "You guys will guide me, won't you?"

The first stop was straight across the top of the hill behind the station. On the west side of the island was a dramatic cliff, where the words "Sid 'n' Eva's Chair" was written on the map. As he trekked over the rise, the spectacular view of the mainland came into sight just before he reached the fifty-foot dropoff to the surging swells below. Chris rechecked the map. *I followed the right path, that's for sure,* he reassured himself, *but what the heck is Sid 'n' Eva's Chair?* He looked around. The path seemed to continue through the bushes right over the edge of the cliff. "That's odd," he said, but the two feline tourguides knew the way and took the lead, forging through the bushes and, seemingly, plunging off the edge. Chris eased his way along to the edge of the cliff and apprehensively looked down, hoping the cats hadn't used the last of their nine lives. He was relieved to see what appeared to be a natural stairway in the rocks which led down to a horizontal outcropping that looked exactly like ... well, a chair; a big, wide, armchair.

The two cats crawled down the stairs, hopped onto the rock formation, and curled up just as if it were a chair in someone's living room. Chris followed suit and settled down in a rather comfortable, albeit, hard, seat. The cats raised themselves and came to rest again, curling in his lap. Above, the sun shone warm and bright in a hazy blue-grey sky. Fifty feet below, the sound of the swells breaking against the rocks was soothing and spellbinding as a gentle southwesterly breeze helped them along. Between him and the mainland a few lobster boats were working, mere silhouettes against the far hazy shore of Southport. He stretched his legs, crossed his feet and settled back in a relaxed pose, his hands crossed behind his head, his body breathing in the salty sweetness of the sea.

It was some time before he got up to continue his self-guided tour ... who would want to leave? The next entry on the map was the west clocktower where lifesavers of old, making their rounds, punched in, thereby verifying they had made that leg of the patrol. The path led back to a fork; Chris headed north and came upon the granite structure. The tower wasn't that high, in fact, the station's watchtower dwarfed it, but there was still a sweeping view of the waters off the west side of the island. The construction was similar to the larger tower; the brass stair treads were made the same, and worn the same.

On the road again to the north side of the island, he took the path along the west shore. To his right were the remains of Poole's dairy farm and the makeshift pasture they had scrabbled out of the rocky landscape. To his left, were the waters of Boothbay, just beyond the surging swells. He passed the remnants of old foundations and remains of barns, pasture fences, milk houses and dwellings. His trek along the shore path eventually brought him through the bushes to the ice pond that was situated north of the harbor, just before the bridge that crossed the causeway to Wood End.

Those guys must have been tough characters to get out here in the dead of winter and saw ice out of this pond by hand, he thought. *It was a convenient source of refrigeration, and I imagine there wasn't much to do on many winter days out here, but it still must have been hard work*, he imagined, picturing hand-propelled ice saws being worked by hardy islanders. An ironic thought on such a fine summer day.

He continued on to the bridge, sat down on its old wooden timbers and decided to eat an early lunch. The causeway was so narrow at this point that the ocean's swells washed up on either side, meeting each other under his dangling feet. The two cats came along and strutted themselves back and forth along the handrails as Chris looked east toward Pumpkin Island and unwrapped his sandwich. The fresh memories of the previous day were still with him; a pleasant experience, yes, but, more, an epiphany of the soul. The ocean had always conflicted him with questions and commitments. The sea is life in its purest form, but it can also be haunting and murderous, taking away that which is most precious. Now it called to him as if it were a trusted companion, ready to share a joyous life together. Looking towards Pumpkin Island, munching on his mug-up, he drifted back to the *Zvezda Rybaka* ...

"Come here, little one," *Starpom* Fedorovich said to young Kristiian as the sun dipped below the horizon of Georges Bank. "Everywhere you look is life ... life from Mother Earth to feed her children!" he exclaimed, making a broad sweep of his arm. "Smell the air ... hear the birds. I tell you, my little friend, once you get used to the life here, there is no finer place for a man to spend his days. We have the best job on earth ... we feed thousands by our efforts."

Young Kristiian looked up at the tall man with the grey chinstrap beard. From under his military-looking hat he continued, "We all came from the sea at one time, you know ... our tears, our blood ... the same salt as the sea. Don't feel homesick for the land ... let those feelings go; you really are more at home right here!"

Chris had never known what *Starpom* Fedorovich meant by those words, but now he understood fully. The kind and gentle man who had saved his life at the border crossing and who had arranged his being smuggled to the United States was more of a father to him than he realized. He had grown up thinking that the factory trawler crews were bound to the sea only by duty. Some were, of course, but *Starpom* Fedorovich loved the life and its rewards, just like Greg and Jim, and most of the other coastal folk that he had interviewed, for that matter. But ... if he had never gone fishing with Greg, he wouldn't have understood the awesome, inexplicable connection between the ocean and its constituents.

It's true what Mackenzie said ... "the more you enjoy it, the more you won't fit into anything else," like starpom said, "You're really more at home right here."

He spoke aloud, "Would the *starpom* be as happy on shore, working in the confines of the mainland? Of course not," he answered. "Then … neither should any other person, of any country be driven off the water due to the whims of those who do not understand! It isn't about having a job that you like, it's about having a life that works for you, and in so doing, you provide one of the very basics that society needs … food!"

His mind wandered back to his memories of playing on the children's swingset mounted on the *shlupochnaya paluba*, (boat deck), of the *Zvezda Rybaka*. When his nineteen-year-old sister took her break from her duties as *ofitsiantki*, (galley waitress and chambermaid), she would come on deck, rain or shine, to share some playtime that a five-year-old would enjoy. Since they spent much of their time crammed together in their bunk reading books from the ship's library, these short recreation breaks in the open air were like heaven to him.

"Tyontaa! … tyontaa, Mari! … korkea!" (in Finnish, 'push, push, Mari … high!).

His heartbroken sister still managed to reveal her luminous smile during these outings, perhaps just for his sake, or maybe she could actually forget their plight for the moment.

"Huvi, Kristiian? … Huvi?" (Fun, Kristiian, Fun?) she would say back to him as he would "whee!" with glee.

Chris looked unseeingly out towards Pumpkin Island. The memory of his beautiful sister haunted his very being. How lovely and pure Mari was. Her light brown hair fell around her pretty face in waves and curls, showing off the blonde highlights that naturally framed her sweetness. Her cheeks were high and glowed like apples, her eyes sparkled with the color of the blue sky on a September afternoon. No softer, more soothing a voice did God ever make; no more caring a being did he ever create. She was as intelligent as any professor at a University, and took after her father with a gift for music that would have led her to the world's most prestigious stages, if ...

"*Amerikkalainen soutuvene, Kristiian! Katsella soutuvene!*" (American boat ... look at boat!), Mari exclaimed, stopping the swing for her young brother to get off. "*Amerikkalainen Kapteeni!*" (American Captain!). Chris was now back aboard the Star, visiting a memory that he hadn't realized he saved from his youth. Coming alongside was an American boat ... one of the many who stopped by to trade cigarettes, coca-cola, milk, perhaps magazines for ... for what?

"What did they get in return?" he again spoke aloud, standing bolt upright and staring out to sea. "What did they trade for?" he quizzed himself again, racking his brain for the obscure memory of a frightened five year old. "What could we possibly have had on that ship that they wanted to trade for?" He rolled his eyes in puzzlement and strained to remember some more details.

"The boats ... they were all like the *Elizabeth Gale*, all eastern rigs ... Starpom *told me we were twenty years ahead of the Americans, and would never see them catching up. They were all like the Elizabeth Gale....all — like — the* "Elizabeth — Gale!*"* Chris stuffed the last bite of his sandwich in his mouth and started running back along the path, the two cats loping behind.

Over the hardscrabble rocks he sprinted, through the low grasses, sending up a shot of dust with every step. He ran to the sandy spot where Jim had his outhaul tackle and stood looking out at the floats, the boats, and in particular, the Elizabeth Gale. Panting and out of breath, he composed himself and studied the vessel as best he could from shore.

"Point Judith ... Point Judith! It was a boat from an island ... Nantucket, Edgartown, Vineyard Haven, Menemsha, Block Island, Long Island, Oak Bluffs or ... Rhode Island? Point Judith is part of an island, in a way. The mail boat ... I've got to get a letter on that return trip ... the mail boat!" he said excitedly as he sprinted off to the station.

Chris ran to the station, threw the door open and hurdled up the stairs, taking two and three at a stride. He burst into his room and yanked the chair away from his desk, panting, out of breath. Fumbling around his papers, he found his tattered book by Edward Rowe Snow, took out a piece of folded paper stored in the pages and then scanned the addresses he had written there. Out of breath and fighting off the adrenaline, he began to write ...

Dear Mrs. Chambers,

My name is Christian Brown and I am pursuing a Ph.D in Fisheries Anthropology at Harvard University. My doctoral thesis concerns the demise of the commercial fishing industry of New England as seen through the eyes of the fishing interests themselves. I have learned from de-classified documents obtained under the Freedom of Information Act that your late husband, Lt. Cmdr. Lee Chambers, USCG, was assigned to Naval Intelligence at Newport, R.I. during the cold-war era and was considered an expert on interactions between the domestic and foreign fishing fleets. Any and all information that you can provide would be invaluable to my research, and would be greatly appreciated. If I may indulge your patience further, I am requesting that you pass this letter on to someone connected with your late husband, if, in your recollection, there is another living colleague of his that could shed more light on this very interesting piece of coastal history.

Thank you once again for any assistance you can lend.

Sincerely yours,
Christian Brown
c/o Damariscove Island Marine Research Center
Damariscove Island, Maine.

Chris's concentration was interrupted from outside the window by the calling of his name. "Hey Slimey!" It was Greg, standing on the ground below Chris's room. "Slimey! ... Hey ... what're you doin' up there?" Greg yelled up at the window, like a parodied version of Romeo and Juliet.

Chris stuck his head out of the window. "What's up, Greg?"

"If you've got time, could you help me gather up the fixin's for the lobster bake tonight? We need to take the punt up to the floats, get the bugs and clams, gather up some seaweed, get a fire goin' for coals, all of that." Greg explained. "I'd like to be squared away before Chappy gets here at three."

"Sure … be glad to … I'll be right there," he answered. Chris found the last postage stamp he had and put it on the envelope. At the bottom of the stairs, he slid the letter in the outgoing mail pocket on the inside of the station door, then went outside into the humid smokey southwest summer day.

"Thanks for the help. I hope I'm not getting you away from anything important," Greg said. The duo started walking toward the float in front of the station.

"I just finished some outgoing mail. I'm all set … what's first, the punt?" Chris asked as they bounced down the ramp to the float.

"Yup. We need to go up to the boats to get the bugs and clams, then stop along the shore and get some seaweed off the rocks," Greg explained. "I like to cook things in layers of seaweed over the hot coals, just like the early folks who lived here before Columbus. It takes a little longer, but the flavor is well worth it."

Greg motioned with his hand for Chris to start the outboard. It started on the first yank, puffing out a small cloud of smoke as Greg untied the bow line. The two motored lazily north to the other boats.

"I'm assuming that the solar components on the floats are for raising clams, is that right?" Chris semi-yelled over the sound of the outboard.

"Clams, oysters, scallops, butter clams. Mack's got God's little acre goin' there, under those floats. 'Course, our lobsters are carred-up under there too. Yup, it looks like just a bunch of floats to tie the boats up to, but, really there's a lot going on there out of sight," he explained proudly. "The solar stuff powers the upweller … that's where all the clams and their cousins live. Mack's got it going with all twelve-volt water pumps to force-feed the plankton to 'em, then he's got the solar water heaters raising the temperature of the water a little bit to boost their metabolism. It's a copy of some systems from Rhode Island, but we added the windmill electrical power and water heating. The water's a lot colder here than it is in some marina in Narragansett Bay!"

"There are two systems there … one on his big boat, too. What's up with that?"

"Same thing … only different," Greg offered.

Chris slowed the small boat, then shut the engine off, bringing them to a coasting stop alongside the floats. "The same thing?" Chris questioned.

"Yeah … someday, get aboard of the Lizgale and get a tour. The place is like a palace inside. There are twelve-volt lights, TV, microwave, stereo, solar hot water. We standardized the systems, but made one for the boat. Same stuff, different applications. 'Course, ya know, we had a lot of help from Ozzie getting these things set up. This was all his brainchild, really. There isn't a thing that he can't do as far as mechanics, electrical, figurin' out systems … you might as well say there isn't anything he can't do, period!"

"The name's not familiar to me, Greg," Chris said.

"Oh yeah, of course … you wouldn't know Ozzie, would you?" he realized. "I first met Oz right there on the Lizgale … he was the engineer when I got aboard. The first day I met him, he was sitting at the galley table doing calculus problems, just for fun. Ozzie never made it past the eighth grade, but he would do stuff like that for fun … you've taken calculus … how much fun did you have?" Greg asked, his hands spread wide, his moustache dancing under his big eyes.

"I mean, the world never took this guy seriously, and here he was, living aboard the boat like a half-a-hermit … designing things, building things," Greg went on. "The engineroom was so immaculate you could eat off the valve covers if you wanted to. Ozzie plumbed it, wired it, rebuilt all the engines, had back-up systems for back-up systems, and he did it all for nothing, so's to speak. He was just happy to have the place to live where nobody bothered him," Greg said with admiration and respect in his voice. "Yeah ... quite a guy ... he's been Mack's brother-in-law for quite a while now. You'd really enjoy Oz, but we haven't seen him for, well, close to three years, now, I guess."

"He sounds like an amazing person," Chris said. "Where is he now, got any idea?"

"Anywhere around the world. Oh ... that's right ... you're probably not into opera music, are you?" Greg asked as he bent over to pick up one of the recessed handles in the deck of the float. "I'm not, particularly, but that's where Ozzie ended up. He was made for it."

Chris's eyes followed Greg's hand to the hatch in the deck of the float as he sorted out the details about Ozzie. "Is he in the stage crew, building sets, or something?" Chris asked.

"Nope."

Greg bent down and pulled open the hatch cover, revealing a stack of plastic crates shimmering below the water's circulation. "How's that look to you?" he asked, looking for the surprised expression that he knew he would get.

Chris's jaw dropped. Below him, the pump's whir was gushing water around bushels and bushels of clams, all neatly stacked in crates, every mollusk pointed up in the same direction. Greg stood back, smiled with raised eyebrows, folded his arms, and waited for the inevitable response.

"Wow!" Chris exclaimed, looking up at Greg. "Wow!"

"Cool, huh?" Every float has something else ... the scallops are at the end, then the oysters, then the butter clams," Greg said, pointing out their locations. "We're standing on about five hundred pounds of lobsters right here!" he said, stamping his foot. "Mack's got about the same over there. We're kinda waiting for the Fourth of July to sell ... ya know ... playing the market a little bit."

"This is incredible! It's like a perpetual motion machine!"

"Nope, not quite, Slimey, but, we're, or I should say, you too, will be working on it during classes. Each year we try something else. The big trick to the clams was to keep their shells closed ... they missed the contact of the mud and started to gape open. Nobody wants to eat a gaper. So ... we put them in these cages with their siphons up, then we put packaging foam on each side of 'em to make 'em feel nice and cozy, then walked the bulk of the warm water right to 'em. I guarantee, you've never tasted a sweeter, cleaner, steamer!" Greg explained with great pride. "We regulate the temperature to make them spawn, then we catch the spat and raise 'em. I know every one of these guys by name, ya know," he winked as he joked, his moustache smiling a proud smile with him.

Chris stood in awe, shaking his head. He took a wide-eyed look at Greg with his mouth still agape. "This is awesome!" he proclaimed.

"Not bad, if I do say so myself, Slimey. Yeah, we figured that this would be a good fill-in for the boats in the fleet, especially since the days at sea are so tightly controlled now. Most of the guys around here are regulated to eighty-eight days at sea a year on the taking of groundfish ... ya know ... cod, haddock, flounders, stuff like that. That leaves the guys scrambling to fill in the rest of the time and try to make a living. We're not so limited on time at sea in the lobster business, but we've got different cannons pointed at us ... trap limits, trap tags ... it just goes on and on." Greg explained. "Meanwhile, it's a great study tool and ... an excellent source of some wicked good mug-ups!"

It wasn't long before the *H&B Too*, Greg's punt, left the floats with a bushel of clams, sixty pounds of lobsters, and a quarter bushel each of oysters, scallops, and the small hard-shell butter clams. The little craft was weighted down with all the seafood and the two good-sized men. They stopped alongside the rocky shore on the east side of the harbor and began filling empty bushel baskets with seaweed.

"Hey Greg?" Chris asked, as they each reached over the side of the punt, gathering the sweet smelling seaweed,

"What were you going to tell me about this guy Ozzie ... something about the opera?"

"Oh yeah," Greg answered. "Ozzie is one of the premier baritone singers in the world. All the gifts that guy was born with, and on top of that, man oh man can he sing! I mean, opera was where he found his thing, ya know, but he can sing anything just as well. He's got a voice that can knock you out of your socks, and it's all purely natural ... no training, no conservatory, just him!"

Chris thought for a moment. "Is that his real name, Ozzie?"

"Well, that's what we always called him. His real name is Kennardson Oswald Marsden. His theatrical name is ..."

"Oh my God!" Chris interrupted. "Not K.O. Marsden, the ultimate Rigoletto of the Met?" he asked, incredulously. "Him?"

"Yeah, that's Oz, alright. Have you heard of him?"

"Heard of him? I waited for months to get the tickets to go see him in Boston when he came and sang with the Boston Symphony Orchestra! You really know him? But ... he has this reputation of being a recluse ... he never gives interviews ... are you sure it's the same person?"

Greg nodded. "That's him. When you can sing like he does, you don't need to say anything else, Slimey."

By two in the afternoon, there was a roaring fire in the cooking pit, as Greg and Chris began the process of making hot coals for the night's mug-up. It wasn't long before they heard the long blast of the *Amanda May*'s horn, signalling the mailboat was passing beside The Motions, with Chappy Lester at the helm. "Let's go down and help Chappy get some docklines on, Slimey," Greg said as he wiped the heat of the fire from his forehead.

Greg and Chris went to the float and waited for the mailboat to ease alongside. The *Amanda May* was typical of the other lobsterboats along the coast, in fact, Chappy was a lobster fisherman on the days he was free from mail duty. She was painted bright red with a white house and a small bit of sea-foam green on the trim pieces. Longer than Mack's and Greg's lobsterboats, the A-May was forty-four feet in length and had a very long roof with canvas side curtains to protect the passengers, if he was carrying any, on rainy days. On deck, he had removable benches so as to accommodate the passengers. The foc's'le was, in effect, a floating post office with mailbags carried in the bunks and storage lockers. Mail sorting pigeonholes were mounted on the galley table so that Chappy could perform his postmaster's duties while being comfortably seated at the makeshift post office desk; he even had a weight scale for packages, and a complement of stamps and mailing envelopes for sale. Next to them were hats and t-shirts for sale with a picture of the *Amanda May* on them. The silkscreened caption read "... neither snow, nor rain, nor gloom of night, but you'll have to wait if there's a good nor'easter blowing, that's all there is to it!" The old Yankee's sense of humor was always on display.

Chappy creased his boat alongside the float and shifted to reverse, curling turbulent water from beneath the hull. Greg and Chris caught the lines thrown by a crew of eager and excited students and began to secure the vessel to its temporary resting place. Captain/Postmaster/Fisherman Lester thrust his bald, be-freckled and tanned head out from underneath the rolled-up side curtain as a puff of exhaust smoke curled away into the haze and the engine idled down to a low hum.

"Greggie, you old lobstah pickah ... you killin' th' breed, Bub?" Chappy asked loudly in a characteristic coaster's greeting.

Looking to the bow, he noticed Chris finishing securing the bow line of the boat to a cleat. "Gawdalmighty, there's Doc, 'imself. I've got a crate on board for ya. Some cussed weighty ... don't need to ship rocks up hee-yuh, we got plenty of granite!" he yelled jokingly.

Chappy turned his harmless bluster to the stern. "Greggie, he's damned near killed me with that cussed thing ... I had t' go over t' th' co-op and use the chain hoist to get 'er aboard, ya know, yuh." Greg shrugged his shoulders and chuckled, as he knew nothing of Chris mailing a package to himself.

Greg and Chris formed a welcoming committee on the float and helped the students disembark while Chappy offered salty words of fatherly advice to each of the passengers: "Be caff-ul they-uh, dee-uh," he said to a slight young woman who obviously found the boat trip outside of her midwesterner's realm and was tottering on the float in search of steady turf. "Yuh, that's right, watch your gourd, there, shorty," he said to a tall, thin, athletic looking student who grazed his head on the overhead as he stepped out. "Be caff-ul they-uh, now ole bud; yuh, that's right, grab ya gear ... thanks for keepin' me comp'ny across th' bay ..."

Greg curled his arm in a 'follow me' motion and led the brigade to the rocky ground at the head of the float's rampway. They all craned their necks, looking at the island, the watchtower of the station, the harbor ... Greg's roaring cookfire ... the staff. Chris followed, and was soon joined by Dr. Grayson and the Burkettes.

"Good afternoon, everyone, I'm Dr. Felicia Grayson and welcome to Dam'iscove Island!" she announced heartily, smiling a motherly smile. The crew was startled back from their visual bounty and all looked to the small woman with the large cache of energy. She introduced Greg, Chris, the Burkettes, and after a minute, Mackenzie, who rowed over from his home and ... Ezekial and Rogers. Each student took a turn introducing themselves and shook hands with the staff members.

It was as diverse a group of students as had ever been assembled at the Marine Science Research Center. They included:

Jake, from Chicago, who was attending Cornell on a basketball scholarship, and had, after three years, no major, but liked to go fishing.

Irene, from Abilene, Kansas, who was gradually returning to a pink face after having worn green on the boat trip over.

She was a pre-med student at Interlocke who was always fascinated by, but cut off from, the sea.

Tiffany, from New York City, a Columbia University poli-sci major who was attending the marine science program to spend some time on an island and fulfill an elective requirement.

Bob and Heidi, two marine biology majors from the University of New Hampshire who were engaged.

Putnam, the heir-apparent to the Middleton Offshore Construction fortune. He was studying ocean engineering at MIT.

Shirelle and Ron, sibling inner-city students from Baltimore, who had distinguished themselves with impressive records of academic achievement at the University of Maryland, after their parents were incarcerated for drug trafficking.

Sewell, a Fisheries and Aquatic Science major from the University of Maine who lived in Machias.

Cindy, the Marine Policy major from the University of Massachusetts' Boston's Harbors Institute who lived in Somerville, Massachusetts.

Zack, the "Wildman from Wilding, Connecticut," who was a terror on the football field of the University of Connecticut, and a cut-up in the classrooms.

Fallon, a dedicated ecology student who hailed from Wilkes-Barre, Pennsylvania. She attended Purdue University.

After introductions, Dr. Grayson and the Burkettes led the students into the station to find their accommodations. As they walked away, Grayson was explaining in her own inimitable style how the school orientation would take place at that evening's lobsterbake, tomorrow would be a day of exploration, then Monday morning, bright and early …

The men left behind began talking amongst themselves …

"Spice, you old puh-dayda, how th' hell are ya?" Chappy yelled out to Mack. "What th' hell do ya want me t' do with all them fish you got in th' tank at th' co-op, annaways?" he asked with his voice wrinkling his forehead.

"Just babysit 'em if you can, Chappy. I'll be ashore tomorrow and take care of them," Mack answered. "They all still flippin'?"

"Yuh, still splashin' water all over th' floor in they-uh."

"They're still alive and kicking?" Chris asked.

"Yuh, that's right, Doc," Chappy offered. "Hey, why dontcha guys get t'geth-uh and help get the Doc's crate off the boat ... it's down at the stern, they-uh," Chappy pointed out with his anchor-tattooed arm. "Gonna take two men anna boy, annaways. I think he's got some dinosaur bones in they-uh!"

As Mack and Chris carried the box to the station, Greg and Chappy brought the rest of the incoming mail and supplies.

"Did you see if Paul's got the research boat launched, Chap?" Greg asked.

"As I went by Sample's Shipyard, they were just puttin' th' finishin' touches on th' bottom paint and bootstripe ... yuh, she should be overboard on the five o'clock high water ... you'll prob'bly see 'em tonight, I 'spect ... there ain't much room to tie up in they-uh ... hah-buh's fulla blow-boats!" he explained. "Greggie," Chappy's voice lowered, "there's a surprise comin' o-vuh on th' *Eva Maker* with Paul tonight ... keep this to ya self, but ...

As the *Amanda May* rounded the harbor mouth and headed for Fisherman Island, Greg, Mack and Chris worked together to prepare the quintessential down-East seaweed-layered lobsterbake.

Dusk fell with a group of satisfied diners sitting around picnic tables remarking on Greg's masterpiece of traditional coastal cooking. As the sun slipped over the west side of the island, all were called to gather around the fire and partake in the Dam'iscove Island tradition of the campfire singalong. Dr. Grayson passed out tattered songbooks as Chris and Mack appeared with their guitars and tuned them to each other.

"It's pretty simple, folks," Mack announced over the crackling of the fire. "I can't sing and I can hardly play, so that means you folks've got to carry the weight ... in fact, to get us into the swing of things, let's turn to number twenty-two, that's the song called "The Weight" by The Band. We'll sing that one, then just yell out another page number and we'll do that one. The chords are right there, Old Scout," he informed Chris. "All easy stuff ... you with me?"

"Step it off!" Chris answered with glee.

The opening chords of Robbie Robertson's song slipped away to Mack's wavering warble ... "I pulled into Nazareth, I was feelin' 'bout half past dead ..." It wasn't long before the group lost their inhibitions and joined in on the classic song from the 60s. "And ... and ... and ... you put the load right on me!"

"Number sixteen!" Irene called out from a lotus position and the group launched into "What do you do with a drunken sailor, what do you do with a drunken sailor, what do you do with a drunken sailor .... ear-ligh in the mornin'?"

On through the evening they sang and laughed. Fun, yes, but really they were building a sense of community and teamwork, a sort of bootcamp without the abuse. More wood hit the fire, more songs drifted off into the night air ...

"Number ten ... I remember this from Boy Scout camp," Jake offered.

"Michael row the boat ashore, al-laylloooooo-ya ...!" they sang.

Greg noticed the lights of the *Eva Maker* twinkling and reflecting outside of The Motions gong buoy, making its way for the harbor. As he sang, he kept a watchful eye on the boat as it slowly crept up to the wharf, unnoticed by the choir of campfire singers.

"Hey ... here's one I've never heard," Chris said. "Can I pick number thirty?" he asked Mack.

Mack looked at Greg, who nodded. Mack's battered guitar came to life with a zealous chord interplay as he yelled to

Chris ... "Follow me and come in on the change!" Then Mack and Greg started off in their half warble/half talk vocal style, the crowd clapping out the time at Greg's prompting ...

> She went down last October in a pouring driving rain ...
> the skipper he'd been drinkin' and the mate, he felt no pain ...
> Too close to three mile rock and she was dealt her mortal blow,
> and the *Mary Ellen Carter* settled low.
>
> There were five of us aboard her when she finally was awash,
> we'd worked like hell to save her, all heedless of the cost.
> And the groan she gave as she went down, it caused us to proclaim ...
> That the *Mary Ellen Carter* would rise again.

Mack and the audience hadn't noticed the three figures disembarking from the *Eva Maker*. Greg shifted his glance, observed this development and sang louder to cover up the sound as they came closer through the bushes ...

> Well, the owners wrote her off; not a nickel would they spend ...
> She gave us twenty years of service, boys, then met her sorry end.
> But insurance paid the loss to them, they let her rest below;
> then they laughed at us and said we had to go.
>
> But we talked of her all winter, some days around the clock,
> for she's worth a quarter million, afloat and at the dock
> And with every jar that hit the bar, we swore we would remain ...
> And make the *Mary Ellen Carter* rise again.

"Rise again ... rise again!" came thundering from the blackness.

Mack and Greg launched into the chorus of the song, and suddenly were upstaged by a booming baritone voice coming from the night, inching closer to the gathering with every step. Greg beamed. Everyone turned and looked in jaw-dropped wonder. Mack just put his head back in awe-inspired surprise, shook his head and kept right on playing with the masterful vocals potently unleashed from the person coming up to them ...

That her name be not lost to the knowledge of men.
Those who loved her best and were with her till the end
will make the *Mary Ellen Carter* rise again!!

"Take 'em home, Ozzie!" Mack yelled, smiling a bearded grin, his hand strumming the chords, tears in his eyes. "Take 'em home!"

The campfire choir peered into the darkness until a short but rugged man with large eyes, a bald head and ears really too large for his face began to reflect the firelight from his cheeks. He walked into the light, then clenched his fists in front of his body and continued in an all-encompassing voice ...

All spring now, we've been with her on a barge lent by a friend ...
Three dives a day in hard hat suit and twice I've had the bends.
Thank God it's only sixty feet and the currents here are slow
or I'd never have the strength to go below.

But we've patched her rents, stopped her vents, dogged hatch and porthole down ...
... put cables to her fore and aft and birded her around.
Tomorrow noon, we hit the air and then take up the strain ...
and watch the *Mary Ellen Carter* rise again ...

For we couldn't leave her there you see, to crumble into scale.
She'd saved our lives so many times, living through the gale ...
and the laughing, drunken rats who left her to a sorry grave,
they won't be laughing in another day ...

And you, to whom adversity has dealt the final blow;
with smiling bastards lying to you everywhere you go.
Turn to, and put out all your strength of arm and heart and brain; and like the *Mary Ellen Carter*, rise again!

Rise Again! Rise again!
though your heart it be broken and life about to end ...
no matter what you've lost, be it a home, a love, a friend ...
Like the *Mary Ellen Carter*, rise again!*

---

* Music and lyrics by Stan Rogers. www.stanrogers.net

"I think Ricky heard that one, Oz," Mack said over the sound of the fire's crackling as he cradled his guitar in his lap at the end of the song.

Kennardson Oswald Marsden, world renowned opera star, fishing boat engineer and trusted shipmate stood in the firelight and nodded a silent concurrence.

Nantucket Lightship

8

THE POINT

LAT. 41 DEG. 22.7 MIN. N.
LONG. 71 DEG. 30.7 MIN. W.

Fog shrouded the island as midnight brought a curtain of wet vapor over everything. A brisk southeast air flow held the temperature cool and raw; the rousing campfire was a short memory away. The station was quiet and dark ... all its inhabitants were secured for the night. A sudden shift of wind blew back the curtains in Chris's room, bringing enough air to rustle the papers on his desk and wake him from a sound sleep. As he groggily slipped to a half-awake state, he heard the fire crackling again outside. Pulling himself from his bed, he went to the window. Beyond the thick layer of water vapor in the night air, he could see the glow of the fire being stoked again. There were figures moving beside the fire, silhouetted against the fog's curtain. He strained his eyes to see what — and who —was still out there? Then he heard the unmistakeable sound of Greg's laughter filter through the thick night air. Looking out the window, he rested his head on his crossed arms and thought for a moment, then snapped his fingers. He quickly threw his clothes on and headed down the stairs.

"It's not polite to come visiting unannounced, unless you bring a housewarming gift, right, Miss Manners?" Chris said out loud as he stocked his arms with firewood from the pile behind the station. He went down the path to the campfire pit to investigate, hopefully looking innocent in his arrival.

"I heard you guys down here," he announced through the fog as he stepped into the warm glow. "Looks like you could use some wood for the fire. I was up rummaging around, so here's some." He set the load down with a wood-on-wood clunk. *Hopefully, they'll ask me to stay*, he thought.

"Have a seat, there, Old Scout, pull up a stump and join the campfire," Mack beckoned. He turned his head to the light, focusing his gaze across the fire. "Oz, this is Chris Brown. He's the guy from Harvard that's doing the study on what happened to all of us nitwits that got into fishin'," Mack announced as he poured another mug of tea and handed it to Chris. "He's okay."

"It's a great honor, Mr. Marsden ... You totally blew me away. I mean, you blew me away at Symphony Hall in Boston, too, but I never expected to meet you ... especially here!" Chris said excitedly as he held out his hand. "This is incredible ... I ... I ... just can't believe it!" he gushed.

Ozzie shook hands and smiled back, silently nodding his thanks for the compliment.

"You know, I've got to tell you guys, I'm also blown away by the upwellers you have underneath the floats! Greg told me a lot of that was your idea, Mr. Marsden ...?" Chris asked with youthful exuberance.

Ozzie shrugged his shoulders but remained silent, then looked at Greg.

"You can call him Ozzie, Chris ... he won't mind ... Right Oz?" Greg asked, then reassuringly added, "he's okay, Oz ... it's just us around here now."

Ozzie grimaced and contorted his face, then with a another shrug said "r … r … r … roy … royt."

Startled, Chris tried to hide his surprise at the speech impediment. *Take it easy,* he thought. *Take it easy. We sing and talk from different parts of the brain.*

"Well you've got three out of the original five pirates of the Lizgale here, Old Scout," Mack butted in, shifting the attention from his old shipmate. "'Course 'The Hellion' is looking down on us and yelling 'Jose Cuervo!' but three of us are still here." Mack looked back into the fire. "Lord luvvaduck! He was a character, though, huh, Oz?"

Ozzie smiled, shook his head and rolled his eyes. "F … f … fi … fine … fine … finest … k … k … k … ki … kind!" he blurted out in a gasping stutter, then eloquently sang, "Excitable boy they all said."

Chris put his chin in his hand and laughed along with Mack, Ozzie and Greg. This was a rare opportunity to gain a window into their lives, and even though he was dead tired, he couldn't pass it up. He took a sip of tea, then asked, "The Hellion?"

"Let's put it this way, Slimey," Greg chimed in, "in any dictionary with the word hellion in it, the definition is Ricky Helliott's picture!" He threw another log on the fire, sending smoke and orange ashes curling skyward into the fog. "I'll never forget the first time I met him …

~ ~ ~

September, 1975. Point Judith, Rhode Island

At the Rhode Runner bus station in Wakefield, Rhode Island, a baby blue Chevrolet Corvair splashed to the curb beside a tall, athletic, but disoriented looking young man standing beside a fully stuffed seabag. The lost look on his face was compounded by the rain pelting down, making his mustache droop over his lips and his salt and pepper hair fall straight to the back of his neck from underneath a hat with the initials OSU on it. The car pulled to a stop and the passenger-side door opened.

"Hi, Greg. How was the bus trip, did everything go all right?" A young Mack Mackenzie asked from behind the wheel. "Throw that bag in the back seat, here," He beckoned as he folded the seat forward. The little car bounced twice as the bag, then its owner, entered. "Wicked day, huh?"

"Do ya want the long story, or the short story, Mack?" Greg answered through his dripping moustache as he looked straight ahead, disgusted.

"Probably ought to start with the short one … if it didn't go too good." Mack answered. "Problems in Boston?"

"Well, let's put it this way … you can't get from North Station to South Station without a long walk or a small mortgage for cab fare. The train came into Boston at North Station … the busses leave from South Station. Get on the wrong color streetcar, or subway, or whatever those things are, and you end up at the Museum of Fine Arts. Boston's a lovely stroll when it's pouring … the seabag was getting a little heavy on the second mile," he answered caustically, watching the windshield wipers slap back and forth. "And oh … let's not forget all the helpful people with directions to their uncle's deli and what in Gawd's name is all that stuff on Washington street … 'Hey, sailor, new in town?'… I didn't stick around to find out why they call it the combat zone …"

Greg turned his head to face his old college roommate. As he looked at Mack's mutton-chop sideburns and brown hair curling over his collar, he shook his head and exhaled.

"Then I had to switch busses again in Providence, once I finally got there … a new Camaro, right? Not just a Camaro, but a Z-28, with mag wheels, right? Bright red, too! You're sure, right?"

Mackenzie reached up to the center of the dashboard and slid the transmission lever into D, then pulled away from the curb.

"Greg, you should see this place … it's like we thought, only better. It's better than what we figured from reading the *National Fisherman* all those years. I'm telling you, The Point is where it's at … It's all there!"

"I probably traveled past two hundred boats comin' from Portland to the New Hampshire line. Then there's Gloucester, Boston,

Plymouth ... all those ports, but you had to go to Rhode Island," he countered. "Are you sure?"

Mack pulled the Corvair out into traffic, then turned down route 107, passing beneath a road sign that read "Pt. Judith, Galilee, Narragansett."

"You should see this place ... every dock has brand new pickup trucks parked next to all these beautiful boats. If there isn't a new truck parked there, there's a Camaro, or a Firebird, even a few 'Vettes! Go around the corner from the harbor and there's one beach right after another, filled with girls from the college right up the road. There's all kinds of nightspots with wicked good bands playing! The Point Judith Co-op is there, just like we've read about ... they've even got a store on the second floor. We're going home for Christmas in new Camaros, Greg! I got us sites on one of the highline boats!" Mack announced exuberantly.

Greg turned his head and managed to smile reluctantly. "I just want a nice car and the down payment on a little Jonesport lobsterboat with maybe a couple hundred traps, by next spring. Do you think we can do that?"

"Greg, we've got a site on the *Elizabeth Gale*! You can buy the whole town of Jonesport by next May!" he answered with a boast. "You should see this place ... and you won't believe how nice this boat is! We lucked out, big time, man!"

They drove on through the rain, then took a right at a sign that said "Escape Road" as they eased onto a divided highway that led over the crest of a hill. At the bottom of a long straightaway across the marsh, the harbor known to tourists as Galilee, but to fishermen the working harbor known as the Point, lay stretched panoramically before them. Mack gazed over at his passenger and saw the expression he expected as Greg's eyes went from mast ... to mast ... to mast. At the stop sign, he took another look towards the passenger's seat. The gloom was replaced by a huge smile. "What do you think, now?"

"A red one, with a spoiler on the back and chrome wheels ... and that's just my pickup truck ... the Camaro's for Sundays. "Mack, we'll be rolling in dough!"

Down the road a little farther, the Corvair slowed across from the revolving windmill of the Dutch Inn, then pulled into a parking lot behind a sign that beckoned weary seamen to grab a frosty mug of

Narragansett beer at Milt's. Mack pulled the car alongside a brand new pickup truck, reached up to the dashboard, shifted into P, then waited for the car to sputter to a stop after turning the key. "C'mon … I'll grab your bag, you've carried it enough today."

The two friends walked down the dock and stood beside the imposing fishing vessel tied up there. Greg's eyes traced the outline of the mast … to the rigging … down to the wheelhouse at the stern … the nets stowed along each rail … the trawl doors nested inside the rails … the winch … the other boats alongside … the seagull flying overhead … watch it! … the splat that hit beside him …

"Good thing cows don't fly, huh? C,mon, let's get your gear down below in the fo'c'sle," Mack invited. "I think the engineer is already on board."

"Wait, Mack!" Greg blurted out apprehensively. "I don't know how to go draggin' … just lobster fishin' and swordfishin'. What am I gonna do if I screw up?"

"Look, Buddy knows we're green hands. I'll explain the gear to you on the way out. We'll take wheelwatch together and I'll just explain it to you from the wheelhouse. It's like my grandfather said … if you can make toast you can go fishin' … just don't put your fingers in things if they get messed up … just like making toast! Buddy's gettin' a good deal with us … don't worry."

"Who's Buddy?"

"The skipper. He owns this boat, too. See, when you start out, everyone has to make a couple of trips at half-share, then you get full share when you prove yourself. Buddy got two crewmen, you and me, for the price of one. Here in The Point, the low man on the boat cooks … everyone starts out as cook, so that's us. You like to cook don't you?"

"Yeah, I love to cook, but …"

"Good … I got all the grub aboard and iced down this morning. We'll split the job, help each other, whatever it takes. Everybody on the boat has a job besides the job of fisherman: cook, engineer, mate, skipper, like that. You know all that."

Greg looked at Mack. "Hey, wait a minute. You told me we'd be making four or five hundred bucks a trip. At half share, that's the same as if we got jobs and made two-fifty a week. We have college degrees. I don't want to do this for the same money we could make in a regular job. I want to get my own boat!"

"Take it easy, Greg … five hundred *is* half share. These guys are pulling down a grand a trip in a lot of cases … it's unreal!"

Greg thought for a second, then jumped over the rail onto the deck of the *Elizabeth Gale*. "A black Camaro Z-28 to match my red Sunday car! Toss me my bag!"

The shipmates went forward and turned under the doghouse to face the ladder leading down to the fo'c'sle. Mack went first, then took Greg's bag as he passed it down the steep ladder. Greg came down next and stood with his back to the galley table, getting his eyes adjusted to the bare-lightbulb luminescence that illuminated the richly appointed mahogany woodwork. Mackenzie threw the seabag into the lower portside bunk, just below the berth he had claimed for himself.

"How's that, okay?" Mack asked Greg, who bounced into the rack to try its comfort.

"Home sweet home!" Greg shot back, his hands folded behind his head.

The two young shipmates were so enthralled, they completely missed the fact they weren't alone. At the far end of the galley table was a short, moon-faced man in his mid-thirties with big eyes and big ears protruding from under a hat with a Detroit Diesel insignia. Strewn about the table were books and papers with numbers, scribbling, doodling and mathematical progressions, written seemingly in a kindergartner's hand. He gathered everything up in haste, like a thief recovers a bag of dropped money, then stared at the two.

"Oh, wow, I didn't see you there," Mack said, half stepping back, when he noticed the man sitting at the table. "You must be the engineer … I'm Jim Mackenzie, and this is Carleton Gregory over here."

Mack held his hand out, but the engineer retreated, clutching his grasp of disheveled papers and books to his chest. Mackenzie caught eye contact with Greg, then turned back to the table.

"What's that?" Mack asked, hoping to start a conversation. "It looks like calculus … are you taking a course or something?"

The man's big eyes looked out from under the visor of his hat, scanning Mack up and down, then shook his head to indicate *no*.

Greg rolled himself up to look over the edge of the bunk. "Hey … that's the same calc' book we had at OSU, Mack." Greg exclaimed. "You're not taking a course?" he asked across the table.

The man looked down and shook his head *no* again.

"You're not? You can't possibly be doing calculus problems for fun ... you can't be! Nobody does that stuff unless you have to. Are you an engineer, or something?"

The visor of the hat lifted as he looked directly across the table at Greg and pointed at the Detroit Diesel patch riding on the front of his hat. "B ... b ... buh ... buh ... buh ... buh-est. B ... b ... b ... bes ... best en ... en ... en ... gin ... eer!" came the labored, stuttered and indignant reply.

Mack turned back to the galley table. "Then you must be Ozzie. They said you were the best engineer in the Point at Milt's last night," he said, trying to be friendly, if a bit patronizing. "Greg ... this is Ozzie ... everyone said to check out his engine room ... you can eat off the engine, they said!"

(As Mack said this, his mind was reflecting on what was really said at the bar at Milt's last night: *Yeah, he's a wicked good engineer, no doubt about it, but he's like this retard or somethin' ... almost like a hermit. He lives on the boat and does all this weird crap like he thinks he's a genius or somethin' ... a guy that numb can't even read, for Pete's sake. He talks like an idiot and sure looks like one, too. I think Buddy puts up with his Hunchback of Notre Dame routine 'cause he's good in the engine room, but, man, he's a nitwit, and ever'body knows it. Buddy's got too big of a heart ... a real fishy guy, and I'm tellin' ya, there's nobody that's got a hangbook like his ... but all the misfits and greenhorns end up with him. That's how you got a site on the Lizgale too ... ha ... har ... harr ...!*)

"Look, man, we don't mean you any harm ... we're just a couple guys that want to learn a little bit about fishin' and make a few bucks. Really ... c'mon ... I'm Mack and this is Greg."

Mack held his hand out again. Reluctantly, the engineer held out his hand and gave back a very strong handshake. Greg rolled out of the bunk and shook hands as well, muttering, "Pleased to meet you ... Ozzie, is it?"

"R ... r ... r ... roy ... roy ... royt!" was the stuttered reply.

A light northwest breeze brought welcome relief from the humid southwest rainstorm that exited to the southeastern sky. A clearing evening gave way to a blanket of stars in the north.

"Anybody home?" came the call from the top of the foc'sle ladder.

"Hello!" Greg yelled back, looking up from his bunk where he was reading a magazine.

"Down here, Buddy," Mack echoed back, putting down his battered guitar.

They rose from their bunks to greet the skipper coming down the foc'sle ladder.

"Buddy, this is the guy I was tellin' you about ... meet Carleton Gregory."

"Glad to know ya, old son," Captain Buddy Folland said with a fatherly smile, giving back a warm handshake. "You're a big one," Buddy chided. "Whatd'ya think, Oz, he oughtta be able to shovel a ton of ice at a time. I think Ricky'll be glad we got a good man for the hold, whatdy'ya say?"

Ozzie looked up from his studying and nodded a silent *yes*.

Greg looked around, then spoke a little apprehensively. "Captain, um, Folland ... Mack's done some draggin' before, but I've got to admit ... I'm no expert ... I'll do the best I can, but ..."

Buddy cut him off in mid-sentence and faked a gruff, stern voice. As he lowered his eyes and cocked his hat on the back of his head, his forehead ruffled like a washboard. "Listen here, mister ... first of all, Captain Folland was my father ... I'm Buddy. Second of all, I've been screwed by experts, and if you're no expert, that's just fine. You know what an expert is, Carleton?"

Greg was unnerved by this interrogation. "Well ... no ... I guess ... I don't, Cap' ... I mean ... Buddy. Um ... What's an expert?" he stammered out.

"If I threw you overboard could you float, or at least tread water?"

"Yeah, I ... I hope so."

"Good. See, an expert is just a duck with a paper ass!" he laughed, reassuringly he added, "Good God, man, take it easy. None of this is hard. If fishermen do it, it can't be that complicated! Just don't ever claim to be an expert. The big pond'll teach ya somethin' ev'ry day if you pay attention. Anyway, welcome aboard! Your compadre here says you put some time in on one of the sword boats ... Lord luvvaduck! If you've been to Corsair Canyon and the No'theast Peak ... that's no swanboat ride you went on! You'll do fine!"

"I'll do my best for you, that's for sure ... thanks for taking us on," Greg replied.

"C'mon up on deck here ... I wanna tell you guys a coupla things." Buddy said.

Greg, Mack and Buddy crawled up the ladder to the evening air and the sounds of a harbor that never stops working. Buddy sat on the fishhold hatchcover and rolled up the sleeves of his flannel shirt, revealing his tattooed forearms.

"Boys, I wanna make m'self clear. The first trip in the Point is half share, and usually the low man, or men, do the cooking, you okay with that?"

Greg nodded as Mackenzie answered, "No problem. Greg's a good cook, I can hold my own. We won't starve."

Buddy folded his arms and lowered his eyes, rippling his forehead. "It's a stupid question, but it's happened before ... you did get grub, right, Mackie?"

"Yes. I got pretty much what you said for a four day trip. I got some other stuff, too. I hope that's okay."

"Good, you can never have enough food. I see you met Ozzie. Once he gets to know you, he'll loosen up. Look, the guys around here ride him awful hard, but he's all there, don't let anyone tell you diff'rent. I own and run this boat, but it's his home ... gotta cut a little slack for that, get me?"

The two nodded.

Buddy took a deep breath and adjusted his gray workpants as he stood up. He took the hat from the back of his head and slung the visor low over his eyebrows, nearly covering his eyes. He folded his arms again so the two tattoos looked like a reaching clippership sailing with an oversized anchor. They looked at him apprehensively. After another deep breath, he asked, "There's one more thing I need from you guys ... can you go down to the 'Tune and pick up the mate, Ricky?"

Mack and Greg looked at each other, relieved. "That's it?" Greg asked. "Just go pick someone up?"

"Well, yuh, you could look at it that way, I guess. Take Oz ... he'll help you find your way to the Neptune's Retreat. It's right over there by Narragansett Pier, a few miles away. Just go in and tell the barmaid, April, that you're here for Ricky ... she'll know where Ricky is. I doubt if you'll need to, but just in case you can't pick him out, ask for the Hellion. We're shovin' off at eleven tonight ... allow a little time."

Along the beaches of Narragansett rode the blue corvair, driven by Jim Mackenzie, navigated by Ozzie Marsden, Carleton Gregory riding shotgun and traveling music provided by Peter Frampton via WPRO radio. Past the BonZoo, past the Twillows, and past Schillet's, the low-slung car rolled along, leaving the neon signs behind as they came into, then faded from view. After a few more minutes, Ozzie motioned to turn left, into the parking lot of a beachfront hotel named Neptune's Retreat. He motioned to go to the right side of the building where the flashing cocktails sign was trolling for the night's catch.

"I'll just run in and get him. I'll be back in a second," Jim said as he put the car in park.

Ozzie grabbed his shirtsleeve before he could exit the car door. "I ... I ... I'm go ... gg ... gg ... go ... goin' in, t ... tt ... tooo," Ozzie blurted out.

"Let's all go," Greg chimed in.

Mack shut the car off and, joined by Greg and Ozzie, headed for the cocktails sign. Ozzie stopped at the door and turned to his two companions. He made the universal signal of *keep your eyes open* by tapping his first two fingers below his eyes, then he turned and opened the door. Inside, the smell of beer-soaked carpets and the sounds of loud laughter, clinking glasses and a blaring jukebox confronted them with the unmistakeable characteristics of a waterfront ginmill.

Through the raucous cacophony, April Mayes looked up from wiping the bar and noticed the three men enter from the side door. She smiled a compassionate smile to Ozzie and motioned for them to come to the far end of the bar, where she slid herself to the corner. As they picked their way through the crowd, Greg and Jim looked around at the nautical decor. Nets hung in place of curtains, over pictures of seascapes that resembled fake windows. One wall was adorned with various sizes, shapes and lengths of harpoons. The restrooms were marked with liferings lettered "buoys" and "mermaids." The jukebox sat in one corner and blared out a Led Zeppelin song with people dancing behind lobster traps that marked the boundaries of the makeshift dance floor. Hanging over the bar was a replica of a Grand Banks dory, oars readied in the thole pins. Charts of the local and offshore waters covered the other walls. The stools were packed with patrons, the air was packed with smoke, the bar was stacked with drinks and beer bottles; some people had three or four drinks ahead, waiting to be consumed.

"Hi there, Ozzie. How are you doing tonight?" April asked in a semi-yell over the noise.

Ozzie just smiled back and shook his head to indicate *okay*.

"Who's your friends here?" she asked, tipping her head to Greg and Mack.

Ozzie looked and motioned for his new shipmates to handle their own introductions.

"Hi, I'm Greg and this is Mack. We're shippin' out with Ozzie tonight on the *Elizabeth Gale*," he shouted back.

April flipped her brown hair out of her pretty face, revealing eyes of the same color. She smiled back at Greg and quipped, "I was hoping the cavalry would get here soon ... you here to pick up the Hellion?"

"I ain't goin' nowheres with that idjut and two farmers!" came a muffled voice from the dory over the bar. "'Sides that, I still gotta couple hunnerd, and ever'one knows, I don't go aboard until all the money's gone ... it's bad luck! Give us another round, will ya darlin'?"

April grabbed a nearby broom and thumped the bottom of the dory until its occupant draped his arm over the rail. He set a one-hundred dollar bill floating in slow motion to April's waiting hand below, then laid back down, out of sight.

"Ricky! C'mon, it's time to go aboard ... and get outta that dory! How many times do I have to tell you ...!" She thumped the bottom of the dory again.

"Another round! Whip' em!" came the orders from the dory. "These flatlanders need a drink ... another tankard of ale for the sheriff and his merry men, ye fine wench!"

A tall man with blonde curly hair came from the end of the bar to offer his assistance. "Did I hear you guys were goin' on the Lizgale with Ozzie, here?" he asked.

Ozzie turned around to see who mentioned his name. "B ... b ... bo ... b ... b ... boz ... Boze!" he exclaimed.

"Hey, Old Bean, howya doin?" he said as he shook hands with Ozzie. He shook hands with Greg and Mack, then introduced himself. "I'm Brad Bozeman ... ever'one calls me Boze. I run the watch on the *Aurora*. Oz and I were shipmates on the Lizgale with Buddy and Ricky for a coupla years. It used to be my job to pick up Ricky, remember, Oz?" He laughed. "You're gonna hafta drink him out when he gets like this ... you'll never talk him out, take my advice!"

April returned with drinks for all, including beers for Ozzie, Greg, Boze and Jim. "Compliments of the Hellion," she said, rolling her eyes. She held a drink up over her head and a waiting arm snatched it back into the dory. "Ricky, this is the last round ... ever'one's got three or four drinks ahead of them now!"

"I ain't goin' till it's safe to go, and it ain't safe until I'm broke! Now give us another round!"

April put her head in her hand. "Ricky, you just bought a round!" she yelled.

"Okay, then ... give ever'one in the place a steak. Yeah, that's it! A round of steaks! Rare! Take off the horns and lead 'em out here!

"Where do you think you are, up in Prahvidence, Ricky?" Boze yelled up to the dory. "The kitchen closed an hour ago!" He shrugged his shoulders and spoke to Ozzie. "You know what you're gonna hafta do, don't you?"

Ozzie just shook his head in frustration.

"Another round ... I still gotta hunnerd here. Another round!"

April looked to Boze for assistance as Greg and Mack watched the spectacle with apprehension.

"Look, Ricky! There's nuthin' else in the place she can give you ... ever'one's got drinks backed up, the kitchen's closed ... all there is left is some t-shirts. C'mon ... Buddy's waiting for you!" Boze yelled. Turning to Mackenzie he said in a half whisper, "There's only one way to get him out, and that's drink him out. Do you like tequila?"

Before Mack could answer, five twenty dollar bills came floating down from the dory above. "A round of t-shirts ... give us a round of t-shirts!"

April, exasperated, went to a cardboard box under the bar and started passing out t-shirts with the Neptune's Retreat logo on them. The last three were tossed overhand into the dory.

"Now, Ricky, that's it! Get down out of there and go fishing!" she ordered as she hit the bottom of the dory with the butt end of the broom handle. "Let's go!"

"Hey Ricky!" Boze said as he winked to April. "Your new shipmate here says he likes Jose Cuervo!"

Mackenzie looked back with horror, shaking his head *no* and holding his hands up in a *stop* gesture. Ozzie could see his fright and whispered into his ear, "Wa-uh."

"Huh?"

"Wa-uh ... wa-uh!"

April slammed two shot glasses down on the bar. She filled one with Jose Cuervo tequila. The other she filled with water and slid to Mack.

One more time, Ozzie offered the drink-him-out plan. "Wa-uh!"

~ ~ ~

"So … then what happened?" Chris asked, motioning with his hands, eager for more.

"Let's put it this way, Old Scout … we were springing off the dock at eleven o'clock, just like Buddy wanted. It was something to see, though, I'll tell you. Greg was coiling up the bow lines. I was stowing the sternlines back aft. Buddy was in the wheelhouse and Ozzie was below in the engine room taking care of things. When we idled past George's restaurant, the whole place turned out to see what the commotion was. Ricky was standing on the hatchcover to the fish hold screaming 'Jose' Cuervooooooo!' … holding the boathook like it was a sword!"

The group erupted in a gale of laughter. Between fits of hilarity, Greg managed to finish the story. "Yup, there he was alright, looking like the Man of La Mancha, wearing a t-shirt on his head, another one on his body, and the last one he had on upside down, with his legs sticking through the armholes like it was a pair of pants!"

9
NANTUCKET LIGHTSHIP

Lat. 40 deg. 30.1 min. N.
Long. 69 deg. 25.9 min. W.

"Don't you gentlemen know that the folks up at the station are trying to get some sleep?" Felicia Grayson asked as she stepped into the firelight, wrapped in an afghan for warmth. "It's past your bedtimes, isn't it?"

"Awww, Mawww," Greg answered humorously. "It's not midnight yet and Ozzie doesn't come for sleepovers very often. Can't we stay up a little while longer?"

She sat down next to the fire and rubbed her hands together. "I've heard this story so many times, I think I was there with you, but I never heard how the rest of the trip went. Did you guys catch anything?" she asked.

"You can't leave us hanging!" Dave Burkette called out from the shadows.

"Yes, please tell us," his wife chimed in as they joined the glow.

"It's my first ever sea story," Irene, the student from Kansas said softly as she adopted a lotus position in front of the fire. "Please, take us fishing!"

It wasn't long before half of the Dam'iscove crew was gathering around the fire again.

"Okay, okay," Greg relented. "I suppose we've got to tell ya about the first trip we all made together. This isn't your standard sea story, it just happens to be true. It's a cocker! Remember when we took the dory out of the rigging?"

Mack and Ozzie nodded, smiling.

"The dory?" Dr Grayson asked. "Wasn't that one of the lifeboats?"

"Yup, it was, but it wasn't like that. Well, not on this trip ..."

~ ~ ~

September, 1975

Buddy steered the Lizgale along the west arm of the Pt. Judith wall, the breakwater that was built around Sand Hill Cove Beach to make it a harbor of refuge. He went past the west gap and changed course to head for the east gap. Their ultimate destination was south of Nantucket, well to the southeast of Pt. Judith. The searchlight's beam streamed forward from the top of the wheelhouse and reflected off the forward rigging as he swung the light around, looking for the next buoy.

"Greg, hey Greg ... come back here for a sec." Mack yelled to his shipmate over the sounds of swirling water, the diesel engine, and Ricky Helliott's midnight choir. "Come back aft for a second and listen ... you won't believe this!"

Greg finished stowing the bow lines around the forward bitt then followed Mack aft to the turtleback, behind the wheelhouse.

"Stick your head in here and listen! I could hear him when I put the lines over there. Listen!"

From the depths of the boat, echoing up the ladder leading to the engine room, came the sound of a powerful, polished singing voice. Over the throb of the twelve-cylinder Detroit Diesel was a musical presence that was almost otherworldly in its effect. The sound seemed to combine with the light filtering out from the engine room as the singing continued …

Ah for just one time I would take the Northwest Passage
to find the hand of Franklin reaching for the Beaufort Sea
Tracing one warm line through a land so wild and savage
and make a Northwest Passage to the sea …*

"Wow! Who's that?" Greg whispered to Mack, his hand cupped to his ear.

"I don't know. But he sure can sing!" Mack answered back in a hushed tone. He put his fingers to his lips, then crept down the ladder to get a closer look. About half way down, he stopped and sat on a ladder tread. Greg came behind and sat next to him.

Five steps below, then through the engineer's stateroom, they could see into the well lit engine room and the gleaming main engine. The sound was much louder now, but the singing still rode over the top of the machinery like a gull flying effortlessly over a storm-tossed sandbar. A man's hand came into view. He was wiping down the engine, even though it needed no cleaning.

From above them, the sound of 'Jose Cuervo' still echoed into the night, but from below, the song changed …

She went down last October in a pouring, driving, rain …*

The hand, and its owner, made its way around to the front of the engine. there was no mistaking who was down there. No one could mistake the ears that stuck out from beyond the black Detroit Diesel hat.

Back on deck, Greg and Mack looked at each other in shock.

"Can you believe that, Mack? I mean, can you believe it?"

"Incredible! You know, I read something about this once. Have you ever heard of that country singer, Mel Tillis?"

"I'm more into Alice Cooper, but I guess I've heard of him, why?"

"He can sing like a bird, but when he talks, he stutters something awful. Because your brain uses one area for talking, and a whole other area when you're singing. You know something?"

---

* Music and lyrics by Stan Rogers. www.stanrogers.net

"What?"

"That guy down there's no idiot. You don't suppose he was really doing calc' problems for fun, like you said?"

"What the hell have we got ourselves into, anyway, Mack? Look at the mate over there … is it too late to turn around?"

"You serious?"

Greg thought for a second. *Everything else about the trip was an adventure, why should it be any different now?* He turned to Mack, threw his hands in the air and humorously declared, "Naaah. It'll make a great story to tell the grandkids, should I ever have any! Let's get this nitwit into his rack and see where in the world we're bound for."

With one man on each arm, the Hellion was shown his way to the foc'sle, and with a deft combination of gravity, physics, manpower and the roll of the boat, he eventually landed in his rack on the starboard side of the galley table. The two greenhorns came back on deck just as Buddy steered the boat past the day beacon marking the East Gap of the Pt. Judith wall. The swells from the sou'west air of the afternoon still lingered as the boat picked up speed, making the Lizgale roll slightly as she forged ahead.

"Hey fellas, thanks for gettin' Ricky aboard and tucked in. He's a handful, isn't he?" Buddy said as the duo entered the wheelhouse from the port side. "Damned good mate, though. He can run the watch as good as any old dog, and sometimes he's got the one place that will pull a trip out when I'm out of ideas. Yup, pretty fishy guy. I'm sure you know by now that he's a better fisherman than he is a money manager!"

Buddy laughed until he coughed, then lit up a cigarette. Exhaling smoke out the port window, he continued, "I think someday April will put her kids through ivy league colleges with the amount of money he's tipped her." He checked the compass, made a slight course alteration, then took another puff from his cigarette. "He comes from a long line of characters. I started out with his father, Bob, over in New Bedford, and he came from Portland, down east. I wish he'd ease up and let someone else ride the wild bull for a while. It took some Jose to get him out?"

"Well, um, I was going to ask you about that," Mack replied. "See, Ozzie's plan worked great for getting him out, but I don't think he'll be too thrilled with me when he sobers up and finds out that I was drinking shots of water."

Buddy turned and looked at Mack with a gaze that combined surprise with respect. He laughed ... and laughed ... and laughed until the ashes fell off his cigarette and he began coughing.

"It was Ozzie's idea?" he hacked out.

Mack looked at the compass, then nodded his head, avoiding eye contact.

"Yup."

The Lizgale steamed along with the sounds of laughter pouring from the wheelhouse, the diesel's power roaring from the exhaust, and Ozzie serenading his engine room. Pt. Judith Lighthouse swept their stern quarter every fifteen seconds, lighting the way off and, hopefully, the way home.

"Hey Buddy?" Greg asked. "Where we goin', anyways?"

"Well, we're gonna start at the Lightship," he explained. "I don't know what we'll find when we get there, the report's not good. Well, I know there's fish there, sure, but so does ever' one else in the world, according to the blue sheet."

"What's the blue sheet, Cap?" Greg asked.

"I got the latest one right here, hang on a sec."

Buddy reached over and put a spliced loop of line over the spoke of the wheel to keep it in check, then stepped back to his bunk behind the wheelhouse. He soon reappeared, carrying some folded blue papers.

"This is a blue sheet, boys. Right off the bat, you can see it's blue. The gummint puts it out. It's got all the New England port landings, the prices, sometimes there's some news for the fleet, foreign fleet surveillance, all kindsa stuff."

Buddy reached up and turned on the light over the chart table, then started pointing things out. "Take a look ... see, there's the Boston boats ... Tremont landed ninety-eight thousand ... fifty-eight of it was haddock at thirty-six cents a pound ... you get the idea. On the last page is the foreign fleet report ... that's what's got me worried. One Coast Guard flyover at the 'Ship ... eight Soviet factory trawlers, twenty side-rigged Soviet catching vessels, ten East German, two Polish factory trawlers, four Spanish pair trawlers off to the sou'west part of Georges ... Japs down at the gully ... and them guys are ruthless!"

"Yeah, I saw the Spanish pairs down at the no'theast peak when we were swordfishin' last summer," Greg offered. "All they wanted was codfish for salting, like in the old dory days. They were towing this huge net between the two boats, and the surface was carpeted with all kinds of flats, flounders, even haddock, and in all sizes, right down to the tiniest … threw 'em all overboard! Everything went overboard except the cod. We gaffed up a couple haddock right off the surface and made a nice meal. Remember I told you about it, Mack?"

He nodded.

"Yup. And the Iron Curtain boats are just the opposite … they take everything, and I mean everything!" Buddy continued. "They tow these gigunda nets made out of the smallest mesh size that man can make. Nuthin,' and I mean, nuthin' gets by. I swear, if they could tow nylon stockings, they'd take the plankton, too! Right on board, they got fish meal factories and fillet lines. Anythin' that can get filleted, does, and everything else, including the guts and heads of the stuff they cut, goes into making animal feed! Then they got fleets of boats just catching, like us, and they even got ocean-going tugs that service the whole lot of 'em, fuel 'em up, you name it!"

"The East Germans were up around us last fall, off Jeffrey's. I didn't see 'em, but I guess they just drove everyone off," Mackenzie added.

"I remember hearing that!" Buddy exclaimed. "That's when the Gloucester guys got rammed and left for dead! I dunno … I can't figure where it's all gonna end, but one thing's for sure … the gummint better do somethin' before it's all gone!"

Buddy motioned for his two shipmates to look at the chart. You boys can see the lightship here, right?" he asked as he pointed out its location. They both nodded. How 'bout if you guys steer southeast for a coupla hours each, then get Ozzie up. That'll give me some time to catch a kink. You'll prob'ly wanna go put on some coffee, get out a little mug-up for snacks, stuff like that. Both you guys have been around fishing boats in one way or another … you all set with the radar?"

They both nodded with confidence.

"How 'bout the LORAN, gettin' our position, you okay with that?"

They both nodded again.

"It's a nice clear night, and the nor'west they're callin' for should give us the fair wind off. There's just one more thing …" Buddy 's forehead rippled as he lowered his gaze. "Take a look off to starboard, here … see that tug?"

Greg and Mack cocked their heads around to look out the starboard window and could plainly see the amber deck lights of a tugboat a couple of miles away. They also saw the white lights in a vertical line off the masthead and the portside red running light.

"See the boat?" Buddy asked.

"Yup."

"A-huh."

"See the three white masthead lights?"

"Yup."

"Sure do, Cap."

"See the barge?"

Greg and Mack looked at each other, then clamored to look out the window. They strained their eyes, but couldn't find it.

"You get that a lot around here," Buddy explained quietly but firmly. "The white lights in a line are tellin' us he's got a tow over six hunnerd feet back. He's prob'bly makin' for Brenton Reef Tower up in the mouth of the bay and headin' for Prahvidence with a loaded fuel barge. Check the radar … you can see the boat, but the barge's flash comes and goes, see? They load 'em 'till they're almost awash!"

They both looked up at the radar screen mounted on the overhead of the wheelhouse. Sure enough, as the heading flash circled around, only about every fifth revolution showed the barge's image. The tug was in the second ring out from the center. At that setting, it was two miles away.

"One more trick, boys. Take that knob there and turn that cursor line until it crosses the tug's target on the screen … yup, that's good. Now … watch the flash and tell me where that tug's heading."

They watched the screen and the tug seemed to be following along the cursor line straight to the center of the picture tube. Buddy looked up over them and checked the radar to see if his assumption was correct.

"Stupid question, guys, but where are we in that picture?" the skipper asked.

Jim and Greg looked at each other, then felt shivers run through their spines.

"I wanna know what each one of you would do if I wasn't here. Mackie?"

"Well, he's on our starboard hand, so either slow down and let him pass, or turn and go astern of him," Mack answered, trying to sound confident.

"That's okay. Good. How about you, Carleton?"

Greg thought for a moment, then blurted out, "Give him any damned thing he wants!"

Buddy nodded and coughed back his smoker's malady. "Okay, boys, it's up to you. I'm turnin' in. You can talk to him on channel thirteen on the VHF, there, if you need to, otherwise, leave it on sixteen so's he can call us. Get Oz up in four hours ... he sleeps next to the engine room when we're steamin.' Tell him we're goin' to the lightship. He'll know the rest."

The skipper went back to his small quarters aft of the wheelhouse, laid down in his bunk, and waited. After about thirty seconds, he felt the boat's rolling motion change to a bow-on jog. He craned his head out of the rack and strained his ears to hear what was happening in the wheelhouse.

"... Roger, Cap, this is the *Elizabeth Gale*, bound out from Pt. Judith. We'll be passing astern of your tow." The voice was Mackenzie's, talking into the radio.

"East bound fishing vessel, Roger, we'll stay on course for Brenton Reef. Thank you, much, Cap. Sea Mist tug *Mystic Sea* standing by on sixteen and thirteen. Y'all have yourselves a good trip," came the southern-accented reply.

Buddy smiled and rolled over. It was the last time he could sleep six hours in a row for the next four days.

"Greg, take a look down on deck, here, and I'll explain how the gear works," Mack announced, breaking the silent tedium of wheel watch. "Okay ... you see the winch right underneath us, here, right? In the Point, they call it the hoister. We'll have to guide the tow-wires on the drums with those bars stowed next to it."

"Hoister," Greg said, never leaving the wheel, splitting his vision between the deck and the compass.

"Okay. The main tow wires run forward from there, then go around the deck bollards, called ballards, then over to the gallows, um, we call 'em gallus frames, then over the hanging ballards that are swinging there. See the doors inside the rail?"

"Uh-huh."

"They hold the net open when you're towing it see? The brackets are made so that the water flow causes them to go to the bottom, then spread apart. They spread and then the net spreads."

"Okay, gotcha."

"Now … when we get to set out, there are ground cables and legs between the doors and the net. The ground cables help cover a wider range of bottom, then the legs are like a bridle, one for the top, one for the bottom of the net. The net is nothing more than a big funnel made out of twine that gets towed along the bottom. They make them with an overhang on the top so that when the fish get startled, they rise up and get caught as the net's being towed along. All the fish end up in the bag at the very end, and that's called the cod end."

"Easy beans, I'm with you so far."

"Now, when we set out, the boat has to turn, in like a half-a-circle, because all the gear is handled off the side," he explained. "I think that the mate and engineer run the hoister until Buddy takes a tow off, but we'll have time to figure that out."

"O.K. … keep goin'."

"The tow wires run aft alongside the hull, so they gather them up in the hook-up block that's hanging off the rail, back aft there," he continued. "That keeps the main wires out of the wheel and makes a common tow point."

"How do we get them in there?" Greg asked.

"We throw a grapple hook over the wires, they winch them in, and one of us will clamp the hook-up block around them. It pins together. Keep the pin in your teeth so that you have both hands to work with … that thing is wicked heavy!"

"Wow … there's a lot to this," Greg said.

"It'll be fine," Mack consoled him. "Hauling back is basically just the reverse of the procedure, except we get out there and take in the slack twine, and hopefully, dump a big bag of fish on deck that we can sort out!"

"Time to do it to it, boys," Ricky Helliott said as he shook Greg's arm to awaken him. "Let's get to it," he semi-yelled at Mack, shaking his foot. "This ain't no disco, ya know, twinkle toes."

Groggily, Mack and Greg shook themselves awake and gathered up their consciousness. The boat's easy roll during the night's steam had given way to a more pronounced snappiness. The sounds of gusting wind could be heard at the top of the foc'sle ladder and spray splashing over the rail. It was just coming on to daylight and the northwest air that had provided a fair wind for the *Elizabeth Gale* was now strengthening with the sun's rising. Mack rolled out and sat at the galley table, yawning, while Greg sat up in his bunk and draped his legs over the sideboard. Both noticed the change in the boat's motion. Mack rose, steadied himself at the ladder, and looked up through the doghouse hatch for an on-site weather report.

"Breezed up, huh?" Greg muttered to Mack.

"I guess so." he answered through his grogginess.

Ricky Helliott was behind the ladder, standing at the galley stove. "There's two coffee pots on this rig, and there ain't no coffee? My mouth feels like the Russian Army walked through barefoot, and now there ain't no coffee?" he exclaimed, disgusted. "Whatsa matter, you didn't learn how to make coffee in college?"

"How did you know we went to college?" Mack asked.

"Ahh … all you guys are stamped right out of a mold … you all look the same. You all make one trip, find out it ain't a luxury cruise, then go off to work in some office somewheres and tell the same damn sea story for the rest of your lives. Meanwhile," he said, squinting his large brown eyes in waves of headache pain, "we need some coffee on this rig 'cause Buddy's gonna blow that horn any second to set in!"

Helliott turned and put his head in the sink, stroking the hand-powered well pump to bring a torrent of cold water splashing from the spout, drenching his straggly red hair and making his wet eyebrows droop almost into his eyes. He looked dirt-road-miles older than his actual twenty-eight years. Without even raising his head, he rasped through his red beard, "Hey … who the hell are you guys, anyways? Instant fishermen … just add water," he gruffed.

Mack snapped his head around to catch eye contact with Greg. "You don't remember us picking you up last night?" Greg asked.

"Naaah!" came the drenched reply from the galley sink. "Was I broke when I came?"

"Yeah," Mack answered. "You spent it all …"

The conversation was interrupted by a loud, long blast of the horn. The three foc'sle mates struggled on with their boots and started for the ladder to the world above. First on deck was Ricky Helliott, still wearing his t-shirt pantaloons from the night before. Buddy rang the bell outside of the port wheelhouse window and yelled down, "Get a care package together, will ya, boys? We're goin' alongside!"

Ricky scrambled back down the ladder before the other two started up. "Get some stuff together for the boys on the ship," he ordered. "A coupla cartons of cigarettes, some magazines, some candy bars, anythin' like that."

Greg and Mack were puzzled. "What ship?" Greg asked.

"The lightship, college boy! C'mon, let's get to it!"

The three rummaged around and put together two cartons of cigarettes, a bag of candy bars, a few magazines and odds and ends then bound the whole lot together with mending twine so that it could be thrown easily. As Mack, Ricky and Greg poked their heads out of the doghouse, they were greeted with a stiff northwest breeze and the awesome sight of an enormous red-hulled ship only a few yards away. Greg and Mack dropped their jaws as they looked up to see the letters 'N' and 'T' towering over their heads. It wasn't just any ship ... it was the Nantucket Lightship!

"I'm gonna come up in the lee of the ship here, then back down hard, okay boys?" Buddy yelled from the wheelhouse over the sounds of engine and weather. "Carleton, throw that package up to the guys on the rail ... aim for a face, you'll never miss that way!"

Greg nervously took hold of the package. When he felt Buddy shifting the engine in reverse, he tossed a hail-Mary pass to a waiting set of arms above. At a safe distance away, Buddy blew the horn, waved, then turned and steamed the Lizgale to the south to find clear ground to set the net in. It wasn't long before Ozzie appeared on deck and took his station at the starboard side of the winch.

The Lizgale steamed away from the ship for about ten minutes. Buddy surveyed the horizon, then slowed the boat and took it out of gear, letting the vessel lay in the trough of the waves with the northwest breeze spraying over the starboard rail. No words were spoken as Ricky, Ozzie and Buddy went to the business of fishing, repeating the same moves they had orchestrated between them thousands of times before.

Ozzie took the handle of the power-take-off and brought the winch to life with a firm jerk on the handle. The outside heads of the winch began rotating as he uncleated a line that ran up through the rigging, terminating with a hook on the other end. Ricky took the hook and brought it forward to the door stowed there. Ozzie took a couple turns around the winch barrel and the door lurched upward from its resting place inside the rail, then, at the proper moment of the boat's roll, Ozzie let the door down over the outside of the boat, where it hung from the gallus frame and slammed and banged in the sea. Mack took the rigging's whipline hook from Ricky and walked aft, repeating the maneuver for the aft door while Ricky pounded the bronze cod-end tripper closed, sealing the net's bag where the fish would eventually be collected after the net was towed along the bottom for two-and-a-half hours.

Buddy put the boat into slow ahead, maintaining a very long, lazy circle to the starboard while the crewmen paid out the twine of the net. Greg shadowed Mack as best he could and joined in guiding the twine of the net over the rail as Ozzie disengaged the PTO. Mack showed Greg how to hook up the g-clip to the flat-link, making the net, the doors and the main tow wires one unit. Seconds later, the wire ropes leading from the winch were taut, the net was streaming aft and Buddy increased the throttle to steaming speed, throwing spray from the bow. Mack and Greg scrambled forward to the doghouse and stood in its relative security as Ricky took his place on the port side of the winch, brake wheel in hand. At a carefully timed moment, Buddy leaned out the port wheelhouse window and yelled "Yup!" Ricky let his brake off slightly, easing the forward trawl door past the rail and into the water, straining against the winch's brakes. Ozzie, meanwhile, let the aft door go quickly for a few seconds, then tightened up his brake wheel. Both winchmen then focused on the wire rope paying out in front of them, watching for pieces of line that were buried into the wire rope at various intervals, marking the length.

"Door mark," Ricky yelled out.

"Y … yup," Ozzie returned, signifying the same amount was paid out.

"Ten fathom."

"Y … yup."

"Fifteen fathom."

"Y … yup."

"Twenty."

"Y … yup." And on it went until seventy-five fathoms of tow-wire were set out.

Buddy slowed the boat as Ricky threw the grapple overboard to gather the two tow wires together for the hook-up block.

"What are you doin' up there?" Ricky yelled to Greg and Mack. "C'mon, get yourselves back aft and hook that up!"

Mack and Greg sprang to life and hurried to the starboard aft rail. Once again, Ozzie clutched in the PTO and began winching in the grapple line. The tow wires sang and bounced under the strain as Mack bent over the rail with the retaining pin in his teeth. As Greg clipped the heavy steel of the hook-up around the two tow wires, Mack slipped in the pin, Buddy hit the throttle and Ozzie disengaged the PTO. The Lizgale was now fishing, towing its net across the sandy bottom in search of yellowtail and blackback flounders, lemon sole, and lobsters.

It wasn't long before the smell of bacon, eggs, coffee and bread toasting wafted up the foc'sle ladder to the hungry skipper aft. This was one ritual that knew no bounds of experience ... it was time for the morning mug-up. As Greg filled the galley table with food, Mack appeared at the wheelhouse door, ready to take over for the skipper.

"You're a welcome sight, Mackie," Buddy exclaimed. "I could eat a horse and chase its rider! Just keep us goin' south by west, just like she is right now. There's a wreck off to our starboard, then we're clear for about twenty minutes. I'll be back by then," Buddy explained through an exhale of smoke. "What didja think when you came on deck and saw the lightship?"

"It blew my mind, Buddy," he replied. "Do you do that often?"

"Well, anytime we're down this way, we usually stop for a second. Doesn't hurt to have friends in the neighborhood, ya know ... besides, that's one lonely buncha bahstidds on that slab! I was talkin' to my nephew ... he's on there ... they got a big radar on that rig. He says the whole iron curtain fleet is just outside of us, headed this way. Look in the radar ... it looks like a city 'bout ten miles away! Lord luvvaduck!"

Mack thrust his head in the radar screen and nodded. "Wow ... it looks like another coastline out there!"

"It might as well be, Mackie ... there's whole cities on them rigs," he said, exhaling cigarette smoke as he opened the door. "Just keep us goin' steady, there, and I'll be back in a few."

Mack watched the skipper go down the foc'sle ladder, took a deep breath and looked around him. The Lizgale was rolling with the wind on her stern quarter, but seemed to enjoy the pat on the rump. The engine gauges all looked good and the compass held steady. Over in the corner, the depth sounder was recording the bottom in a straight, horizontal black scribble. Behind him, the oscillators of the LORAN sets hummed while the digital readouts spit out numbers that constantly tracked their position, while off in the distance, the lightship stood guard, her massive light looking like a small city building. Gulls flew overhead and shadowed the boat's movements, swooping and diving, waiting for the engine to slow when they knew it would be feeding time. Mack looked over his hands on the wheel, looked beyond the deck and gazed over the bow of the boat ... Water ... ocean as far as the eye could see. He was far away in a strange new world, with a crew of characters like no other, in a small ship rolling against a stiff breeze, but with the wheel's spokes in his hand, he was ... well ... home. Very comfortably home.

It seemed like seconds, but the skipper returned in about fifteen minutes. "Let's see ... where are we?" he asked, checking the LORAN units for their position. "There's a bad wreck at 3760-6180, a hang at 3745-6200, another at 3740-6203; some more down the other way at 3675-6085 and 3712-6028 ..." he recited off the top of his head. "We're looking good here, though, Mackie. You thread the needle in fine style."

"How can you keep all that stuff in your head like that?" Mack asked. He'd heard Buddy had a hang-book like no one else's, but he didn't realize just how much of it he could keep in his head.

"It just comes to ya, that's all," Buddy explained. "See, you're prob'ly lookin' at the water out front of us ... I don't see it. Well ... I mean, of course, I see it, but what my mind sees is that net goin' along the bottom ... bumpin' along the sand, missin' this wreck, that hang. Fish live on streets, same as people. We're goin' down that way," he said, sweeping his hand out the window, "Then we're gonna take the first left, come up a few blocks, turn before the spot where the *Mary Tapper* got into trouble, go down the boulevard, stay on the right fathom of depth, come around and end up here. If we do okay, we'll know where they are, we're on the right street ... if not, then we know where they ain't!"

Buddy grabbed the wheel and lit a cigarette. "Carleton's got your mug-up on the back of the stove ... you'd better head 'fore Ricky tears into it," he said, exhaling smoke. "I'll blow the horn in a coupla hours or so."

Below, Greg was beginning to wash dishes, Ricky was lying in his bunk, half asleep, his hat's visor pulled over his eyes, and Ozzie was sitting at the far end of the table, sipping a coffee and working on a crossword puzzle. Mack filled his plate and sat down at the galley table. The Lizgale rolled and rocked with gentle creaking sounds as she made her way down what Buddy called the street.

Sometimes, two hours at sea is an eternity. Sometimes it goes by in an instant, but in general, time is slower and more gentler to the soul when you're on the big pond. There are reasons for keeping to a makeshift schedule, of course: tow the net for the same amount of time so that you can make comparisons as to your productivity, don't tow too long, because you might be filling up with junk or trashfish, or you may be just prolonging the time that you towed around a torn-up net, catching nothing. Five minutes one way or the other means nothing. But five minutes one way or the other on shore means you've missed your train, you're late for an appointment, you're caught in a traffic jam, you're irresponsible ... you're caught up in all the trappings of society. Five minutes out there was, well, just a little longer. Two or so hours is a second, or a whole day. Man invented the clock; the ocean doesn't have one — never did.

The horn blew a loud, long blast, bringing everyone to their senses. The Lizgale had towed her net for a total of two-and-a-half hours, covering six-and-a-quarter miles, and was basically back on the same bearings she started from. Buddy maneuvered the boat so that the wind was on the starboard rail — the working rail — as the crew donned their boots and oilers. Down below, Ricky Helliott was giving the orders of the day: "Shimmy up the shim-sham! Hoist the Goddam! Oil up your oilskins and grease the foc'sle!" he announced to no one but seagulls as he arrived on deck.

Ozzie chimed in with a parody of Jimmy Durante's "Fairy Tales Can Come True" as he crooned,

"Yellowtails can come true ... they can happen to you ... if you're young at heart!"

He took up his position at the starboard side of the winch, his hands ready on the PTO lever.

Greg and Mack pulled their oilskins on and went up the ladder. The ocean was a deep blue, heartened by the sun's arrival. The sky was crystal clear and the wind was breezing at about twenty knots out of the northwest, making white caps as far as the eye could see. Other boats were beginning to show themselves. New Bedford boats to the east, a couple of Newport boats to the north, and on the shimmering horizon to the south, the outlines of the superstructures of the iron curtain fleet hovered in suspended animation. It did look like another coastline off there; the foreign ships were inching closer.

Ozzie clutched in the PTO as Ricky joined him at the starboard side of the winch. Mack and Greg stood on deck, not knowing quite where to fit in. Buddy came to the starboard wheelhouse window and yelled out to them, "Mackie, why don't you and Carleton come back aft and knock out the hook-up! Just yank the lanyard on the pin, then trip it open with the prybar hangin' on the gallus, there ... and boys ... be careful hangin' out over the rail!"

With a bit of hesitation, they both leaned out over the rail, and by timing the roll of the boat to their own internal sense of balance and innate fear, they managed to unlatch the hook-up, sending the main wires slithering off to a point leading from each gallows frame directly perpendicular to the rail. Ozzie and Ricky clutched in the frictions of the hoister, and the haulback started as the gulls in the area circled, cackling.

Buddy leaned out the window again. "Boys, guide them wires, will ya?" he yelled over the sounds of engine and machinery as he increased the engine speed. Mack motioned for Greg and they each took up a station at the head of each winch drum. Mack showed Greg how to use the guidebar to push and pull the tow-wire, making the coil smooth as it wound on to the drum.

"That's good, boys!" Buddy yelled reassuringly, throwing his cigarette butt overboard. "Keep 'em nice and smooth, we don't want any bird's nests in there ya know! How do they feel, Ricky, we got the mother lode or what?"

Ricky listened to the crackling and popping of the wires as they groaned onto the winch, then announced, "I think we did okay ... prob'bly sixteen hunnerd!" he yelled over his shoulder.

"Any dogs?" Buddy yelled as the boat rolled and heaved under the strain of hauling.

"Naaah ... she's trying to float up ... no dead weight ... we ain't catchin' no green eyes on this trip, Cap! I'm sayin' eighteen bushel of yt's, a couple of bb's, some odds and ends, maybe a few lemons and a couple bushel of bugs. That's my guess, Cap!" Ricky yelled back to the open window above his head.

"Whadya you say, Carleton?" Buddy yelled out in fatherly jest. "It ain't like swordfishin' is it?"

Greg looked up, smiled and shook his head *no*, then went back to intently watching the winch drum.

"Door mark!" Ricky yelled out. Buddy slowed the boat to an idle speed. In an instant, the heavy doors broke free of the water and slammed into the hull at each gallus frame, as the two winchmen turned the brake wheels, locking them. The doors hung and slammed in the wind, water streaming from the brackets. Spray came over the rail on every roll as seagulls mounted overhead, knowing breakfast was about to be served.

"Mackie, you go forward!" Buddy ordered. "Carleton, you go aft! Throw that dog hook down through the door brackets and hook 'em up on the d-ring, then stand back."

Each did as ordered, and the winchmen eased the doors down onto the hook, bringing most of the banging and thrashing in line with the boat's roll. Then they unhitched the g-clips and the winchmen started the drums turning again, retrieving the ground cables and legs until the wings of the net came to rest inches from the hanging bollards. Ricky came out from behind the winch and Ozzie remained, waiting to work the overhead rigging.

"Okay, boys, here's where we haul hard, so's she'll come easy! Over here with me, and no fakin'!" Ricky ordered as he headed for the net trough inside the starboard rail. "Untie that quarter rope offen your forward wing, Twinkle Toes, and pass it around the fairlead block, then give it to me." Mack did as ordered, then stood by for more instruction. "Okay, Farmer! Do the same and hand yours to Ozzie!" Greg followed his orders as well.

"Now look," Ricky continued, "when the sweep of the net comes up, we're gonna break it down inside the rail and hold it with our knees. Whatever ya do, don't bury your fingers in the meshes to hold the twine … if she goes over … you're goin' with it … got me, frat boys? Work with the roll of the boat and it will do the job for you! It's time to use your back, forget your head!"

Buddy came down from the wheelhouse and worked the forward quarter rope on the port winch barrel as Ozzie did the same at starboard. The sweep, the part of the net that actually has contact with the bottom, broke the surface and hung at the fairleads, its bights of chain shining and glistening in the sun, polished by their ride over the sandy bottom. In the orderly entanglement, the floats of the net clunked together as the twine spewed water in the wind, spraying the railmen in the face.

"Okay, boys, get ready!" Ricky ordered as he put his hands on the top of the net. When the boat rolled down in the wave's trough, the twine went slack for a moment … It was at this precise juncture that Ricky yelled out, "Yo!" Buddy and Ozzie slacked their hold on the quarter ropes and the sweep, floats and slack twine fell into the net trough. "Get your knees on it, boys!" Ricky yelled to Mack and Greg. "Stick with me!" As the boat rose on the next wave, they pushed hard to keep the gear bent over the rail and stopped off. When the boat rolled down, Ricky ordered to pull again, and the three took up more slack twine, gathering up the net's length in small increments. After four or five more roll/pulls, the weight was beginning to be too much for them to hold.

"Get the whip, Twinkle Toes," Helliott ordered loudly. "Grab that strap, Farmer!"

Mack retrieved the hook of the topside rigging as Ozzie threw a spliced piece of heavy line to Greg, who in turn, handed it to Helliott. Ricky wrapped the strap around the remaining part of the net and put the hook of the whip into the spliced eyes, then yelled "Yup!" Ozzie brought the whipline high into the rigging, carrying much of the net with it, driving the fish down into the codend. "Grab that other strap, Farmer, then get the tay-kle!" Helliott ordered. While the twine was still in the air, he wrapped the other strap around the net, then hooked the block and tackle into the final strap. "Now pay 'tention, boys … when Buddy comes up on the tay-kle, Ozzie's gonna let the whip go … we break the twine down, pull in the slack on the bullrope, then get out of the way 'cause that bag's comin' over the rail!"

Greg found the only rope that had slack and figured that must be the bullrope. Mack readied himself for the change of strain and at the right moment, dodged the hook coming down while the other went up. Helliott swept his arms and warned, "Now get the hell outta there!" Buddy winched in the tackle, and at the right point in the roll of the boat, the bag of fish came careening over the rail and hung a few inches above the starboard side of the deck. Ricky reached underneath and pulled the line holding the tripper, opening the cod end … a teeming mass of fish spilled out, filling the whole side of the deck in one enormous, wet, whoosh. Flounders flipped everywhere, small hake fanned their tails in the fracas, a few codfish peeked out from under the crush of sea life, and a good many lobsters were sprinkled through the catch, some waving their claws in a futile act of defiance. The trip was well underway.

"Whatd'ya think, Ricky, didja get your hail?" Buddy yelled to the foredeck.

Ricky kicked around through the pile and gave his report. "Yup, it looks like more bugs than I thought, but that's okay. We'll work 'em over!" he yelled back as he pounded in the tripper, getting ready for the next tow.

~ ~ ~

"So how did the rest of the trip go?" Dr. Grayson asked as she threw more wood on the fire.

"Oh, great. For the first couple of days, the iron curtain boats stayed off a few miles and we had some real good goin' there for a day, night and a day," Greg answered. "We had most of the trip by then."

"By the time we put the gear on deck after the fourth day, we needed a traffic cop to control all the boats that moved in," Mack added. "Remember when that Russian research boat cut us off and checked out the haulback? He called in the fleet! Within six hours, the whole of eastern Europe had us surrounded."

Sewall, one of the students from Maine asked, "What about the dory ... the lifeboat ... what happened, anyway?"

Ozzie smiled and nodded. "B ... bu ... bu ... bugs," he replied.

"Bugs?" the newcomers chanted in unison, confused.

"Yup, bugs," Mack jumped in. "Lobsters. We had a tank on deck to hold six hundred pounds of lobsters. By the end of the first night, that was full. The lobsters came on heavy in the night, that's when they crawl more. Ozzie had the idea we should use one of the dories as a lobster tank, so we took it down out of the rigging and set it up on deck, back aft. He ran some hoses and plastic piping from the engine room and we had enough room for another eight hundred. We ended up the trip with eighteen thousand of yellowtails, seventy-seven hundred of blackbacks, four thousand lemon sole — those are really just big bb's — and fourteen hundred of bugs. Plus, we saved most of the hake and skates to pump out at the trash plant ... back then, we had that option, too. Not a bad first trip, huh, Greg?"

"It was a magic time, back then, that's for sure. I just wish Ricky and Buddy could be here, too," Greg said longingly. "Finestkind-a-folks."

Jim Mackenzie rowed alongside the float that held his homeboat and the other boats and tied up. It was 1:30 in the morning. At 5:30, he had to bring Ozzie to the mainland, then check on his fish experiment at the co-op. It was a great night at the campfire, and it was wonderful to see his old, dear friend again. He climbed the short set of stairs leading to the wheelhouse of the Lizgale, stepped in, shut the door and looked around. The binoculars still hung in the same place where Buddy had kept them those many years ago. He picked them up and looked through the starboard side window, seeing nothing but fog and a distant memory …

~~~

"Here, take a look! Lord luvvaduck! Mackie! You won't believe it! They've got ever'thin' on there, and I mean ever'thin'! Look back aft there, on the deck … take a good look! Lord luvvaduck!"

Mackenzie took the binoculars from Buddy and peered through them as the Lizgale increased speed to begin the trip back to Pt. Judith. He focused in on what appeared to be a beautiful girl standing at the rail of a Russian factory ship, the wind blowing her dress above her knees just like that famous scene with Marilyn Monroe standing over the subway grate. She had long, light brown hair that flowed in the breeze, but although she was strikingly beautiful, she looked sad. She turned her head, then momentarily went out of sight. When the two vessels rolled back towards each other, he found her again … She was pushing a child on, of all things, a swing set.

10
THE BRIDGE

Lat. 43 deg. 46.1 min. N.
Long. 69 deg. 36.5 min. W.

"**G**uess. Just take a wild guess!"

"Half that amount would be unthinkable."

"You're so far off, you're nowhere close. Someone else give a wild guess. C'mon, go crazy!"

"I'm clueless. This is a joke, right? We would have heard this. It would have been all over the news. It would have been the biggest story of the year! Twice?"

"Not even in the ballpark. Not even in the same state as the ballpark!"

"I went up there as a volunteer intern. The place was devastated. It was, well, it was environmental carnage. I can't believe this ... not even twice? It's larger than double the size?"

"You were up there? Bravo, but it's larger than double, yes. You saw what went on up there ... can you imagine anything like that happening again, much less every year and on a much grander scale? Anyone else want to hazard a guess?"

School was definitely in session, and professor Chris Brown had picked the footbridge to Wood End as his open-air classroom. "Give up?" he challenged.

"We worked on a community project stenciling storm drains back in the old neighborhood in Baltimore. It must be a phenomenal figure. I don't think people realize, I mean, I don't think they do it to directly cause harm. Owning a car is a major thing to some people, they just want to try to take care of it."

"Anyone else want to take a chance on the oil spill lottery?"

"Well, if it's bigger than double, how about triple?"

"No way. Putnam, what's your guess?"

"Quadruple?"

"Uh-uh. No. Nada. Not no way, not nohow," Chris quipped. "It's sixteen times. That's sixteen, folks!" Chris announced. "One-six — sixteen!"

"Sixteen times? C'mon, you're kidding me, right, Prof?" Zack asked.

"One thing you can count on, I'll never kid you on something like this, not for a moment. That's right ... it's sixteen times," he answered.

"But, Mr. Brown, the *Exxon Valdez* was a disaster of immense proportions. It will always be a big story in history," Fallon said incredulously. "I just can't believe that it's sixteen times, and every year, too. Why doesn't something like this ever get to the news? How can they possibly do this, and get away with it, year after year. How?"

"Well, the way I look at it," Chris Brown answered his students, "this is a situation of us, not them. We change our oil over storm drains every year and it eventually runs into the sea, but because it's just us trying to save some money, and maintain our cars ... it's just little guys! But ... when they run their tanker aground, it's them, and they're a big corporation! We buy their oil, then we don't dispose of it properly, but, is it still them?"

"Yeah, but how can they do that? Sixteen times the amount of the *Exxon Valdez* oil spill reaches the ocean every year from people who change their oil over storm drains, and nobody even knows? How can they do that?" Tiffany asked. "When we work on urban models in community planning courses, we never see or hear this. Why?"

"That makes you think doesn't it?" Chris addressed the class. "If you get nothing else out of this course, remember that the problem is always us, not them. It's all of us, all of the time ... Remember, I'm an anthropologist, as well as an oceanographer. If anything brings you around to the concept of a global community, it's anthropology. It's us who created the demand, not them. Us dumping millions of gallons of oil into the sea.

"Hey, I live on a farm in Kansas," Irene said indignantly holding her long blonde hair out of her face as a seabreeze caught it. "I've never put any oil down any storm drain. I never even saw a storm drain until I was eighteen years old." Her blue eyes grew wider as she grew angry. "I don't live anywhere near the ocean, I only saw it for the first time a few days ago. How can you say it's us? *I've* never dumped oil into the ocean!"

Before Chris could answer, Fallon looked out from under her brown bangs and shook her head. "You grew up on a farm in the midwest and you never did anything to the ocean?" she asked sarcastically. "How about the dead zone in the Gulf of Mexico. It's hundreds of square miles of ocean where nothing lives, because the fertilizer and topsoil from you and your big corporate farm runs down the Mississippi and pollutes the Gulf. How can you do that?"

"You mean, how can *we* do that, right?" Chris was deliberately being the antagonist, playing the situation but hoping to spark a debate between the students, raising their awareness. "What do you mean, Fallon?" he asked. "Do you eat? Do you grow your own food?"

"Ahh, you're like all the rest of the tree huggers!" Putnam chimed in. "Our construction company is always blamed for everything, but we've built hundreds of miles of sewer lines, built treatment plants, put in special storm drain runoff collectors called 'stormtreat' systems ... lots of things. One time, we were installing an emergency pumping station for raw sewage spilling into the harbor. A group of neighborhood residents shut us down for two weeks because the equipment was too loud, they said. By the time we got that resolved, about two million gallons of raw sewage spilled all over their beach and made it off-limits for the summer. They didn't get it, and you don't get it, either, Fallon!"

Jake stood up and stretched his six-foot-seven athlete's frame. "You know, I read somewhere that sixty percent of the oil pollution in the ocean comes from runoff from the streets. I never really thought about it, but I guess if we all drive cars, we all contribute."

Chris nodded. Cindy jumped into the discussion. "I can give you a good example," she said. "Last year, we worked on a commuter rail project. The MBTA was resurrecting a couple old commuter rails to get some mass transit back to Boston. One of them was on the North Shore ... it ran from Newburyport to Boston, right through the middle of this pristine salt marsh. There was a lot of concern on the part of the locals, but, if it keeps a lot of cars off the highway, then the runoff from those cars never gets into the marsh that the train is riding by, right? The plans for the rail project had very elaborate filter systems to prevent runoff contamination from the trains. On top of that, all these little creeks that were restricted or blocked off when the original line was built in 1856 were supposed to be re-opened. That brings back acres of critical habitat. There's always two ways to look at anything, but people don't want to consider the other view."

"Well, that's a great argument for mass transit, but I've worked on fisheries issues, and I'll tell you, you can point the finger right towards the greedy fishermen who over-fished the oceans!" Bob, the marine biology major from U.N.H. exclaimed. "Overfishing! One word says it all! Shut 'em down and go all out for aquaculture. There's your answer!"

"One word, huh? One word?" Tiffany interjected. "Even a New Yorker like me knows that seventy-five percent of the commercial fish species depend on the estuaries for part of their life cycle. Yeah, that's right, big boy, I did a little homework before I got here! Where've you been? We've been talking all along about all this pollution going into the ocean ... it goes through the marshes and bays first!" She stood and ran her thumbs along the straps of her tank-top and shook her bobbed hair in the breeze. "Everybody plays their little part. You're picking on Irene, over here, for having a farm. What's up with that? You guys don't eat?"

"There'll be plenty to eat when Heidi and I get our fish farm going, right, Hi?" Bob snapped back. "It's the future, and this country better get with the program! And another thing ..."

Sewell Gordon, up to this point, had remained silent, taking in the whole fracas and contemplating the ongoing debate. He'd had enough and cut off Bob in mid-sentence. "Wellsuh, I think you've gotcha cart before the hoss, there, old man. I useta think that aquaculture was the only way to go, but it's not foolproof, ya know, yuh. By godfrey mighty, they got sea trout farms over in Scotland that quadrupled the levels of sea lice in the coves over there. One of them big salmon farms up in Washington State produces the same amount of untreated sewage as a hundred thousand people. There's the use of antibiotics, genetic mixin', the harvesting of baitfish off third world countries to make feed for these operations. Remember what happened when they took all the capelin, the baitfish, off of the Grand Banks? Wiped out the fish at the secondary trophic level ... no cod food, no cod, mistah! And most of the capelin went to eastern Europe and Russia, in factory ships ... the same damn factory ships that are now off the third world shores, doin' the same damn thing, yuh. By godfrey mighty, you wanna blame it all on the fishin' guys! It's like blamin' it all on the farmin' guys or the construction guys, or …

"If I could jump in here, folks," Chris interjected. "I'm glad to hear the spirited debate, and I think we've raised our collective consciousness level a little bit, but the spirit of the whole discussion is to work together. Those who ignore the lessons of history are doomed to repeat them, I mean, most of the world's great wars were out of finger pointing, don't you agree? Here's the scoop about aquaculture. It's figured that 150 to 160 million metric tons of fishery products will be needed to provide protein for the world's ever-increasing population. The wild, or capture fisheries are expected to provide about two-thirds. That leaves 50 to 60 million metric tons that will have to come from aquaculture, and that's no small figure, Bob. Once again, we've got to have both, and in some sort of harmonic balance."

Chris checked his watch. "Well, that looks like that's about it for today, we should be heading back. We're all here for one reason, you know," he said. "It's up to us to find some solutions. I dare say we've stated some of the problems!"

The students cast their eyes on each other and smiled. They realized that Chris Brown had an unorthodox, challenging, seat-of-the-pants method of inspiring his students to be their own teachers. They'd been fooled into creating their own enlightenment.

"Okay, Brownie, what are we going to be up to next class?" Zack asked, not out of disrespect, but from the comfortable familiarity that was just forged out of the class debate. "What've you got for us next?"

Chris smiled and nodded. "Glad you asked, Wildman. I think we all can agree that no matter who you are or where you live, everyone impacts the oceans. That's why our course on fisheries anthropology starts, realistically, on shore. We can also agree that the population of the world is growing faster than we can feed it, and the oceans are needed for both wild and cultured harvest. Next we're going to look at things from an anthropologist's view. Let's say you're doing an artifact dig about ten thousand years from now, and a chemist crashes the bone party. Okay then, your chemist does a routine check of the ground water ... that would make a nice place to look for clues of life from the past, don't you think? ... " Puzzled looks came back.

"I'd be looking for a Corvette or something buried there," Jake offered humorously. "Maybe a Coke bottle."

"But think about it, Jake," Chris challenged. "When we dig up an ancient site, we're looking for clues to their technology, which gives clues as to how they lived ... why their culture died out, et cetera."

"Why groundwater? For signs of industrial pollution?" Ron, the student from Baltimore, asked seriously, his dreadlocks swaying as he spoke.

"It's a little like that, Ron," Chris answered. "See, a German study just found traces of antibiotics, caffeine, personal care items and other things like that in groundwater. Guess where that comes from! Oh, and before you answer, we'll also be talking about nitrogen loading of the atmosphere that eventually finds its way to the oceans, and guess where that comes from! Again, it is always us, it's never 'them,' got it? Why don't you folks head along ... I'll be right behind you."

Twelve students started to hike along the island's rugged trail, jabbering, joking and bonding. Between the chuckles and good-natured ribbing they were realizing this was no ordinary class in an ordinary place. Chris followed behind, far enough back, but just in earshot so he could overhear if they were beginning to think as a team, not a group of individuals.

The smell of tea rose through the watchtower's staircase. Chris vaguely recognized the aroma and the sound of footsteps approaching him but was too engrossed in looking through the binoculars to pay attention. Dr. Grayson startled him when she spoke.

"Well, Mr. Brown, if the chatter at the table tonight is any indication, it seems as though you've got your class off to a flying start. Is there a reason why you didn't join us for supper tonight?"

"Oh, good evening, Dr. Grayson," he answered. "Actually, yes, there was a reason. It's because I don't have Kay Summersby here."

"Who?"

"Kay Summersby. She was Eisenhower's secretary during World War II."

Dr. Grayson sipped her tea, puzzled. "Please continue."

"See, Dr. Grayson, Kay Summersby was General Eisenhower's personal secretary. I've always been a student of life in the past, as you know, and World War II has always been a fascinating visit for an anthropologist, believe it or not. You can learn a lot from that old guy."

"Eisenhower, you mean?" she asked.

"Yes, Eisenhower," he continued. "His philosophy was to give out all the credit when things went right and take all the blame when things went wrong. He was there to win the war, not to get his name in history. He knew that if the war was won, he'd get his just rewards then, but it had to be won first."

"I'm starting to see what all the hubbub was at the student's table. There's a point to this, it just isn't obvious. Correct, I hope?"

Chris smiled and nodded. "When General Ike wanted some hard facts about the activity at the front, he'd gather a roomful of sergeants ... not colonels or generals ... sergeants. Then he'd say something to tick them right off ... for instance, 'I'm sending the fifth army to the west and taking all the tanks away.' Something ... anything ... to get them going. He knew they'd be angry and frustrated, but he also knew the chain of command prevented them from saying what was really on their minds as long as he was there. This was

Kay's cue ... she'd come in the room with a phony excuse to get the general out of there, then they'd both listen outside the door and she'd write down what they said."

"So he had his own front line report from a source that otherwise wouldn't give straight information. I still must confess I don't follow, Chris," she said.

"Well, I took a page out of Eisenhower's book," he continued. "I got them all riled up in class today, then left them alone so they'd say what was on their minds, and hopefully, bond into a more cohesive unit by rallying around a few issues. I'm here to win the war, so's to speak, not get my name in the history books."

Dr. Grayson sipped her tea and thought for a few seconds. "The cats ... the cats were nowhere to be seen during supper. They usually rub everyone's legs looking for a handout, but not tonight," she realized. "The cats were out in the kitchen eating with you, weren't they?"

"I've sworn them to secrecy. You'll never make them talk," he joked.

"You were listening to what the students said without you there! You're wise beyond your years, Chris Brown!" she declared. "Sneaky, maybe, sly, even underhanded, but wise, nonetheless!"

Dr. Grayson sat down and silently enjoyed the view of the night's stars. She smiled and sipped her tea while Chris went back to his binoculars. In the distance, the glow of the lights inside the Lizgale illuminated the rigging above the deck skylight. *There's something about that boat,* he thought. *They all look the same, but they're not.*

11
MAIL CALL

LAT. 43 DEG. 45.2 MIN N.
LONG. 69 DEG. 36.95 MIN. W.

LAT. 41 DEG. 29.55 MIN N.
LONG. 71 DEG. 19.3 MIN W.

It was a hazy, hot July afternoon as Chris Brown began to paddle his kayak back to Damariscove from the mainland. The morning fog had burned off slightly to leave an eighth of a mile visibility. The fishing folks at Pemaquid Harbor and Round Pond had been most cordial and enjoyable to visit with. They were also very free with their information regarding his Doctoral research.

Kayak paddling can be a lonely, solitary activity, but alone-time on the sea is a time for organizing one's thoughts. As he paddled, he began to sort out his mental notes from the trip. Comparing fishermen's comments seemed to be, in many ways, moot. There were so many commonalities between everyone along any coast, involved in any manner of fishing, they seemed to be grown from the same roots, his research showed. "Why can't they just leave us alone?" they always ask. "Why do there have to be so many regulations, and why aren't they enacted from common sense?" they say in frustration. "They make us throw perfectly edible fish overboard because they don't fit into a quota scheme."

"We were fine until the fleet got overbuilt with cheap government money and tax breaks for people who were never involved in fishing before."

"Why do they think we're stupid when we're the guys that are out there every day?"

The words of Tashunkewitko, also known as "Crazy Horse," the Ogala Sioux Chief who defeated Custer, flashed across his mind: "All we wanted was peace and to be left alone."

"That's it!" he exclaimed out loud as he paddled. "That's it! It's been staring me in the face all along! I've ignored my own mantra ... history repeating itself! I'm here to study an ancient culture under duress," he muttered. "Of course!" ... *the Native Americans. When they lost their land, they also lost their way of life. All they wanted was to live the same way they always had, and, more importantly, they just wanted to be left alone. Government programs brought the settlers, who eradicated the buffalo, fenced in the open range for ranches, even brought the railroad. Modern government brought trickle-down economics that brought investor boats, that put too much pressure on the fish stocks too quickly after the distant water fleets left. Are the fish analogous to the buffalo? Are the fences analogous to frustrating regulations? They've all said it a million times ... everyone from* Starpom *Fedorovich to Jim Mackenzie to the people at Round Pond and Pemaquid:* "'We don't fit in anywhere else ... just leave us alone ... leave us alone!'" he repeated aloud.

As he paddled along, following his 255 degree compass course, he thought, *What if there was a sweeping law passed that fishermen of today couldn't use any modern technology and were required to fish as in the days of sail, like the 1700's ... No diesel engines, no radios, no electronic aids ... would they still go fishing? They probably would because the way of life is still, in most ways, preserved. They might even like it better if the regulations were the same, which, effectively, were non-existent.* "I'll have to ask the next group I meet with. Of the two choices, would they go back to the past if the only other choice was leaving fishing?"

Chris hove-to from paddling to make some notes on his newfound revelations. He reached into the front storage compartment of the kayak and retrieved his clipboard. Drifting along outside of Thrumcap Island, he began to recollect to himself, occasionally muttering, "I'll have to ask Mack for clarification on this."

Writing away, deep in thought, with the southwest breeze in his face, he wasn't paying attention to the boat that was slowly but squarely running directly at his stern. The vessel steamed closer and closer, oblivious to the low silhouette of the kayak that was hidden in the murky sun glare just beyond the edge of the haze. On and on it came, until at the last possible moment, the startled skipper caught sight of something in the water and veered the course to starboard while he blew the horn in a long, loud, spine shaking blast. The bright red boat doubled back to check out the situation and came alongside.

"Gawdalmighty, Doc!" came the yell from the cockpit of the *Amanda May*. "You cussed near gave me a heart attack! What in hell you doin' out he-ah? Damn near got yourself run down, dammit!" Chappy bellowed as he poked his head out from underneath the starboard side curtain. "Dammit, man, that thing don't show up on the radar, ya know, yuh. What the hell you doin'? You all right out they-uh?"

Chris shook off his initial shock and waved his hands high. "I'm really sorry, Mr. Lester," he yelled apologetically. "I guess I wasn't paying attention. I stopped to make a couple notes, and ... are you all right?" he yelled back over the sound of the A-May's engine.

"Me? Gawdalmighty, I s'pose I'll make it, but you cussed near gave me a shock! Paddle that damn thing ov-ah he-ah and get aboard he-ah before you get really run down, yuh. C'mon, I ain't got all day!"

Chris came alongside the A-May, caught Chappy's hand, then climbed aboard the boat. The two of them slid the kayak over the rail and stowed it in the cockpit. Chris came forward and leaned beside the helm as Chappy put the boat in gear and set a course to split the difference between the Hypocrites Ledges and White Island.

"I'm takin' the mail ov-ah to th' island, annaways. You're safer he-ah than on the pond," Chappy lectured. "Where in Gawd's name you comin' from, annaways?"

"I've been doing some research over in Round Pond and Pemaquid Harbor, Mr. Lester. Mack set me up with some meetings with the guys from those ports. Nice group of people over there."

"Well, if I'm gonna keep runnin' into ya, we might as well get somethin' straight, okay, Doc?"

"Sure ... what can I do for you?"

"First off, call me Chappy like anyone else does, mist-ah was my fath-uh. Second, next time you go off in that damned plastic log, make sure you pay attention. Deal?"

Chris smiled. "Sure, Chappy."

"How long you been ov-ah to th' mainland, annaways, Doc?"

"Two days," Chris answered over the engine noise. "I stayed in Norbie Hackett's fish house at Round Pond last night. The fish house he has on his dock is bigger than some people's main house. Beautiful spot, too," Chris marveled.

"Yuh, I know where you were, they-uh. It is a pristine lookin' view from they-uh, that's for sure."

The red hull of the *Amanda May* sliced along on her course to the Motions buoy outside of Damariscove Island Harbor. Periodically, Chappy checked the radar screen for any other boats in his path, and to adjust his course to the Motions buoy. The afternoon southwest breeze threw up a small amount of spray as they motored along.

"Ya know, Doc, I think I got some mail for you. Yuh ... pretty sure I do. Small package, I think, yuh. Got a small package for Spice, too." Chappy said, ticking off his fingers. "Got some stuff for the students ... Dr. G ... gee, I guess everyone gets somethin' this trip, come to think of it. If you want yours now, the plastic box for the island is right down below on the galley table. Help yourself."

Chris went down the foc'sle ladder and found the box marked "D-cove I." He poked through the letters and packages until he found the item addressed to him. It was rather heavy and marked with the words "fragile-photos enclosed." His heart was pounding as he sat down at the table and opened it. Inside was a letter, a manila envelope marked "copies of documents" then another manila envelope marked "copies of Dad's pictures from Newport." He set the two envelopes aside and began to read the letter ...

Dear Mr. Brown,

Thank you for inquiring about my late dad, Lieutenant Commander Leeland J. Chambers. Originally, you wrote to my mom, but, I'm sad to say, she also passed on this last winter.

A lot of what my dad did while he was stationed at Newport he could never tell us about. It was a lot of cold war secrecy, from what I can gather. As you know, he was assigned to Naval Intelligence. Like you, I've also been working through the Freedom of Information Act to recover whatever documents I could on his life. He was gone for months at a time, especially when I was a little girl, and this is the only way I'll ever really get to know him, through his work.

I can tell you he was the recipient of many awards and his papers show many instances where his superiors felt he was the only man capable of handling some tough assignments. I've included some things I've received from the War Department. I hope it helps. Please keep in touch if you uncover anything that might help me to know and understand my dad.

Sincerely,
Caroline R. (Chambers) Williams
Scarborough, Me.

"Didja find it, Doc?" Chappy yelled down the foc'sle ladder.

Chris answered back, "Yes, all set." Then he opened up the documents envelope. Inside were about twenty papers, some faded copies, some looking remarkably original in their quality. The words "sanitized," "declassified," "authorized for release" and "sensitive information deleted" were prominent in various places. Some documents had actual words cut out of them, some had words covered up by thick marker before they were copied. Near the end of the stack, he pulled out one document entitled "National Security Action Memorandum 1198." It was addressed to the Secretary of State, Secretary of Defense and the Secretary of the Treasury, with copies to the Secretary of the Navy and the Commandant of the Coast Guard. The subject of the memorandum read: 'Interactions of Soviet Bloc Fishing Vessels with Domestic Fishing Vessels.' Chris scanned the document, reaching the bottom of the first page …

> 6) Fishing vessels from domestic ports that engage in illicit trading with Soviet Bloc vessels shall be, under the terms of this directive, considered under suspicion for the passing of intelligence, and should be closely monitored in port, as well as underway. The so-called "spice trade" may, under certain circumstances, be considered prima facie evidence of suspicion of treasonous activity.
>
> 7) Any means necessary, including the use of force, may be used to enforce these provisions if the security of the United States and/or its environs or allies are put in jeopardy …

"Spice trade?" he whispered to himself, puzzled. "More references to 'spice.'"

He slid the papers back into the envelope, then looked inside the envelope containing the pictures. One was of the staff at the Newport Naval War College standing for a group photo; several were of various fishing boats, American and foreign; a couple were of aircraft; some of old Liberty ships and freighters from World War II. One picture caused Chris to stop and catch himself. "Oh my God," he breathed, clutching the picture in his hands. "I can't believe it! If this is what I think it is, it could be the best clue so far! *Kaunis*!"

The Burkettes, the husband and wife geology team, were just heading for the door of their room when a knock startled them. Sandy Burkette opened the door.

"Oh, Chris, how are you? We don't get people knocking on the door very often," she mused. "We're just leaving to go next door to watch Mack's video, care to join us?"

"Sandy, Dave, do you have some type of high powered magnifying glass, a loupe, or something?" he asked, nearly out of breath. "You must have something to check minerals or crystalline structures in the field, don't you? I don't think a microscope will work too well."

Sandy and Dave looked at each other, speaking in glances like most married couples. "What's the matter, Chris?" Dave asked in a concerned tone. "You weren't at the evening mug-up again. Everything alright?"

"You okay?" his wife chimed in. "You look like you've seen a ghost."

"No, no I'm fine. I've received some pictures from a contact of mine. Some of them are old aerial surveillance photos from the '70s and I'd like to see if I can decipher them a little better, that's all. It's ... it's ... for my research."

"Sure thing," Dave offered. "Sandy, why don't you go ahead to the mess hall, and I'll be right along. I'm assuming this can't wait until after Mack shows his video. You look like a man on a mission, Chris."

Chris composed himself, still standing in the open doorway. "I'm sorry, I didn't realize you had plans. I guess I missed the whole thing. I've been reading my mail. What's going on in the mess hall?"

"It's a tradition. Mack's wife plays cello in the Boston Pops Orchestra in the summers. She always sends us the tape of the Fourth of July concert on the Esplanade in Boston," he explained. "He just got it today."

"That's where they end the show with the '1812 Overture,' timed with the cannons and fireworks. I certainly don't have to explain that to you, do I, though. You're a Harvard

Man. The great thing about this year is, his daughter won an honorary seat from the Conservatory to play alongside her mother. They're both playing! Where've you been? You haven't heard?" Sandy asked.

"If you could just point me the way, I'll leave you alone. I'm sorry … please!"

Dave Burkette grimaced. "You go ahead, dear," he told his wife. "I'll be right behind you. "C'mon, in Chris," he beckoned as Sandy strode off down the path to the mess hall.

Dr. Dave reached down behind his desk and took out a wooden case containing a large, free-standing magnifying glass. "Slide your pictures under there, then if that doesn't give enough resolution, use this hand-held glass, too. If you get the focal length just right with your arm, you can double the mag power. It's crude, but effective. Works real good in the field."

Chris thumbed through the envelope, pulled out a photo and slid it under the large magnifier.

"Well, there's the hammer and sickle," Dave said, looking over Chris's shoulder. "She's a Soviet ship, that's for sure. Factory trawler?"

"It's definitely a catcher/processor, yes," Chris answered without looking up. "I need to get the number off the stack."

"Simple," Dave explained. "Take this mag-glass and go up and down until it comes into focus through the other one. "We've started campfires in a minute flat with this baby," he chuckled.

Chris moved the magnifier until the numbers on the stack came clearly in view.

"Hmmmm," Dave said, still looking over Chris's shoulder, becoming fascinated. "Well, she's number six-ten, that's for sure."

"The *Zvezda Rybaka* … The Fisherman's Star," Chris mumbled, sitting back in the chair, almost lifeless. He ran his fingers through his hair, then rubbed a hand over his eyes, as if the image would change when he opened them again.

"The *Zvezda Rybaka*," he repeated. His blood ran cold.

"Do you speak Russian?" Dave asked. "I don't see that anywhere here."

"I learned a little when I was a kid," Chris stumbled out.

"That's some childhood you had, there, Chris. Hey! Look here!" Dave guided Chris's arm, still holding the hand-held mag-glass, until another feature of the ship came into view. "Well, at least this kid had some time to play. Can you beat that? They even had a swingset on there for the kids. Can you beat that?"

Dave reached into the envelope and pulled out another photo. "May I?" he asked, not waiting for an affirmative answer. This was a close-up of an American boat alongside a Soviet factory ship. Both watched intently as the image became clear. A fisherman was standing on the steps outside of the starboard wheelhouse door of an eastern rig. His arm was outstretched and a package was in mid-air. It was evident that he'd just thrown something to the Soviet ship. Dave moved the glass to see who was about to catch it.

"Man, oh man, look at that!" Dave exclaimed. "They had everything on there! Look at that! She's beautiful!" he spouted. "Can you believe that? What in God's name is a gorgeous girl like that doing out there?"

Chris sat cold and limp, exhaling loudly, rattling his lips. Dr. Dave tapped him on the shoulder. "You all set here? I've got to catch up with the wife. She'll sharpen a knife and shoot me if I'm late for this thing," he joked.

Chris shook himself halfway back to the present. "Sure ... go ahead. Can I just stay and look at a couple more?"

"Take your time, help yourself, but you don't want to miss the show, if you can help it. Mack's wife said in her letter that there were a couple guest stars in it, too. A surprise. And ... Greg's made some of his famous applesauce cake. Don't take too long!"

"What's going on, Old Scout?" Mack whispered as Chris sat down beside him in the mess hall. On the TV screen, Keith

Lockhart was conducting the Boston Pops, his trademark smile as wide as the screen. "Thought you'd miss the whole show. Well, you already missed the big cello scene where my wife and daughter were shown. Her letter said that's the only time they put the TV camera on them. They never show the cellos, dammit!" he grumbled, half joking, but with frustration showing nonetheless. "At least you haven't missed the surprise ... besides my wife and daughter, that is."

The VCR played on, with the Pops' lilting melodies filling the mess hall. Staff and students were swaying to the music, enjoying the culture and familiarity imported from the mainland. Keith Lockhart announced his two guest stars, but Chris was still in a daze. He appeared to be paying attention, but inside, he was deep in another time and place.

"And it gives me great pleasure to introduce Mr. K.O. Marsden, and from Canada, Mr. Garnet Rogers!"

The whole room applauded, as did the taped audience on the banks of the Charles River, when Ozzie and Garnet Rogers took the stage. Mack sat bolt upright, clenching his fists in front of him like Ozzie did when he sang. Ozzie and Garnet blended their powerful voices to soar above the Boston crowd as they tore into one of Stan Rogers' great songs:

Once again with the tide she slips her lines ...
Turns her head and comes awake.
Where she lay so still at Privateer's Wharf ...
Now she quickly gathers way.
She will range far south from the harbor mouth ...
And rejoice with every wave ...

... and who would know the *Bluenose* in the sun?
... and who would know the *Bluenose* in the sun?

Feel her bow rise free from Mother Sea ... *

---

*Music and lyrics by Stan Rogers. www.stanrogers.net

It wasn't until Garnet dropped his hands from his guitar and picked up his fiddle that Chris finally came back to the present. The thick, haunting, echoing strains of the instrument in the master's hands ran chills through everyone listening. Even the seasoned musicians of the Pops violin section were captured by the TV cameras showing awe and respect in their expressions. The next song they combined their talents on was one of Garnet's own compositions, "Night Drive:"

> How bright the stars ... how dark the night ...
> How long have I been sleeping?
> Before it took me on a westward flight ...
> Held me in its keeping.
>
> Had a dream it seemed so real ...
> Its passing left me shaking ...*

No one spoke, moved, or scarcely breathed until the otherworldly reverberations settled from the stentorian voices and the electric guitar that testified so brilliantly through the control and channeling of Garnet's hands.

"Who was that?" Chris whispered, leaning over to Mackenzie's ear above the combined TV/messhall applause. "I missed the introduction ... who was that with Ozzie?" he asked again, wiping away the moistness from his eyes, feeling the goosebumps settle on his arms.

"That's Garnet Rogers, Stan's younger brother. He toured with him all those years, but he's a tremendous virtuoso in his own right," Mack answered, still watching the television. "There's a lot of history on that stage ... my wife ... my daughter ... Ozzie ... Stan's brother, Garnet. "Finestkind," he marveled, staring straight ahead, his fists still held erect and clenched after all those minutes. Through his welling eyes he mumbled again, "Finestkind."

---

*Music and lyrics by Garnet Rogers. www.garnetrogers.com

12

THE RIGHT WHALE

LAT. 43 DEG. 43.0 MIN. N.
LONG. 69 DEG. 35.0 MIN. W.

LAT. 41 DEG. 29.55 MIN. N.
LONG. 71 DEG. 19.3 MIN. W.

First Monday of August, 1995.

Dr. Grayson rose from the evening mug-up table and rattled her spoon against her cup. "Good evening, folks. We all know that tomorrow's classes will be canceled so that this important experiment can be carried out. To say the least, I'm very pleased to see what you can accomplish with relatively nothing, when you need to," she announced. "More than once, I felt we went down the wrong road by not running prepared, independent experiments, like we did in the past, but this project has, once again, proven the amazing resolve and creativity you students have. I tip my hat to all of you, and to Mr. Brown, over here, for molding you into a cohesive unit.

"Remember, scientific results set to an agenda is just politics," she continued. "Strive for truthful, workable answers, and believe in yourselves! And now, I'd like to turn this over to our three principle investigators, who will outline their project for our evening's peer review."

Putnam, Irene and Fallon went to the front of the mess hall.

"You probably witnessed the small but spirited discussion we had a couple of weeks ago concerning the right whales," Fallon began, as the audience laughed. She blushed, smiled and rolled her eyes.

"Chris wouldn't let us get away from this issue, or ... each other ... and assigned us to work together," Irene continued. "I think we've got a great idea for solving one of the major problems facing the endangered right whales. We tried to blend history, human nature, technology and good old-fashioned know-how, along with the fact that Putnam is a real-live MacGyver," she joked.

"To state the problem," Putnam jumped in, "the Northern Right Whale is under threat of extinction. Shipping traffic and fishing gear entanglements have been singled out as two causes of mortality. You will remember that one of my co-conspirat- ... make that co-investigators ... felt that all ships should be banned from the sea, and all fishing gear should be removed from the earth." More laughter filled the room.

"We looked at some of the facts, and found out that since the 1970's, sixteen right whales have been killed by ship collisions and only three by fishing gear entanglement. I was, um, really surprised," Fallon said. "It seems that even though the whales have great hearing, they can't pick up the low frequency of a ship's engines, especially since they are located in the back, umm, the stern of the ship. Sometimes, they can't get around some of the buoy lines without getting tangled, though, I guess, this doesn't happen very often. Bob gave us some info he had about how the fishing boats in New Hampshire have started using these little underwater acoustic devices called pingers. They attach them to their fishing gear, and the whales can hear them, and avoid them.

"I figured that we could try a couple things," Putnam continued. "First off, we made a real crude bell-buoy that takes the place of a lobster buoy. The wave action works this little hammer in there, and makes kind-of a bell sound. The second thing we did was make a buoy line with some of those pingers that Bob alerted us to. They're attached to it every fifty feet."

Irene joined in, "What we want to do is see if the sound carries far enough and strong enough to warn the whales about a ship coming or the presence of fishing gear. We thought that we could make our second million installing these devices in the bows of ships and inside buoys and attached to lines that fishermen use."

Zack interrupted, "What do you mean, your second million? Like you've already made your first million dollars?"

Irene smiled and tucked her long blonde hair behind her ears, her blue eyes twinkling. "I've been waiting to get you all summer, Wildman! We're working on the second million because we gave up on the first!" The mess hall erupted with hoots, whistles and applause. "I learned that in the mean streets of the prairie," she said proudly. "Gotcha!"

The next morning the half-awake crew filed out onto the wharf in front of the Damariscove Marine Science Center. The air was chilly, the wind was from the southeast and the skies were hurling rain. The students, staff and boat captains milled around and huddled for warmth before receiving final instructions from the student team that was leading the day's cooperative experiment.

"I've made up a station bill so that we're all split up evenly between the three boats," Putnam began. "Each of the three principle investigators will be in a different boat with three other students whose names were picked randomly out of a hat. The noise makers are going on the research boat, the *Eva Maker*. The other two boats will be sent to various locations on the grid with listening devices. Sailing on the *Eva Maker* with Captain Paul is Fallon, and her crew will be Jake, Tiffany and Ron. Sailing with Captain Mack on the *Susan G.* is Irene, with her crewmates Heidi, Sewell and Shirelle. I'll be sailing with Captain Greg on the *Haley and*

Blair, and the crew will be Zack, Cindy and Bob." Putnam looked up from his clipboard, turned it upside down to shed the rain, then looked at the assemblage. "Any questions?"

"How about food?" Jake asked.

"Greg was very kind in outfitting each vessel with plenty of food. All the boats have a galley, so coffee is available, and I think we're going to need it today," Putnam answered hiking his shoulders to shake off the chill. "All we need to know is how well, and how far, the sounds carry underwater, so the rain really doesn't make any difference to the experiment. For the most part, we should be able to stay under cover, but let's hope it doesn't get too severe."

Chris raised an index finger. "I have a question, Putt."

"Sure."

"Would it make any difference to you in which boat I came along in? I was thinking that if it was okay with Mack, I'd ride with him and pick his brain on clarifying some issues I have in my research. Only when we're steaming between stations, that is, and only if it's all right with the three of you."

"Fine with me, no problem at all," Putnam answered. The other two nodded.

Mack nodded an affirmative, shedding some raindrops off the visor of his hat. "That's what I'm here for, Old Scout," he offered, turning his head to face Chris. "I can tell you everything I know in five minutes anyway, but it would take a lot longer to tell you everything I don't know," he dryly joked.

As they went to board the boats, Greg caught up with Chris and detained him long enough to impart some advice. "That was a good move, going with Mack to ask him some stuff. Most guys will be glad to talk to you, and God knows Mack wants you as his messenger to the masses, but take my advice, Slimey, you'll get more information from a waterman if he's on his boat. If you meet any real crotchedy guys on shore, chances are, they'll be a peach of a guy when they're on the pond," he said. "Mack'll tell ya more without him even realizing that he will."

"Greg?" Chris asked, stopping on the float while everyone else was boarding the boat. "Can I ask you something?" he asked over the sound of the engines starting.

Greg cupped his hand to Chris's ear so he didn't have to raise his voice. "What's up?"

"I need to ask Mack about a variety of issues, but ... I'm not sure about one particular item."

"What's that?"

"Have you ever heard of a guy named Chambers? Lieutenant Commander Lee Chambers?"

Greg turned his back, climbed over the rail of the *Haley and Blair* and pushed the start button. After a few seconds he came back to the rail of his boat, shook his head and stared silently back at Chris through eyes as cold as blade steel. Greg's normal big-brotherly poise was gone, replaced by twenty years of seething anger. "So he got a promotion, huh, the sonuvabitchin' bahstidd! He's no longer a chief, huh? I wonder how many guys he had to send to the bottom to get that rank, that lowlife piece of hookbait! Where in the name of God did you ever run into him?"

Shocked at the violent reaction, Chris replied slowly, "He's listed in some old documents I've obtained from the State Department. I don't know if it matters to you, but he's dead and buried ... he's passed away. I'm just trying to ascertain the level of foreign fishing back in the cold war days. I'm sorry, Greg, I didn't know it would upset you. Forget it, please," Chris retracted. "I'm sorry."

Greg grabbed Chris's arm, sprung from his boat, and pulled him along down to the end of the float, out of earshot of the others. "Look Slimey, innocent or not, you've gotten yourself into something that should stay locked away and forgotten. You mention this and Jim Mackenzie will fly over the moon and back again! You have no idea what that man did to us ... no idea!" he gritted his teeth, grabbing both of Chris's shoulders. "Just let it go ... you hear me?"

Chris was shaken and confused, but felt deep-down that this could be a link to solving the mystery of his sister's death. He had to know. He put his good relationship with Greg on the line and risked continuing.

"Greg, he was a decorated serviceman with many commendations. What's the problem?"

"What's the problem? Decorated! Commendations! The only guy in the history of the free world to be decorated for killing innocent civilians, and from his own country, to boot! He may as well as stuffed that howitzer shell right in Ricky Helliott's shirtpocket!" he glared. "That sonuvabitch! What's the problem? Look, Chris … you're in way over your head! Whatever you do, don't ask Mack … it'll kill him!"

Chris stood his ground. If there was that much emotion attached to this, it could be very important. Important enough to go all the way with his inquiry. "Greg, I need to know. If I don't hear it from you guys, it will probably be in the next mail, anyway. All this information is de-classified now. Chambers is dead. The cold war was fought and won … the Berlin wall is a memory … the spice trade is over … the …"

"The what?" Greg demanded. "The spice trade?" Listen, mister … not a word of this!" he ordered, his finger firmly thrust in Chris's face. "You've got to promise me you'll never mention this to Mack … not today, not ever! Okay?" Greg spouted, shaking his head in frustration, spraying raindrops from his moustache. "He got a commendation, huh?" he demanded, his words on fire.

Suddenly, he realized that he could be making a scene and stopped when he saw the crew on his boat waiting for him. "Maybe it's time to set the record straight," Greg said more quietly, looking at the students waiting for him. "I was your age, for Pete's sake." He snapped up his oil-coat while thinking for a moment, then put his hands on his hips. "Yeah, I guess you're right … he's dead and gone now. Unfortunately, so is Ricky, and the guys on the *Barnacle Two* and the crew of the *Naviless*, and who knows who else." He drew a long breath, then said, "Meet me after mug-up tonight, Slimey, and remember, not a word of this to Mack!"

"So where did you ever get the idea for the home-made underwater headphones, Old Scout?" Mack asked over the sound of the *Susan G*'s engine.

"It was in *Sea Kayaker*, a magazine I subscribe to. A few months ago, I think it was," Chris answered. "A few bucks worth of parts from Radio Shack, a short piece of copper pipe, a nine-volt battery, some goop, and that's about it. I built a couple myself, and the students built their own. It was one of the lab projects we saved for a rainy day."

Mack nodded and checked the compass heading he was on, then gazed into the radar. The picture was covered with interference, so he switched on the rain clutter setting. The radar screen now clearly showed the harbor mouth trailing behind the Motions buoy and the *Eva Maker* up ahead about a half-mile. The *Haley and Blair*'s blip was seen heading off to the westward to take up its position in the triangulation underwater listening grid. The rain hit the ocean in sheets and actually beat down the whitecaps that rode on top of the southeast chop. The *Susan G*. made her way to windward, bucking into the head sea. Down below in the foc'sle, the four-student crew checked their underwater devices, their search grid and their preparations.

"Ralph Stanley's boats love to go to wind'ard," Mack said. "Why don't you take her and I'll sit over here on the tank and answer your questions."

Chris grabbed the wheel, beaming. "This really is a beautiful boat," he marveled, looking at the varnished mahogany all around him at the helm. "Someday, boats like these will be considered works of art, not just nice boats. Do you suppose he'll still be an active builder when I can afford to get one built?"

Mack frowned. "I sure hope so, I really do. All the boatbuilders are under the gun to get bought out of their waterfront property. I mean, the taxes are wicked, and the realtors want their locations for condos and such. It's going to be tough sledding, just like all the farmers being driven out by high taxes and selling out to developers. Same thing," he lamented. "I guess you could build a boat up-country and have it trucked to the water ... God knows there's some talented people doing it ... but it seems to me the artwork of the whole situation would suffer. Look at the Lizgale. Are Newbert and Wallace just another pair of boatbuilders? I don't think so! I'm no artist, but my wife and daughters sure are, and they've convinced me that an artist needs their creative space. Susan knows where she's comfortable when she practices her music, and it shows. It was three years from the time a luthier buddy of mine up in Thomaston fixed that old cello until she won a seat in the Pops ... never even played one before then!"

As he steered, Chris thought, *Greg was right .... Mack is more open when he's out here.*

The *Susan G* sliced along to the southeast, still following in the wake of the *Eva Maker*. Greg steered his *Haley and Blair* along a westerly course to eventually be at his pre-determined position two miles east of Seguin Island. At the start of the experiment, the research vessel *Eva Maker* was to be five miles east of Greg's boat, and one mile east of Mack's boat. They would then begin to determine the range of their acoustic warning devices by moving the boats around in search patterns, taking advantage of the increased carrying capacity of sound underwater as opposed to in the air. By staying in radio contact, the three boats expected to be able to decipher the signals sent, and codify them so that the range and effectiveness of the system could be determined. Conversely, they'd try to work an effective system against the current flow.

Chris steered the *Susan G* along her course, watching the LORAN coordinates count by, checking the radar. Sheets of water rolled off the roof every time the boat lunged forward into the next chop. It was a dirjeen day, but it was like heaven to him ... so enthralled with running the boat, he nearly forgot why he came.

"So what's on your mind, Old Scout?" Mack asked, snapping him back to the tasks at hand. "You've got some things to iron out?"

Chris reached into his backpack, brought out a clipboard and set it down next to the compass. "I've jotted down a few things that I need your expertise to clarify," he said, maintaining his control of the helm. "I've sifted through most of the comments in the meetings I've had and have come up with a handful of common points. Sometimes these guys get so wrapped up emotionally, their articulation of the problem isn't too clear."

"Yeah, I know what you mean. A couple times I've testified at public hearings and damned near escaped with my life, and I was on their side! Oh well ... what have you got?"

"First off, what happened during the Reagan years? A lot of the older folks said they would have been able to ride out the rough times if it wasn't for him. What's up with that?"

"Well, Ronnie had Reaganomics as the cornerstone of his economic policy," Mack began. "Trickle-down economics. Simply put, you ease up on some of the tax burdens of the wealthy investors, they'll take this money and invest it in businesses, then the benefits will trickle down to the working man. More jobs ... stimulate the economy ... investors make money. Sounds great, right?"

"On paper, sure, but what's in the fine print?"

"In the case of the fishing industry, it got overcapitalized right after the foreign fleets got kicked out. The fish stocks never had a chance to regroup before the Americans had built our fleets up to the same level of exploitation. It only took a few years after the two-hundred mile limit was passed. We were fishing like never before ... couple that with the technological advances, and a guy didn't need to serve a lengthy apprenticeship, so's to speak, to learn the trade. He didn't need to scrimp and save for half his life to be skipper, either. Five lawyers could get together, throw in ten grand apiece, build a boat, then make money by losing money on their investment through tax breaks. This was okay in the big picture, though, because the shipyards were humming, and that created jobs, and the fuel guys sold more fuel ... the gear shops sprung up, the fish truckers bought trucks and hired drivers, the packing houses created more jobs … you get the idea."

"The American way, you could say," Chris interjected.

"I guess so, Old Scout, the rich got richer, only now they could tool around in their golfcarts and puff their chests out because their boat was out conquering the sea. Macho. It did create a lot of jobs on and around boats for a little while, and it's a proven fact that a dollar of fish sitting on the dock will generate nine dollars in the surrounding community. That's big numbers! It was fun while it lasted, which wasn't too long, unfortunately. It was all built on the backs of the fish, and like I said, the fish were beat to a pulp by the distant water fleets long before Ronnie took over."

Mack adjusted his hat to the back of his head, the visor sticking up at a jaunty angle. He crossed his arms and unconsciously bent at the waist at every wave to compensate for the boat's motion. "We also lost the Public Health Service under Ronnie, too," he continued. "It used to be that fishermen were considered merchant mariners and were eligible for free medical care under the Public Health Service. If you needed major surgery or something, you could go up to the Brighton Marine Hospital in Boston and they'd patch you up … free. I don't have to tell you what losing that did. Fishing is the most dangerous occupation in the world; the insurance companies didn't exactly rush in to fill the void, and when they came, it was at a premium price."

"I never realized that. So that's why one of the fellows over in Round Pond said Reagan wouldn't let him get his hip fixed. He was in a wheelchair. Hmmm," Chris said as he checked the compass and jotted down notes at the same time.

"Yeah, I know who you met over there. Sad story … came home from 'Nam and all he wanted to do was fish, then got crushed by a door that broke lose in a storm. There he is, like someone out of an old movie. He can't get the money together to get the operation he needs. Wicked."

"How about some of the regulations. Didn't some of the conservation measures help? And why is it called the shell-game?"

"Ahh … the shell-game. First off, no one, and I mean no one, would deny that something had to be done, and fast, otherwise the fish stocks were going to be a memory, but … every time a conservation measure was enacted, the landings went down. What shell is the fish under? Okay … stay with me here … this is the simplest concept in the world, but, for some reason, most people just don't get it," Mack explained. His hands were making animated movements showing his frustration. "This is the one thing that really galls me, and the one big thing that has destroyed the public's perception of the fishing industry. This is where we crossed the public relations line from noble, romantic seafarers to eco-terrorists. As I said, every time a conservation regulation was enacted, the landings went down … which necessitated another regulation, which made the landings go down again, which hit the media, which made a new regulation needed, which made the landings go down again! Meanwhile, we look like jerks because we can't rein in our own industry, the sportfish people organize a huge lobby saying there will be no fish left … it's a public relations debacle!"

"I don't get it … a conservation measure should make the fish landings go up, shouldn't it?"

"Ah-hah!" Mack countered, his right index finger high in the air, almost causing him to topple off the lobster tank when the boat plowed into the next wave. "You're a Ph.D. and you don't get it, either! Let's say you've got ten fish in a barrel, okay? They're all swimming around enjoying themselves. Now what if you tossed an M-80 firecracker into the barrel … you'd kill all of them, right?"

Chris looked over from checking the radar screen, "I guess so, Yes."

"Obviously, that's no good, so we need a conservation measure, correct?"

"I'm with you so far."

"Alright, we say that you can only use a little tiny firecracker, you know, regulate the effort ... and with a short fuse, too, got me?"

"Yeah."

"Well, now you might only take three fish out of the barrel instead of ten. You've enacted a regulation to save fish, but what happened to the landings ... the landings, Old Scout? What happened to the landings?"

Chris smiled. "You just cut your landings to a third, more or less."

"Right. Only three made it to the dock, and if they do get landed, they did, in fact, exist ... The others are still in the barrel, sight unseen ... but, we've only caught a fraction of our previous catch, so now we need a new regulation. It's obvious the previous one didn't work to help land more fish, so now we cut down the number of days we can go fishing. Let's see if that works ... you can only toss in one tiny firecracker a week with one arm tied behind your back, and blindfolded. More regulations. Now, what happens to the landings?"

"The landings should go down, once again." Chris answered.

"True, but are the landings a good assessment of what's out there, that's the point. The fleet made these great sacrifices for the good of the stocks, but the media couldn't get beyond the fact that the landings went down. They were supposed to go down ... we reduced the effort! See the reasoning? ... the damned, bald-faced common sense reasoning! How numb can you get?"

Chris chuckled in the realization that he now knew why Mack wanted him to be his mouthpiece. He could also see that, as learned a man as Mack was, he would never be recruited to work in a public relations firm. He was a bulldog!

"Now, here's a real killer! You've done some fishing on a dragger before, right?"

Chris's mind shot back to his days aboard the *Zvezda Rybaka*. "Sure have," he replied.

"Good. So you know that you're effectively towing around a funnel made of twine. The water pressure and bottom contact are the keys to its efficiency, right?"

"Absolutely."

"What if I told you that the government's fisheries research ship didn't check their tow wires for two-and-a-half years? They were reporting that there was no fish out there, and meanwhile, the net wasn't hardly fishing because it was being towed way off skew. It didn't tend bottom correctly, either. In short, a total screwup!"

"C'mon. Are you sure? Checking the length of the main wires is normal maintenance. I'm no skipper, but I remember that. Checking the gear was a religion."

"Well, they finally got a New Jersey boat to fish alongside and the results were a lot more than embarrasing, they were totally ridiculous! Two fluke for the Feds, a hundred and ten fluke for the Jersey guys, in the same time. How's that make you feel?"

Chris just shook his head. "Wow!"

"Yup, wow! No fish, right? What else have you got?"

"What about the Hague Line?" Chris asked, keeping his voice raised to accomodate the engine and rain hammering off the overhead.

"The World Court decision. Basically, we lost the No'theast Peak of Georges Bank to Canada. Politics as usual. See, we always used to fish the peak with the Canadians, we used to fish the Bay of Fundy with them, the Boston boats went to Brown's Bank a lot ... that's off the southern tip of Novi ... they came over here ... no big deal. Good people to fish with, actually, but then the two governments began haggling when we both declared two-hundred mile limits. Two hundred miles off either coast put the lines into each other's mainland, so that didn't work. In short, when the World Court in The Netherlands was through with us, we lost the Peak, where, out of all the square area of Georges is concerned, a fifth of the fish came from. Of course, it goes without saying that we lost the rights to Brown's and the Bay of Fundy, and a lot of the offshore lobster grounds out in the Gulf of Maine. So now, here we were with this big, brand-new fleet all built up, and we just lost a lot of the prime grounds to fish in ... same number of boats ... much smaller puddle to play in! The increased amount of effort now became concentrated into a much smaller area."

"And that brought in closed areas?"

"Well, sort of. Now, once again, I don't think anyone denied that we should leave the spawning fish alone, but the combination of all this pushed the boats into each other's territory. You've got big, offshore boats that would rather be working outside somewhere stuck on the beach because it made no economic sense to go elsewhere. They're alongside the day boats who can't go anywhere, even if they wanted to. So now, we need another conservation measure and that gave us days-at-sea. I finally turned the Lizgale into my homeboat and got into this one here because we could only fish her for eighty-eight days a year ... we used to go straight out at about two-hundred twenty days."

Chris nodded his head in understanding as he wrote on his clipboard. "I see. It's incredible, to say the least. What's really sad is that you're one-hundred percent right about the media's reporting of all of this." He checked his clipboard, gazed at the compass, and continued. "I have a good, clear understanding of the quota issue and the needless discards that came from that. How about the mesh sizes?"

"Okay ... when I bought the Lizgale from Buddy's widow back in 1977, we were the laughing stock of the fleet because we were using nets with the mesh size of four and three-quarters inches. All the boats were using a lot smaller windows in their twine, but I'd read a study by URI that said you could reduce the mortality of juvenile fish, but still catch just as many marketable fish. Everyone laughed at us ... 'Look at the college kid ... he's towing around that coarse twine and leaving half of 'em in the water,' but you know what? ... we could run the boat with one less guy on deck because we weren't handling all the trash. We shared up the same money with less effort, and we didn't have to run a big crew for long trips to do it. Back in those days, though, anything that came on deck could be sold if there was a market for it, hence, the scrod cod and scrod haddock. You know that they were a small size, but the fillet fit perfect on a restaurant plate. Now, the mesh sizes are up over six inches, by law, so you don't even see a true scrod any more ... did you know that?"

"No."

"Didn't think so. The mesh sizes were increased, and enforced, so that the small fish could get away. Sound thinking there, wouldn't you agree?"

Chris nodded an affirmative, not wanting to interrupt Mackenzie's tirade.

"The smaller fish got away ... never hit the deck in the first place ... what happened to the landings?" Mack asked as he put his hat back to its normal visor-down location. He didn't wait for an answer.

"Now, here's a new twist ... we come in with minimum sizes of fish, too, Mack continued. "Not enough that the gear is being more selective, now let's get picky ... a minimum size on fish and no exceptions, no percentage of error. None! Let's say you've got two codfish laying beside each other on deck ... one's nineteen inches, he's legal, the other's eighteen and seven eighths, he's obviously from the same year-class, but he's illegal. What happens?"

"I guess, if he's illegal, he's got to be thrown back, correct?"

"Yup ... Thrown back dead ... Dead! ... Not landed ... didn't exist!" Mack was getting more testy by the minute, but Chris knew that the only way to get this information was to ride out the verbal storm. "When the mesh sizes went to six inches," Mack ranted, "we were burning just as much fuel as before, but were taking about fifty percent of the fish as before. After we measured the ones on deck, another ten percent went over the side. Dead. To make the sacrifice was alright, and everyone that was in it for the long haul gritted their teeth to try to get through to better times, but ... but ... to get home and read in the papers that I was upsetting the balance of the world's oceans! That I was greedy? Throwing money overboard, and I'm greedy? That fishing was only for profit! Dammit, we were producing food! Food! Wouldn't you think that food would have a little importance to a consumer society that loves to stuff their pie-holes? Millions of people starving, and we're throwing food overboard? But, but ... you know what it is?" he asked in total frustration, his fists clenched before him. "Know what the problem is?"

"What's that?" Chris asked as he pulled back the throttle, slowing the boat to an idle.

"A lot of people can't get it through their damn fool heads that the ocean isn't a farm," Mack continued. "On a farm, you can spread fertilizer to enhance growth. You can spread pesticides to keep out unwanted species, be it plant, insect, whatever, too. The American farmers are the best in the world, but the fishermen can't produce the same way ... in an orderly, pigeon-holed fashion. How numb can you get? You can't modify the ocean like it's land! Why aren't fishing boats like combines you see in the wheatfields, lumbering along, harvesting away, feeding the world; they don't have a clue, Old Scout! The sacrifices were made, dammit ... and they weren't easy ... still being made, too. I just think the guys should get some credit for it. I mean, you don't see car manufacturers running an assembly line and crushing every other car to keep production down, do you?"

"I think it's because the fishermen are a different culture and work under different rules, Mack," Chris interrupted as he took the boat out of gear. "It's so sad, to say the least. That's what I hope to write up in this great American thesis I'll be working on. Should I call it 'the death of fishing,' or 'the death of common sense'?"

Changing the subject, even though he hated to, he smiled and said, "Hey … we're on the bearings Putnam gave me … want to see if we can save the whales?"

Mack jumped off the lobster tank and stepped out into the rain. He called back from the aft deck, "Old Scout, you know what good luck is?"

Chris shrugged a puzzled *no*.

"In the boat business, water from the top down is good luck!" he yelled, the rain drenching his oilskins as he steadied his balance when the boat rolled in the trough of the southeast chop. He caught a handful of rainwater and threw it forward.

"Why's that?" Chris yelled back, ducking the splash of water thrown at him.

"Because water from the bottom up is definitely bad luck in the boat business!"

Chris laughed. "Where'd you learn that?" he asked, hands outstretched, waiting for the next salvo.

"School of H-N, Old Scout! Lord luvvaduck, what a nice day!"

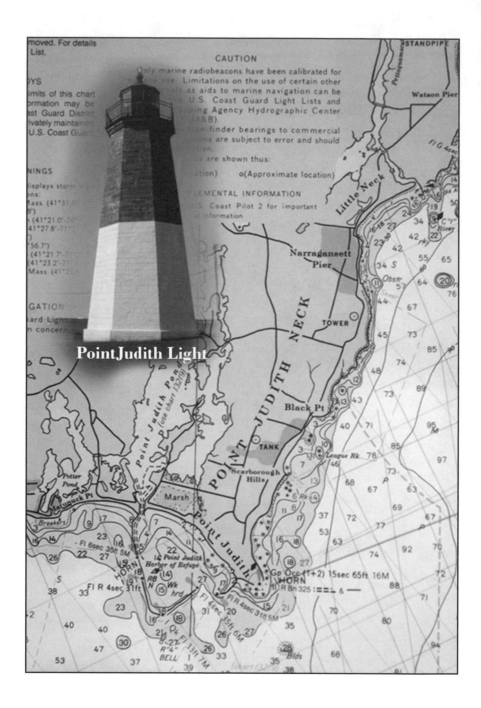

PointJudith Light

13
THE CORNER

LAT. 40 DEG. 44.5 MIN. N.
LONG. 70 DEG. 0.5 MIN. W.

"C'mon in, Slimey and have a seat. I made us some applesauce cake and coffee. I think we might be here a while, that is, if you're still interested. What did ya think of today's research ... think the warning devices will work?"

"Sure ... someday they'll be standard items around the water ... why not? I think the best product that came from today, though, is that they're all trying to solve problems rather than blame someone else for them. That's something you can build the future on. All in all the day was an unqualified success, I believe. Greg, did you see their faces light up when they could hear that underwater signal, and from miles away?"

"Yup, they did that on my boat, too ... what a great moment, huh? I guess that's why I feel that someone has to know the truth. I'd hate to see a repeat of what happened to us. Those kids made me realize that."

Chris exhaled, rattling his lips. "Greg, I don't want to push you into something you're uncomfortable with. Really. Please … if you don't want to talk about it, let's just call it a night."

"Naah. If history's gonna show Chambers as some type of hero, somebody's got to set the record straight. I guess that will have to be me," Greg said, rubbing his hand over his moustache as he sat down. "My mind's made up … was the moment I heard that name. You're sure you saw the lights on the Lizgale go out, right?"

"I watched from the tower until they went dark, yes."

"And not a word of this to involve Mack in any way, right?"

"You've got my word, Greg, I swear to you." Chris' heart was pounding with anticipation. "If it involved the fishing fleet, then it's important that the information be documented. It will only show up in a summary, and won't link to anyone … not Mack, not you … no one." Chris leaned forward and looked directly into Greg's blue eyes. "What in God's name happened to you guys, anyway?" he asked sympathetically.

"Like I said, Slimey, it's a long story …" Greg stopped in mid-sentence, rose from the table and went into the kitchen. When he came back, he sat down and forcefully placed a container of cinnamon on the table with a hard, metallic 'clunk.' "See anything you recognize there?" he asked.

Chris picked up the cinnamon can and looked at it questioningly. It was just a can of cinnamon. "I guess I don't follow, Greg," he said.

Greg went back to the kitchen and repeated the same maneuver, only this time it was nutmeg he brought back. "How about now … anything similar?"

"Well, they're both made by the same company." Then the realization hit him. Chris felt a bolt of cold energy climb his spine as he muttered out, "Oh my God … I've never paid any attention to this before … all these spices are made by a company named Mackenzie!"

From the darkened hallway came an unexpected voice. "No relation."

Chris and Greg snapped their heads around in horror as Jim Mackenzie stepped into the light of the mess hall.

"Mack, I, I just wanted to ..."

"Never mind, Greg. Don't give it a thought. We both hoped this day would come, even though we'd never admit it to each other. I was thinking today that I'd tell the Old Scout the day before he left, but now's as good a time as any, I guess."

Chris sat silently, hoping that he hadn't ruined his good relationships with these two men who he had come to regard so highly.

Mackenzie cocked his hat on the back of his head and looked at Greg and Chris. "I overheard Dave and Sandy talking the other day ... when I heard the name Chambers, I knew it was just a matter of time."

Greg turned his head to Chris and conveyed an unspoken expression of relief through his upturned eyebrows. "Slimey, would you mind going into the kitchen and getting our coffees and the cake, please?"

Chris left the mess hall and could be heard clinking mugs together out in the kitchen. Greg leaned over the table and kept his voice low. "Mack, what about Mari?"

"Who? I married Ozzie's sister, Susan Gwendolyn Marsden, remember?"

Greg rolled his eyes. "Ya know, I didn't think too much about this until the other day," Greg whispered, "but one morning I went to wake him up and he was talking some gibberish in his sleep. I think I recognized the word *Starpom*. It didn't register at the time, but ... I dunno ... I think we should be careful before we get too far down the wrong road ... just to be safe. Another thing ... one day he asked me why Chappy called you Spice."

"What did you tell him?"

"I told him exactly why Chappy calls you Spice ... no other reason. He came up with the 'spice trade' from some old documents he got from the State Department. That's where he found Chambers, too."

Mack took a long inhale and rocked his chair back on two legs. "Mari always said they'd come after her," he whispered, a tremble of fear in his voice, "but hell, that's ludicrous now that the Soviet Union is long gone, isn't it? ... unless ..." Mack looked into Greg's eyes with a look Greg hadn't seen for twenty years. "You don't suppose that he's with the Russian Mafia, do you? That's where a lot of the old KGB operatives ended up ... they were perfectly trained for the job."

"I dunno, Cap, actually, my thought was maybe he could be a link to her long lost brother."

"Greg, do I have to remind you why we live on a boat now? I went to the wire to find that kid ... even sold that beautiful house we had on Ring's Island and went around Finland and Eastern Europe until the money ran out. There's no record of him anywhere ... not over there, not at the INS, the FBI, the State Department or the CIA. They dumped him overboard just as sure as they dumped her ... you know it and I know it ... and I knew it the whole time we tramped around the other side of the world! That's why there's no records! Who keeps records of the first-degree murders that they committed?" he said in a fierce whisper.

Greg grimaced and tweaked his moustache from side to side. He folded his hands across his gray hair, leaned back in his chair and spoke aloud, "It's your cow, Henry Huckett, what would you like to do?"

Mack thought to himself, stroking his beard and curling his moustache. "Tell him about Chambers, like we agreed, and see what we can find out in the meantime, I guess," Mack said softly. "He'll be here for a couple more weeks ... let's give him enough to chew on and see where that goes. What other choice do we have?"

As Chris set the tray of coffee and cake on the table with a rattling of porcelain, Greg looked once again into his old shipmate's eyes. He hadn't seen that look since the last time they were together with Ricky Helliott. The very last time. He looked away from his friend and gave Chris a nod. "Slimey ... do you know what George Washington said before he crossed the Delaware and went into the battle of Trenton?"

"No."

"Untie the boat."

~~~

October, 1975. Point Judith, Rhode Island

April Mayes was engrossed in studying for a big exam between calls for drinks from the bar. When she looked up, she caught sight of an adoring smile in front of her. On top of that smile was a moustache, and centered above that were two blue eyes that were admiring her. She cascaded her long brown hair back over her shoulders, radiating femininity through her brown doe eyes as she straightened up. Her voice purred, "Greggie, how are you? Can you stay for a little while before you shove off?"

"Maybe just a cup of coffee, if you have one back there," he answered, looking around for a glimpse of the Hellion. "What are you reading?"

"Oh … I've got a huge exam coming up in my grad course in special ed. I've got to ace it! Someday," she added, "I'm going to have my own school, and a summer camp, too. Just to help all the kids that need it."

April went over to the other end of the bar before Greg could say another word, her hair swaying with every step, then came back with a steaming coffeepot. She pulled out the largest beer mug she could find and filled it to the very top with coffee. "I know all you guys drink it black, anyway," she said. "Ricky staggered up to his room. He said to keep you around until he comes back."

"How is he tonight?"

April smiled. "I'm sure you can handle him." She reached and took Greg's hands in hers. "Cold hands … warm heart," she whispered, then ran to the end of the bar to answer a patron's overvoiced demands for beer. Greg couldn't take his eyes off her … his emotions were a jumbled-up mess. Even though the only time he had ever spent with her was as a customer, her forwardness today was surprising, to say the least, and was intoxicatingly delightful. A pretty woman is one thing, but a gorgeous woman who works hard and cares about others is a rare beauty … a keeper, as the fishermen say. In any setting, she was a stunner.

When she returned, she reached across the bar for his hands again. "Greg," she said, "Boze was in earlier … he said something that really scares me. You'll be careful out there, won't you?"

Greg shrugged his shoulders, "What's the problem?"

April clutched his hands and let her eyes travel over his face before coming to rest in a solid eye-to-eye gaze. "Boze said the *Naviless* is missing. All hands … not a trace of anything. They were steaming home a few miles behind the *Valiant Mistress* and the lights disappeared, I guess. There wasn't any distress call, no flares, no nothing. Boze said he heard one of the other boats saw a flash, or something, then she was gone. The guys on the *Naviless* were just talking to the V-M a few minutes before … they didn't say anything was wrong, they were just cleaning up the deck and icing down the last tow of fish."

Greg worked his hands free and cupped her face as if it was the most precious thing in the world. This was a dream come true, though he didn't have a clue as to how he had been so fortunate. He looked at her, pushed his OSU hat on the back of his head, then bent to kiss her forehead. "I'll be home, darlin', don't worry."

"You'd better come home … my dad and my brother are still out there, somewhere. They went down on the *Barnacle Two* about a year ago. Make sure you come home!"

"Darlin' … you hardly know me," Greg stammered out in confusion. "What's goin' …"

"I know you, Carleton Gregory. I knew you a month ago when you first came in here with Ozzie and your friend Mack. Sometimes a skipper's daughter just knows things … I can't help it. Now go get Ricky and get going so you can get back home."

Buddy blew a long, loud blast on the horn and put the Lizgale in forward gear. The boat came tight against the forward springline, causing the stern to lurch away from the dock.

"Back'er down, Cappy!" Ricky Helliott yelled from the bow.

Buddy blew three short blasts, then put her into reverse, the exhaust roaring as the water of Point Judith Harbor swirled beneath the hull and careened against the bulkhead. Ricky coiled up the bowline and tied it firmly around the forward bitt as Mack and Greg each stowed their docklines back aft in the turtleback. Below, Ozzie was wiping down his engineroom, singing a merry tune as usual:

Oh the year was 1778, How I wish I were in Sherbrooke now!
A letter of marque came from the king,
to the scummiest vessel I'd ever seen ...
God damn them all!
I was told we'd cruise the sea for American gold
we'd fire no guns — shed no tears ...
Now I'm a broken man on a Halifax pier
The last of Barrett's Privateer's ...*

To the lone person watching from the rocks at the foot of Point Judith Lighthouse, the white sternlight of the Lizgale began to fade over the southeast horizon after about twenty-five minutes. The vessel was no more than a pinpoint of light against the mighty sweep of the lighthouse, and in less than a half-hour, she was gone from the view of land. April reached around and twisted her hair into a ponytail, then let it go and walked back to her car, her hair still blown by the wind. She looked into the southwestern sky and whispered, "Please bring them home."

"Mack, it's your watch."
"Wow ... seems like I just nodded off. What time is it?"
"It's two. Buddy said to put it on the bearings he left on the chart table."
"Where we going?"
"I dunno, somewhere to the east'ard, Buddy called it the corner, I think. I left it on the autopilot, but you don't want to leave iron mike steering for long, if you can help it. Want me to go back up?"
"Nahhh, I'm okay, Greg ... go ahead and catch a kink."
Mack climbed the ladder of the foc'sle, maintaining his balance with one hand while holding a coffee mug in the other hand and a package of twinkies clenched in his teeth. He made his way across the rolling deck to the port wheelhouse steps, climbed up and stepped in. The hum of the LORAN oscillators greeted him with a high-pitched whine. The autopilot, or iron mike, eerily held the compass course that Greg had left it clutched in to, the wheel turning and compensating with no one touching it. The radar set swept the sea, but no targets

*Music and lyrics by Stan Rogers. www.stanrogers.net

showed on the screen. The depth sounder clicked along, sweeping the paper with its stylus, drawing out a jagged profile of the sandy bottom twenty-three fathoms below. Were an unititiated eye to view the scene, the vessel might appear haunted except for the constant rumble from Buddy, sleeping in his stateroom aft. Mack checked the compass, the radar and the engine gauges, then propped himself in the corner to drink his coffee. The engine, the roll of the boat and the electronics lulled him into a sense of contentment until he was startled by the radio coming to life.

"*Aurora* callin' the Lizgale ... you on, Buddy?"

"*Elizabeth Gale* standing by," Mack answered.

"Hey ... is this Mack? ... this is Boze! What's goin' on, old daaag?"

"Boze! Where are you ... you out?"

"Yeah ... we're headin' off to the gully on the cable patrol this trip. AT&T hired us to patrol the offshore cable and keep the fleet out of it ... should be interesting!"

"I guess so ... good luck on that assignment, old man!"

"Hey, Mack, I'm sure you guys heard by now. I guess the *Naviless* isn't coming home this trip. Boys went to Fiddler's Green."

"Yeah, we heard, Boze ... wicked, huh?"

"Somethin', I'll tell ya ... really somethin.' They were okay one minute, then nothin'. Coast Guard's still on the scene with two big cutters, but they only found one guy, and I don't know who yet. Wicked! Where you bound for?"

"Somewhere off to the east'ard. I just got up here and haven't checked the final bearings."

"Well look, old daaag, be careful out that way. I heard a couple of the New Bedford hard-bottom boats talkin'. They were steamin' off to the channel and barely made it through the Soviets ...could've used a traffic cop!"

"We'll watch out, Boze ... check in from time to time if you get bored."

"Bored? All we've got to do is jog along that cable for eight days. I brought every eight-track tape I own, but that won't last me for three hours. We'll probably wear out the cribbage board."

"Just don't get caught hauling lumber! Thanks for the call, Boze."

"Give it hell, old daaag! *Aurora* standin' by sixteen and seventy-seven."

Mack turned on the light above the chart table and looked for the LORAN bearings that Buddy had left for the final watch before set-out. His hangbook was left on the chart table, open to the pages marked 'Corner'. A fisherman's hangbook is the sum total of all his 'bottom knowledge.' Some information is traded, some overheard, some gained by inheritence, but mostly it comes through years of hard work and some very hard lessons learned. Buddy's hangbook was considered legendary among the Point Judith fleet, and Mack took the sly opportunity to thumb through its pages, figuring he might not ever see it again. The LORAN bearings were handwritten in neat columns of pairs:

3900-6149	buoy
3900-6150	*Kessly* lost net
3905-6050	*Dorothy and Mary*
3820-6160	*North Sea* hung up
3836-6130	*Lisa Mae*
3920-6150	hang
3880-6202	took out belly

The bearings went on for another two pages … just on the section marked "the Corner." There were pages of bearings under the heading "Nomans" … there were pages in a section called "The Gully." All in all, there must have been a hundred pages of LORAN bearings covering all the waters from the Northeast Peak of Georges to Cape May, New Jersey, not including the ten pages covering Nantucket Sound, another twenty for the outer shoals then another twenty pages of landmarks in a section called "beach." In the beach section, there were detailed landmarks, not LORAN bearings, written out by hand …

"When working Cow Cove, make sure you keep the monument on Block Island lined up with the light until you reach the sand bank, then turn NW to the line of the buoy on the second house on the bluff."

Mack read for a few more moments then carefully replaced the hangbook exactly where he found it. *It's like they all say,* he thought, *his hangbook is amazing, to say the least!* Mack then looked for the skipper's instructions. In the corner of the chart table was a note: "Put her on 3920-6060 and wake me up."

Mack scanned the chart for the crossed lines of the LORAN grid and found the spot where the two lines intersected, then checked their present position by the two LORANs in the wheelhouse and figured the distance and compass course to the final bearings. The Lizgale was right on course for an imaginary point in the ocean that was called "the corner." He adjusted the range knob on the radar from six miles to twenty-four. The empty picture tube lit up like there was another coastline over the horizon. He double-checked their position … it was fifteen miles to the bearings that Buddy wanted to set-in on … it was twenty miles to the fleet of boats fishing beyond.

In a little over an hour-and-a-half, Mack was feeling quite proud of himself. Buddy had entrusted him with the job of putting the Lizgale on the set-out bearings. When he slowed the throttle and pulled her out of gear, the LORANs beamed his accomplishment in their digital readouts. The slowing of the engine woke Buddy up and he came rasping and coughing behind Mack, lighting a cigarette. He cleared his eyes a little, scanned the horizon, then took the wheel as he exhaled a plume of smoke.

"Where are we, Mackie?" Buddy asked as he looked at the LORANs. "Good. Right on the mark! Lord luvvaduck, Mackie, nice job," he said, balancing himself against the roll of the boat. "I heard you on the radio … what didja hear on the boys off to the south'ard?"

"I was talking to Boze. He said there were still two big Coast Guard cutters at the scene and they only found one guy … he didn't know who it was or if they were okay. Wicked, huh?"

"Been a lot of that the last coupla years. Who knows? There's a lotta stuff out here from World War II. It's not too awful uncommon to tow up a bomb or somethin'. Hell, we steamed right past 'the dump' gettin' to here. That's the dumpin' ground, Mackie, where all the extra bombs were dumped harmlessly into the sea, so they'd never bother anyone again."

Buddy chuckled, which set off his coughing reflex. When his voice cleared, he continued, "When there's fish in there, the boats go in, whether they care about those unexploded bombs or not. At 3922 and 1280 there's some depth charges … that's right over there." Buddy pointed out the portside window as the boat rolled in the trough.

Mack was impressed on two counts: Buddy's encyclopedic knowledge of every square inch of the ocean bottom, and the fact that the bottom was littered, to some degree, with explosives. He swallowed hard and looked back at the skipper, but he'd learned to trust and respect Buddy implicitly in the month that he'd spent with him. Buddy had his life, and the rest of the gang's, in his hands every moment they were out there. No problem.

Buddy furrowed his forehead. "Okay Mack, it's up to you. Should we be good to the gang, and wake 'em up gently, or should we blow the horn, as usual?" he quipped. He reached above his head to grab the horn lanyard, but didn't pull it. He looked to Mack for his instructions.

"How many years did you have to work on deck before you got this boat, Buddy?" Mack asked.

Buddy smiled and dropped his hand to his waiting cigarette. "Yup, you're right. Eighteen years listenin' to the skippy blow the horn before I got to blow mine. Why don'tcha go forward and rattle 'em, and I'll check on Oz, back aft, here. We'd better get this rig set in."

It wasn't long before the Lizgale was set in and going about its business. Buddy managed to stay just outside the big fleet for most of the daylight hours the first day, working on the start of a good trip of yellowtails, bb's and lobsters. The same crew had worked the Lizgale for a month now. Every set and haulback was a timed choreography of a well-meshed team. Every fourth tow, Buddy turned in and Ricky took the wheel, Ozzie lavished love to his engine room in between deckwork chores, and Mack and Greg still split the galley detail when they were off deck. At late afternoon of the first day, a Soviet research ship appeared on the western horizon, and within an hour, the same ship was cutting across the bow of the Lizgale ... almost too close for comfort.

"Lord luvvaduck! Ain't they got better things to do? What's he want to know, the kind of underwear we got on, too?" Buddy fumed.

Mack climbed the steps to the wheelhouse with two cups of coffee and propped himself in the corner. "Brought a coffee for you, Cap," he said. "They going to ram us, or what?"

"Naaah ... just want to see what we got so's they can call in the rest of the fleet, that's all. That, and they're so damned bored out here, a little game of chicken is all they got for entertainment. They say that's where the real jerks are. Supposedly, the research boats are also the spy boats for the Russkies. The fishin' boats just fish."

"Spy boats? What could we have to offer them?"

"Well, they know they saw us somewhere last trip, right? So now, Lord luvvaduck, they look back through their records and find out where. Then they cross-reference that with our landings, which are in any number of public reports on shore, and bingo … you've got yourself a winner … we become their scouts! Actually, they've watched us here, alone, and watched the gulls around us all day, so there's no chance we'll be left to ourselves. We'll have company shortly, Mack," Buddy said gloomily, his forehead looking like a rippled sea. "As far as spy stuff goes, they're in the perfect spot to watch for all the Navy ships from Newport, the subs comin' and goin' from Groton, the planes from Otis Air Force Base on the Cape … they're bahstidds, I'm tellin' ya!" Buddy looked at the ship's clock. "We should be haulin' back in fifteen minutes, but maybe we'll let her go another ten, just to let them get by a little. I dunno," he lamented, "the gummint better step into this mess before there's nuthin' left, that's for sure."

As the Soviet research ship steamed off to the eastward to rejoin the fleet, Mack saw the despair in Buddy's eyes and decided to change the subject. "Hey Cap, how come this area is called the corner?"

Buddy smiled. "See the buoy at the end of the 'shoals, here, Mackie?"

Mack looked at the chart where Buddy's massive, gnarled index finger was pointing to a buoy on the chart located thirty-two-and-a-half miles south of Nantucket. "You make this buoy, the corner buoy, and you're clear of Nantucket Shoals, see? Then you turn the corner and head on down to Georges, or off to the east'ard. Clear run from here, see?" Buddy explained. Mack smiled and nodded.

Buddy's prediction was right on the mark. By late evening, a few boats started moving closer from their positions to the eastward. By midnight, the Lizgale was surrounded on all sides by enough lights to make it look like they were towing their net down Fifth Avenue. The fishing remained steady … and good. In the afternoon on the second day, Mack, Greg and Ricky had finished cleaning up the deck and were talking around the galley table when Buddy's voice carried down from the doghouse above. "Hey Mackie … she's back again … come take a look! Lord luvvaduck!"

Three confused glances were passed around the table. Mack scrambled to the top of the ladder and looked out. Buddy hung his head out the starboard side wheelhouse window and pointed off the port bow. The bow of the *Zvezda Rybaka* was fifty yards away and closing … she was going to pass by as close as two draggers can pass without entangling their gear. Buddy held up the binoculars and made a waving motion to come get them. Mackenzie hurriedly went back aft and bounded up into the wheelhouse.

"Keep lookin', Mackie … I'm goin' as close as I can without scrapin' the paint. I can play chicken, too, ya know!"

Buddy knew that since they were towing their own net off the starboard quarter, the Lizgale would turn to starboard very easily and keep their net out of harm's way before the massive Soviet trawl crossed paths with theirs. He maneuvered the port side of his boat to within five yards of the side of the Soviet ship, then slowly eased off to starboard. At the rail above them, people were waving and smiling. Some were yelling things in Russian, one man even had his hands clenched together like he was praying for them to rescue him. There were children watching in silent awe, their hands held by their mothers, there were two men who appeared to be in some kind of officer's uniform, and then, from the blur of faces … there she was!

"Right there! There she is! Lord luvvaduck, I don't even need the binoculars to see how pretty she is! She sure is a looker!"

Mack took one long look, then sprinted from the wheelhouse to the forepeak, waving his arms like a madman.

He'd thought about her since the first day he saw her. He just couldn't get her out of his mind. There were plenty of attractive girls at the "Tune" that were more than willing to share themselves with him, but he clung to this stupid, stubborn, notion that he'd see her again, and anything else would be like cheating on her. Even Greg tried to talk him out of it, but he knew that talking Jim Mackenzie out of an idea he had in his head was like shifting the Apollo rocket in reverse two seconds after blast-off. Mack looked at her and waved frantically. "I love you!" he yelled. She caught sight of his ridiculous antics and realized he was looking straight at her. "I love you!" he screamed, not caring that he was making a complete fool of himself as he pointed directly at her.

The factoryship crew erupted with laughter … Mack's yelling needed no interpreter, the phrase was very much universal. Every person at the ship's rail looked aft to see what the girl's next move would be. The middle-aged women smiled happily, one of the officers began to laugh, the other crossed his arms and harshly looked on.

She began running to the stern as the boats passed. Jumping, smiling and waving, with her hair blowing in the breeze, her quick steps began bouncing gracefully like that of a ballerina's. *"Amerikkalainen Kapteeni!"* she yelled back, waving her hands. *"Amerikkalainen Kapteeni!"*

As she ran to the stern of her ship, Mack inched along the rail towards the stern of the Lizgale, never releasing his eye-to-eye gaze with her. She took the scarf from around her neck, balled it up and threw it to him. In a dangerous stretch out over the rail, he just caught it, getting soaked in the process. Mack was so overwhelmed, he almost forgot that both vessels were moving, but he snatched the OSU hat off his head, tucked a shackle into it for weight, then threw it across to the ship. The officer in the gray chinstrap beard reached out and caught it, then quickly took it to her.

As Buddy creased the Lizgale off to a hard starboard rudder, barely missing being sucked into the wheel wash of the huge ship, she stood at the stern rail, waving her arms, Mack's OSU hat on her head. As the *Zvezda Rybaka* faded from view, she was joined by a small boy, but she never moved from the stern rail.

14

MUSKEGET CAN

LAT. 41 DEG. 15 MIN. N.
LONG. 70 DEG. 26.5 MIN. W.

t daybreak on the third day, the ocean took on a jumbled, confused quality. The wind had come around to the northeast and swiftly worked up a steep chop against the currents flowing around the tail end of Nantucket Shoals. The sky was heavy with dark thick clouds which shortly began raining. All day the wind freshened until, by late afternoon, Buddy was faced with considering his options ... continue the trip temporarily stopping fishing and laying-to, or running to shore to beat the worsening weather. The skipper used his extensive knowledge of the grounds by setting up courses to keep the boat fishing, at least for now. He still had the Lizgale slogging along, but she only towed her net to windward. The turns he made were to come around hard, to go to leeward or haul back. The sea frequently broke over the bow and washed over the deck, barely draining from the scuppers before another wall of water took its place. In the wheelhouse, he lit a cigarette then turned the VHF radio to the weather channel for the 6 P.M. updated forecast:

"... The offshore forecast for the waters south of Martha's Vineyard, from the Great South Channel to Hudson Canyon, out to one thousand fathoms ... Gale warnings upgraded to storm warnings at 6 P.M. Tonight, northeast winds of forty-five to sixty knots with frequent higher gusts. Rain heavy at times in areas of intense atmospheric activity. Seas fifteen to thirty feet, locally higher in areas with conditions of tidal interference ..."

Buddy exhaled, blowing smoke up into the overhead of the wheelhouse. He looked down from the windows, watching water curl its way down the deck, hit the base of the house, then drain aft. Forward, the glow of the foc'sle lights could be seen through the crack where the doghouse hatches came together. The rain would come and go, but at times it swirled in torrents, beating the boat with a wild fury. Buddy now knew that one decision was already made for him ... this would be the last tow for a while, but then what? Lay-to and the boat would ride just fine, but the northeast wind would push her right out into the shipping lanes that ran from Nantucket Lightship to Ambrose Lightship at New York ... that was risky. Jogging into the wind and holding her position here was risky, too, considering the fact that the Soviet factory ships would probably keep fishing and certainly wouldn't care if he was in their way.

Run for Muskeget Channel and head for Edgartown? Nantucket? Steam downwind across the shipping lanes and lay-to, but risk getting too close to the edge of the continental shelf? "Nope." Buddy said to himself. "The last time we tried that, we ended up off Cape May," he muttered through a cloud of cigarette smoke. The decision of what to do was made for him in the next second, however, when the VHF interrupted the sound of the wind whistling through the rigging ...

"Mayday ... mayday ... mayday! Fishing vessel *Monte Christo* in need of immediate assistance! We're at 3960 and 1260! ... on fire and have lost part of our sternquarter in an explosion! We're goin' down! 3960 and 1260! we're go ..." The radio went dead.

The hair on the back of Buddy's neck stood up straight and his heart began pounding. The *Monte Christo* was a Point boat, not like the *Naviless* who was from New Bedford. A Point boat with his brother-in-law on board making a mayday call!

Buddy grabbed the mike from the radio. "Lanny, this is the Lizgale ... we're at 3940 and 1305. We'll get the Coast Guard on it and be right there as soon as we can! Hold on, Lanny, we're coming!"

Buddy turned on the full set of decklights and blew the horn five times ... the signal reserved for times of immediate danger. In the foc'sle, Mack, Greg, Ricky and Ozzie were playing cribbage at the galley table. Everyone was still in their full oilskins, waiting for the horn to go haul back, but the unexpected danger signal sprung Ricky into instant action.

"Somethin's wrong! Let's go, boys ... let's go, LET'S GO!" he shouted.

The crew scrambled up the ladder and rushed out onto the deck, into a wall of water crashing over the doghouse. Ricky went hand-over-hand down the center of the deck, stopping once to let the water clear from the scuppers so it wouldn't wash him overboard. When he reached the port side of the winch, he yelled up to the wheelhouse, "Buddy, you alright? Buddy!"

The skipper slowed the engine, then dropped the port window. "Lanny's goin' down ... he's about ten miles away! Get that gear on deck. Now!"

Ozzie traversed the roiling confusion on the deck, safely made it to the starboard side of the winch, but not before he lost his balance and caught himself on the fish hold hatch cover. Mack and Greg stayed close to each other, but got separated half-way down the deck. Greg made it to his station at the front of the port winch drum, but Mack was nowhere to be seen ... he'd tripped over some loose fish baskets and fallen. The rushing deck water swept him to the starboard rail, but he managed to hang on and ducked low as the next wave came crashing over the bow, sending a surge of seawater aft and carrying him with it. At the aft gallows frame, the water drained out of the scuppers long enough for him to regain foothold while he held onto the swinging dogchain for dear life. It was his turn to knock out the main tow-wires from the hook-up block on the stern quarter, and that was where duty, and a shipped sea, took him. Timing the seas, he reached out over the rail to attempt to pull the pin, but the roll of the boat threw him back against the turtleback. At the next try, another sea came roaring down the deck, almost washing him overboard as he clung to the aft gallows frame with a death grip. Mack stayed rigidly glued to the frame, water swirling around him, the boat heaving from rail down to rail high. He had to get the hook-up block knocked out ... there was no way to get the net hauled back until he did, and until the net was on deck and the doors were secured at the rail the Lizgale was, for all intents and purposes, anchored by its own gear. Between soakings, he saw the hook-up block only a few feet away, and his shipmates fighting to hang on for themselves.

"M ... M ... M ... Maa ... Mack! M ... Maaa ... Mack!" Ozzie blurted out as he appeared at the turtleback door. He had gone down the portside rail and come across through the turtleback to the starboard side. Ozzie held out his right hand for Mack as he held a firm grip on the door latch with his left. When Mack grabbed a hold, Ozzie motioned his head to go get the hook-up block, now singing in a loud, clear, operatic voice: "You go on out but leave one hand for me ... pull the pin with your other ... she'll come free with the roll of the sea."

Soon, Mack had the tow wires knocked out and Ozzie was reeling him back to the deck. Buddy pushed the throttle ahead to an engine rpm double that of the usual haul-back.

The hoister violently sprung to life as Ricky clutched in the PTO and pulled both drum frictions into gear. The winchdrums were wildly spinning around at twice the normal haulback speed. Greg was trying to keep his balance, guide both drums and look for his shipmates at the same time. One false move, one slip in a moment of sea, and Greg would be hauled into the winch and crushed by the tow-wires in a horrible, grisly death. But he held on, bracing himself against both guide bars like a makeshift pair of ski-poles and kept the tow-wires coming aboard smoothly. Mack and Ozzie reappeared at the winch, having taken the return trip through the turtleback and up the port rail.

"Thattaboy, Carleton!" Buddy yelled from the wheelhouse. He knew that if the wires got birdnested, they would be impossible to untangle in this weather. He'd have to cut the tow wires and leave the gear behind ... and waste precious time. "Stay with 'em, boy!"

With the tow-wires unhooked and the winch engaged the Lizgale now swung directly sideways to the wind and sea. The boat rolled from rail to rail, seawater breaking across the boat from the starboard side, rolling across the deck and slamming into the opposite side. The hoister strained, groaned and labored when the boat rolled up on a sea, but spun wildly when the boat rolled down, causing the wires to go slack. The baskets, picks, knives, fish boxes and deck checkers, the planks that separated the deck for fish sorting, broke loose from their storage points and began to slosh around in the turbulent deck water, then, one by one, were swept off the deck. The wind howled through the rigging like the wrath of the devil himself. The rain flew in sheets and the waves pounded.

In the wheelhouse, Buddy tried to maintain control of the vessel, keep a watchful eye on his crew and get the gear on deck and secured, all while trying to co-ordinate a rescue from the mainland for the *Monte Christo*. He kept his eyes out the starboard window as he talked into the VHF's microphone …

"Roger, that was 3960 and 1260. The boat's name is the *Monte Christo*, from Point Judith. Request you send a chopper to their location. I have no more communication with them, over."

"Fishing Vessel *Elizabeth Gale*, Coast Guard Station Nantucket, roger. Say again … the vessel in distress reported an explosion and was on fire? I repeat, say again, over."

"That's a roger, Nantucket, affirmative on the fire and explosion."

"Fishing Vessel *Elizabeth Gale*, Coast Guard Station Nantucket, roger on last. What is your present position and ETA to the vessel in distress, over?"

"We're about ten miles to the southeast. Our present position is 3940 and 1305. ETA about two hours, or less. We still have to get our gear aboard, and the weather is lousy, over."

"Fishing Vessel *Elizabeth Gale*, Coast Guard Station Nantucket, request you standby this frequency, over."

"*Elizabeth Gale* standing by channel two-two, over."

From the wheelhouse, Buddy watched the wires madly spinning on the winch drums, then slowed the engine as the doormarks became visible. After a few seconds, the trawl doors popped free from the water and slammed into the side of the boat. Ricky and Ozzie secured the brakes, Mack went through the turtleback again and managed to get the dog chain through the aft door then unhooked the g-clip while Greg went hand-over hand up the center of the deck and worked the rigging on the forward door. The Lizgale rolled down to the rail, but now didn't recover quite so quickly since the weight of the net, and the fish it held, was hanging from the starboard side, freed from the sea bottom.

Mack ducked back into the turtleback, Greg found shelter in the forepeak as a huge sea drove itself over the starboard rail. The boat groaned and shuddered with the extra water weight, adding to the weight of the gear. Another wave surged across the deck, breaking over the winch, slamming into the base of the wheelhouse. Ricky and Ozzie clung to the brake wheels of the winch as their feet drifted sideways from the force of the rushing water, but kept hauling the ground cables aboard until the wings of the net appeared at the hanging bollards. Ricky, Greg and Mack watched for their chance. On Ricky's signal, they rushed to the starboard rail. In-between the repeated battering of the waves rolling over the rail, they caught hold of the quarter ropes and got them to the winch, wading and crawling through swirling knee-deep deck water.

"Okay, boys, here's where we haul hard, and she'll come easy!" Ricky yelled. Buddy came down from the wheelhouse and took a position on the port side of the winch. The net's sweep came free of the ocean with Ozzie and Buddy hauling in the quarter ropes.

"Ready ... Yup!" yelled Buddy.

"Yo!" came the unison response from the deck crew at the rail.

"Ready ... Yup!"

"Yo!"

The boat rolled down into the trough of the next wave, making the sweep go slack. This was the split second that Buddy and Ozzie spun the quarter ropes off the winch heads and let it fall to the deck. Mack, Greg and Ricky jumped next to the rail and pulled slack twine as hard and as fast as they could. When the boat lurched up on the next wave, they grunted and strained to keep the sweep from going back overboard. The boat rolled down again and again they pulled twine as fast as they could, only to be on the verge of losing it all when the boat rolled back upright.

"Keep your fingers out of it!" Ricky yelled. "If she wants to go, let 'er go, we'll get 'er on the next sea!"

All the time they were riding this amusement park ride gone beserk, the doors were crashing and banging off the boat's side rails, thundering and shuddering the whole vessel. Finally, after strapping the twine and hauling it high into the rigging, the cod-end came sailing over the rail, surfing on another huge wave. At last, the crew could relax a bit and return the Lizgale to a better state of seaworthiness.

"Lash it down, boys, don't pop that bag open, or we'll lose 'em all!" Buddy yelled from the stairs leading back to the wheelhouse. "I'm gonna bring her around and jog into the wind so's you can get everythin' secured and get the doors aboard! Do the best you can to hurry, we've got to get to Lanny. I can't raise him on the radio!"

Greg went forward, Mack went aft and eventually got their respective doors hooked-up and winched aboard. Buddy jogged the boat ahead while the crew finished lashing everything down for their next endeavor. The easy part was over … now they had to steam to the *Monte Christo* with a living gale beating their starboard bow.

The drenched, exhausted crew crowded into the wheelhouse, taking up all the available room, including Buddy's stateroom.

"Everybody here?" Buddy asked, his eyes fixed on the bow of the boat.

"Yup, we're all here, Cap." Ricky answered.

Buddy shut off the deck lights to increase their night vision, then pushed the throttle ahead to a point where the vessel could maintain headway speed without pounding herself to pieces. The Lizgale met every wave like it was a mountain to climb, her bow reaching clear of the water for the sky. At the top of each wave, she shuddered, took a slanting roll to port, then surfed down the other side, spilling water that rushed aft and crashed into the wheelhouse as she buried into the trough and started her ascent again. She was free and able now, no longer burdened by the weight and strain of towing tons of gear and fish over the bottom.

"Ricky … get on that chart table and figure how much the wind and tide set us while we were hauling back. We started at 3940, 1305," Buddy ordered calmly. "I got to hand it to you boys … all of you … that was some damned fine seamanship out there. Finestkind!"

Ricky was busy at the chart table with the dividers and parallel rules, figuring out Buddy's request by looking at their present position on the LORANs, then backtracking to their previous one. "We got set almost two miles to the sou'west, Buddy," Ricky reported.

"Two miles … Okay … check the tide vector at the top of the shippin' lane, there. What's goin' on with that?"

Ricky measured the vector with the dividers, then checked the time of high tide in the tide tables book to co-ordinate the information. "High water's in an hour, Cap. That gives us a knot and-a-half tide on our ass for about an hour of the run to the nor'thard." Ricky answered. There would be time later to find out the details on Lanny … right now was the time to help the skipper get to where he needed to go.

Buddy figured in his head and clicked his mouth like a farmer trying to plod a horse to work. "Alright … keep her on nor'd by west, will ya, Carleton? That should hold us up into the wind, but we should still catch up with Lanny if he's driftin' like we did. Good God, I hope he's still driftin' … didn't sound very good."

"Have you heard any more?" Ricky asked.

"Naah. One second I was talkin' to him, the next he was gone! Said he was on fire 'cause of an explosion in the sternquarter and he was goin' down … that's all I know."

"Should we keep trying to get him on the radio?" Greg asked.

"Coast Guard's doin' that, Carleton. They told me to keep it on channel twenty-two so's they can tell us when the chopper is coming. Ricky, stand by the VHF, will ya? I'm gonna see if I can get some dry clothes on, then I'll get you guys to the foc'sle so's you can get changed up. Oz, why don't you get a dry fit-out on too, then we'll take over for these guys. It's gonna be a long night!"

When Buddy came back from his stateroom in dry clothes, he took the wheel then slowed the boat to a jog so Ricky, Greg and Mack could inch their way to the foc'sle to change clothes. Before they went below, Ricky ordered a lifeline rigged from the wheelhouse to the foc'sle so that there was a hand-over-hand way to make the journey across the deck. When Buddy saw that all three were safely off deck, he increased the engine speed, then shut off the decklights.

The VHF came to life, startling Buddy: "Fishing vessel *Elizabeth Gale*, fishing vessel *Elizabeth Gale*, this is Coast Guard Group Wood's Hole, Coast Guard Group Wood's Hole, Coast Guard Group Wood's Hole, channel two-two, over."

"Wood's Hole, this is the *Elizabeth Gale* standing by."

"Fishing vessel *Elizabeth Gale*, Group Wood's Hole, roger, Cap. Request to know your status and ETA to the distressed vessel *Monte Christo*, over."

Buddy thought for a moment. "ETA to the *Monte Christo* approximately one-and-a-half-hours, over."

"Fishing vessel *Elizabeth Gale*, Group Wood's Hole, roger, confirming your ETA to be one-and-a-half hours to the *Monte Christo*. Request you proceed at all due speed to render assistance, over."

"Wood's Hole, *Elizabeth Gale*. Any word on the arrival of a chopper, over."

"Fishing vessel *Elizabeth Gale*, Group Wood's Hole. Negative, I repeat, negative on hee-lo deployment, Captain. Coast Guard hee-lo from Otis currently rendering assistance in Gulf of Maine. ETA to your position approximately four hours, over."

"Wood's Hole, *Elizabeth Gale*, roger. Will any cutters be on scene when we arrive?"

"Fishing vessel *Elizabeth Gale*, Group Wood's Hole. Negative, I repeat negative, Captain. Closest cutter ETA to your position approximately five hours, repeat, five hours, over. Request you use all due speed to proceed to the distressed vessel and render assistance, over."

Buddy lit a cigarette and took a long drag. "No assistance? That's just great! Lord luvvaduck!" he smoldered, smoke escaping from his lips at every syllable. He keyed in the microphone for his reply, "Wood's Hole, *Elizabeth Gale*. Roger ... will proceed. Standing by on this frequency. Out."

He checked the ship's clock. It had been fifteen minutes since Ricky, Greg and Mack went forward. He turned on the decklights, slowed the engine and gave one blast on the horn. The doghouse hatches opened up and three figures came on deck, the first two carrying a plastic milk crate between them. They inched along the deck using the time-tested "one hand for the ship, one hand for yourself" method and eventually got to the port steps, climbing quickly and coming inside.

Ozzie came from the turtleback and went up into the wheelhouse. Buddy shut off the decklights and pushed up the throttle until the Lizgale was once again climbing mountains and diving into valleys.

In the wheelhouse, everyone found corners to wedge themselves into. Mack and Greg were waiters. They had a pot of coffee, mugs, snacks, cold cuts, a loaf of bread, some fruit and a few sodas crammed into the plastic crate they brought from the foc'sle. They devoured everything in about fifteen minutes. Their bodies were crying for sleep, but food was the next best thing.

"Fine mug-up, boys," Buddy said. "That hit the spot." The skipper winced a little as he spoke, touching his chest with his fingers. "Let's see if we can make some kind of a plan for when we find Lanny, okay?"

Everyone nodded, not wanting to bring to words the very real possibility that they might not ever find Lanny, his boat, or his crew. "I think we should stay together here until we see what's goin' on. I'll come up on 'em on the loo'ard side, so's we can work off the starboard side and bow, okay?" Buddy explained. "Look, let's stay together so we know where we are at all times ... the five of us are okay and we're gonna stay that way, roger that?"

No disagreement there.

"Fishing vessel *Elizabeth Gale*, fishing vessel *Elizabeth Gale*, this is Coast Guard Group Wood's Hole, Coast Guard Group Wood's Hole, Coast Guard Group Wood's Hole, channel two-two, over."

"Wood's Hole, *Elizabeth Gale* standing by."

"*Elizabeth Gale*, Group Wood's Hole, roger Captain. Have received transmission from fishing vessel *Monte Christo*. Please be advised that distressed vessel is now at position 3960, 1301. Fire is extinguished. Vessel is still taking on water. What is your ETA to this position, over?"

Before Buddy could even turn around, Ricky had figured the new ETA. "Tell 'em an hour and fifteen minutes, Cap."

The skipper reached for the microphone and felt a shot of pain travel down his left arm, but the good news that Lanny was still afloat and alive obscured any small inconvenience that a sore arm could cause.

"Group Wood's Hole, *Elizabeth Gale*. Tell Lanny we'll be there in an hour and fifteen minutes. Bring him up to channel two-two so we can have direct contact, over."

"What course, Ricky?" Buddy asked.

"Same course, Cap ... Nor'd by west."

"Fishing vessel *Elizabeth Gale*, Group Wood's Hole. Roger, will relay one hour and fifteen minutes ETA. Request you continue to standby channel two-two and monitor frequency for transmission from the *Monte Christo*. Request you keep your working traffic to a minimum ... how on that? Over."

"Wood's Hole, *Elizabeth Gale*. Understood, that's a roger ... break, break ... Monte C., you there, Lanny?"

It was a very long, very full minute of silence, but finally a static-laden reply came from the skipper of the *Monte Christo*.

"Buddy! Buddy! ... come get us, Cap! ... 'Charlie Golf' says you're right around us, somewhere!"

"Lanny, how you makin' out, you all right?"

"Yeah, so far, Cap ... (static) ... We got all the mattresses out of the foc'sle wedged in by some of the pen boards from the hold ... (static) ... we're still takin' water, but the Lister's keepin' up, so far ... where are ya? ..."

"We'll be there in a little over an hour, Old Son. Hang on! What happened, anyway?"

"By the Lord Jaysus, bye, we're all here in one piece, thank the Almighty. We were just haulin' back and we got a shell in the bag. It got away from the gang when we took a sea over the rail and it rolled down onto the stern bul'ark and blew it right off. Opened up a big hole in the hold and part of the engine room ... got the fuel tank on fire ... (static) ... a sea and that doused the fire. Killed the main, though." ... (static) ... room's got quite a bit of water in her ... (static) ...

"You all right on keepin' the radio goin'?"

"So far, Buddy. Once we started the Lister, we took the battery off of it and brought it up into ... (static) ... 'house to run the radio. We got no LORAN, now. Lister's still clackin' away, but don't know for ... (static) ... longer ... I don't dare go ... (static)" The radio went dead in mid-sentence.

"Lanny, if you can still hear me, we're comin' as fast as we can! Do whatever you have to do to hold on, Old Son!" Buddy hung up the microphone, not noticing or caring that his arm felt weak and fuzzy when he reached overhead.

The crew of the Lizgale exchanged fearful glances, but remained silent as they steamed along. The next hour seemed interminable. The Lizgale bolted on through wind and rain, climbing up one side of a thirty-foot sea, cresting like a breaching whale, then plowing down the other, plunging headlong into the next. The fair tide helped with the boat's speed but it was flowing against the nor'east wind, making the waves steep with crests curled and fist-like; fists that packed a mean punch.

Ricky watched the LORAN bearings count down until he told Buddy they were about a half mile off the bearings. Buddy slowed the boat to headway speed. Ozzie stepped over to the starboard side of the wheelhouse and manned the searchlight, scanning the seas ahead for a sign of ... anything. The seas were so high and steep, the radar was virtually useless. The cliche' "a needle in a haystack" couldn't begin to be analogous to finding a boat and four people in a thirty foot sea in raining blackness.

Onboard the *Monte Christo*, the situation went from "worse to worser" in the time it took for the next wave to hit. Captain Lonwood "Lanny" Raymond and his three-man crew were huddled in the wheelhouse listening to the two-cylinder Lister, the auxiliary engine mounted high in the engine room that drove a generator and pump. A Lister on a good day sounds like a model 'T' on steroids, but right now, it sounded like heaven. It was the only thing keeping them afloat and, to them, the venerable engine's clanking was like a choir of angels.

As the *Monte Christo* lay wallowing in the troughs of thirty-foot seas, her starboard side was vulnerable. With the main engine out of commission, there was no way to turn the boat up into the weather unless they rigged a sea anchor forward, but Lanny wanted everyone to stay together. One dory was still nested above the wheelhouse if Buddy didn't get there in time.

Lanny's engineer, mate and cook had risked their lives to go below in the foc'sle of the stricken boat and bring all the bunk's mattresses on deck. They cheated fate when they pulled some of the pen boards from the gaping hold aboard after they were washed overboard in the seas that pummeled them following the explosion. They were put to the ultimate test as they wrestled all of these items down into the flooding engineroom and fishhold and wedged the mattresses into the space where, only a few minutes before, there were the thick oak planks of a vessel built in 1948 for the exploration of the Arctic. Any lesser boat would have been blown to pieces, but master boatbuilder Harvey Gamage of South Bristol, Maine had built her to withstand the rigors of the ice floes and Arctic Circle seas. Still, she was a crippled lady.

Even though she had a few bandages applied, water was pouring into the engine room and hold every time the *Monte Christo* laid down in the trough. The Lister's diaphragm pump was fighting at a forced stalemate; it was only two feet from immersion. Lanny watched the power indication light on the radio go dim, then fade away … the battery they had dragged up to the wheelhouse and jury-rigged to the radio had run low, then died. The Lister kept chunking away, but for how long? The water was four feet high in the engine room when the courageous crew waded in to try to plug the damaged hull with mattresses and penboards. How long until the water takes over? Where was Buddy?

"C'mon, Lanny," Buddy whispered. "Where the hell are you, anyway?" He felt a short pang of stiffness shoot down his right arm as he talked. "Lord luvvaduck, they've got to be right here somewhere … the wind should've brought them right to this spot," he said, never looking up from scanning the sea. "C'mon!"

Buddy slowed the boat to a jog. The Lizgale held her position in the wind while the seas rolled along underneath her. Every eye and ear was trained on the water around them. Every heart was racing. Ozzie kept the searchlight going in a steady arc from beam to beam.

"You don't suppose we went by her, do you Cap?" Ricky asked.

Buddy shook his head in disgust. "Damned if I know. He's gotta be right here ... just gotta be!" He reached up over his head, winced, but managed to grab the horn lanyard and blow the horn to give a long blast signal ... Nothing in return. "Mack, why don't you man this horn lanyard, here ... give her a tug about every thirty seconds or so. Lord luvvaduck, my arms are tired." he said.

Mack moved into position to follow orders. "Okay, Cap," he replied. In his head he started counting, 'One, Mississippi. two Mississippi ...'

Ozzie rippled his forehead. He might have seen something on the last pass of the searchlight, but wasn't sure. He swung the searchlight quickly from port to starboard and dropped the window. About forty yards away, he could just make out an instant of a reflective flash going over the crest and down the backside of a wave. "B ... Bu ... BB ... Bud ...!" he yelled as he grabbed Buddy's shoulder and pointed off the starboard bow.

Buddy spun the wheel to starboard and pushed the throttle up to gain headway. The engineer kept the searchlight trained on the top of the waves to try and catch another glimpse of the small reflective image. All eyes were peeled ... all hearts were hopeful. Mack kept blowing the horn every thirty seconds. Ozzie found the flash again. When they finally caught up to it, he went out onto the starboard stairs, took one look, then shook his head 'no'. It was the reflective tape on a life ring — an empty life ring with no heaving line attached. Where the boat's name would have been stenciled was now just burned and charred plastic.

"Lord luvvaduck, where is he?" Buddy fumed in frustration. He reached for the radio microphone, but felt his arm go weak and drop back to the wheel as he shook off a small jolt of pain in his chest. He rasped out, "Ricky, see if you can raise 'im, or see if 'Charlie Golf' got ahold of 'im." He lit a cigarette and kept steering ahead.

Ricky did as ordered. "Lizgale callin' the Monte Christo ... come back, Lanny ... Lizgale callin' the Monte Christo ... come back, Lanny!" No reply.

"Break, break. Fishing vessel Elizabeth Gale, this is Coast Guard Group Wood's Hole, Coast Guard Group Wood's Hole, channel two-two, over."

"Lizgale by. Go ahead," Ricky answered.

"Fishing vessel *Elizabeth Gale*, Group Wood's Hole, roger. Understand you have not made contact with the distressed vessel *Monte Christo*, is that affirmative, over."

Before Ricky could answer, Ozzie began sputtering and pointing to the port bow with his arms flailing in frustration as he tried to speak. Then he stamped his foot, waving his arms and pointing ahead as he shone the searchlight square onto the stricken *Monte Christo*.

"L … Lllll … Lan!!"

"Lord luvvaduck!" Buddy exclaimed. "There he is!" He reached for his chest with both hands and made a grimacing gesture as he excitedly yelled the news.

"Wood's Hole, the Lizgale," Ricky spoke into the microphone. "We found her! We're at 3908 and 1285!"

"Fishing vessel *Elizabeth Gale*, Group Wood's Hole, Roger. Understand you have located the *Monte Christo* at LORAN coordinates three-niner-zero-eight and one-two-eight-five. How on that, over?"

"Yup … look, we've got work to do here!"

The Coast Guard radio operator knew it was his turn to stay out of the way and to wait for further information. He answered simply, "Roger."

The stricken *Monte Christo* looked like a vessel out of a war zone. The Lizgale had overshot her by a little bit, so the crew saw her starboard side before Buddy brought his own boat around to leeward and came up on her port quarter. The starboard quarter and hull was charred and splintered. Half of the bulwarks, from the fishhold to the aft quarter were missing. The aft gallows frame, once a sturdy structure of steel, was now completely missing, reduced to shards and shrapnel which was now embedded into the turtleback. Pieces of the net and ground cables swayed in the wind and sea from the forward gallows frame. Mattresses stuck out where the top two planks of the hull once joined to the upper bulwarks.

The wheelhouse didn't look much better; the starboard side was sooty and burned, a pillow from Lanny's stateroom was sticking out of the broken window, the radar antenna swung wildly, clanging into its broken stand. Even the starboard dory was blown apart and its launching davits now looked like bent, twisted question marks. She was dark, beaten and burned … and showed no signs of life.

As the *Monte Christo* heaved and rolled in the trough, the seas careened over her deck, having their way with her. She had seawater in her engine room and hold, making her sluggish, but the taking on of deck water was compounded by the fact that the starboard bulwark was missing. The seas broke over her like she was a low sandbar. They rolled across the deck, smashing the opposite side, then backlashed into the next wave to come aboard.

Buddy maneuvered the Lizgale to a safe distance along the port side, then grabbed the horn lanyard and laid into it until someone finally came out of the lee side of the wheelhouse and started yelling back.

"Hey … It's Buddy!" The tall, thin figure yelled to his crew in the wheelhouse. "It's Buddy!" He turned directly into the searchlight that was shining on him and began waving his arms over his head. "Hey Buddy!" he screamed over the sound of the wind, waves and engines. "Am I glad to see you!"

"Okay, Ricky … you, Carleton and Mackie go forward and get those guys offa there and down into the foc'sle. I'll bring us up on the port quarter of the Monte C and you guys grab 'em anyway you can, got it?" The three nodded. "Maybe, if we're lucky, we can come back and rig up a towline from their bow bitt."

"Oz, I want you to be thinkin' about some way we can save the Monte C from goin' down … if anyone can save that rig, it's you. Lanny can't afford to lose her; I don't think he's even got enough insurance on her to replace the bucket they use for the head. The insurance company canceled her 'cause of her age. It's twenty-three miles to Muskeget Can. If we can keep her afloat until we get in the lee of Nantucket to break up this wind, we might be able to get her into some harbor somewhere when the wind goes around … might not, too, but I think we should try. If anyone can cobble somethin' together, it's you!"

Mack, Greg and Ricky pulled their oilers on and started for the wheelhouse door. "Hey!" Buddy said as he switched on the decklights, "we're all still together … be careful! Now go get them poor bahstidds offa there!"

As they cracked open up the wheelhouse door, Ozzie's face lit up with an idea. His moon-pie face got even bigger as his eyes and big grin became framed by his large ears. He stuttered his idea out. "W … w … w … ww … wai … wait!" he yelled, waving his hands, desperately trying to communicate his plan. At … at … At … las!! … Atlas!! … Wa … w … wait! … Sea anc … sea a … a … a … anc … anch … or!!

Ozzie motioned for everyone to gather around the chart table, then he took a scrap piece of paper and diagrammed his plan. Crudely, he drew an overhead picture of the *Monte Christo* with a towline leading off the port bow and a sea anchor rigged off the starboard quarter. Buddy looked over his shoulder long enough to see what he had in mind.

"Okay Oz, we rig a sea anchor off the quarter so's when we put her under tow, the damaged area stays in the lee … good thinkin'. What about the other thing you were sayin'?"

Ozzie began clenching his hands and stamping his feet in frustration … the words just wouldn't come out of his mouth. Ricky grabbed both of his shoulders and gave him a sharp shake. "Listen, Oz … we gotta go!" he forcefully said. "Calm down and sing it! Just sing it!"

Ozzie broke into an extemporaneous song. "She's got an Atlas engine … slow turnin' … block off what is dead! She's got the arctic air-start … don't need no batteries! She'll run on just three cylinders, if they're any good … we'll take her into Edgartown … Rise Again!!"

Buddy thought for a split second. "Lord luvvaduck, you've got it, Oz! You guys get up forward and get Lanny and his gang onboard. Oz, you get goin' on what you'll need. Make sure you take some flares! One signal and you're outta there! Everybody's goin' home, got me?" Ozzie waved him an affirmative as he went out the port wheelhouse door and dashed for the turtleback between waves.

Buddy called up all of his boathandling skills to deftly maneuver the Lizgale's bow next to the port quarter of the wallowing *Monte Christo*. One false move and the two vessels would collide, creating more problems and possibly leaving Lanny and his crew stranded or crushed. Ricky, Greg and Mack followed their lifeline to the bow and waited for Buddy to time his helmsmanship with the wind and sea.

Over the roar of the storm, Ricky yelled some last minute orders, "Don't do anythin' stupid! Just grab for the guys and get 'em over here, first! Whatever ya do, wait for my signal. Don't do anythin' until! Buddy'll get us there!"

On the first pass, the seas weren't co-operating. When the bow of the Lizgale reached to within inches of the port rail of the Monte C, the bow was thrust wildly upward by a surging sea. Greg, Ricky and Mack looked down into the frightened faces of the crew as they soared skyward. Buddy put the boat in hard reverse, regrouped, then tried to time himself with the sea again. He eased the Lizgale forward, then lunged the throttle so that the boat was momentarily steaming toward the Monte C. When the stern of the Monte C went down in the trough of the wave, he pulled the throttle back and put the Lizgale in hard reverse. When the Monte C rose on the next wave, the bow of the Lizgale was right next to the Monte C's waterline, making an opportunity for Lanny and his gang to jump aboard.

"Now!" Ricky bellowed. "Jump! Now! Now!"

Two crewmen jumped into the waiting arms of Ricky, Greg and Mack. All five of them fell into a jumbled mass that immediately became drenched with a wave breaking over the bow. Greg reached up for the forward gallus frame and, with one hand, stopped them from being washed down the deck and overboard. Ricky and Mack hustled the two shaken fishermen to the foc'sle ladder after the deckwater momentarily cleared the scuppers.

There were still two more men to rescue, however, and Buddy started his approach once again. After three tries, one narrowly missing having the two boats crash together, the seas relented again. The Lizgale eased up to the stern quarter of the Monte C again, riding the waves in anticipation. "You're gettin' over here this time, Lanny!" Ricky yelled. "Get ready!"

When the boats rolled down in the trough, Buddy gunned the throttle to catch up, then quickly backed-down hard, bringing Ricky's outstretched hand to within a foot of Lanny's. Lanny didn't grab ahold though, instead he pushed his other crewman over the rail and into the waiting arms below. After a few seconds, Lanny jumped himself, but missed the deck and just barely made a hand-hold of the heaving rail of the Lizgale. As Buddy backed away, the boat rose high on another sea, with Lanny outside the hull holding on for dear life. Greg shook himself free from the confusion and waddled through rushing deck water to catch up with the last man to be rescued. He grabbed a hold of the gallus frame with his left hand, then swung his body on top of the rail with his right arm overboard. Greg found the hood of Lanny's oilcoat and buried his fingers into it. The days he captained the basketball team in high school came into play now as he held a relentless, teeth-baring grip on Lanny's hood ... and life. When the Lizgale went nose-down into the next sea, the rising water swept Lanny upward and Greg reeled him in single-handedly, twisting his body so that the sputtering skipper landed face down, spread-eagled on the deck.

"Get 'em below!" Ricky screamed. "Grab 'em!"

Seven drenched, relieved and exhausted men gathered around the foc'sle table. Lanny wiped his face and realized his nose was broken; blood was streaming out of his nostrils. One man laid his head down in his crossed arms and immediately dozed off, probably out of shock as much as tiredness. The other two stretched out on the benches alongside the table. Ricky, Greg and Mack stood near the ladder, surveying their rescued victims.

"Sorry, Cap. I guess I got carried away," Greg said to Lanny as he caught sight of his face. "You Okay?"

"Okay? By the Lord Jaysus, man, you saved my ugly carcass from goin' to Fiddler's Green! You got some mitts on ya, I'll tell ya that … saved my life, you did! You byes saved all of us," he croaked out between twinges of pain, tears and blood blocking his breathing. "Saved us all! Finestkind!"

The conversation was interrupted by Buddy blowing the horn. "Make yourselves at home, boys," Ricky announced. "If anyone feels up to it, I'm sure Buddy could use the help back aft."

"Where you goin?" Lanny demanded. "You ain't thinkin' of goin' back for the Monte, are ya? Suicidal!" he said, trying to get up. "I'm goin' to talk to Buddy! Lord Jaysus!"

Ricky held out his hands, palms down. "Lanny, take it easy … we're just goin' back aft. Take my bunk over there and catch a kink." Ricky turned and gave a stern look at his two shipmates as he quietly said, "Let's go."

Ozzie was waiting in the lee of the doghouse as the crew went topside again. Buddy maneuvered the boat to within an inch of the Monte C's rail. "Go!" Ricky yelled and Ozzie, Greg and Mack jumped aboard. Greg inched his way along the port rail until he was standing at the forward bitt of the stricken vessel. Buddy brought the Lizgale alongside and Ricky heaved the bitter end of the anchorline to him. The line cut across Greg's neck, but he managed to grab it, keep his balance and make the line fast to the Monte C.

"Put it on the port bow, Greggie!" Ricky screamed upwind.

With the towline secured to the Monte C's forward bitt, Ricky felt his way aft along the lifeline, paying out slack as Buddy backed away. When the time was right, Ricky tied the line to the Lizgale's aft gallows frame. He waited there, paying out line until the two boats were in-step, each riding the upward sides of different waves. Ozzie and Mack waited in the lee of the Monte C's wheelhouse until Greg scampered back aft to join them. Oz smiled and waved a clenched fist to signify a good job done. Then the beam of the searchlight of the Lizgale momentarily left them in darkness as Buddy brought the boat ahead to a towing position. When Ricky was satisfied that the towing arrangement would suffice, he joined Buddy in the wheelhouse and manned the searchlight, illuminating the Monte C once again. The two vessels moved slowly ahead, climbing the up-sides of respective waves then rolling down the next.

Ozzie pulled a flashlight from under his oilcoat and looked through the turtleback trying to find something that would make a sea anchor. A sea broke over the Monte C's bow breaking the lobstertank loose, washing it down the deck. The tank came to rest against the port sternquarter with a thud. Thinking quickly to use this serendipitous moment, Ozzie took one of the stowed docklines and tied it in a bridle arrangement across the mouth of the tank. Using hand movements illuminated by his flashlight, he instructed Greg and Mack to drag the tank through the turtleback and throw it over the starboard quarter. Ozzie paid out the line, then made it snug around the aft tie-up bitt. As the makeshift sea anchor changed the boat's attitude in conjunction with the towline, the Monte C now towed a little off-center, but the sea no longer drove in through the makeshift patches in the side of the hull. The damaged portion was now in the lee.

So far, so good, Ozzie thought. *If that Lister keeps going, it should be able to catch up now.* Ozzie's mind was as keen and distinctive an instrument as a Stradivarius even though his communicative skills greatly belied the fact. He motioned for Greg and Mack to follow him. They went down below into the engine room.

In the beam of Ozzie's flashlight, the engine room looked like something out of a war movie. The Lister thankfully still clacked away, working the push-arm that kept the diaphragm pump slowly draining the hull. A slick of oil and fuel was about an inch deep, sloshing around on top of cold seawater that was now two feet below the top of the deadened Atlas main engine.

Ozzie held up the flashlight and put Mack's hand on it, then he tapped his chest and signified he was going in. Mackenzie lit the way as Ozzie waded into the cold water and felt his way along the main engine's sides. *Sixth cylinder threw a rod ... didn't get the jacket, though*, Oz thought as he felt the connecting rod protruding through the broken engine block. *Let's see ... firing order is probably 1-5-3-6-2-4, so let's see if the number two is gone, too.* He waded ahead and felt along the number two cylinder … it too had a connecting rod protruding through the block, but neither thrown rod had smashed through to the water jacket. *Okay, let's see about the number four,* he reasoned to himself with the calm confidence of a surgeon. *Beautiful! Four is okay! Gotta love these old slow-turners ... can't kill 'em. So when she took a gulp of water, the six and two cylinders locked up and stopped her cold.* He felt along both sides of the big Atlas engine. *Okay, we block off the six and the two while the Lister is pumping us out, then we flush her with some diesel fuel from the daytank ... gotta find some wrenches and some lube oil.*

Now, Ozzie sang eloquently to his two apprentice engineers, "Find me the inch-and-a-half socket and breaker bar and all the oil you can find. I'll feel my way over to the Lister and make sure she's okay. After that, bail with whatever you've got to help the pump and I'll get her fired up!"

Aboard the Lizgale, Lanny noticed that they were doing a lot of backing and maneuvering. Now it felt like they were towing something … that lunging, snapping feeling definitely felt like they were towing. He ripped the sleeve off his shirt, tied it around his face to stem the flow of blood from his nose, then hobbled up the foc'sle ladder.

"By the Lord Jaysus," he wondered aloud, "am I dreamin'?" He looked down the deck, then followed the stream of light that led aft from the searchlight. "Can't be," he said, but as the Lizgale started down the backside of another wave, the bow of the *Monte Christo* rose into view a few waves back. Lanny jumped to his feet and wobbled his way along the lifeline, reaching the wheelhouse in an out of breath panic. "Lord Jaysus! You guys crazy? Let 'er go!" he blubbered as he burst into the wheelhouse, looking like a beaten, skewed version of the Lone Ranger. "You crazy, Buddy?"

Buddy laughed heartily, rasped, then lit a cigarette as he felt another twinge bolt through his chest. "Lord luvvaduck, I always knew you were ugly! I think the mask is an improvement! How in hell could my sister marry someone as butt-ugly as you?" he joked. "Whatsa problem, Old Son … you don't want the old girl?"

"By the Lord Jaysus!" Lanny choked out. "Is Ozzie over there?"

"Yup ... got two guys with him. If anyone can save that rig, it's him."

"Buddy, you're nuts ... get them offen there!" Lanny demanded through his three day old beard and sunken eyes. "Let 'er go!"

"She's towin' fine and I think she's comin' back up on her lines since we've got her bad side in the lee. Whatdya think, Lanny?" Buddy said calmly. "The Monte C. looks pretty good! You still look some cussed ugly, though!" he laughed.

"Yup, she's definitely comin' back up," Ricky joined in, watching through the searchlight's plume. "I've been watchin' her since we got her hooked up ... she's fine. Oz'll get 'er goin' ... I betcha!"

"All we gotta do is keep her goin' until we get in the lee up by Muskeget Can. The island should give us a good lee by then if Oz can't get her goin' ... but by the look on his face, I think he will, Lord luvvaduck!"

Onboard the Monte C, Ozzie was pulling the heads off of the engine's sixth and second cylinders. He had already disconnected the fuel lines from those two cylinders ... now he was going to insure that they couldn't make any compression by leaving them wide open, letting the pistons sit naked in the light from the flashlight. He reached around the engine block and disconnected the two broken connecting rods, feeling his way around through the water, oil slick and half-blackness. *At least the holes in the block make this part easy,* he thought.

Greg and Mack bailed hand-over hand with five gallon buckets, taking turns passing the water up the ladder and emptying it out on deck. Each time they filled a bucket, they drove it down deep into the bilge so as to keep the oil slick contained within the boat.

In about an hour's time, the top half of the main engine was sitting above water, its two gaping wounds where the connecting rods had pierced the block in plain view. Ozzie began bailing lube oil and water from the crankcase by hand. When he had removed all he could, he drained fuel from the daytank mounted above the heating boiler and ran it into the crankcase, filling it full, spilling out the last of the contaminants. He crawled forward, pulled the compression release open so the engine wouldn't fire, then slowly released the air valve from the accumulator of the start mechanism. The engine turned over slowly, blowing fuel and oil from its cylinders in popping, hissing sounds. When Ozzie was satisfied that the engine was cleaned of water, he bailed out the crankcase again, this time, adding fresh oil from five-gallon buckets.

"Keep bailin' boys," he sang. "I'll be right back!" He scrambled up the ladder and returned shortly, carrying the chart table, a mattress, a locker door and a pillow.

"Stuff 'em in the holes, then wedge the wood against 'em to keep the oil from splashin' out," he sang. When Greg and Mack had plugged the holes in the engine block, Ozzie grabbed the lever to the compression release in one hand, the air-start valve in the other and sang, "Rise Again!"

The engine turned over with a loud, high-pitched whoosh from the air accumulator, then smoked to a disjointed, "ka-chunk-ka-chunk-ka-chunka" mis-firing life. The excess fuel from washing the cylinders began to let the engine race uncontrollably, but Ozzie feathered the compression release in and out until the threat of the fuel-rich engine "running away" was past. Soon, the *Monte Christo* had four cylinders of its main engine running … not smooth, but running nonetheless. Ozzie clutched in the main bilge pump manifold, and within ten minutes, the engine room was free of excess water … only the oily bilge slops remained.

"G … G … G … Go … b … bl … blow … th … th … the … h-h-h-horn!" he stuttered out in celebration. He pointed for Greg and Mack to go topsides as he pulled his clenched fist in a signal to pull the horn lanyard. There wasn't one square inch of him that wasn't covered in oil, grease, water and filth except his wide, victorious smile.

When the two boats passed Muskeget Can, the towline was no longer needed and Ozzie, Greg and Mack steered the *Monte Christo* behind the Lizgale until, at nine the following morning, they rafted up both boats beside the New Bedford scalloper *Iver and Jens* at the bandstand in Edgartown Harbor.

15

EDGARTOWN

Lat. 41 deg. 23.5 min. N.
Long. 70 deg. 30.5 min. W.

G reg ran down the hill, huffing and out of breath. "They'll be here as fast as they can," he panted out. "I hope they hurry!"

The cook from Lou's Worry, the restaurant where Greg ran for the phone, arrived shortly behind. "I called the police and they'll pick up my wife ... she's a nurse ... they'll be right here!" he said between breaths. "Sometimes it takes ten or fifteen minutes or more for the ambulance if they're over to the other side of the island. Hang tight ... she'll be here!"

In a couple of minutes, the police cruiser arrived carrying the cook's wife in the passenger's seat. A husky policeman cleared the way and they entered the wheelhouse of the Lizgale. Ozzie, Ricky, Lanny and Mack were ushered from Buddy's cramped stateroom by the officer. "Why don't you boys wait outside," he suggested in a tone that needed no reply. "Give Karen some room to get in here."

The nurse felt for Buddy's pulse, checked his eyes for dilation, felt his skin, took note of his labored breathing and pain ... all the things that were second nature to nurses. "I think he's definitely having a myocardial infarction," she said, never turning around. "Got oxygen in the cruiser?"

The police officer ran to the trunk of the cruiser and returned with an oxygen bottle and facemask. He handed the mask to her, then reached down and turned the valve on the tank. "Just hold on, Cap," she said soothingly. "We'll get you fixed up in a jiffy. This should make you breathe a little easier." She turned around, still holding the mask on Buddy's face, and spoke in a low tone. "He didn't just come on with this ... my guess is he's been infarcting for a matter of hours." She arched her eyebrows to signify her grave concern to the police officer. "Let's hope they get here real quick," she whispered.

A few hours later, Ozzie, Greg, Mack, Lanny and Ricky silently rode in the taxi carrying them back from the hospital.

"Well, I guess I'll have to call Doris," Lanny choked out from the back seat. "Better tell the wife, too, I guess ... she was his sister. I should be the one to break the news to her. I don't get it ... he saved all of our sorry arses but didn't know he had to save himself. Lord Jaysus, what a shame. Dammit, he never stopped to think of himself."

"We're all together and we're gonna stay that way ... that's what he said," Greg muttered. "I just can't believe he's gone. I can't believe it."

Ozzie looked out the window and held back his tears.

As the taxi reached the top of the hill and began to descend to the bandstand, the driver stopped the car short. "What the hell is goin' on down there?" he wondered. The waterfront was covered with police cars, their lights flashing and revolving. Uniformed police officers were standing guard over the bandstand. A yellow "police line" tape was stretched across the road. An officer stopped every car, making each one turn around, and head back up the hill to town. The taxi driver finally inched the car up to the policeman and rolled down the window.

"What's goin' on down there?" he asked the policeman.

The policeman bent down and leaned on the door of the taxi. "That boat tied up outside the *Iver and Jens* has got some sort of explosive or somethin' on board," he answered. "Crew found it when they were pickin' through the fish. I guess they left the fish in the net on deck 'cause it was too rough to sort 'em out in last night's blow. That boat just rode out that whole storm and rescued the other one rafted up outside of it, never knowin' they could have been blown to bits at any second!"

The crew in the taxi was momentarily stunned, then simultaneously came to the realization: "The bag of fish!" Ricky blurted out. "We never opened the last tow of fish! There must have been something in the bag just like what you got tangled up with, Lanny!"

Over the protesting yells of the policeman, five men vaulted from the taxi, ran to the bottom of the hill and forced their way into the fracas, trying to get through the police standing guard at the bandstand. Three Massachusetts State policemen stopped them as they tried to continue.

"Where do you think you're goin', boys?" one of them asked. "No one gets aboard those boats!"

"But the *Monte Christo* is my boat, and the Lizgale is ... um ... my brother-in-law's boat! These guys are from the *Elizabeth Gale*," Lanny protested. "Those are our boats!"

"Well good, then," the State Trooper answered. "You come right over here with me, gentlemen ... you've got some explaining to do." He called to his superior officer, "Lieutenant! This is the missing crew!"

The five were led to the far corner of the bandstand where a State Police Lieutenant was interrogating the other three members of Lanny's crew.

"Yeah, it's like I just told all them cops over there," Dan Garrett, Lanny's engineer, was explaining loudly. "We figured we'd pick the fish while the other guys went to the hospital to see how Buddy was. It was the least we could do for 'em. I'm tellin' ya, man ... that's the same kind of shell that we got that blew off our stern quarter yesterday. Same exact thing! Even got some Russian writin' on it, or somethin'! Them bahstidds meant to kill us!"

Lanny shook his head in disbelief. "Danny ... they had one of them shells onboard too?"

"Sure thing, Cap! We figured we could just start the engine, hoist 'er up, pop the bag, clean ever'thin' up and kind of help out, ya know?" he said in a frustrated tone. "Instead, we got world war three goin' here. Once we saw that shell roll out of the pile, we booked it on outta there and ran for the nearest phone!"

"And it's like the one you guys saw that blew us up?" Lanny asked.

"Yup. If there's one thing I'll never forget, it's what that thing looked like. Same thing, Cap ... same thing!"

Lanny sat down. He put his head in his hands. In the last twenty-four hours, he'd lost his brother-in-law and best friend, he'd almost lost his crew and his boat, and his own life, to boot. He took a deep breath, but before he could muster enough strength to speak, the air was filled with the thumping, pulsing noise of a helicopter. Louder and louder the sound reverberated until the chopper was hovering directly overhead, blowing a hurricane of air and deafening noise earthward. Through the PA system the pilot ordered, "Move those police cruisers, and give us a fifty-foot circle to land! Now!"

The sound of the rotors was overwhelming and the backwash of air turbulence whipped everyone's clothes into fluttering sails. The heads of the two crewmen were thrust out the side door; the rifles they were carrying were pointed muzzle-up, but looked ready to be used. It looked like a surprise armed assault landing on enemy territory.

After a scurrying flurry of activity, the landing spot was cleared and the aircraft set down in the parking lot next to the bandstand. The two gunners stepped out, weapons drawn, then between them came a man in a Coast Guard uniform. He looked surprisingly overweight and out of shape. He turned to the chopper pilot and gestured to him to kill the engine. The engine and rotor sounds died as the armed escort marched into the bandstand.

"Who's in charge here?" the Coast Guardsman demanded. "Speak up! I haven't got all day!"

The officer interrogating Lanny's crew stepped forward. "I'm Lieutenant Henry from the Mass State Police special tactics unit. And who the hell are you?"

"Chief Lee Chambers, United States Coast Guard, assigned to Naval Intelligence at the Newport War College, that's who I am, and you are relieved of anything further here, Deputy Fife! This is a matter of national security. This is a military matter!"

"Relieved? On whose orders?"

"The President of the United States! He's the Commander-in-Chief, remember, Gomer?"

The Lieutenant beckoned to one of his men, explained the situation and sent him to patch a radio call to the Mass State Police headquarters in Boston.

"Listen, Chambers. My men and I aren't moving an inch without authorization from Boston," Lt. Henry said. "Until I hear otherwise, you're this close from being hauled off for butting your nose into my investigation. Now stand clear, tell your goons to secure their weapons and get out of my way!"

The two sides began a stare-down through air thick with tension. The police officer returned and whispered something to the lieutenant.

"What? ... Are you sure?" he asked incredulously.

"That's what they said, Lieutenant, H-Q wants you to talk to them personally, right now."

"Damn straight I'll talk to them! Watch these clowns until I get back!"

"Bye-bye, flat-foot," Chambers muttered through his surly smile and squinted eyes. "Oh ... I'll take mine with cream and sugar. Now run along and make yourself useful!"

After a few moments, Lt. Henry re-appeared. "My orders are to assist you in civilian control. Your bomb squad is on its way now from Newport in another chopper ... we'll clear a place for that to land, also." He turned to the bewildered fishermen. "You boys should come with me and stay out of his way. Right now, both vessels are impounded," he explained. "I know you guys have been through a lot. I didn't realize that you just lost your skipper, too. One of my men will take you up to Lou's and stay with you until I can settle this fracas a little."

"And don't think of leaving!" Chambers shouted over to them. "You people will all be interrogated as soon as I can get up there. Right now, you're all witnesses under an official military investigation and can be shot if you decide to run! And ... drink nothing stronger than coffee, I want your minds nice and clear when I get to you, and that's coming shortly!"

~ ~ ~

"So that's the first time you met this guy? No wonder you didn't want to re-tell the story. It was harrowing!" Chris said. "Hey, I apologize to you two, I had no idea what you went through ...

Before Mack or Greg could speak, Dr. Grayson came into the mess hall, surprising them.

"Don't you guys ever take a break?" she asked. "It's ten o'clock, and you're still going strong!"

"Just tellin' some old sea stories, Doctor G.," Greg said. "Did we wake you?"

"No. Greg, April's on the phone. She sounds upset."

"Prillie? She okay?"

"She says she's fine and the girls are fine, but needs to talk to you right away. She's on my office phone."

Greg followed Dr. Grayson out of the mess hall.

"Is that the April from the Neptune's Retreat?" Chris asked Mack.

"Yup, that's Prillie. Greg's wife, and a very lovely person," he answered. "I hope everything's okay with her."

"Both of you guys are out here while your wives are ashore? I didn't want to ask, but … doesn't that cause problems?" Chris asked.

"Naah. You've got to let your mate be who they are, Chris. Both of those girls knew what we were before we got married, and Greg and I supported them in their hopes and dreams, too. Sue plays cello in the Pops, Prillie finally got her summer camp up at Sebago for all the kids she wants to help. They couldn't do that out here. 'Course, Greg and I can't very well do what we do unless we're on the water, so it all works out."

"Mack, whatever happened to the girl on the factory ship?" Chris asked. Now he was certain that it *was* the *Elizabeth Gale* he'd seen and he had been face to face with Jim Mackenzie twenty years earlier. Now, here he was, face to face with him again.

"Did you ever see her again?" he pressed.

A bolt of cold energy rushed upwards through Jim Mackenzie's spine. It might be just a harmless question born from curiosity, or he might be looking for something much more. Mack had been trolling for his own information, the bait was out. If this kid was on the up-and-up, then okay. If he wasn't, then ...

"We're talking about Chambers, aren't we, Old Scout? Didn't you ask about Chambers? Maybe we should just call it a night ..."

"No! ... please continue. I'm sorry I interrupted."

Greg rushed to the phone at Dr. Grayson's desk. "Prillie, what's the matter, darlin', is something wrong?"

"Oh Greggie," she cooed back in the receiver. "It's so good to hear your voice. I'm fine, the girls are fine, everyone here is doing great ... are you guys okay out there?"

"Sure, darlin' we're finestkind out here, couldn't be better. What's the matter?"

"I don't know. I was asleep and then I got dreaming about that awful time when we lost Uncle Buddy. Are you sure everything is okay out there? Is Mack alright?"

"He's fine, darlin'. We're just sittin' around tellin' old stories. You remember I told you about Slimey? We're just helpin' him with a few issues, that's all."

"Greg, how's Sue-Mari, is she there?"

"Sue? God love ya, darlin', she's not here! Mack talked to her last night. She's playing music out at Tanglewood. They were having the time of their lives when they spoke. You know, Liz is playing with her too. They're thrilled."

"You mean she isn't in the corner room upstairs? She isn't even there?"

"Prillie, you're worryin' me, darlin'. Nope, she's not here ... hasn't been since the week before Memorial Day when you were here too. Are you sure you're okay?"

"I guess so, Greggie. Just a bad dream, I guess. Will you call me tomorrow when you get in from hauling?"

"Sure thing, darlin'. Now get some sleep. We're finestkind out here."

"Everything okay?" Mack asked when Greg came back to the mess hall.

"Yeah … she's got her radar goin' again, I guess. They're all set up at Sebago."

"The skipper's daughter," Greg muttered to himself.

~ ~ ~

Edgartown, 1975 …

The Pt. Judith fishermen and their state police escort were gathered around a table at Lou's Worry beginning to sip their coffees when the second helicopter arrived from Newport. Five Navy ordinance experts ran out from under the whirling rotors and went directly to the Lizgale. In fifteen minutes, the chopper lifted off again, carrying the disarmed shell and the crew it had brought from the mainland. It wasn't long before Chambers climbed the stairs to the second floor and sat down at the table to join the crews from the Point boats, out of breath from the short climb up the hill and the flight of stairs.

"I'll ask the questions and you guys give me the answers," Chambers blurted out when he finally composed himself. "Just give me the straight scoop." He dismissed the state policeman with a back-handed wave.

"Lord Jaysus, you're treatin' us like we're criminals or somethin'," Lanny retorted. "We didn't dump that stuff out there, you military people did! Haven't we been through enough?" A round of angry nods circled the table.

"Easy, Newfie," Chambers fired back. "I can have you flown outta here in handcuffs and put in the brig at Newport if you give me a hard time. This is a military investigation … you've got no civilian rights with me!"

"Well, by the Lord Jaysus, this is still America, and …"

"That's right! It still is America, and I don't have to tell you that the whole of Russia and Eastern Europe is right over the horizon, watching our every move." He reached into his briefcase and retrieved a packet of photographs. Chambers pulled out a picture of a Soviet research ship and flipped it onto the table. "Ever see this rig before?"

Mack was the first to speak up. "It sure looks like the ship that cut us off. They went right across our bow."

"You sure, son?" Chambers pressed.

"Well, I'm not a hundred percent sure, but I'm fairly certain."

"They cut us off, too," Scotty Wecker, Lanny's cook, offered. "Sure looks like 'em, anyways. Don't you think so, skipper?" he asked Lanny.

"Lord Jaysus," Lanny came back, "they all look the same to me. What the hell difference does it make?"

"Because, gentlemen, this so-called research ship also got chummy with the *Naviless* a few days ago. See anything familiar?" Chambers asked.

"By the Lord Jaysus," Lanny whispered.

"You guys that were on the *Monte Christo* ... did any of you see anything that could help us identify the shell that detonated?"

Danny Garrett put his hat on the back of his head and rolled his chair back on two legs. "Yup. I saw a few letters of somethin' engraved on there. I'm no 'A' student, but I do know it wasn't written in English. Saw the same thing on the shell on the Lizgale, too."

"Tell me whatever you can remember," Chambers said. "How about the first few letters?"

Danny thought for a moment. "Well, it started out with Y-H-D-Y-S, then I don't remember the rest. Oh! ... wait a minute! ... There was some other stuff! When we first ran across that thing, we just saw the very end of the shell ... you know, the round part. When we picked some fish around it was when I saw a little bit of the side of it, then we took a sea, it rolled down to the stern, and blammo! Believe it or not, it all happened in a few seconds ... once we realized what it was, it was blowin' us up!"

"So what else did you see?"

"I think there was a bunch of numbers ... I dunno, but ... I can remember the letters c-n-g. It didn't look like any of the practice bombs we get in the dump from time to time, I thought it was a round piece of brass off of an old ship's telegraph or somethin'. Sure was shiny, though ... looked brand new."

"And the same thing was on the *Elizabeth Gale*, correct?" Chambers asked.

"Yup, though this time we didn't hang around to read it! It was 'legs do your duty!'"

Chambers rolled back in his chair and put his feet up on the restaurant table, barely missing three coffee cups. He folded his hands over his beer-belly and studied everyone's face before he spoke again. "Well, the shell's been disarmed and is on its way to Newport where we can study it further … I guess you guys can head back to the Point when the weather permits. We'll get in touch with you if we need anything else. Oh, one more thing … Anyone been trading anything with the Soviets? Any contact with any of the catcher boats or the factory ships?" Chambers asked as he looked around the table again, studying their faces. "Anybody know of anything like that?"

16
NOMANS

LAT. 41 DEG. 15.3 MIN. N.
LONG. 70 DEG. 49.8 MIN. W.

October is a month of opposites and transitions, ironies and intervals. The earth begins its descent into winter with storms that hint of its fury, but nature also manages to bestow some of its finest weather of the year. Sweeping the harbor with one's eye, there was definitely something amiss with the view; almost every boat that called the Point home was tied up. The Lizgale was riding safely in her usual docking place, the battered *Monte Christo* was tied up in the million dollar corner, the dock near Gallard's Engine shop. Only the *Aurora*, stuck on cable patrol for AT&T was still at sea.

No fish? Hardly ... there were yellowtails and lobsters at the Corner ... butterfish and scup south of Block Island ... squid and fluke making their way to heap up at the Gully ... whiting off Montauk ... a handful of flats at Whistling Eel ... codfish and haddock in the hard bottom south of the BB Buoy ... big lobsters at Oceanographer and Gilbert's Canyons. It wasn't a lack of fish or bad weather that brought the fleet home to rest, it was the fact that Buddy Folland had made his last trip.

It was a crystal clear, calm, warm and delightful bluebird day that greeted the overwhelming throng of people amassed on the State Pier in Pt. Judith. The crowd extended back into the street.

The words were simple and the thoughts reverent. No one had to hold back any ill feelings out of respect for the deceased — there just weren't any. The vessels floating at the piers, the Co-op, the members of the fleet who now owned their own boats, the crewmen who never filled a full seabag at high school but were very successful in their chosen trade, all either directly or indirectly owed a word of thanks to Buddy. Those who could, spoke this aloud ... those who couldn't knew the facts only too well. When the chaplain said that he would be missed, he had no idea how much.

"Ozzie, would you please sing one of your songs for Uncle Buddy?" April asked. "He loved your singing. You were like one of his sons he never had."

"I ... I ... ca ... can ... I ... c ... c ... c ... can't." Ozzie whispered. "N ... n ... no," he stuttered with tears in his eyes. Th ... th ... they ... a ... all ... th ... th ... th ... th ... think ... I ... I'm ... an ... id ... idj ... idjut."

"Oz, Uncle Buddy never thought that. He thought the world of you. Where would you be without him?"

Ozzie looked down into April's compassionate face and nodded. "R ... roy ... royt," he stammered back.

April pushed her way through the crowd and spoke to the Chaplain. "We will now hear a musical tribute to Captain Folland from his shipmate and engineer, Mr. Kennardson Oswald Marsden," he announced.

The somber crowd drew a collective surprised breath as Ozzie worked his way through the people to stand at the right side of the chaplain. He raised his head, looked around the crowd at the disbelieving stares that greeted him, then clenched his fists in front of him and closed his eyes tight. Soaring in song, he unleashed his inner soul ...

There used to be a Pharisee, cynical and wise,
Telling unGodly lies of humanity.
But in the marketplace was seated, a cripple with a lyre.
I looked at him and said, "I've been rich but so unhappy ...
What sets your soul on fire?'

He said, "Look upon me brother, I am a man with peace of mind,
I know I was never much good at nothing …
But the words I wrought and rhyme.
But I've a good woman to feed me, and friends to share it too,
Evenings we sit around and sing together … it can be the same for you.

"Just hold on, to young friends you made of old,
and please too, the one who keeps us whole,
Keep a warm fire for all your friends who come in from the cold.
Love them as brothers, you don't have to know their names …
For you it might be different,
But for us it always stays the same.

"Tonight the smoke is rising from around the room,
And judging from the warmth and smells from the kitchen,
there'll be supper ready soon.
And our table's set for twenty … room for more if they should come,
And later on we'll pass around the wine for our pleasure,
and sing until the morning comes.

"Just hold on to young friends you made of old,
and please too, the one who keeps you whole.
Keep a warm fire for all your friends who come in from the cold.
Love them as brothers, you don't have to know their names …
For you it might be different,
but for us it always stays the same."*

The stunned crowd stared at Ozzie, their disbelief changing to surprised admiration. At the end of the service Buddy's widow and their daughter clutched a wreath of flowers in the shape of a ship's wheel and threw it overboard into the harbor. The falling tide picked up the wreath and swiftly delivered it past George's Restaurant. The current brought it past Sand Hill Cove Beach, then took it out to sea through the east gap. Within two hours, forty diesel engines had started up and one hundred and seventy men had gone to sea. Point Judith was again a working seaport.

"What in hell do you guys think you're doin'?" Ricky Helliott asked as he came down the foc'sle ladder. "Where do you guys think you're goin'?"

---

*Music and lyrics by Stan Rogers. www.stanrogers.net

Greg and Mack looked up from packing their seabags. "Well, we're all done here, aren't we?" Greg answered. "It looks like it's time to head along."

"Yup ... typical," Ricky said. "You guys run out and go get a real job now. Better yet, you've bought a few rounds of beers at the 'Tune, now you can go out and write a book. I can see it now ... Greg and Mack actually lived and worked among the Point Judith fishermen. I thought you guys were gonna amount to somethin'!"

"Well, we were only on half share anyways," Mack countered.

"College nitwits," Ricky said. "Wait right here."

Ricky turned around and bolted up the foc'sle ladder. After a few moments, he came back down, holding a copy of the Coast Pilot he'd retrieved from the wheelhouse. "You guys never were on half share," Ricky explained. "Both of you guys held your own from the time you stepped aboard. Buddy, Ozzie and I agreed on it ... we set your money aside ... every dime of it. Buddy figured that you had to go half share like ever'one else so that you had the feeling that you earned your site, but the other half of your money has been right here all along." He opened up the Coast Pilot, pulled out two envelopes and threw them on the foc'sle table. "There's the rest of your money. Buddy figured you'd stay around awhile ... well, I guess we all did. We didn't think you two would pack up and desert us. Guess we were wrong."

"But Ricky, aren't we all out of a job?" Greg asked.

"This is more than a boat ya know, this is Buddy's family business. Doris can't pay the bills on this boat; the Lizgale pays her own bills. How's Doris supposed to take care of herself? The Lizgale was her paycheck, too. And their daughter ... it was always Buddy's dream to put her through medical school. Elizabeth's in her third year. What are we gonna do, tell her to quit med school and go get a dishwashin' job? You guys might be runnin' out on Buddy, but Ozzie and I ain't! This boat is goin' back to work. The Lizgale still has to support his family, just like always."

"So ... who's going to skipper her?" Mack asked.

"I talked to Doris. It's about time I got my act together, I guess. She said the hangbook goes to me if I stay on. Oz will still go engineer but he said he'd run the watch if needed. We didn't think you guys would leave, though, but if we have to, we'll go two-handed until we can find somebody. Buddy's family comes first."

Mack and Greg looked at each other. They had thought that their time on the Lizgale had come to an end and this revelation came out of the blue.

"I dunno, Ricky," Greg said softly. "I got into this to get the down payment on a little lobsterboat, not to get blown up. I dunno ..."

"Whadda you say, Mack?" Ricky asked.

"I didn't realize we still had a site here. I'm staying aboard. I've been thinking about it for awhile. I want a down payment for a boat, too. A boat just like this one. I'll do something with my degree when I get older and want to slow down a bit. Besides ... I can't leave her out there."

"Her who?" Greg asked.

"I don't know her name, but I can't leave her out on that factory ship."

Greg sat down at the table. "Are you out of your mind?" he asked. "Are you crazy?"

"Nope. I'm staying aboard," Mack declared, his arms folded. "I have to."

"What about you? You sorry sack of monkey dung!" Ricky fired back at Greg. "Every guy in the Point has been after April Mayes and she wouldn't hear of it, but you waltz in here and she's gah-gah over you. You're makin' good money on a high-line boat, you've got the prettiest girl in the Point throwing herself at ya and you're gonna go back to stuffin' bait bags? You can't believe that Coastie ... there's all kindsa stuff out there. He's just makin' work for himself ... probably tryin' to get a promotion. Every now and again, someone stumbles across a few World War II practice bombs. It happens. You could get run over right out in the street, for that matter. You don't pick your time, ya know!"

"You really want to stay, Mack?" Greg asked, already knowing the answer.

"Yup."

"Look," Ricky interjected. "I've watched you two. You're fishermen, whether you like it or not. I had my doubts sometimes, but when you guys jumped aboard the *Monte* without even thinkin' about it, I knew. If you leave here, well ... that's your decision, but you'll never leave the ocean, and it's the same risks no matter what piece of water you're on or what you're doin'. Period. We're takin' the rest of today and tomorrow off and we'll be leavin' at eleven the followin' night after we put on ice and fuel. Should I grub-up the boat for me, Mack and Ozzie or should I go across the street and tell Allen that you'll be over to put in a grocery order?"

"Lord luvvaduck," Greg sighed. "Tell him I'll be over to get the biggest porterhouse steaks he can cut." He thought for a moment … "One more thing or I'm leaving …"

"What?"

"I'll be glad to pick you up, but if you're our new skipper, you're gonna leave the dock sober."

Ricky Helliott lowered his eyebrows. He hadn't gone to sea sober for as long as he'd been shipping out.

"You can't tell the captain how to run this boat! It's bad luck to go to sea unless you're broke! That's what happened to my father and my grandfather, dammit! The one time they went to sea with money in their pockets …"

Before Ricky could continue, a voice echoed down from the doghouse above, "G … g … g … gget a s … s … st … stock … b … b … b … bro … bro … bb … broker! G … Gr … Greg's … royt! I … I … a … ain … ain't … g … gg … g … go … goin' … ne … nneith … neither!"

"What a beautiful day. Where are we goin', darlin'?"

April pulled her long tresses back then let them go over her shoulders. The delightful scent of her hair filled the car as Greg folded himself into the passenger's seat of her VW bug. She turned and looked at him. Her big brown eyes gazed directly into his blue eyes. *I wonder what the color of their eyes will be?* she thought.

"We're going on a mystery ride," she cooed.

April steered her VW up the Escape Road and turned north on Route 108. Through Narragansett, Wakefield, Peace Dale and on to Kingston she drove. Greg kept up a small-talk chat, all the while becoming totally enchanted by his chaffeur. He wondered where they were going, but really didn't care as long as he was with her. April turned left onto Route 138, then drove right past the main gates to the University of Rhode Island.

"Hey … so that's where U.R.I. is," Greg said. "I knew it was right up the road, but we've been so busy, I haven't had any time to explore. 'Course, havin' no car kinda slows you down, too," he joked. "Darlin', where we goin' anyways?" he asked, puzzled.

April looked over and smiled as she turned right onto Keaney Road. "There's someone I'd like you to meet. Would you mind stopping for a minute?"

"Of course not, darlin'."

April parked her car in the Keaney Gym parking lot. "We've got to walk up the hill a little bit, Greggie. Is that okay?"

"Great day for a hike," Greg chimed in. The beautiful October day showered them with crisp air and warm sunshine. As they walked to the main campus of U.R.I., the trees showed a hint of fall color change, but strolling hand-in-hand, they gave off their own inner glow.

After a few minutes, April had guided them to a low building called the Childhood Development Laboratory.

"There's someone I'd like to introduce you to here ... come on in," she beckoned. April led Greg into the main hallway, then down a corridor to a room to the left. She opened the door and five young children turned from their Lego blocks. Four smiled and came to her, grasping her legs with affection.

"Hi, everybody!" she said gleefully. "How's all my best pals today?"

At first, Greg was taken aback, but then joined in. He got down on his knees and waved 'hello' at eye level to the children gathered at April's feet.

"Want to read a story today?" she offered. "Pick out a favorite."

Two boys and a girl toddled over to the small bookshelf and had no trouble making their selection. *Make Way For Ducklings* was a favorite for any generation. They carried the large book back to her as she sat down in a toddler's chair and the four children gathered in a semi-circle in front of her.

"Is he okay?" Greg whispered to April, noticing that one little boy wouldn't leave the Lego blocks and join the rest.

"Oh ... that's Petey," she whispered back, cupping her hand to his ear. "He's got a condition called neurofibromatosis, a learning disability. He came to us because he'd been incorrectly diagnosed with autism. He has 'islets of competence,' in other words, he's real proficient in music and mechanical things, that's like autistic kids, but he's not autistic. He's sweet and affectionate once he knows you. He's really withdrawn ... lost his dad in Vietnam. Sad."

Before she could begin reading, a staff member came into the room. "April, you're wanted on the phone," she said. "Can you get it now? Please."

The four youngsters let out a collective groan when April stood up to leave. "Greggie, would you mind reading to them? I'll be right back," she pleaded. Greg awkwardly shrugged, but contorted his basketball captain's body into a toddler's chair as April left the room. He began reading and showing the pictures. "I used to love this book too!" he exclaimed as the children looked on.

Just outside the room, but still in view of the kids and Greg, April and her fellow staff member, Joan Tarasmith, stopped. "Why did you want me to say you had a phone call, April?" Joan asked in a whispered tone.

"It's a long story, but I needed to know something."

Joan looked puzzled, but was easily distracted as she looked back into the room. "He's gorgeous, April! Is that him?" she asked in a low volume.

"Yeah, that's Carleton Gregory," she answered.

"So ... that's Mr. Right, huh? He's certainly all right in my book!"

April was watching the children and Greg. "Shhhh," she said, putting her finger across her lips. She pointed to the room as little Petey slowly made his way over to the other children. Greg was still reading but never lost a beat as he scooped up the shy, awkward little boy in his rugged forearm and plopped him on his lap.

April and Joan silently exchanged glances of wonder as they watched the boy snuggle under Greg's arm. Greg was reading away, totally engrossed in the story but enjoying every minute. Near the end of the story, Petey held out his right index finger and in a small but determined voice, labored out, "D ... d ... d ... ddu ... du ... duck ... duck!"

"Hey!" Greg said, surprised. "Hey April!" he raised his voice. "Did you hear that? Petey said 'duck'!" Greg looked around, but saw no one as April pulled herself and Joan out of sight in the nick of time. "Oh well," he said to himself. "Okay, then ... on with the story!"

"April, what are you doing?" Joan asked, perplexed. "You tell us all about this great guy, then you bring him up here and leave him like that? If you don't want him, I'll take him! Didn't you say he was Mr. Right?"

April looked around the corner and watched one of the children go back to the bookshelf for another book. This time it was *Mike Mulligan and his Steamshovel.*

"Oh man! This is one of the best books ever written!" Greg exclaimed as he turned the page to begin reading again. "Great choice!"

April leaned against the doorcasing and took in the full view of this massive man sitting in a chair ten times too small for him reading to five special needs students, and enjoying every minute of it. "There'll never be anyone more right than him," she whispered.

Greg, Mack and Ozzie walked into the Neptune's Retreat. It was 9:30. April came from behind the bar and was instantly swept up by Greg's embrace. "I'm gonna miss you," he said. "Will you be here when I get back?"

"If I'm not here, you know where you can find me," she coyly answered.

Greg smiled and looked deep into her eyes. "Just make sure that Petey knows he has to share you with me."

Ozzie and Mack raised their eyebrows. "Who's Petey?" Mack asked.

"He's an old friend of ours," Greg answered. "You might say he introduced us to each other." Looking around the bar room he asked, "Darlin' where's the Hellion tonight?"

April silently motioned them to the bar. She pointed to the far stool where a red haired man sat drinking coffee, one leg folded over his other knee. The three shipmates did a double-take ... It was Ricky! ... Gone was the scraggly beard ... only a neatly trimmed mustache remained. His hair was cut, he was clean clothed, sober and sitting like a judge.

"About time you gentlemen got here," he said. "April, will you attend to my finances in the manner in which we discussed?" Ricky asked, sounding like a member of the bourgeoisie. He reached into his shirt pocket and handed her an envelope.

"I'll open up a bank account for you tomorrow, Cap!" she proudly answered.

"Well, then, if there's nothing further, gentlemen, I suggest we make our way to the big pond and ply our fare with the noble fishes! Ice and fuel first, of course."

Greg, Ozzie and Mack were grinning, looking and feeling foolish, dumbfounded and overwhelmed. They exchanged looks of surprise, then threw up their hands.

"Skipper says it's time to go, so let's go!" Mack exclaimed.

In the back corner of the bar room, over behind the dance floor, two men spoke quietly to each other. "That's your answer to our problem? Him?"

"Yup. It seems he's got himself a head-over-heels crush on one of the Russky sweethearts on the *Zvezda Rybaka*. Ain't love grand?"

"How are you going to orchestrate this maneuver, Chief?"

"Simple. I see that the lad is a fan of clean living. It doesn't appear that he smokes."

"So what?"

"Well then, he might have a few extra cartons of cigarettes to trade if he had the right circumstances, now wouldn't he?" Chambers thought to himself for a moment. "What's his name again?" he asked. He fished around in his shirt pocket and brought out a small notebook, flipped through the pages, looked, took another look, then chuckled to himself. His rotund belly began jiggling as he laughed in the half-light of the bar. "Oh, this is beautiful!" he chortled in a low volume. "This is too good!" He reached down to the far end of the table and held up a pepper shaker. "Son, the 'spice trade' is about to begin!"

"Back 'er down, Cappy!" Greg yelled from the foredeck. Ricky blew the horn with three short blasts, then put the engine into reverse.

"Shimmy up the shim-sham! Hoist the Goddamn! Oil up your oilskins! Grease the foc'sle!" Captain Helliott yelled from the port wheelhouse window. "Let's go fishin'!"

Nomans Land is a small island located almost three miles off of Squibnocket Point, the southwestern corner of Martha's Vineyard. On the chart it is marked as a "prohibited area," because it is truly a no-man's-land. The overgrown sandbar has had a dubious history, including being used as a military installation and a target for practice bombing and shelling. At 3:00 A.M., the Lizgale passed twenty miles west of Nomans as she steamed off to the eastward.

The sea was flat calm, the sky was perfectly clear and a bright moon shone across the water. No one aboard the proud vessel bearing the name of Buddy Folland's only child knew that the funeral wreath bearing his name washed ashore on the west facing beach of Nomans when the Lizgale passed by. It came to rest beside a similar wreath bearing the name of the skipper of the *Naviless*.

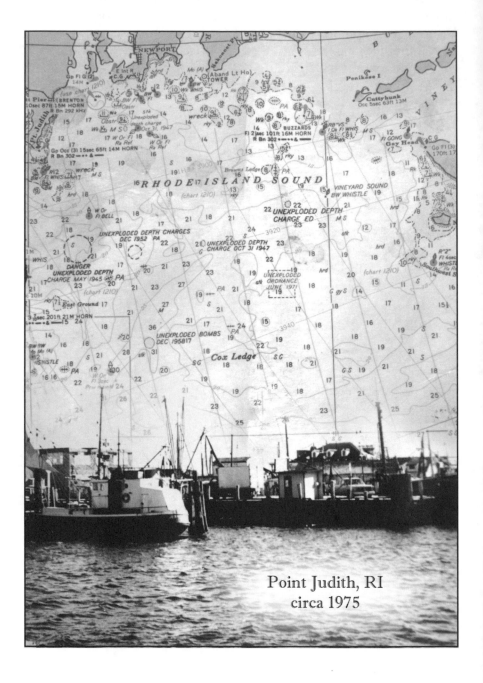

Point Judith, RI
circa 1975

17

NEWPORT

LAT. 41 DEG. 29.55 MIN. N.
LONG. 71 DEG. 19.3 MIN. W.

Marty Farmagano slowed his car and stopped at the guard post leading to the Newport Naval War College. He rolled down the window and passed a set of papers to the guard. "Martin Farmagano here to meet with Chief Leeland Chambers in Intelligence," he said. "I assume he's set up the channels for me, as usual."

The guard told him to wait as he stepped into the brick enclosure and made a phone call. After a few moments, he nodded his head, hung up the phone and stepped outside. "Chief Chambers is expecting you. Please wear this visitor's pass, sir. Do you need directions?"

"Naaah. I know the way. Thanks."

Marty parked his white government issue Ford Pinto in the parking lot, grabbed his briefcase and entered the front hall of the War College's main building. After checking in with the guard, he took the elevator to the fifth floor, checked in with another guard, then went down the hall to Chief Chambers' office.

"You're late," Chambers said upon his arrival.

Farmagano checked his watch. "I'm three minutes early, Lee."

"You are? Well don't let it happen again. What have you got for me?"

Farmagano sat down and put his briefcase in his lap. He pulled a comb from inside and, before he spoke, slicked his black hair back, bringing the smell of Vitalis hair tonic into the air. Marty looked like a cross between Jerry Lewis and Dean Martin, but was all business. "I think I've got everything you need, Lee," he answered. "Plenty of smokes for ever'body!"

Marty Farmagano worked for, well, the Government. It was his day job to ensure that the fishing and merchant fleets got their fair share of tax-free cigarettes since the boats and ships were covered under the same blanket policy as the military. It was common knowledge around the waterfronts that you could make a few extra bucks selling off your smokes in a gray — not really black — market. Even seamen who didn't smoke took the cigarette cartons they were allotted — they could be traded, sold, or given away.

"Our boys in Montauk sailed yesterday," he reported. "Ever'one that I could find in the Point and Newport got some yesterday, too. They should get traded shortly, I mean … who's going to smoke Tareytons, Kools and Raleighs?"

"No Marlboros?"

"Just one carton per boat. I told ever'body that we were out and I had to ration them. Did you find a Point boat to watch?"

"Oh yeah, I certainly did," Chambers said. "They left last night."

"Headin' to the east'ard?"

"I'd bet my life on it."

"I didn't quite get what you said, Lee. Why is this called 'Operation Spice Trade'?"

Chambers rolled back in his chair, nearly upsetting the point of balance and almost toppling over. "Marty, this is such a beautiful story," he said sarcastically in a high tone. "Boy meets girl, boy falls in love, boy forgets that she's stuck on a …"

A knock on the door interrupted his narrative as a Navy seaman in a crisp white uniform burst in. "Chief Chambers, sir, the Pentagon is on the phone for you. Code three!"

Chambers motioned his arm in a dismissive back-handed swing, then picked up the receiver.

"Chambers here. I'm a busy man. Speak."

The receiver came alive. "Chief Chambers, this is Ensign Simons at the records archives at the Pentagon. Sir, we've identified the source of your request, but it wasn't easy and it leaves some unanswered questions. We've been up all night and ..."

"Spare me the sob story and give me something I can work with, Ensign."

"Well, we've made a positive ID on the serial number of the disarmed shell you airlifted down here. It was manufactured in Manitowoc, Wisconsin at the C.N. Grove Machine Shop."

"That's good, I guess. Got any idea when?"

"The records indicate that it was December of 1943. World War II."

"I know when the War was, so what? There's a million of those shells out there!"

"Here's where the trail got sticky, Chief. This is what took so long to verify ..."

"Look, I haven't got all day, Ensign. Spit it out!"

"Well, sir, these shells were never loaded with explosives. They never got to a munitions facility. They were sent along a lot of different rail routes until they reached Portland, Maine. We're not sure why but that made it real hard for us to track. Then they were loaded on an old freighter that the government conscripted. Now here's where it really gets weird ..."

Chambers thought for a second. "What was the name of the ship?"

"The ship? Let's see ... um ... oh ... here it is! It was the *Rowley Knight*, but ..."

"I know the ship. Are you absolutely positive, Ensign?"

"Like I said, we've been on this thing for about thirty hours straight. We're positive, Chief. Did you know that the ship sunk off of ... let's see ... Jeffreys Ledge. It never made it to Boston like it was supposed to. Probably got hit by a German torpedo. Subs were in that area then, according to our records. One body washed ashore on Plum Island. No survivors."

"You're positive that these shells weren't primed?"

"Chief, listen to me! The shells are now exploding off Nantucket Shoals but the ship sunk off of the Northern Coast of Massachusetts over thirty years ago. And! The shells never made it to the facility to be primed! Repeat, never primed!"

Chambers put the receiver down on his desk and leaned his head in his hands, lost in thought. The shouts of the ensign through the phone finally brought him back to the present. "Chief Chambers … are you still there? … Chief?"

"Right here, son," Chambers said as he put the receiver back to his ear. "What about the so-called Russian inscription? What's that all about?"

"Another mystery, I'm afraid, Chief. It's not Russian … it's Finnish. The word that is spelled y-h-d-y-s-v-a-l-l-a-t is actually 'United States' in Finnish, and i-s-a means father. Those guys are awful lucky. That shell was being towed along the bottom in that trawler's net, then it came ashore with them! I'll tell you, it's amazing that it looks brand new, too, all polished up and ready to go! What do you make …?"

The Navy Ensign was still talking but the shocked Chambers absentmindedly rolled ahead in his chair and hung up the phone.

"Problems, Lee?" Marty Farmagano asked.

Chambers rose and went to the window, gazing out through glazed eyes on Newport Harbor and Narragansett Bay beyond. "All I want to do is get through this last assignment, get the big promotion they promised me, then retire. I joined up when I was sixteen … lied about my age. Now I'm sixty-three. That's enough of this crap. I just have to get that sub out of Electric Boat in Groton without the iron curtain fleet finding it."

"So what's the big deal, Lee? You've seen plenty by now, haven't you? You're the best, by anyone's estimations," Marty countered. "That's why you always draw these assignments. At least that's what the brass at the Pentagon told me. You're the only guy that can make this work! The last time they tried this, the *Suzy and Anne* caught the sub in its net, remember? Talk about a compromised mission!"

Lee Chambers came back to the task at hand. He turned and faced Marty Farmagano with the look of a hunter with game in his sights. "As far as anyone's concerned, they're World War II shells, so that's not that uncommon," he said, squinting his eyes as he spoke. "Unfortunate, yes," he said, "but it happens, doesn't it? No need to put out the word and get everyone all upset and compromise the mission. That sub's gonna sail on schedule, and on the surface this time, where nobody's gonna expect it to be."

"I don't follow, Lee. What's the prob …?"

"Well, Marty," Chambers interrupted, raising his hand. "It might be nothing, or it might be the start of World War Three. It's already war ... the enemy is off our shores. And if it is a war, then collateral damage is unavoidable, isn't it? I can't blow the whistle, it'll kill the whole operation. Besides, the fishing fleet is our cover. We might sustain a few losses, but ..."

"Well, I don't know if we're at that stage yet, Lee, but if there's a problem, shouldn't we warn th' ..."

"Marty, have you ever heard of the *Mount Washington*?"

"Sure, ever'body's heard of Mount Washington. Worst weather in the world, so they say, but getting back to what I was just saying ..."

"Not the mountain, Marty, the excursion boat. It takes passengers around Lake Winnipesaukee in the summers. Heard of it?"

"Nope. Lake Winni-what? What in hell are you talkin' ...?"

"Winnipesaukee, Marty. Win-ni-pe-sau-kee. I wonder if our new skipper aboard the *Elizabeth Gale* has. What's his name again?"

"Ricky Helliott. He ran the watch for Buddy. Ever'body knows him as the Hellion around the Point."

Lee Chambers scratched his head and went into thought until his eyes were nothing more than lines drawn across a flesh colored beach ball. "Helliott. Helliott? I thought that name sounded familiar," he realized. "The *Rowley Knight* ... Helliott!" He turned away from the window and looked at Marty Farmagano. An unpleasant grin swept across his face as he attempted to fold his arms across his barrel-shaped physique. "This is beautiful!" he announced, leaning against the windowsill. "The spice trade! God, I love this job!"

F/V Elizabeth Gale
Point Judith, RI

18

NORTH OF VEATCH'S

LAT. 40 DEG. 15 MIN. N.
LONG. 69 DEG. 30 MIN. W.

About thirty miles south of the Nantucket Lightship, the continental shelf takes a deep plunge. The bottom slopes from fifty fathoms, to ninety, to over three hundred fathoms in a very short distance. Carved into the face of this sheer dropoff are gullies and canyons, reminders of ancient rivers that existed when the sea was three hundred feet lower at the end of the last ice age. One hundred miles southeast of Staten Island lies Hudson Canyon; south of Block Island lies Block Canyon; south of Nantucket is Atlantis Canyon and a little west of south of the Lightship is Veatch's Canyon. The lobsters that, two weeks earlier, marched past the Corner and the Lightship were headed there to winter-over in the deep shelf water inboard of the canyon. Mackeral made the journey to lay in the fifty fathom depths for the winter. Scup, butterfish, squid and fluke also headed to the outer reaches of the shelf on their late fall pilgrimage.

Ricky Helliott steamed past where they fished the previous trip, partly out of a feeling that he didn't want to retrace Buddy's last route, but mostly because his instincts told him that the storm that swept through the shoals would get things moving. Moving off. Moving south.

He steamed past the Corner, leaving the foreign fleets in his wake. He decided to set out below the southward edge of the outbound *Ambrose* to *Nantucket Lightship* traffic lane. From *Nantucket Lightship* it's a straight steam to the westward to reach *Ambrose Lightship* off New York harbor. To the southward of this imaginary line connecting the two lightships lies a parallel lane that creates a highway for the ship traffic outbound from New York to Europe. Conversely, to the northward lies the traffic lane for ships inbound from Europe to New York.

Some Point boats, a handful of Newport boats, some New Bedford boats and some Soviets were working around the shipping lanes, but the Lizgale went on. It wasn't long before she was back in her element, doing what she did best.

"We're here. Time to do it to it!" Ricky yelled from the wheelhouse as he blew the horn at four-thirty a.m. and flicked on the deck lights, illuminating the thick mist that enveloped them. As three shapes in yellow oilers gradually appeared on deck, Ricky pulled on his boots, took the engine out of gear and went down on deck, letting the Lizgale roll in the trough.

"First thing we're gonna do is swap the gear for the fine twine," Ricky announced. "I'm not gonna fight that big fleet if I can help it. Should be some butters and squid around here somewheres."

The crew went to work, bringing the spare net of smaller mesh size from the port rail to the working starboard rail with the boat's rigging and brute strength. Then they stowed the large mesh yellowtail net alongside the port rail. When the three-and-a-half inch mesh, four-panel Shuman box net was shackled onto the legs, Ricky gave his next orders:

"Okay, college boys, we gotta come up with a new system for workin' the deck," Ricky explained. "Mack, you and Oz hop on the hoister for this set-out, then next tow, Greg rotates in and Mack comes up here with me. After that, we keep switchin' until ever' one's run through all the jobs. To hell with tradition, dammit … if we're gonna run this rig four-handed, we all gotta know all the jobs."

Three yellow hoods nodded their groggy understanding.

"If we have to, we'll all take a turn in the galley and someone can spell Oz down in the engine room. We talked it over, and we think you guys can run the watch once in awhile, so I figure the best thing to do right now is just get the boat catchin' again, okay? I'm gonna stay in the clear ground here, out of the fleet, and hopefully, the butters and squid have come to us. If not, well, we'll cross that bridge when we come to it."

Ricky looked at Ozzie and Mackenzie. "We'll need a hunnerd-fifty of wire. I'm gonna work the edge a little bit." he said. They both nodded and all three moved forward to get the doors and gear overboard.

The set-out went smoothly and Ricky settled into his new/old routine in the wheelhouse. Buddy's hangbook was, of course, constantly referred to as he worked the Lizgale through the southeast swells that rolled on a twenty-knot breeze. The sounder clicked along, drawing out the bottom in a slowing descending line. When Ricky came back to relieve Mack after the breakfast mug-up, the VHF radio uttered the first sounds it had made in hours …

"*Aurora* callin' the Lizgale, you on, Ricky?"

"Standin' by, Boze," Ricky answered. "Where the hell are ya?"

"Aw Jeez, I gotta tell you guys, we were all real sorry to hear about Buddy. We're all sick about it. We couldn't get home, Ricky, they wouldn't let us leave! We're still on the cable patrol for AT&T, Cap! Lefty Miller was comin' out of Cape May to relieve us and he blew his reverse gear somewheres off the old tower inboard of Hudson Canyon. He had to get towed into Sandy Hook so here we are! Still!"

"I wondered why you guys didn't make it back to the Point. Where's here anyways?"

"Oh yeah … we're on the eastern cable right where it crosses the fifty fathom curve. Lots of boats here … mostly Japs workin' on squid and butters. Looks like they're doin' some business. Hey … did Lanny make out alright?"

"Yup … he's gonna be fine shortly. No insurance on the boat, but the bank gave him a ninety-day note on his house. Barry's puttin' in a rebuilt Vee-twelve, Swera's gettin' the hull fixed up. She's comin' along real nice. Hey … how'd you hear about Buddy?"

"Ray Fender's over to the west'ard of us here. He filled us in. Said he'd never seen the Point so jammed full of boats since the last hurricane. He said you guys got a little package, too!"

"Oh you know the score, Boze. That stuff's ever' where. Hey … how you guys fixed for grub and such? Need anythin'?"

"Naah, we're finestkind, Cap. The phone company's helicopter dropped off all kinds of things a couple of days ago. New fit-outs of clothes, books, magazines, tons of all top-shelf grub … we even got prime rib! Cigarettes left somethin' to be desired, though. They dropped us three cartons of Tareytons, one Raleighs and two of Kools. Like smokin' bag twine!"

"Yup, that's all we got too. I don't get it, but Marty said that was all he had."

"Okay old daaaag, I gotta let you go here … looks like one of these Jap rigs wants to play chicken with us. These guys are bahstidds! Gotta protect the cable, ya know! Bridget Bardot might be tryin' to get a call through from France!"

"Yeah, to me! Alright Boze, go get 'em! Lizgale standin' by."

Shortly after Mack had helped Greg with the breakfast dishes, he came back up to the wheelhouse carrying two coffee cups. He found Ricky with his eyes glued to the depth sounder. The sounder paper showed small clouds of sealife slowly settling to the bottom as the sunrise was trying to make its presence known through the mist and drizzle.

"If this is what I think it is, we're in for a decent tow of squid, Mack," Ricky said, never moving his gaze from the sounder. "Look at this bunch here," he explained, pointing at a dark 'haystack' that was being drawn on the sounder paper. "This one here could be ten thousand if they're big enough," he said, his red moustache dancing with animation. "Never know, of course, but I think we'll haul back in another fifteen minutes just to be sure. This stuff here," he continued, pointing at the paper, "looks like a good bunch, just settlin' down for the daylight hours. We might be right on the heap!"

Mack went forward, crawled down the foc'sle ladder and sat down at the table. Greg was reading a *National Fisherman* magazine and Ozzie was studying a book of quantum physics. He was so engrossed in the subject matter that only his ears were sticking out beyond the open covers.

"Ricky's got some promising stuff showing up on the sounder," Mack announced. "He said we were going to haul back in fifteen minutes."

Greg set the magazine down and furrowed his forehead. Ozzie was deep in thought, oblivious to the outside world.

"What's he think we're on?" Greg asked.

"Squid. The sounder's showing a nice bunch settling down for daylight."

"No Russian research ships showin' up, are there?"

"Naah. We're all alone." Mack went into a pensive moment, then asked, "Do you think I'll ever see her again?"

"Who?"

"You know who! Man, I wish I at least knew her name. Do you think I'm barking up the wrong tree here, or what?"

Greg laughed and shook his head. "Well, let's review our situation here. You're in love with a Russian girl on a factory ship from God knows where. She's probably head over heels for you, considering the fact that you gave her a smelly old hat with a shackle in it. That's the closest thing to an engagement ring you can get in Russia, ya know," he chided. "Nothing spells romance like a worn out hat soaked in scales and fishguts, let's face it," he joked. "Now," he continued, "in order for you two to get together, she'd either have to jump ship or we could probably wait for Communism to fall apart ... like that's just about to happen in this century, or the next, for that matter. I'm not sayin' it's not possible, but ..."

"I hate it when you beat around the bush," Mack interrupted, adding his own slice of sarcasm to the conversation. "Oz, am I going to get together with her or what?"

Ozzie looked up from his studying long enough to croon a few bars from one of Frank Sinatra's chestnuts:

"I did it myyyyyyyy ... wayyyyyyyy!" he sang to a chorus of Greg's laughter.

The three foc'sle mates shared in the laughter, but before Mack could speak, Ricky blew the horn for the haulback. "You guys are saved by the bell for now," he sputtered back, "but you'll see!"

Ozzie got up from the foc'sle table and put his arm around Mack in a brotherly gesture, then sang, in a doo-wop style, complete with finger snaps, "Why do fools fall in l-ove?"

~ ~ ~

"So how'd the trip go?" asked Chris. *Vaieta!* he calmed himself as his heart was pounding and his pulse was racing. *He's seen her ... he even fell for her!'* he thought. Normally reserved and low key, his patience was being strained by a lifetime of grieving and wondering and waiting.

Chris kept his cool and tried a simple question to keep the conversation flowing. "Squid?" he asked.

"Oh yeah," Greg answered. "We were buried in 'em by the first tow and there was no end in sight." Greg was surprised that Mack would offer that much information about his Russian romance. He showed his alarm and confusion as his eyes met Mackenzie's, but all he got back was a slight shrug. He decided that Mack must be using a smoke-'em-out strategy ...

"Remember what we got in the late afternoon tow of that trip, Greg?" Mack asked. "That was fun, huh?"

"Wicked."

~ ~ ~

The southeast swells and drizzle gave way to a bluster of northwest air and the seas had settled to a deep blue sprinkled by whitecaps under the bright, clear sky. Every hour and fifteen minutes, another haulback yielded another five thousand pounds of squid. Clean. No sorting. No junkfish, except for an ocassional skate and a few butterfish. One man on deck could just stand at the deck plates and run the irridescent 'tubes' down to the two men chopping and shoveling ice below. Buddy had the net rigged so that it would just barely skip across the bottom, not like the yellowtail net that had to work its way along the sand.

By mid-morning, there were twenty thousand pounds of iced-down squid riding in the Lizgale's hold, enough weight to make the boat slap off the chop like Goliath swatting a mosquito. After the sunrise tow was iced down, though, the horizon to the northward became alive. It looked like Manhattan was floating towards them on a giant raft.

Ricky was cursing and fuming when Mack brought him a coffee after the deck was cleared. "Take a look in the radar. You can kiss this trip good-bye! How in hell did they even know we were here, anyways?" he muttered in frustration.

Mack looked into the radar, gazed back at the horizon, then stared incredulously back at the screen. "There must be twenty boats headed our way!" he exclaimed. "I didn't think they were interested in cheap stuff like squid."

"It's protein and it weighs up, that's all they care about, Mack. As soon as they fill the hold they can go home, same as anyone else," he said with a dejected tone. "Dammit! It's my first trip as skipper. I knew it was goin' way too good! I knew it!"

He went back to the skipper's stateroom, then returned, slamming a pack of cigarettes against his hand. Opening the pack, he lit one up.

"I didn't know you smoked," Mack said, surprised.

Ricky slid the port window down, then blew a trail of smoke outside. "Can't quit all your vices, ya know, college boy. I came sober and already the trip's goin' to pieces. I quit for two years, but right now, even this thing ... whatever the hell it is ... tastes good. Dammit! Couldn't they have just given us a couple days? Would that be so much to ask?"

Ricky gripped the wheel and steered the boat to wind'ard along the fifty fathom edge, muttering his frustration, all the while watching the sounder intently as Mack scanned the horizon with the binoculars. When he had smoked the cigarette down to the butt, he dropped the starboard window. "Look at them bahstidds! They'll be all over us by noontime."

Ricky threw his cigarette out the window in contempt, but the wind caught the glowing ember and in a you-wouldn't-believe-it-unless-you-were-there-to-see-it moment he watched it fly around on the breeze, then get carried right around the wheelhouse and enter the portside window. He grabbed it out of the air, put it back in his mouth and continued to puff away. He turned to a drop-jawed Mack and muttered," I guess I won't be quittin' today. Pissah! My first trip!"

It was only ten o'clock when the first of the foreign fleet steamed into the area. By noon, there were nineteen Soviet vessels working the same piece of shelf as the Lizgale. By two in the afternoon, the Soviets had realized what the stocks of squid would amount to and began a unified push to eliminate their one and only competitor. The vessels fanned out over the entire area, moving along the continental shelf in one big flotilla, effectively claiming the ground by towing their gear in a rail-to-rail formation, spread out across forty-five to fifty-five fathoms. The Lizgale was out-classed and out numbered and was, by late afternoon, pushed to the westward, out of the good fishing.

"Lizgale callin' the *Aurora*, you on, Boze?"

"Whatd'ya say, old daaag?"

"How's the Japs doin' down your way, Cap?"

"Oh, they're doin' great. Most of our guys that tried to set in with 'em have gone off to easier workin', though. They pushed ever'one out but us. They'd have towed up the phone cable long ago if it wasn't for us bein' here. Wicked!"

"Yeah, I gotcha, Boze. Same thing here, only with the Russkies. They got alongside of each other and there was nowhere to go but to the west'ard. I'm just wonderin' if we should keep comin' that way, that's all."

"Negatorry, Ricky. You're better off there than comin' over here. These guys have hammered this place for a few days now. At least where you are you might get a little gravy before the bones are picked clean."

"Roger that. I guess I know what my next move is …"

"Good luck, Cap! We'll be here if you need us."

Ricky pulled down the visor of his hat, lit a cigarette, then swung the Lizgale around to starboard and towed back towards the oncoming Soviet fleet. Before long, the squid began to show again on the sounder paper. When he was a half-mile away from the iron curtain boats, they curiously all turned and went back to the eastward, too, staying in the same formation that they had been using. Ricky watched them through the binoculars and was puzzled at his next view. *Seagulls … Seagulls? … Seagulls? They never have gulls around them,* he thought to himself. "They don't ever throw anything overboard … what could they be doing?" he muttered.

Ozzie, Greg and Mack were sitting around the foc'sle table, still wearing their boots and oilpants. There was no time, or need, to remove them and get comfortable between haulbacks. They looked at each other as they felt the boat swing around and tow to leeward again. It wasn't long before Ricky blew the horn to haul back.

As they strained at the rail to strap the twine for lifting the codend aboard, Greg and Mack noticed that something about the net wasn't right. It felt heavy and sluggish and bubbles were beginning to rise next to the boat. Mack and Greg had the same frightful thought at the same time and began to hurriedly make way for the turtleback as they alerted Ricky and Ozzie.

"There's something in there!" Greg yelled. "It's not floating up and now there's some bubbles!"

"This don't look good!" Mack chorused in as he ran back aft.

"Ease it up real slow, Oz," Ricky ordered through the starboard wheelhouse window. "Get it up so's we can see what's in there, but don't bring it over the rail! We'll cut it loose if we have to!"

Ozzie did as ordered and cautiously brought the bag to the surface. Ricky scrambled down the wheelhouse steps then cautiously crept up the deck and peered over the rail as the Lizgale rolled in the trough. He looked, took a double take, looked again. He turned around and raised his clenched fist towards the receeding Soviet fleet, his face contorted in anger. "You sunuvabitchin' bahstidds!" he bellowed at the top of his lungs. "You red commie bahstidds!" The frustrated skipper turned towards his own crew, yelling, "Take it aboard! Oldest trick in the book! Take it up and clean it out! He cursed, muttered and kicked in seething anger.

The startled crew did as ordered, although they were wary of the net's unknown contents. When the bag cleared the rail and came swinging aboard, however, everyone onboard knew what the "oldest trick in the book" was. Mack very gingerly tripped the bag open, then ran for cover as the contents oozed out and spread over the deck like a scene from a B-grade Japanese horror movie. The stench of rotting garbage, galley tailings and trash filled the air as bottles and cans clanked and smashed against the deck checkers. Oily rags were seemingly embroidered into the cod-end twine by the net being towed across the bottom. Soaked cardboard boxes with Russian writing on them formed a paper mache', with potato peelings and egg shells as decoration. Every Soviet ship, catcher boat and even the oceangoing service tug had dumped its trash right in the path of the oncoming Lizgale before they swung off to the eastward.

Ricky Helliott was beside himself. He had both hands in the air and was cursing and swearing in tirades. "I told you guys it was bad luck! Damn college knot-heads! Jonahs!" He looked up at Greg and his eyebrows fused themselves together in rage. Ricky ran up to Greg and snatched the new Caterpillar Diesel hat off his head. "A yellow hat! Don't you know a yellow hat is bad luck?" he screamed as he frisbee'd the hat overboard and watched it float away.

After a few more epithets, the skipper calmed down enough to issue some coherent orders. "Clean this deck up and soak the codend in some bilge cleaner in the lobstertank. It looks like there's a few bushels of squid in there, but you'd better throw 'em over, too." He sat down on the hatch cover and regained himself. "Let's see if we can get workwise again while I figure out our next move. I'm gonna go look through Buddy's old logs to see if there's somethin' we can do around here, but God knows what's left after them bahstidds get through with killin' another piece of ground!"

Ricky went up the steps of the wheelhouse and closed the door behind him with a resounding bang! Greg, Ozzie and Mack looked at each other and exchanged raised-eyebrow glances. "MMMmmmmann I ... is ... is ... h ... h ... he ... ug ... ug ... ugl ... ugly!" Ozzie stammered out as he shook his head.

"That was my brand new hat!" Greg groused angrily. "What the hell was that all about? We didn't cause any of this!"

"Ahhh, just let it go," Mack said. "I don't know what to think, but I've got another hat you can borrow. It's blue and white, from Cummins engines ... that should be okay. I guess I'll go down below and get some bilge cleaner and some Joy detergent. At least we can just open the scuppers and run this crap overboard. It won't be that bad, do you think, Oz?"

Ozzie's reply was a head-shake "no."

Mack came back on deck with some bilge cleaner, some Joy, and a couple of brushes. He turned on the water valve to fill the lobstertank, then tossed Greg the new hat. Greg, Mack and Ozzie started pushing the deckload overboard with shovels when Mack suddenly came to a realization ...

"Wait! We can't throw this over! Wait a minute!" he screamed. "This is it! It's staring us right in the face!" he yelled as he pointed to the disgusting mess on deck. "This is our ticket into the Soviet fleet!"

"What in hell are you talkin' about?" Greg asked as he leaned on the shovel handle. "I think these toxic fumes gave you brain damage."

"Greg, remember when we took Sociology 202? Remember?"

"Yeah, I remember that every Monday, Wednesday and Friday from twelve-thirty to one forty-five I took a nap. So what?"

"C'mon, man!" Mack exclaimed, his hands shaking, palms up. "You don't remember the field trip? The field trip to the suburbs of Corvallis? The dumpsters? Tell me you don't remember that!"

Ozzie put down his shovel and grabbed hold of Mack's sleeve questioningly.

"Here's the deal, Oz. We were sent to pick through people's trash. Garbage cans, dumpsters, landfills. You name it, we picked through it." Mack began.

"Yup," Greg chimed in. "That's right. That was the only thing that made sense to me about the whole course. It grossed me out, but it was good training for digging bait out of the bottom of bait barrels, though!"

"Oz, the point is, you can learn a lot about people when you see what's in their trash," Mack continued. "Go to a house with trash cans filled with whiskey bottles and macaroni and cheese boxes and you get some idea for how they live. Another house might have a lot of fresh vegetable peelings, junkmail from some upscale catalogs and expensive wine bottles and you've got a window into their lives, got it?"

Ozzie's face brightened up with a huge grin as he nodded his head in excited enlightenment.

"Okay. So we keep a mental note of what the Russkies have and don't have as we shovel this crap overboard, then what?" Greg asked.

Mack picked up his shovel and dug it into the deckpile. "We go trade them something that we have, that they don't have, for something they have, that we don't have," he yelled over the sound of the clacking seagulls attracted by the garbage. "Simple!"

Ozzie stopped shoveling, put his hands on his hips, then listened for Greg to ask the next obvious question:

"What do they have that we need?"

Mack looked up and smugly replied, "Our trip of squid."

"I dunno boys," Ricky answered as he stroked his moustache. He looked up from reading one of Buddy's old log books and sat up in his bunk. "What in hell would we trade 'em, anyways?"

"Cigarettes is always a good start. We've got carton upon carton that'll never get smoked in a million years. I gave my last month's allottment away and we've still probably got twenty-five brand new cartons on board here," Mack explained. "I got a spankin' new pair of Levis in my seabag," he continued. "That's like gold to them, but if we keep catching like we were, that's nothing to replace when we get home."

"They don't have anything in their trash like empty maple syrup bottles, or apple cores, or empty spice containers, or even an old Bic pen," Greg offered. "No kleenex's, no toilet paper rolls ..."

"N ... n ... no ... no ... Ru ... RRRR ... Russian d ... d ... dr ... dr ... dres ... dressss ... ing!" Ozzie added.

When the laughter died down, Ricky's tone became serious again. "It doesn't make much sense to try to go anywhere else now. We can only go a day, night and a day with these things onboard anyways. I guess it's either try to stay here for another day or go unload this stuff now. What makes you think you can talk to them?"

"I've thought a lot about what that Coast Guard guy said. I'll bet you they've got people on those boats that speak better English than we do. It wouldn't surprise me that they were listening in on every radio conversation on every channel," Mack said.

Ricky laid back down in his bunk and thought for a couple of minutes. With his eyes closed, he lowered his voice and asked, "Would you have a particular vessel in mind that you'd like to contact?"

Mack smiled and clenched his fist in a sign of victory. "I thought you'd never ask ..."

19

ON THE HEAP

LAT. 40 DEG.15 MIN. N.
LONG. 69 DEG. 30 MIN. W.

"Look, I'm willin' to go along with this knot-headed educated idjut plan, but I'm gonna draw the line at that!"

"C'mon, Cap, they'll know we're really serious if we give it to them."

"Nope. Not no way, not no how!"

"It … it … it'llll sh … sho … show 'em wha … what … a g … g … gr … great coun … tttt … try we've g … g … got."

"I don't care! That's Barbi Benton in that centerfold and I ain't givin' her up for nothin'!"

"C'mon, skipper. We've got the makings of a nice little trip, and you yourself said we're better off trying to finish up right here. I promise you I'll replace it when we get ashore. Really."

Ricky Helliott lit a cigarette and exhaled smoke out the side of his pursed lips as he reluctantly mulled over his latest dilemma. "You guys are killin' me … Promise?"

"Yup. Scout's honor. You can make it a day or two without her, can't you?"

The skipper opened the venerable magazine and turned it sideways, then let the full length of the centerfold drop open. He took one long, winsome look, took a deep puff on his cigarette, then pointed to the photo in his view as he exclaimed, "Barbi, please forgive me. It's up to you to show them damned Russkies what America's really made of!" He handed the magazine to Greg with his final instructions, "Put her where she can't get hurt when you throw her over there, okay? Handle with care ... that's a national treasure you're trading away!"

"Will-do, skipper," Greg jibed as he issued a fake salute.

Ricky took a deep breath then grabbed the wheel. "Alright, let's get this show on the road," he ordered. He put the Lizgale in gear and started jogging ahead for the largest ship in the Soviet fleet. "Just so we're all on the same page, boys, I'm gonna head for the mothership. Half of these guys in the smaller rigs are just catchers, so we should set our sights on the command post. Mack, if there's a six-ten on that ship, great, but if not, we've still got a job to do, roger that?"

"I understand, Ricky."

"Okay. Now here's the way I see it. Boze said the Japs have got that bunch of squid down to the west'ard all sewed up. Besides us, I don't think there's gonna be anythin' for squid goin' across any dock sometime soon, so we should be lookin' at a good price for this stuff. Now ... if, and I mean if ... they let us set in with 'em, I say we finish this short trip, steam for the Vineyard, unload there, gather up some more trinkets, then head right back here for another day-night-day trip. If that works, then we'll head to the Point with that load. By the time we could turn around and get back here again after that, they'll have this place beat to a pulp anyways, so we'll make a new plan at the Point. Roger?"

Three heads nodded "yes".

"O.K. Get to it. Whatever you guys think should be bundled up along with Barbi, go to it. We'll be over there in about twenty-five minutes. Oh ... and one more thing ..."

"What's that, Cap?"

"Keep the 'Boros and don't give 'em all the cigarettes. We might need to bribe 'em again before we're out of there. If this plan doesn't work, I'm gonna be back to skipperin' the dory over the bar at the 'Tune'."

The three shipmates went to the foc'sle and began gathering things up. They made four bundles, each at a comfortable size and weight for heaving to the top rail of the ship. Each bundle held four cartons of cigarettes and some assorted goodies such as Mack's new Levi's, a package of Bic pens, maple syrup, Russian salad dressing, cinnamon, powdered sugar, cans of coke, bags of Hershey's Kisses, fresh apples and oranges, and a few magazines, including Ricky's donation. Mack wrote a very simple note and taped it to the top of each bag-twine secured bundle: "Trade for a clear LORAN Line." When Greg and Ozzie weren't looking, he added a note of his own to the last package, addressed to "the girl with the OSU hat." When the fourth bundle was receiving its finishing touches of duct tape, Ricky blew the horn.

The crew scrambled up the ladder, carrying their packages like Joe Namath on a fake lateral. They rounded the doghouse and stopped in awe. All around them were iron curtain catcher boats, each about one-hundred-fifty feet long. Curious Soviet deckhands watched in wide-eyed amazement as the Lizgale slowly crept past them towards the largest and most central vessel of the fleet. Greg and Ozzie looked ahead to pick the best vantage point for the toss-over, but Mack's gaze was frozen on the name of the oncoming bow: "610 *Zvezda Rybaka* … It's her! It's her!"

Ricky passed by the ship, then made a turn to starboard and came around to keep in step with the forward movement of the ship as it towed its own gear. He slowly eased the Lizgale's starboard side up to the port side of the ship as the rails above became thronged with Russian crewmembers smiling, jabbering and waving. Ricky leaned out the starboard window and yelled, "Go ahead! Toss that stuff up there!"

Greg, Ozzie and Mack each picked out a willing set of arms and tossed the packages above. Three down, one to go. Mack took the fourth, special package and ran back and forth, looking again like Joe Namath, only this time trying to avoid a fourth-down sack. He desperately looked for the object of his affection to appear at the rail. "C'mon, where is she?" he asked himself. "C'mon! … she's got to be there!"

"Throw the damned thing!" Ricky bellowed from the wheelhouse. "Throw it, you stupid college idjut!" But quarterback Mack continued to let the clock run as he looked upward. "Throw it!" Ricky shrieked. "Damned book-brained nitwit!"

"Where are you?" Mack yelled. "Where are you?" he screamed at the straining point of his voice. "OSU girl!" He ran back to the stairs at the starboard side of the wheelhouse to get a better view, and just as he cocked his arm to fire in hopeless adrenaline-fueled fury he heard the words he had been praying for:

"*Amerikkalainen Kapteeni! Amerikkalainen Kapteeni! Tassa! Tassa! Kapteeni!*"

She was at the far end of the quarter rail, jumping up and down over the crowd to get a glimpse of her 'American Captain.' It was her! Even at that distance, her blue eyes glistened with radiant azure excitement. As she waved her arms, the breeze caught her long, light brown hair which sent her curls and waves bouncing alluringly over her shoulders. She forced herself between two people to get to the rail, reached inside her blouse, then threw something directly at Mack. He reached out and with one hand, caught her offering from the wavering breeze as the other arm fired his package with all his might. It went up … up … over her head. She strained as she jumped to catch it, but it was too high. It went to the tallest man there who thrust out his left hand and knocked it down, much like a wide receiver bringing down a ten-second-to-go touchdown pass. He laughed a robust laugh through his gray chinstrap beard, then handed it to her.

Ricky pulled off about a hundred yards, then jogged along on a parallel course, waiting for an answer from the Soviet skipper. As he watched through the binoculars, he noticed that the officer with the gray beard went forward carrying all the packages except for the one that Mack's girl had. When a couple more minutes had passed, another officer came along and herded everyone off the deck, presumably back to their shipboard jobs. The ship towed along for another ten minutes before there was any sign of life, then the officer with the gray beard came out to the rail and waved his arms for them to come over. Ricky called everyone into the wheelhouse with him as he brought the Lizgale alongside.

"Not that I don't trust these guys, boys, but I don't trust these guys, get me?" Ricky said firmly. "Let's all stay here. I'll do the talkin' if we need to."

Ricky maneuvered the Lizgale to a loping course alongside the *Zvezda Rybaka*. He handed the wheel to Ozzie, then cautiously stepped out onto the starboard wheelhouse steps. He looked up at the Russian officer and put his hands out, palms up, giving the best body language he could to ask the question, "what gives?" The gray bearded man leaned over the rail and threw a potato directly into Ricky's outstretched arms, then motioned in no uncertain terms for him to pull the Lizgale away ... now!

"Get us outta here, Oz!" Ricky ordered as Ozzie cranked the wheel to port and pushed up the throttle. When they were a safe distance off, Ricky slammed the potato down on the helm in a rage, splattering its juices on the compass and wheelspokes. "Any more bright ideas, college nitwits? Huh? Any more brilliant plans?" he blasted.

"Wh ... wh ... wait a m ... m ... min ... minute!" Ozzie realized. "L ... I ... llo ... look!"

Everyone looked at the smashed potato. Inside was a rolled-up piece of paper taped to a stub of a pencil covered in plastic. Greg grabbed the pencil stub and carefully unwound the plastic and tape from it, then handed the scrap of paper to Ricky. On it was a message from the Soviet skipper:

5835 — 3700 — 3780
bolshoe spasibo [Thank you very much.]

Ricky cocked his hat on the back of his head and stared at the paper while his three crewmen stared at him impatiently. "What's it say?" Mack asked. Ricky handed the paper to him as he shook his head in disbelief. Mack gazed down, then clapped his hands together. "It says we can work the fifty-eight-thirty five line from thirty-seven-hundred to thirty-seven-eighty! They gave us a clear line right through the middle of the best fishing! We did it! We did it!"

In amongst the Soviet fleet the Lizgale looked like a hummingbird among vultures, but the other skippers left the 5835 line alone for her. One-and-a-half hours later, the American crew was dumping another tow of squid on the deck. Six thousand pounds of the tube-like creatures slithered out of the codend, making the deckload glow in irridescent, undulating, pink/purple colors. One particular color, however, showed out of place when the crew began to send the squid below to the hold.

As Greg worked the deck plates above while Ozzie and Mack shoveled ice below, he noticed something quite different showing up in the deckpile. A shiver of fear ran up his spine as he cautiously inched closer to the foreign object, but once he got a good glimpse, he suddenly started laughing and pointing back at the wheelhouse. Greg reached down, pushed some squid out of the way, then fished the yellow object out of the pile.

"Hey!" he yelled back aft to Ricky. "Hey you guys!" he screamed down into the hold. "Look at this!"

Greg went over to the deckhose and lightly washed off the yellow object. Next, he removed the new hat Mack gave him and tossed it down the doghouse to safety. He then triumphantly thrust the yellow object, his sea-soaked yellow 'Caterpillar" hat on his head. Scales, water, mud and squid ink ran off the hat, dripping on his moustache and running down his shoulders but he didn't care; he was wearing a big ear-to-ear grin.

"Hey Cap!" he yelled to the wheelhouse. "Whatd'ya think of my bad luck hat now?"

Ozzie and Mack scurried up the hold ladder to see what the commotion was on deck. Just as they both cleared the hatch, Ricky put the wheel in the becket to keep the boat on course, then came down on deck to confront Greg. The skipper plowed his way through the deckpile and walked up to Greg until they were face to face. Ricky scowled at him for a few seconds, then removed his own hat and snatched the Cat hat from Greg's head. He stared Greg down again in mock anger as the skipper himself donned the yellow hat and stuffed his own on Greg's head.

"You can't have this hat, Greg … it's mine!" Ricky barked.

"Yours? But you said it was …"

"Never mind what I said … it's my hat now. You can't have it … it's good luck!"

Twenty-four hours later, the Lizgale left the Soviet fleet, steamed past Muskeget Can buoy, headed through Muskeget Channel, swept safely around Cape Poge, then tied up at Steve Bogeau's packing house in Vineyard Haven Harbor at 3:30 A.M. On board were forty-eight thousand pounds of squid, five hundred pounds of assorted fish and … four jubilant Point Judith fishermen. At 6:00 A.M., unloading began. By noontime they were all packed out; by 1:30 P.M., they were loaded with ice and fuel. Ricky came down the foc'sle ladder with the final tallies of the trip and handed it to Ozzie.

"You're our math whiz," he said. "What's a rough guess-timate of the take?" he asked as he sat down at the table and pulled his yellow hat low.

Ozzie looked over the figures, calculated in his head, then looked up with a broad smile on his moon-pie face.

"I ... I ... s ... s ... say cl ... clo ... close ... t ... t ... t ... to ... Oh ... ov ... over ... o ... ov ... over t ... t ... tw ... twe ... twel ... twelve ... h ... hun ... hun ... hunnerd ... a p ... p ... p ... piece!"

"Yup, that's what I thought, too," the skipper said proudly. "Not bad for a two day trip, huh, college boys? I learned a few things in college, too, ya know."

Mack and Greg were stunned. They'd heard of trips like this, and heaven knows they were making good money right along, but this was like something out of a dream. Before they could speak, Ricky threw two hundred dollars on the galley table.

"I called a taxi for you guys when I was up in Steve's office gettin' the settlement sheet. While I go over the net and fix a few crow's feet, I want you guys to head into town and get whatever you think we need so's we can go back out there and buy our way back into the fleet again. It worked once ... let's see if we can do it again."

"Aye, skipper," Greg joked. "Muskets and firewater for trading, it is!"

"I never heard you say, Cap. What college did you go to?" Mack asked, puzzled.

Ricky nodded then shook his head, faking his disgust. "If you two eggheads ain't a pair. My father said his Dad called it the school of H-N."

"H-N?"

"Yup ... Hard Knocks!"

"Message received and understood," Mack said, laughing. "Coming to town with us, Oz?"

"R ... r ... roy ... royt!"

"Where to, boys?" the taxi driver asked.

"A liquor store that has coloring books, crayons, magazines, dungarees, and oh ... I almost forgot ... potting soil," Mack answered.

20

SID 'N' EVA'S CHAIR

Lat. 43 deg. 45.3 min. N.
Long. 69 deg. 37.1 min. W.

"Wow. Look at the time ... my God, it's after midnight!" Mack exclaimed through a wide, protracted yawn. "I'm going to have to continue this some other time, Old Scout. You understand, don't you?"

"Yeah, me too," Greg agreed. "Mornin' comes quick around here." He gave Mackenzie a long look, then left the mess hall and headed for his room. "You'd better catch a kink, too, Slimey," he yelled over his shoulder. "I'll see you in the a-m."

Chris was drained and frustrated. He was careening from the top of the emotional roller coaster to the plunge at the bottom, and having a hard time holding on. He was tired, and angry too. The obvious physical fatigue of a long day was compounded by a lifetime of unanswered questions. The two people he'd spent the last few weeks with had definitely seen his sister aboard the *Zvezda Rybaka* twenty years ago. As Jim Mackenzie walked towards the door, Chris realized he had nothing to lose by asking, "That girl ... the one you kept seeing on the rail of the *Zvezda Rybaka*. Did you ever see her again?"

Mack stopped short, keeping his back to Chris. "Why?"

Chris swallowed hard, then blurted, "That was my sister, Mari! I was the little boy on the swingset, Mack. That was me you saw out there! I remember when she gave me one of the coloring books and crayons! They told me she jumped overboard and committed suicide, but I never believed it. Did you ever see her again? I mean, she could have been rescued by someone! Did you?"

Jim Mackenzie's blood turned to ice. His worst nightmare had been sitting across the table from him. Hell, that was nothing ... he'd been with him all summer! There was no way that he could be her brother ... they looked for him for many long, anguished weeks. Months of searching without even a single trace. No records anywhere ... no witnesses, no family members left alive, no farm left in Ladoga Karelia in Russia ... no lost brother. Period.

She said they'd come for her, Mack reminded himself. *She said they'd never give up!*

"Well, we went back, traded some more stuff, got another nice trip out of there, and that was about it," he answered. "Nope. Never saw her or the ship she was on again. Sorry."

"You said she threw something to you. What was that?"

"That was a long time ago now, Chris. The whole thing was silly, now that I think about it. Crazy. I was just some stupid lovesick kid, that's all. It was a note with some writing that I couldn't understand anyway. I never hung on to it. There were lots of those ships out there and we weren't the only ones who had contact with them. Maybe you're mistaken ..."

Chris took a deep breath. "Yeah, you're probably right," he said more calmly. "Thanks for the info, Mack. I'll see you tomorrow," he said, sounding sincere and appreciative.

"Have a good night, Old Scout."

Chris heard the door of the station close behind Jim Mackenzie. He pounded his fist on the table in frustration. "He knows a lot more than what he's let on, I'm sure of it! Easy, Kristiian. You still have to find out the truth. *Vaieta!*"

It was almost twelve-thirty when Jim Mackenzie tied his peapod up to the float and jumped over the rail of the *Elizabeth Gale*. "Man, what a night," he said to himself, "and the nightmare is only just beginning. What am I going to do?"

He went below and sat in the main salon, a spacious, beautifully varnished 'room' that had once been the fish hold. He exhaled heavily then lay back in his easy chair and looked at the moon glimmering through the skylight above his head. Startled, he became reminded of something and jumped up in panic. "Oh my God, she'd kill me if I forgot!" he said aloud.

Mack dashed to the galley, drew a pitcher of fresh water from the sink then returned and pulled a chair over to the skylight. The green leaves of the vine curled back and forth around the molding of the skylight making a soothing rain forest effect within the confines of his home-boat. Tucked among the leaves were small, star-like flowers in full bloom, showing in suspended pink clusters. Delicate, fragrant flowers, that even though they were living, resembled flowers finely crafted of porcelain.

He finished watering the plant then went to a bookcase and retrieved an old copy of the *Coast Pilot*. Inside, was a tattered note carefully hand printed, as if each letter was selected individually:

To *AMERIKKALAINEN KAPTEENI*
MY MOTHER'S PLANT — FOR FREEDOM.

He sat down again and put his head in his hands. "What the hell am I going to do?" he muttered in anguish. "They came back for her — and after all these years."

Chris Brown watched from the tower until the glow of the lights shining through the skylight of the *Elizabeth Gale* grew dark. As he pondered his situation, he continued to fix his gaze on the darkened vessel at the north end of the harbor.

"All right, let's calm down," he whispered to himself. "You're not going to accomplish anything if you can't think straight. I don't get it … what difference would it make to him if I was her brother or not? Why would he just shut off? What's he trying to hide? Well … I'll be here a couple more weeks, so if I can play it cool, maybe things will work out. And … what about Greg? He was there, too! Maybe I can get something out of him … he's always been more open than Mack. C'mon, Chris … don't blow it now. This is the closest you've ever been. Stay cool, man! He's got the answers, but after all the stories of explosives, could she possibly still be alive? … What did Chambers do to those guys? … I still didn't get the whole story on that, either."

Chris sat up in the tower working out different strategies until nearly two A.M., when he finally went to his room. He tried sleeping, but all that did was remind him more of Mari, so he got dressed again, took a couple of blankets and hiked across the island to the rock outcropping that the cats, Ezekial and Rogers had showed him.

After crossing the top ridge of the island, it took a few minutes to find the trail down along the cliffside in the dark. Thankfully, the moon was reflecting off the waters on the west side of the island and he managed to reach Sid' n' Eva's chair safely. The sounds of the surf washing over the rocks below had a calming effect in the slighty chilled night air. He stetched out, then covered himself over with the blankets. Just as he finally got his emotions under control, the two feline islanders hopped down the trail and curled up with him, one under each arm. He was dead tired, wide awake, running on nerve and falling on fatigue, but right there, in Sid' n' Eva's chair, the world seemed to stop long enough for him to catch his breath. As he relaxed and watched the clouds drift by the moon to the gentle cadence of the waves below, he began to organize his thoughts:

You're forgetting that you were there, too, Kristiian, he reminded himself. *Think ... think! Jim and Greg just gave you a lot of background information. Try to remember what happened ... it will probably make more sense now. Try to remember the packages they traded ... try!*

The keen mind of the world-hardened scholar Chris Brown stopped short when his memory settled on a terrifying recollection. The *Matros Rulevoi*! The helmsman who worked under the third mate! What was his name? Peter ... Peter? No, wait! Petrovich Kochen!

As Chris racked his brain trying to make sense out of the disjointed memories of a frightened five-year old, he scarcely noticed when the two cats heard a rustling in the bushes on the high ground above and left to investigate. Recognizing the visitors, they rubbed their bodies against their legs, then went back to the comfort of the rock-hewn chair and settled in with its conflicted inhabitant.

"Those stupid cats could screw up a free lunch," Mack whispered to Greg. "What am I going to do with him? Who is he?" he asked.

"I dunno, Cap," Greg whispered back as he crouched in the bushes alongside his old shipmate. "What would they do in the school of H-N?"

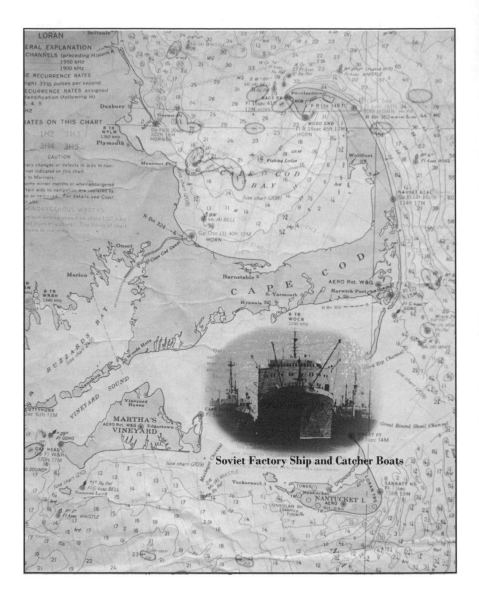

Soviet Factory Ship and Catcher Boats

21
ABOARD THE *ZVEZDA RYBAKA*

LAT. 43 DEG. 45.3 MIN. N.
LONG. 69 DEG. 37.1 MIN. W.

LAT. 40 DEG. 15 MIN. N.
LONG. 69 DEG. 30 MIN. W.

"*K*apteeni* came again! He brought more things. He brought something for you, too!"

"For me? But Mari, what could he give to me?"

"Look, Kristiian, look! Coloring books and crayons! Oh, and see this happy green frog puppet. What is a Kermit? Shhhhh … We must look!"

Kristiian grew to love the times that the *Amerikkalainen Kapteeni* came alongside. It was the only time that his sister glowed with her rare spirit of inner beauty. She used to exude her infectious personality and love of life every waking moment, but that was before they witnessed their parents' murder. These days, stuck on the factory ship, just to see her smile was an extraordinary occurrence.

Mari cautioned Kristiian to be quiet as she closed the privacy curtain to their bunk. "Over here," she whispered as she felt around under the mattress. "Shhh! Not a word! *Vaieta!*"

"Mari!" Kristiian blurted out when he saw what was happening. Admonished by her silent glare, he whispered back, "A book from the library! They will punish us if they find out!"

"Do not worry, little brother. The librarian will not tell. I gave her the *Amerikkalainen* cigarettes! You don't need them to smoke, do you?" she asked jokingly.

The saucer-eyed five-year old answered with a forceful shake of his head.

"Come here," she said as she sat on the bunk. "You hold the paper and I will find the words. Don't be afraid," she soothed.

Kristiian snuggled into her lap and unfolded the American *Kapteeni*'s note as she put her arms around him. Mari held the English-Russian dictionary out for the both of them to see, then began deciphering the message.

"It says here … 'hello' … that's a good start. Then these words say … 'pretty lady'." She began by translating the English words to Russian with the dictionary, then spoke the words in Finnish to her brother. "He says here that he missed me … that's nice … Here he says he wants to know when we will be in port so he can come to Russia to take me to America."

"You wouldn't leave me, would you, Mari?"

"No, Kristiian, I won't leave you. Don't worry. If there is a way to get to America, we'll both go. The Soviets took our farm and our freedom, but they won't separate us."

"What else does the *kapteeni* say?"

"He graduated from university in Oregon."

"Where?"

"It's a place in America. *Katsella!* Look here! He has mother's *kasvi* in a pot with nice soil. I gave him a sprig of her freedom plant, you know."

"What does this say, Mari?"

The *sovtuvene* he is on is from Point Judith, Rhode Island. That's another place in America, not too far from here, about ninety kilometers. We are so close to *Yhdysvallat*. Can you believe it?"

"Will *kapteeni* take us to America?"

Before she could answer, the shipboard P.A. system announced the change of the watch. It was time for her to become what the Russians call an *ofitsiantki*, a galley waitress and chambermaid. As she changed into her uniform, she gave some last minute instructions:

"*Vaieta*, little brother. No more talk of America, please! Stay here, be quiet and play with your new coloring book. You'll show me a work of art when I return. Maybe you can make a nice picture for the *kapteeni* and we'll pass it to him when he comes back again."

"When is he coming back, Mari?"

"I don't know when, but I know he'll return, perhaps to *pelastaa* us. I know in my heart that he will find us again. He has a piece of mother's *kasvi* now ... at least one dream of America will come true for her. He is a good *ihminen*."

"I *rakastaa* you Mari."

"I *rakastaa* you, too, Kristiian. Be brave. We'll get to America someday. The first thing we'll do is *suudella* the ground!"

She hurriedly shoved the note into the dictionary and thrust the book under the mattress. "*Kapteeni* will come, you'll see."

The companionways became crowded at the change of the watch. Filletting line workers, bridge and deck officers and their crews, engineering and mechanical crews, galley workers and ancillary staff such as the *sportsmenska* and the librarian all exchanged their watch with the fresh people coming on. Despite the ruthless stereotype of Soviets, their distant-water crews were very well-staffed and cared for. There were no round-the-clock marathons with a short-handed gang, common to the American fleet. Safety was a main consideration. Fatigue and its associated safety implications were well planned for, as such, the well-manned watches were only for eight hours duration, with eight hours off. This compromise, however, was tempered with the fact that the trip length for the ninety-three crew members was five full months. To a five-year old living on the edge of confused terror, it meant long hours left alone in his bunk wondering when his sister would return.

This was the watch that Mari hated the most; the times she had to serve as chambermaid to some of the lower officers' quarters. It wasn't the work that was taxing, it was the fact that she would have to enter the helmsman's quarters, in particular, Petrovich Kochen's room. Petrovich Kochen resembled Josef Stalin in his younger years. He was, by most accounts, a handsome figure with his dark hair, eyes, moustache and muscular build, and indeed, many of the female crewmembers found him very attractive until his romantic intentions quickly turned to terror. He was sent to sea by his father, a high-ranking Kremlin official, to obtain some real-life experience away from his privileged upbringing in Moscow. Onboard the *Zvezda Rybaka*, he was the leader of the ship's *Komsomol*, the Young Communist League, in addition to his helmsman's duties. Petrovich Kochen, like the man whose looks he resembled, was not accustomed to being refused anything that he wanted … ever. He used his party connections to his benefit whenever and wherever he saw fit, much to the frustration of the professional sea folk he was shipping with.

Mari reached the companionway where *Matros Rulevoi* Kochen bunked. She had her arms full of cleaning supplies as she made her way along, bracing herself against the slight roll of the ship. When she reached his cabin, she took a deep breath, mentally readied herself, then knocked on the door. No answer. She knocked again … Silence. What could this *sika-aivot* be up to now? she wondered. One last knock … nothing. She tried the door and entered, then breathed a sigh of relief. Could it be that she could just clean his room without his constant, overbearing demands? A watch where she would not have to repel his comments, his remarks, his groping, his attempts to force himself upon her? "*Kaunis!*" she said to herself and began cleaning.

After a few minutes, Mari began to wonder where 'pig-brain', as she had come to nickname him, was. Perhaps he finally got the hint and was off in another part of the ship with some other female crew member. 'That must be it,' she comforted herself. When she swept under his bunk, though, a horrible thought flashed across her mind: 'Kristiian! … The dictionary! … The note from *Kapteeni*!'

Mari dropped her broom and raced back through the ship's companionways, went down two decks, then ran to her bunk in the women's quarters. Out of breath and frightened, she was met with a chilling scene.

"Your small man does not speak, my dear Mari," Kochen said from his sitting position on the bunk beside a terrified Kristiian. "But it is no matter, I knew you would come … and isn't it interesting that everyone else here is on watch? It is just us three here, now, my dear. Aren't we cozy!"

"What do you want, Kochen?" Mari hissed.

"I want nothing other than to show you what you are missing. The months at sea are so long and lonely. I can help make the trip more interesting for the both of us. The, how would you Finns say, *sukupuoli* would be magnificent, don't you think?"

"I'd sooner die first, Kochen. Leave us alone or I'll call *Starpom* Fedorovich."

"Ah yes, your adoptive uncle, your big brother, your guardian ... Deputy Captain Fedorovich! Isn't it a shame that *Starpom* Fedorovich never had the presence of mind to join the Communist Party ..."

"Leave us alone, now, Kochen, or I'll go get him!"

"I don't think you will, my little Finnish *puristaa*. You see, I was wondering if little brother, here, could swim." He reached over and grabbed Kristiian's ankles, then hoisted him into the air upside down as he stood up. "Can you swim, little brother? Can you make like the fishes that we catch? Perhaps we could run you through the filleting machines after you bounce along the bottom and come flopping out of the net. Or maybe, the sharks could have a little *poldnik*, a snack, with you."

"You're insane! Put him down, now!" She screamed.

Kochen began striding triumphantly down the companionway, swinging the little boy from one arm while fighting off his sister with the other. "Just say the word, my dear and the three of us will be very happy!" he taunted.

While Petrovich Kochen ambled along, shouting his boisterous jeers, Mari's efforts to fight him off and Kristiian's hysterical crying masked the sounds of the men rushing up behind him. In a split second, Kristiian was returned to his sister's arms and the helmsman was backed against the bulkhead, lifted clear with one hand that had a firm grip on his throat. As big as Kochen was, he was no match for the awesome might of the man in the gray chinstrap beard who had spent his life at sea.

"Let us see now who is the better swimmer!" *Starpom* Fedorovich gritted through his seething anger as he held the sputtering, gagging Russian at bay. "It would give me great pleasure to see you dance with the waves below, wouldn't you agree, Captain?"

"Pleasure, yes, but his carcass would sour the bottom and ruin the good fishing, don't you think, Vladimir?"

"Respectfully, I answer there is but one way to find out, Comrade-Captain."

"I was against taking you to sea with us, Petrovich," the Captain added, "But your father prevailed with his party connections. I will just have to inform him that your lack of sea experience resulted in your falling overboard. A shame, yes, but these things happen, do they not? Three months we have put up with your *dermo* [crap]!"

In an emergency shipboard meeting of all the officers, the charges brought against Kochen were read by *Starpom* Fedorovich:

"Petrovich Kochen did so willingly endanger the safety of the ship by threatening a crew member with harm and attempted murder."

"*Da!*" came the affirmative chorus of the ranking officers.

"Kochen also was disruptive to the productivity of the ship and was disrespectful to female members of the crew, forcing himself upon them, many times against their will."

"*Da!*"

"Kochen was inept at his job of helmsman, endangering the ship and its crew with his total incompetence."

"*Da!*"

"All of these acts are *nelzya!*"

"Are we in agreement that we enter his name in the *Klasifikator* and give his rating at point nine?"

"*Da!*"

"Petrovich Kochen, you are a worthless *padlo* [scoundrel], and your record shows it. Second mate! Call a general assembly of all crewmembers that can be spared. Fifteen minutes … on the *schlupochnaya paluba!*"

When the meeting was cleared, just the *starpom* and the captain remained behind.

"Vladimir?"

"Yes, Comrade-Captain."

"Was he really that bad on the wheel?"

"Hopeless. He said he knew how to steer a course, but when I told him the heading, he asked me what the course was in degrees. Degrees! He's a total *mudillo* [dumbass]!"

"I agree with your handling of this case, but one thing still perplexes me …"

"Yes, Captain?"

"Did he really accost the *sportsmenska*? Olga!"

"*Da.*"

"Vlad, she must be as old as you are, my old friend!"

"*Da*! Give her a couple of days and she could probably grow a beard like mine, too!"

The P.A. system announced the special assembly and in fifteen minutes, the boat deck was filled with crewmembers. The charges and their dispositions against Kochen were read aloud as he listened from where he was hand-cuffed to the rail. At each item, he yelled, "*ot 'ebis*" to the charge, but the crew, especially the female members, were noticeably relieved that his short reign of terror was over.

"I will get you!" he yelled. "When the Kremlin learns what you have done, you will freeze in Siberia, Fedorovich! *Yeb Vas*, all of you!"

"The Kremlin is thousands of miles away," *starpom* addressed the crew, keeping his back to the prisoner. "The Kremlin appreciates what we do here and gives us the power to maintain safety for all! We are here to do nothing more, or less, than feed the hungry mouths that await our return, including those that are at the Kremlin! We are paid well for our hard work, and we take that as a reward as well as the satisfaction of *kachestvenny trud*, the job well-done. *Tak derzhat!* Steady as she goes!"

The grateful crowd gave a hearty applause to the deputy captain. "And now, will the two most senior members of the *obrabotchiki* come forward, please?" he announced.

A middle-aged husband/wife team of factory line workers stepped forward sheepishly, looking perplexed and nervous as to why they had been singled out.

"For many years, the Selichovs have been model stakhanovites," *starpom* continued. "They have been very productive workers. It now gives me great pleasure to promote Nicklos to the rank of *Matros Rulevoi*, and to promote Rula to the position of *sportsmenska's* assistant!"

The crowd cheered as the couple hugged each other, overjoyed by their new fortune. When the applause died down, *starpom* gave his closing words:

"And as for you, Petrovich Kochen, you will become our new *obrabotchiki* ... for two watches a day. And if you are ever seen on the deck for any reason, you will surely demonstrate your own swimming lesson after the ship's security throws you overboard! Work well in your handcuffs ... they will be your only true shipmates."

It was two o'clock the next morning when *Starpom* Fedorovich was awakened by a loud knock at his cabin door.

"*Starpom* Fedorovich! This is third mate Chernitsky. Captain Minolin wants to see you in his cabin! ... *Starpom*! ... Are you awake?"

The tireless seaman had heard this a thousand times before, for any number of reasons. To be rustled from your rest was a common occurrence for any seaman of any age, rank, or nationality.

"What is it, Mikhail?" Fedorovich raspily asked through the closed door. "A torn net again?"

"No, *Starpom*, I'm afraid it is not that simple. The *nachalnik* is coming alongside in the *Spasatel*! He wants all officers to meet with him and the captain immediately!"

"I will be there directly, Mikhail," Fedorovich answered.

The fleet manager is coming alongside in the support tug? he wondered. *What would he want that he couldn't ask over the radio ... and at this time of night?*

In the captain's cabin, the *nachalnik* got down to business. "Your gifts from the American boat were greatly appreciated ... especially the fine cigarettes. They were a welcome change from the *morflot* cigarettes they issue us,comrades," he began. "*Da!* ... They proved to be very interesting when I shared them with our crewmembers who monitor the activities of the Americans ..."

As the *nachalnik* spoke, he alternately maintained eye contact with all the officers assembled in the captain's cabin. He studied their facial expressions as he continued, "I understand you have received more. May I examine them, my fellow sea-comrades? I will be glad to wait while you go get them ..."

Nervous glances were exchanged as the captain silently motioned for them to follow the orders of the fleet manager. Even though it sounded like a simple request, the *nachalnik* out-ranked him in every way, including party affiliation. The friendly banter was most assuredly a direct order, and at that, it was laced with suspicion. Captain Minolin, though he didn't let on, was just as concerned about this situation as his crewmen. The fleet manager kept him in the dark as well.

It wasn't long before the officers returned. Among them they had four unopened cartons of cigarettes and a handful of packs, mostly Raleighs and Kools.

Nachalnik Sokhorov looked each pack of cigarettes over closely, then set them aside. He opened every carton then examined every pack in those as well, leaving every pack of cigarettes laid face down on the Captain's chart table. He turned to address the worried crew assembled in front of him, once more piercing each set of eyes with his before he spoke. "It is my understanding that these all came from the same boat ... is that correct?"

"*Da*. That is correct, *Nachalnik* Sokhorov," *starpom* answered.

"Have you obtained any of these brands of cigarettes from any other vessel?"

"*Nyet*," offered the third mate.

"I also understand that one of the American crewmen is ... how would you say ... attracted to one of your crew. Is that true?" Sokhorov pressed further.

"That seems to be the case, yes." Captain Minolin answered. "Harmless, I assure you, but ..."

Sokhorov raised his hand to cut off the captain in mid-sentence. He thought to himself for a moment, then dismissed all the officers but Captain Minolin and *Starpom* Fedorovich.

"Comrades, do you know what is written on the packs of cigarettes before you?"

"*Nyet*."

"In the strictest of security, I will tell you that someone in the Pentagon is trying to contact us to become a double agent. I did not see it myself, but our intelligence experts are the best in the world! Embedded in the printing on these cigarette packs are offers to sell us some of the details of the new composite-framed bomber that is being sent for testing at two American air bases. You are now under orders to continue trading and cooperating with the American vessel. Use all due caution, but if necessary, maintain radio contact with them to apprise them of your whereabouts on the fishing grounds. This is your new mission. Am I fully understood?"

"But, *Nachalnik* Sokhorov, what about our fishing trip?" Captain Minolin asked. "Our primary mission is food production."

"That should be no problem to you, Captain. The Americans have always led us to the fish anyway. You know yourself that if you find this vessel, the *Elizabeth Gale*, you will find the fish nearby. Finish your last two months on the grounds working with them, like brothers of the sea."

"But what if they do not go along with this arrangement, Comrade?"

"Then use the *ofitsiantki* to insure that they do!"

At three o'clock in the morning, Chief Lee Chambers was startled awake by the incessant ringing of his phone.

"Chambers here," he croaked out. "This better be the President because no one else can wake me up without regretting it."

"Lee, it's Marty," came the voice on the other end. "I just received contact from their agent! The cigarettes, Lee! They bought it hook, line and sinker!"

22

IN THE LEE

Lat. 43 deg. 45.3 min. N.
Long. 69 deg. 37.1 min. W.

Lat. 43 deg. 45.2 min. N.
Long. 69 deg. 36.95 min. W.

Saturday morning. Stiff and exhausted, Chris Brown was awakened by the sunshine glowing over the ridge behind him. It had been a restless, virtually sleepless night. His mind was reeling. He had pieced together some answers to a plethora of questions that he had carried with him since childhood.

But every new piece of information seemed to create a new set of questions. He was convinced that James Mackenzie had the answers but he couldn't begin to fathom his own next move.

Rubbing some circulation back into his extremities, he stretched, walked up the path from Sid 'n' Eva's Chair, got his bearings on the watchtower, and, with the two cats navigating, strode across the crest into the eastward sunrise.

When he reached the Marine Science Center, he by-passed the breakfast mug-up and went straight up to the watchtower, binoculars in hand. The morning sun was in full glory, reflecting off the eastern sea's ripples from a light westerly air. A quick look showed both the *Susan G* and the *Haley and Blair* were missing from their tie-up floats at the north end of the harbor. Chris scanned the horizon in all directions; lobster boats worked their gear in all points of the compass from the tower, but two particular boats caught his eye. About two miles to the northeast, he made out the distinctive, longer house of the *Susan G*. She was rafted up to another boat. *That's Greg next to him, for sure*, he thought. *At least I know where they are for the time being.*

Chris's eyes remained glued to the binoculars as he tried to work out his next move in this game of cold war chess played on a board built from nerves. He didn't have all the moves figured out, by any means, but he did know who the pawns were.

"Coffee, Mr. Brown?" It was Dr. Grayson coming up the steps to the top of the tower. "You didn't make the morning mug-up," she said laboring to the top step, nearly out of breath. "Late night?"

"Thank you, Dr. Grayson," Chris said. He managed to work out a smile of appreciation as he took the coffee mug from her hand. "Yes, I guess you could say it was a very long night."

Dr. Grayson looked him over, studying his face, his hands, his hair, his eyes. She narrowed her gaze and stayed focused on his features ... making him feel uneasy.

"Anything wrong, Dr. Grayson?" he asked.

Dr. Grayson found a chair behind the stairwell and sat down, still looking at him. She sipped her tea, then, finally, looked beyond him out to the bay beyond. "Mr. Brown, you're a Ph.D. candidate ... what is the function of a university?" she asked firmly. "Any idea?"

"Well, it was always said that a university exists to disseminate knowledge," he answered half-heartedly as he went back to his binoculars. "Dr. G., really, it's been a long night, and ..."

"And it's only going to get longer," she snapped. "Wrong! Now get it right this time!" she barked. "And put down the binoculars … this is between you and me, not Greg and Mack! Knowledge can also be a case where you know something, but don't understand everything you know. That is precisely where you are right now! The function is one thing and one only … to disseminate what?" she demanded.

Chris let the binoculars hang down around his neck and leaned on the safety rail, maintaining eye contact with his interrogator. "I guess you could qualify that statement by saying that a university exists to determine and disseminate the truth," he answered.

"Very good. Good answer. Now … how much truth have *you* disseminated and how much have you conveniently left out? Are you doing research to determine and disseminate truth, or research to further your own agenda? They don't co-exist, my friend, do they?" she pressed. "You haven't been honest with me, and therefore, you haven't been honest with your research. It's time for you to disseminate some truth."

Chris felt a twinge of cold energy shoot through his abdomen. As usual, the wily professor knew the score, and, also as usual, she wouldn't bend her rules for anyone. She was right. He was cornered. He pulled a chair over and sat down and exhaled, rattling his lips. "How'd you know?"

"Let's just say that I don't have Kay Summersby working for me, either."

Countering, he asked, "Is your eavesdropping an act of integrity as well? What made you think you should do that? Last night's discussion was on my own time, and they were volunteering information freely, like we had all agreed at the outset."

Felicia Grayson took a deep breath, quelled her anger and continued: "When I was a little girl … twelve years old … my aunt took me and three of my cousins to Popham Beach for the day. It was a beautiful, bluebird day and we were having a ball. About eleven o'clock in the morning, my aunt suddenly became very agitated and made us pack up and leave. Four kids having a great time at the beach, but she just tore us away. No explanation. When we got home, the Coast Guard was at Aunt Sally's front door ... they lived next to us. Uncle Jake's lobster boat was found going around in circles, but no sign of him ... there never was another sign of him. Aunt Sally *knew*, even though she was on that beach miles away. She knew it. Not only knew, but was aware at the exact time the Coast Guard records show they found the boat. The call from April Gregory, Mr. Brown. She knew something was wrong with her husband. She always knows. Most water-women know ... I knew too."

"They were re-living some of their experiences. They weren't in any danger at all."

"Maybe, but the emotional level was just as high. April was quite upset when she called. Besides, what gives you the right to force these people to undergo such questioning?"

"You said it yourself. I was looking for the truth."

"Really? What about this crap about you being on a Russian factory ship?"

"One hundred percent true."

"Care to expound upon that?"

"Actually, I'd rather not talk about it. It's too pain ..."

"Too painful to re-live again? You call yourself an anthropologist! What are the three common traits that soldiers who survive the ordeals of war exhibit? You've studied enough! C'mon this is history repeating itself, Mr. Brown. Save your questionable credentials and answer me!"

Chris stood up and looked out at the sea, finding the two boats again. "Well, the first is that they don't want to talk about their experiences because they are too painful to bring up," he began.

"Continue."

"The second is the feeling of guilt that they were the ones to survive while the person next to them died, or was seriously maimed, whatever."

"Good, the third?"

He thought for a few moments. "I guess I'm not sure on the third."

"I'm not surprised. It's the feeling that you are fighting someone else's war and not yours. Most soldiers are caught in the middle of someone else's conflict. The governments make war ... the soldiers have to go fight it, then live with the nightmares if they are lucky enough to survive. Where do you place yourself in all of this? What gives you the right to subject these men to the horrors that they'd rather forget?"

"Because I still need to know what happened to my sister and I believe James Mackenzie has the answer to that question. I don't care what it costs to find out! I didn't ask to be thrust into ..."

"Someone else's war, Mr. Brown?"

The watchtower fell silent for a few painful minutes. Chris Brown stared out to sea while Felicia Grayson stared at him, waiting for a crack to show in his exterior. When at last he turned around, Dr. Grayson took the lead again. "Do you know who Jim Mackenzie's wife is?" she asked.

Chris was surprised by the change of subject, but mumbled out, "Greg said he married Ozzie's sister. Her name is Susan ... at least that's the name on his lobsterboat. Correct?"

"Susan Gwendolyn Marsden was the name on the marriage license."

"So?"

"So you're going to tell me how you came to be caught in someone else's war. That is, if you want my help fighting your way out ..."

Between the South Ledge of Heron Island and the buoy at Heron Island Outer Ledge, the *Susan G* and the *Haley and Blair* were rafted together, drifting along in the lee that Heron Island afforded them.

"Did you get ahold of her, Mack?"

"Yup. Called her on the cellphone late last night after we left the 'chair.' She wasn't happy, to say the least. I hope I'm not pushing the panic button."

"Hard tellin', not knowin', Cap. He seems to have a lot of information and dammit, he knows what buttons to push. I can't help thinkin', though, what Prillie said last night when she called ..."

"What's that?"

"You know her, Mack. She wanted to know how Sue-Mari was. She even asked if Sue-Mari was in the corner room upstairs."

Mack stroked his beard and thought for a moment, then took his hat off and let the breeze blow his hair around. Putting his hat on with the visor low, he theorized, "Prillie ... well ... as far as that goes, we all know that was Sue's favorite room. She even calls it the cello room."

"Those two are the closest thing to sisters. Amazing, isn't it? So what did you tell her last night?"

"She was awake and next to the phone when I called. Like I said, Greg, she wasn't thrilled, and I'm damn sure Keith Lockhart won't be happy either when he gets their note saying they drove off into oblivion for parts unknown. She and Liz had to leave Tanglewood at three A.M., then drive to Boston to pick up Gale, then they're headed for Sebago."

"Sebago?"

"I didn't dare say much, anyone can intercept a cellphone call. I just told her that the *Fisherman's Star* was in the area and to head for the lee."

Greg nodded in understanding. "Good thinkin', Cap. Best spot to weather out a blow is right in the lee of the old girl's ass! What do you think our next move should be?"

"Keep an eye on Chris Brown, or whoever the hell he is. What an alias, huh? Two of the most common names in the world. I just can't help thinking that he's tied to the guy that damn near killed her on that Russky rig. He did get high up in the Kremlin before the whole house of cards came crashing down."

"We don't know that for sure, by any means, Mack. What if we go back and bottle him up workin' on one of the student's projects? At least we'll have an eye on him. Or, I suppose we could shift some of the oysters and mussels in the upweller."

"What if we bagged up some of the soft-shell seed clams and took them over to the New Harbor co-op for the boys to transplant up back in the bay? That would keep us busy," Mack offered.

"And, if we involved all the students, he wouldn't be trying to dredge up the past. I don't think he'd try anything with them around. Do you, Cap?"

"Let's hope not."

"From what I can see, it looks like Mack and Greg are turning to head back," Dr. Grayson said as she looked out over the ocean. She thought for a quick moment, then said, "Mr. Brown, gather the troops from the mess hall and have them assemble onboard the *Eva Maker*. Now!"

"Wha … what's going on?"

"We're going on a field trip!

"But … where?"

"Forward into the past. It's about time we did some gut-level research at the school of H-N. We'll be studying from the curriculum of Life 601, a graduate level course. You can give us the undergrad pre-requisite course as we travel."

"What's that called?"

"The truth and why people will help you for free if you offer it as pre-payment."

23
RULES OF THE ROAD

Lat. 55 deg. 00 min. N.
Long. 20 deg. 30 min. E.

Lat. 40 deg. 30.1 min N.
Long. 69 deg. 25.9 min. W.

Chappy Lester bumped along Route One in his trusty, rusty 1968 Dodge Powerwagon carrying a full load. In the back of his truck were barrels of salted redfish racks, the head and bones left after filleting, that he'd use for lobsterbait between mail days. Chappy had to take it easy ... he had to drive slow, otherwise the "whole damn lot of 'em would be scattidd 'cross old numbah one road." Coming back on the long trip from Portland, he turned right to make the final swing to Boothbay Harbor, much to the chagrin of the line of cars and much to the delight of the seagulls that had followed him for miles.

"What in hell?" he asked himself. He craned his neck out the window in disbelief as the Damariscove Marine Science Center Van passed him, heading to the westward. "What in hell they doin' hee-uh?" he asked himself. "Where the hell they goin'?"

The nine-passenger van with fourteen people in it passed him with all students waving and Dr. G. blaring the horn from the driver's seat. She could scarcely see over the wheel and barely reached the pedals, but the van roared ahead with the elderly fireball at the wheel.

Chris leaned over from the front passenger seat so he could be heard over the excited chatter coming from the students in the back. "You still haven't told me where we're going, Dr. Grayson," he said. "What's up?"

"We're going to see a friend of mine to see if she can check out your story. If you come up clean, I think we can help you. If not, it's a long walk home," she answered, staring at the road with her hands firmly at ten and two on the wheel. "It's about time we put some things to rest once and for all. Ever heard of Madeline Langhorne, Mr. Brown?"

"Can't say as I have."

"She was quoted as saying, 'We are not to get over our greatest griefs, they make us who we are.' She inspired this trip."

"You're not going to give me a straight answer, are you, Dr. G.?"

"Want a straight answer? We're on the road to find out who you and Mack Mackenzie are. In the meantime, you may start with your preliminary remarks."

Chris shook his head. He was no match for Felicia Grayson. "Alright, then ... Where should I start?"

"The beginning."

As the van rolled along, the passengers became quiet while Chris began a narrative of his life. It soon became clear that this was no ordinary field trip; the jovial, carnival mood was soon replaced by somber, awestruck silence as he related events that he'd once hoped to never re-live again.

"To start this off at a comprehensible point, we've got to recount some history that happened before I was born. Between Finland and Russia, there is an area known as the Karelian Isthmus. The Gulf of Finland is on the west and a large lake, called Lake Ladoga is on the eastern side. You probably think of the climate of this area as all snow, but really, the proximity to the sea keeps Karelia in rather temperate weather, in fact, the finest climate in that whole geographic region. For a long time, it was part of Russia, but in 1917 it became part of Finland. That's where my family lived, in Ladoga Karelia, on a large and highly productive farm close to Lake Ladoga. Because of the two ethnic factions there, we learned to speak some Russian, but Finnish was our main tongue. Anyway ...

"During World War Two, the Russians took the isthmus back in 1940. They breached what was called the Mannerheim Line. When that happened, hundreds of thousands of Finns fled to the main part of the country, leaving this beautiful, fertile area behind. The Finns and the Germans fought together to get Karelia back, and from 1941 to 1944, they held it secure enough for three hundred thousand Karelians to go back and re-establish their farms. My grandparents and parents went back during this 'continuation war,' they called it.

"Around the time of D-Day in Normandy, the Russians went back and re-captured Karelia again. This time, four hundred thousand Karelians were thrown out, but some, like the good productive farmers that my grandfather and father were, weren't allowed to leave. The world was so fixated on the ending of the world war that this wasn't even a bump in the road of world history, but it meant that our family ... my grandparents, my parents, and later my sister and me, were essentially stuck in Russia, even though we were Finns. My sister and I were raised as Finns, we were taught religion by our parents, we kept our traditions alive ... all in secret of course ... and we were always reminded that someday we would be free again. I was born in 1970, but my sister was quite a bit older ... she was born in 1956. There we were. Stuck."

"What happened next, Brownie?" came a voice from the back of the van as they sped along under Dr. Grayson's leadfoot driving.

Chris smiled and continued, becoming more at ease. "Okay, you've all heard of the Underground Railroad, right?"

"Yeah."

"Sure"

"Well, there were a few similar set-ups in Karelia. The *Amerikkalainen ihimen* were the people we got tangled up with. To get smuggled out, you had to give them your land, but if you were going to America, it didn't really matter to you, right? Well, my mother and father decided to go for it. What they didn't know was that this was a scheme that garnered land for the KGB 'railroaders' and left no witnesses behind. People left and they weren't heard from again, so it was just assumed that they made it to America. In reality, they bought a one-way ticket to hell."

"Everything went pretty good when we left the farm. We made all the checkpoints and got all the way to the Finnish border crossing at Vaalimaa. That's the busiest checkpoint to Russia, located in the city of Virolahti, which is now becoming somewhat of a resort area. Not then. We got right to the border … we could see Finland on the other side of the gate. We could see freedom. We could even taste it and smell it, we were that close. You've got to remember, I was just five, and my sister was nineteen," he continued with his eyes welling. "We were scared out of our wits, but my mother calmed us down and gave each of us a sprig of her porcelain plant … she called it the freedom plant. She told us we'd plant them when we got to our new home."

No one spoke as the van continued on. Irene, the student from Kansas, finally broke the tension and asked, "I hate to ask … did things go as planned?"

"It was a set-up. There really were some good people getting folks across, but not the ones we were entrusted to. It all happened so quickly. The shots were fired before we even knew what was happening, and if it wasn't for *Starpom* Fedorovich coming through the checkpoint at that precise moment, I wouldn't be here telling this story. My mother and father were cut down in cold blood. My sister and I were left standing in the road. I was in shock, she was in hysterics. Just as the rifles were trained on us, *Starshi Pomoshnik* Vladimir Fedorovich pulled his car right alongside to shield us. He scooped us in and then we sped off into the Russian countryside with the border guards still firing at us. I mean, it all happened like that. Just that quick." He snapped his fingers. "Like that! We got to see Finland, but at the end of the night, we were deep in Russia again, with a complete stranger at the wheel going to who-knows-where."

Chris turned back around and looked blankly out the windshield of the van. He wiped his eyes and rode along in a state of near shock. After a few miles, Tiffany got up enough courage to simply ask, "*Starpom?*"

The van went along for another mile, "Deputy captain on the Russian factory ship number six hundred and ten, the *Zvezda Rybaka* ... the *Fisherman's Star*. Homeported in Kaliningrad, Russia. On the Baltic Sea."

"Russia? By godfrey mighty! Bound for where?" Sewall asked from the back of the van.

Chris turned around and looked at the students. Every set of eyes was on his. He faced forward again and focused down the road before he answered, "Within a day's steam to America."

When the *Susan G* and the *Haley and Blair* headed past the Motions buoy, both skippers noticed at the same instant that the *Eva Maker* was gone from her usual tie-up spot at the Marine Center's float. Greg was in the lead, so he took advantage of the open dock and slid in to tie up, saving the run to the head of the harbor. Mack came right alongside and rafted next to him. After they had their boats secured, they came to the same realization ... there wasn't anyone around.

"That's funny. I don't remember Paul saying he had a trip today, do you, Mack?"

"Nope. Maybe I'll check with him to make sure." Mack went back to the helm and grabbed the microphone from the VHF.

"*Susan G* calling the *Eva Maker*. You on, Paul?"

"E-M here. Go ahead, Mack."

"I just got back in. It looks deserted over here … is everything alright?"

"Oh yeah, finestkind, Cap. Dr. G and the students are goin' to take the van up to Acadia and bicycle around for the day, I guess. I'm just about to leave Boothbay. You need anything over here?'

"No, thanks. Is Chris Brown with them?"

"Yup, that's a roger. They left a few minutes ago."

"Are they okay?"

"Couldn't be better as far as I can see, Cap. Yeah, Felicia said it was such a nice day, she decided to go on one of her mystery rides. Never seen her more upbeat, and the kids are thrilled. Good morale booster. Why?"

"No reason, Paul. Okay, I'll let you go. *Susan G* by."

"Uh, Okay. E-M standing by."

Mack turned and looked back at Greg who was waiting on the stern deck. "Paul said they're all going to Acadia for the day. They're already on the road in the van."

"They okay?" he asked.

"He said everyone was fine. It's just another one of Dr. G.'s spur of the moment field trips, I guess."

"You don't suppose we've thrown the harpoon too soon, do you, Mack?"

"Can't be too careful. Actually, this works out to our benefit, though. Let's check out his room, then we can head over to the harbor and drive down to Sebago without worrying about him. It'll be nice to see the girls, won't it, Greg?"

"Sounds like a plan I could vote for, Senator." Greg said.

The pair went into the old station and took a cursory look around. Dave and Sandy Burkette were already up at Wood End, working on their glacial era research. Everyone else was either on the mainland or in transit on the bay. They climbed the stairs to the second floor and went to the end of the hall where Chris's door was. Both exchanged glances, then Greg slowly tried the doorknob. It was unlocked. He turned the knob to unlatch the door, then pushed it open a crack and peered inside. The morning sun streamed through causing Greg to stop to get his eyes adjusted, but Mack gave the door a good swift push, opening it wide. Mack's eyes were wide open above his gaping mouth as he slowly walked to the window. He reached out and felt the leaves of the plant that Chris had left climbing up his window casing. A porcelain plant ... A porcelain plant!

"Greg! Look!"

"Wow. I didn't notice that before. It looks just like the one ..."

Jim Mackenzie reeled around with horror in his eyes. "Greg! We've got to get to the boat! We've got to get to them before it's too late!" he yelled. He ran for the stairs and bolted out through the door with a sprinting Greg following.

Mack and Greg ran down the rampway, out onto the float, then hopped across the *Haley and Blair* to get aboard the *Susan G.* Mack started the engine while Greg released the docklines. When he saw that they were clear, Mack turned the wheel hard over, put the throttle up to wide-open, then headed for the Motions buoy, black smoke streaming from the exhaust.

"You thinkin' what I am?" Greg yelled over the engine, terror in his voice.

"Yup. He's already left his calling card. Who else would know about that plant than that sadistic psycho from the ship that ended up at the Kremlin? He must have sent Chris Brown."

"And he's got a whole vanload full of hostages, heading for those cliffs on Acadia!"

"Greg!" Mack yelled. "Take the cellphone and call the State Police. Tell them to start looking for them between Boothbay and Acadia. They can't be too far away yet!"

"Roger that, Cap!"

In the Marine Center van, Chris continued with his narrative of life in the hands of the Russians. Suddenly he realized that they were travelling southwest, not northeast to Acadia.

"Dr. G?"

"Yes, Mr. Brown."

"Is it my imagination or are we traveling in the wrong direction? Acadia would be to the northeast of Boothbay, correct?"

"No, and yes, respectively. We're going in the right direction, although it is southwest and yes, Acadia is in the northeast direction, however, that's not where we're headed."

"We're not?"

"No."

"Can I ask where we are going?"

"You just did. Continue teaching the class. We haven't got too much farther to go."

Bob, the marine biology major, yelled a question over the heads of his fellow students. "Chris ... if you ... um ... lost track of your sister ... how did you get to America? I mean obviously you did make it!"

"Yes. After she turned up missing ... I won't say she jumped ... *starpom* kept me sheltered in his cabin for the remaining two months of the trip. I don't remember much ... it was late fall and winter and I was too frightened to move from my bunk for the most part, anyway. When we got to Kaliningrad and were docked, *starpom* woke me in the middle of the night, told me to dress warm, then he took me on deck. He put a life jacket on me, tied a rope onto the straps of the life jacket, tucked my mother's plant in my coat and lowered me over the side. I was petrified. Scared more then than ever before, if you can believe it. In total, absolute shock with terror. It was below zero, too."

You could hear a pin drop in the van as he continued, "I was lowered down but before I hit the water, a boat came from out of nowhere and a pair of arms grabbed me. They untied the rope, *starpom* hoisted it up, and it was the last I ever saw of him. When the boat touched shore again, twenty-two people walked out onto the dock at Helsinki. My great aunt from America, Lydia Hamalainen, ran out and hugged me. That's how I got to Wisconsin. She gave me a generic American name, Chris Brown, that was similar to my real name, Kristiian Brueen. No adoption papers. No customs. No border checkpoints. No records of me going aboard or getting off the *Star*. My passport said I was Christian P. Brown from Manitowoc, Wisconsin. The rest is, well, history."

The van reeled along for a while longer, then turned off the highway onto a secondary road. After a few miles, Dr. Grayson turned onto a dirt road after the sign that said, "New Beginnings-A Camp for Special People." At the parking lot, a distinguished looking man smiled a broad grin when he saw the van pull in. He waved and began running, his arms wide open.

"Doctor Grayson! April said you might be coming!" he said when the van stopped and she rolled down the window. "She said you'd come!"

After she had embraced the man through the window of the van, Dr. G. turned around and addressed the members of her entourage. "Folks, I'd like you to meet an old, dear friend of mine. This is Doctor Peter Lamell, assistant director of the camp.

"Hi everybody!" he said, waving to all the faces in the van. "Call me Petey. All my friends call me Petey!"

The *Susan G* came roaring into Boothbay Harbor on the pin at full speed, throwing a wake that angered and tossed everything and everyone that thought they were sheltered within the no-wake zone of the harbor. The boat steamed along with a bone in her teeth, curling water off the bow, until Mack backed her down hard at the co-op dock, threw out some docklines and shut her down. Greg tied up as fast as he could, then the pair ran up the ramp towards town, nearly causing an accident when they sprinted across the street through the startled drivers caught in summertime traffic.

They ran to the back of the parking lot where they kept their pick-up trucks. Mack fumbled for his keys, then unlocked the doors of his dirty seagull splattered truck. They both jumped in, slammed the doors and … nothing. The battery was dead. It was the middle of August but he hadn't run his truck since May. No need to until now.

"Pissah!" Mack exclaimed as he hit his fists on the steering wheel.

Greg was already out the door and ran for his truck. He lay down on the parking lot and, in a panic, felt around the inner lip of his back bumper until he retrieved his keys from the hiding place. Greg tossed his keys to Mack who unlocked the doors and they both jumped in. The truck started right up and Mack popped the clutch, chirping the tires as they sped for … Brakes! … Nowhere! The summertime tourists had completely blocked them in.

Greg climbed out of his truck and scrambled to the roof then scanned the harbor with his cupped hands extending his hat's visor. Left … right … back … "Chappy! C'mon, Mack! Chappy's truck is over there! Let's Go!"

Mack and Greg high-tailed it over to Chappy's bait cooler near the wharf where his truck was backed in. Seagulls circled overhead as the old coaster stood in the back of his truck, pitchforking his bait out of the barrels into others on the ground so he could re-salt it. They huffed their way into Chappy's yard, then jumped into his truck, oblivious to the presence of the owner working in the back. Mack dropped his hand to where the keys should be …nothing!

"Gawdalmighty, Spice, what in hell you doin' in they-uh?" Chappy yelled from the back of his truck. "You lost your marbles or what?"

Mack jumped out on the pavement and turned towards the back. "Chappy! We've got to take your truck! Greg and I can't use ours! It's an emergency!"

"Where's the fire?" Chappy drawled as he scanned the horizon. Seeing nothing, he croaked, "You been drinkin'?

"Chappy, we don't have time to explain!" Greg shouted, hands flailing. "The kids ... Dr. G ... they're in great danger! We've got to go after them!"

Chappy thought for a second, then tossed the pitchfork aside. "I don't know what you two are up to, but get in they-uh. I'll drive. Tell me on the way."

Mack and Greg lunged for the cab and Chappy hiked himself behind the wheel. Chappy fumbled around in his shirt pocket until he found a lobster plug which he jammed into the ignition switch with the palm of his hand. Next, he reached down to the dashboard, pulled a length of dangling twine and tied it tight around the steering column. Finally, he reached into the glove compartment and crossed two bare wires that shot sparks when they touched. The old Dodge Powerwagon cranked, started ... and purred like a kitten. The truck lurched ahead, toppling the remainder of the bait barrels into the bed of the truck, which in turn sprayed leaking baitjuice on the hapless tourists who were unlucky enough to be adjacent to the truck's path out of town.

"Where we headed, boys?" Chappy asked as he drove. He'd warmed up to the spirit of adventure and the sense of duty that was thrust upon him. "Sounds like it's urgent, yuh."

"We've got to get to the van! Dr. G. and all the kids are in the van headed for Acadia. Chris Brown will kill them if we don't get there in time!" Mack yelled over the loud engine and the wind from the open windows as they bounced along.

"Who? ... Doc? You sure you guys ain't been drinkin' somethin'?"

"It's a long story, Chappy," Greg said. "It goes back twenty years to when we were in a real mess with the Russians, and ..."

"Russians! Gawdalmighty! Them bahstidds! We should stop by the VFW and get the rest of the guys! We still talk war down they-uh, mis-tah!"

Mack shook his head and buried his eyes in his hands. "Chappy, it isn't like that. Please!" he yelled. "Just head for Acadia! Greg already called the State Police. Just drive, will you?!"

"Sure, Spice, sure I'll drive alright, yuh," Chappy said, a touch of hurt feelings showing through. "But if Felicia was headed to Acadia, it's gonna be a while before she gets they-uh. It's twenty-six thousand miles the way she was goin'."

"Whatd'ya mean?" Greg asked.

"Well I passed the whole lot of 'em when I was comin' back from 'Pottland', yuh. Could barely see the ole' girl behind the wheel. Prob'bly she couldn't see at all, 'cause she was drivin' to the west'ard. Now I don't know much, but I think Acadia's still off to th' …"

"Sebago!" both Mack and Greg screamed in unison.

"Turn left up here, Chappy, turn left! Head to the west'ard!"

Mack felt around all his pockets until he located his cellphone, then dialed 9-1-1. Instantly, the answer came: "Maine State Police. This call is being recorded. Sergeant--" … beep-beep-beep.

Mack threw the phone on the dashboard of the truck in disgust. "The battery went dead! What next?"

"We'll tell the person in the tollbooth to call them," Greg said. "Drive, Chappy, give her all she can stand! Put your foot to the floor!"

24

THE ICE DOCK

LAT. 41 DEG. 22.69 MIN. N.
LONG. 71 DEG. 30.7 DEG. W.

Chappy drove his old truck for all she was worth. After all, he reminded Greg and Mack several times, he drove one of the lead trucks in Patton's Red Ball Express in "the big one." The Powerwagon bumped along the road, tailpipe barking, fenders flapping, seagulls following. Cars passed them as fast as they got behind them, especially after they got a few drops of leaking bait juice spattered on their windshields and smelled the potent fish/salt stench in their open windows, or sucked in by their air conditioners.

They alerted the Maine State Police at the first tollbooth to the Maine 'Pike, but it took some coaxing to get the toll-taker to believe them after Chappy started giving instructions on hand-to-hand combat because the Russians were about to attack. It also took a few minutes to get the message straight, then put into a believable form, since the other call that Greg made earlier was now deemed a hoax. When the toll-taker started the call off with, "Sergeant, there's three guys here who say the Russians have landed, and one of them says that he sent you the wrong way to Acadia. Now he says they're landing at Sebago, and ..."

Time wasted. Precious time wasted. Every second was time wasted when something horrible might be happening. Were the girls all right? Were the students alive? Dr. G.? What about the kids at April's camp ... did the Saturday morning bus already leave? Where are Mari, the girls ... did they get out of Boston? Did that psychotic murderer phone the island with a ransom demand? Dave and Sandy out there alone ... is another kayak landing there?

They finally got on the road again after about fifteen excruciating minutes. As they were rolling along, neither Mack nor Greg had a firm feeling that the Police would take them seriously and dispatch the proper manpower. They were supposed to wait at the side of the toll stop for a patrol car to come, then substantiate their story face-to-face, but all three felt that was a waste of more time. Probably they were considered a drunk driving call trying to perpetrate another hoax. The Powerwagon flapped and rumbled its way to the southwest.

Mack was sitting by the window watching the landscape roll by, mile after long mile as Chappy regaled them with stories of his ... and Patton's ... exploits. Mack rested his elbow out the open window, put his chin in his hand, then blankly watched the rushing green roadside blend into a blur as the wind loudly whistled through the cab of the truck.

It wasn't supposed to be like this, he thought, trying to fight off the adrenaline his body was churning out in gallons. All we wanted was to be left alone so we could work our asses off ...

~ ~ ~

Mid-November, 1975

"That's right, Lee. The Lizgale's gettin' ice and fuel tonight at ten. I checked the blackboard up in the co-op."

"Okay, we'll give 'em a little peptalk then. Did you make arrangements with Peepers about the *Aurora*?"

"Yup. He's pretty happy about the arrangement, let me tell ya. I told him to order the best radar money could buy and he'd be paid the balance in cash when it's installed. I gave him half down, in cash, already. He knows the deal about security, too. Peepers, I mean, Bob, still has top level clearance from when he developed the echosounder back in the war."

"Good. He knows we need the old one, right?"

"Yup. We figured that he'd tell them that the new one was a gift from the phone company for puttin' in the extra time on the cable patrol. How they gonna find fault with that? They're gettin' a nice new Kelvin Hughes. Twenty four mile … a real beaut'."

"Just make sure he doesn't do anything to change the signature of the way the old one transmits. We've got to make sure the Russkies think that's the *Aurora* jogging along the cable, got me?"

"No problem. With the *Aurora*'s old radar installed on the sub's escort tug, it'll throw them off. That's their route to open ocean?"

"Yup, right under their nose, along the phone cable. It'll look just like the *Aurora* patrolling it, from the radar signature. They'll never see the sub just below the surface, ahead of the tug."

"Gotta hand it to you, Lee, it's a stroke of genius. Oh … I heard from our contact with the Russkies. The boats down to the west'ard scored, too. They really think there's some kind of new bomber that's going to be tested over the water! I think we might have 'em roped in and tail-wrapped, Lee. If half the fleet goes off Jersey and the other half is looking for a plane off Cape Cod, we'll be golden."

"I love this job," Lee Chambers remarked as he chomped into another clamcake. "How about another dozen? I'll buy if you fly."

"Lee, the restaurant's about twenty feet away." Marty Farmagano gestured over his shoulder with his thumb as another boat steamed out the gut past George's Restaurant. "Can't you … oh, never mind, I'll get it. Anything else?"

Lee Chambers tossed a dollar bill across the front seat of Marty's car. "Well, how about a couple dozen clamcakes, a couple chocolate cabinets, and then, whatever you want."

Marty picked up the crumpled dollar bill and tossed it back into the car. "How about if I get it?"

"You're buyin'? Great! I'll take a scallop plate to go, too. Growin' boy, ya know."

"Believe me, I know."

The high-pitched whine of the ice blower filled the cold night air as Mack and Greg guided the heavy hose around the deck, filling the aft pens of the hold through the open deckplates. Ten tons of ice were being loaded through the large diameter black rubber hose. The power of the blower propelling that large amount of heavy frozen water could easily sweep them off the deck if they didn't maintain a constant vigil, consequently, they were both paying attention to their duties when two shadows slipped over the rail unnoticed and went down the foc'sle ladder. Ricky was aft checking Buddy's hangbook and Ozzie was down below putting the finishing touches on polishing his engines.

When it came time to blow ice down the deckplate for the foc'sle icebox, Greg signalled the dockmaster for the blower to stand by while he went down below to check the proper placement of his meats and perishable foodstuffs for the trip ... beef in first, chicken next, pork and lamb on top, milk, butter, bacon, cold cuts and cream iced down evenly from top to bottom. Mack braced himself against the rail to be able to handle the power of the hose by himself, but there was no call from Greg to start filling.

Not wanting to let go of the hose in case it inadvertently got switched on, Mack yelled down the deckplate, "Hey Greg, you all set to let 'er go? Greg? Hey, you alive down there?"

"Just barely," came the answer. "You'd better get Oz and Ricky. We've got company!"

Mack gave a slashed-neck signal to stop the ice blower then poked his head down the doghouse. "What are you talk ..." He stopped in mid-word when he heard the bolt of a carbine engaging and saw the barrel pointed directly at him.

"You! Down here now!" an order barked from below. Mack slithered down the ladder then went behind the galley oil stove with his hands up, shaken, confused and bewildered. Exchanging glances with Greg, they both quickly concluded that neither knew what was going on as two Navy men in pea coats and watchcaps held them at close riflepoint. "Don't speak unless spoken to!" the shorter of the two commanded.

"How many POB's are on this vessel?" The other intruder asked gruffly, motioning his rifle. "Don't play 'johnny dunce' with me ... talk! How many people are on board?"

"Two more ... besides us," Greg stammered out. "The skipper and engineer. What's ..."

"I told you not to speak unless spoken to, and I meant it!" He turned to his partner, then ordered, "Go find them and bring them here."

Soon, all four crewmen of the Lizgale were sitting around the galley table as two rifles were pointed directly at them from the aft end of the foc'sle. An hour went by ... two hours went by. The situation didn't change and no information was given out. After another half-hour went by, the two Navy men were noticeably concerned, judging from the way they frequently checked their watches and shrugged at each other. After three hours and ten minutes, someone appeared at the top of the foc'sle ladder and began a labored, out of breath descent into the foc'sle.

"Looks like the gang's all here," Lee Chambers said from the bottom step. "That all-night breakfast buffet over at the Denny's in North Kingstown ... now that's a damn good deal! You fellas really ought to try it sometime. I'm tellin' ya, I just couldn't drive past without givin' it a go. Went back for seconds three times! Hey! Good job, boys," he said to the Navy men. "Why don't you wait on deck while I have a little chat with my buddies here. A little of that crisp night air will feel good."

The two Navy riflemen climbed the ladder, grumbling under their breath, "Over three hours he leaves us here!"

"Yeah and he stops for breakfast? Breakfast!"

Chambers leaned against the ladder and addressed the four fishermen trying to hold back their rage and frustration. "Ut-tut-tut, now," Chambers spoke as he wagged his finger. "Don't speak unless spoken to. My good friends are right upstairs."

"So shoot me. I've had enough of this crap! Whadda you want, anyways?" Ricky demanded. "You've got no right to hold us like this!"

"I most certainly do! I've been informed that you people are carrying on an illicit trade with the iron curtain fleet. That's treason in my book!" Chambers shot back. He took a manila envelope from inside his pea coat and threw it onto the table. "Go ahead, Cap, take a look ... exhibit number one!"

Ricky opened the envelope and took out an aerial photograph showing the *Elizabeth Gale* alongside the *Zvezda Rybaka*. The next photo showed a package flying from the hands of someone standing on the Lizgale's wheelhouse steps towards the ship. The third item to be slipped out of the envelope was a copy of National Security Action Memorandum 1198. Ricky snorted in disgust and tossed it aside.

"So what?" Ricky sneered. "We're on the high seas. Whadda you want, the tax money on the duty-free cigarettes?"

"Do yourself a favor and check out the directives on the memo." Chambers waited, arms folded, while Ricky read the memorandum aloud:

"... 'Six. Fishing vessels from domestic ports that engage in illicit trading with Soviet Bloc vessels shall be, under the terms of this directive, considered under suspicion for the passing of intelligence and should be closely monitored in port, as well as underway. The so-called "spice trade" may, under certain circumstances, be considered prima facie evidence of suspicion of treasonous activity ...

"Seven. Any means necessary, including the use of force, may be used to enforce these provisions if the security of the United States and/or its environs or allies are put into jeopardy'..."

Ricky threw the paper down and put his face in his hands. "Lord luvvaduck," he mumbled through his fingers.

"Ever heard of the *Mount Washington*, Cap?" Chambers asked.

"Big hill in New Hampshire," the skipper answered, his face still obscured. "So what?"

"Not the mountain, the tourist boat that goes around Lake Winnipesaukee."

"Nope. Who cares? What the ..."

"I checked the boat document up in Providence today. Richard B. Helliott, that's you ... is listed as the master. I see that Doris Folland, the owner, has dutifully followed through on endorsing you as master of this vessel. As master, do you know if the war risk insurance is up to date?"

"The war risk insurance?"

"That's right. In case this vessel was to be conscripted in time of national peril, I mean. The Russians are right off our shores, and ..."

"Conscripted?"

"Yup. The *Mount Washington* was conscripted in World War Two. Actually, a lot of boats were, but the M-W was cut in two, hauled overland to the coast, then re-assembled and used in the war. Conscripted means it's taken by the government to be used for military purposes ... it's a standard part of your boat document, Mr. Master."

"You couldn't possibly take this boat!"

"Oh really? Well, I guess you're right, Cap, I don't need to conscript it ... I've got enough evidence to seize it outright and arrest all of you to boot! What a shame that would be for Buddy's widow, huh? 'Course ... There might be a way we could help each other out ... For the good of the country, of course!"

Ricky stared down at the table and felt the life go out of him. He couldn't lose Doris's boat. He couldn't fight his way out with two armed guards at the top of the ladder, either. "Okay," he managed to squeak out. "If you came to take the rig you would have by now. What have we gotta do to keep Doris's boat? First Buddy, now this ..."

Lee Chambers smiled and sat down at the table. "Now you're talkin'! This will actually be kinda fun for you guys, and you," he pointed across at Mack, "will get to see your little Russian sweetheart. Ain't love grand?"

Ricky silently glared across the table at Mack as he addressed Chambers in no uncertain terms. "Just tell us the deal and let us get away from the dock!"

"Easy, Cap. No need to get testy. Just continue trading your little goodies with the number six-ten, that's all. Just give 'em the cigarettes and stuff like you've been doin'. Now that isn't so bad, is it?"

Ricky brightened up slightly and removed his gaze from Mack. "That's all you want, just to know where they are?"

"Well, not quite, Cap. We, the military, I mean, know where they are twenty-four hours a day. But, the whole of the US of A, needs you to brother up with them, you know, work together. Think of it as a good-will gesture. I'll let you know where they are ... you just steam out and fish along with 'em. That's it. No more to it."

"What if they're someplace I don't want to fish, or have never been?"

"You've got the fabled, Holy Grail of hangbooks! Whadda you care if you've never fished in a certain area before? If you've never been there, there's a damn good chance that Buddy Folland has been there before you and wrote it down in his priceless fishing bible. You know the Russkies have scouts all over the place … on shore as well as on the water. If you set in with 'em, you're gonna have a nice trip. It's a no-brainer, Cap!"

Ricky cocked his yellow Caterpillar hat on the back of his head and thought for a moment. "Where's the catch? What's the purpose of all of this?" he asked.

"Presidential order going back to Eisenhower, actually. I guess old Ike thought that the way to avoid conflict was through cooperation. That's why he started exchange students and stuff like that. I don't want to sound corny, but you boys are on a historic mission. One by one, if we can break down the barriers between us, maybe someday the threat of nuclear war will be a distant memory. Help 'em catch some food … they help you catch some … toss 'em a few things from the good ole' US of A … make some friends … sounds like a winner, doesn't it?"

Ricky shrugged and thought to himself, *What a sack of crap. So you want to play poker with me, huh?* He played his first card with Chambers. "I'm goin' to the gully this trip, somewheres inside of Hudson Canyon lookin' for some butters and fluke," he explained. "They near there?"

Chambers snapped his finger in an arm-sweep motion. "Missed it by a little bit, Cap. Actually, you're headed for the Highlands and Nausets, off the Cape. Surveillance aircraft says they're slammin' the codfish, pollock and greysole in the deep water off there. Thirty-four sixty and ten-eighty are the LORAN bearings. Just ride the fair wind down, then you can hide in the lee of the Cape if it blows up hard. You know all that, anyways."

"Okay, I guess we can go down to the east'ard," Ricky relented uncharacteristically. "Last time I fished the Highlands was with my father on the old *Renegade*."

"Good. Any more questions, gentlemen?"

Mack spoke up. "Why the guns, the show of force, the scare tactics, if it's true you came here in the name of detente? One minute we were going to be arrested, the next, we're all brothers. Sounds like something Nixon and Haldeman dreamed up …"

"Sorry, son. I don't know who Dave Taunt is. Never met the man … Anyway, I just wanted to make sure you guys weren't a bunch of wimps, and man, oh man, you fellas certainly impressed me! You guys are some tough bahstidds, steamin' into the Vineyard with that live shell on deck ... you guys got spunk, I'll say that!"

"But ..."

"Look, I'll send word when you get in," he said as he started for the ladder. "You boys'll thank me when you see what happens when you've got your own private spotter plane! Remember this is a military operation. Loose lips lose ships to conscription."

"Back 'er down, Cappy!" Greg yelled from the forepeak.

Ricky blew one long, then three short blasts on the horn, put the Lizgale in reverse, then pushed up the throttle as the grand eastern-rigged lady once again entered the channel of Point Judith Harbor. Mack was coiling up the sternlines and Ozzie was in the engineroom, singing as he admired his machinery:

> No rail on the mess room table,
> And you're dead if you spit on the floor.
> No grog allowed, no singing too loud,
> And no locks on the doors;
> But there's always a fire in the card room,
> And the tucker is always the best,
> And they'll end it all together....
> Down at the Sailor's rest!*

April Mayes stirred from her sleep, got up, and went to the east-facing window of her bedroom. Try as she might, she couldn't see beyond the darkness. But she kept trying.

---

*Music and lyrics by Stan Rogers. www.stanrogers.net

25

THROUGH THE SOUND

Lat. 41 deg. 28.3 min. N.
Long. 70 deg. 30.0 min. W.

Lat. 41 deg. 54.1 min. N.
Long. 69 deg. 31.2 min. W.

Lat. 41 deg. 29.55 min. N.
Long. 71 deg. 19.3 min. W.

There were six pages of bearings and information in Buddy's hangbook concerning the eastern side of the Cape. Many entries were like this, even though there are just a few written here:

Highland Light hangs and wrecks (note: some of these I got from Bob Helliott — I traded him some of the Gully stuff, 3/15/65)

3510	1212	30-32 fm.
3505	1214	34 fm.
3465	1249	49 fm
3400	1240	85 fm.
3478	1252	46 fm.
3470	1185	62 fm.
3429 ...		

And so on for two pages more of LORAN bearings, then:

Nausets (Some I traded for with Junior Revello 1/24/71 — I gave him Davis Shoal. Got a few from Frank, "Abba Jabba" from Boston — on 2/16/72)

3622	1090	45-47 fm.
3515	1115	68 fm.
3638	1101-1102	36 fm.
3502	1102	81-82 fm.

From 55-60 fath. tow SE bet. 3560 and 3570 until you get to 68-72 fm. Then hold that bet. 3560 and 3580. When in 30-36 fm you can't go further than 3585 to N and can tow 3640 line …

The Lizgale finally cleared the East gap of the Pt. Judith wall at 2:50 A.M., four hours and fifty minutes after she began to have her ice topped off. She headed down to the eastward, making good time with a twenty-five knot northwest fair wind patting her on the port quarter. The stars were as bright as they could be, lighting up the celestial dome in constellations that now became more visible in the middle of November. The air was clear and crisp, and not bashful in hinting that winter was on its way.

Jim Mackenzie was worried. Worried that he'd gotten them into something that would end in Doris losing Buddy's boat, and Ricky and Ozzie losing their livelihoods. Worried about the implications of what this Chambers would come up with next. Worried about his Russian romance … Is she okay? Right now, in the short-term, he had first watch and was very worried about what Ricky Helliott's reception would be when he stepped into the wheelhouse. The way he glared when they were all in the foc'sle a while ago. If looks could kill …

There was nothing he could do, and there was certainly nowhere to hide. It was time to face the music. Mack made himself a coffee, stuffed two Ring-Dings in his jacket pockets then climbed the foc'sle ladder and quickly went along the deck. He climbed up the starboard steps, took a deep breath and entered the wheelhouse. The warmth felt good compared to the chill air crossing the windy deck.

Ricky was at the chart table, back to the wheel when Mack closed the door behind him. Iron Mike, or the autopilot, was steering the course as Ricky pored over Buddy's hangbook, familiarizing himself with the list of bearings and where they led on the chart. Mack sipped his coffee and stood at the wheel, watching as it turned, making small rudder adjustments to keep the boat on course. The skipper never looked up or even acknowledged his presence. After a few long minutes, Mack figured he'd better take the lead and break the ice.

"What course, skipper?" he asked. Ricky never moved. He tried again. "Ricky, I need to know what course you want me to hold."

"There's a lot you need to know, college idjut." Ricky grumbled. "We're goin' in the right direction, just check the radar. See if you can do that without creating an international incident, will ya?" Ricky went back to his charts, never lifting his head.

The Lizgale steamed along for another mile or so before Mack got up his courage to speak again. "Look, Ricky, I'm ... I'm ... well ... really sorry for the way this turned out. I had no idea that ..."

"It's not your fault. I'm the skipper. It's always the skipper's fault, good or bad. I broke one of the cardinal rules the old man always drilled into me ... find your own fish, don't take anyone else's."

"But we just had two big money trips on the squid you knew would be there. You found 'em first, Cap."

"Maybe so, but I'm not gonna make the same mistake twice. We bought our way into 'em after they found us, but not this time. That guy Chambers thinks I'm an idjut, so I'm gonna let him keep thinkin' that. They all think we're just stupid dumb fishermen tryin' to dance with our pants down around our ankles. The old man always said to use what you've got, and that's about the only advantage I've got with that jerk. What I've got is he thinks I'm stupid ... but he ain't seen nuthin' yet!" Ricky lit a cigarette and blew smoke into the overhead. "He ain't seen nuthin'," he repeated as smoke puffed from his lips at every syllable.

Mack breathed a sigh of relief. At least Ricky was conversational and took the blame for things, even though Mack still felt just as guilty. The big plan for trading with them ... that was his doing. Still ... how in hell was he supposed to know they were being watched from some spyplane? No matter now. He gathered up some inner strength and asked, "What have you got in mind, Cap?"

Ricky looked up and smiled a sinister smile. He took his Cat hat off and frisbee'd it onto the chart table, then squinted at Mack, imitating Lee Chambers. "I'm gonna show 'em what a semester at the school of H-N is like!"

Mack looked at him with raised eyebrows, puzzled. "But what can ..."

"Mack … is Greg asleep yet?" Ricky interrupted with his hand raised.

"I don't think so. He was still arranging the grub when I left. He's got a special meal planned for the beginning of the trip, I think."

"Go get him, and Ozzie too. We're gonna have a strategy meeting. If this plan's gonna work, we've all got to be on the same page, roger that?"

"Roger that, skipper."

As the iron mike steered the course that took them a few miles off the entrance to the east passage of Narragansett Bay, Ricky called the meeting to order.

"Awright, boys, first of all, we're all in this together. Sink or swim."

"You could use a better choice of words, Cap, but you've made your point," Greg said. "What's up?"

"First up, that jerk Chambers thinks we're all a bunch of dummies. While you guys were blowin' ice in, I was readin' the bluesheet about where the Soviets were. His big tip is general knowledge to anyone who can read. Ever'one knows they're there, but what's a Point boat gonna do with a trip of pollock? We wouldn't get jack squat landin' that stuff back here."

"We're a … qu … qu … queerf … queerf … f … f … fish p … p … por … port, C … Cap!" Ozzie stammered out.

"Right! We wouldn't take a trip of butterfish to Boston, or scup to Gloucester. By the time they figured out where to sell it, the trucking costs would kill the price. Same thing, only different. Now, I was gonna go to the gully, but we all know that we would have been beat to death scrapin' a trip out in this nor'west breeze. S'posed to blow twenty-five to forty for the next three or four days straight … so actually, Chambers did have a decent idea … head to the east'ard and work in the lee of the Cape. Better than the Gully."

Ozzie nodded a well understood and appreciated approval of that piece of information. Mack and Greg were still listening quietly.

"Okay," Ricky continued. "You college oceanographers know about upwelling? They teach you anythin' about that for your twenty thousand bucks?"

"Sure," Greg answered. "The wind blows the top layer of water offshore, drawing the bottom layer up, bringing nutrients with it, starting the food chain rolling, right?"

"Correct-a mundo." Ricky answered. "Now, it's gonna blow out of the nor'west for a few days. What's gonna happen to the water off the Cape?" The skipper looked to Mackenzie for the answer.

"Well, I guess you'd have the upwelling thing going on there, right?"

Ricky nodded his head. "I don't know why ever'one says you college guys are so dumb … well, maybe I do! Anyways, we've got two things goin' for us so far, right?"

Three heads nodded in unison.

"Awright. Now … take a look here on this chart that I made up out of the hangbook."

The three crewmen gathered around the chart table and looked at a section of chart that was covered in hangs and wrecks that Ricky had plotted.

"Wicked, huh?" he asked.

"How are you going to get a net through there and keep it in one piece?" Mack asked. "Looks like a pretty tough spot."

"Yup … sure is," Ricky answered. "But this ain't the first pair of boots I've worn out, ya know. Look here where Buddy wrote this down. Where'd he get the info for this place?"

The three crewmen looked. In Buddy's own hand was written, "some of these I got from Bob Helliott." Ricky flashed his eyebrows like Groucho Marx.

"Yup, the old man taught Buddy how to get by up there. He had to learn somewhere, too, ya know. Some of the old tricks came back to me when that lard-ass Chambers mentioned the Highlands. I never would have thought about it, but …"

"I wondered why you agreed as easily as you did," Mack said.

"Thanks a lot for callin' me a wimp, college idjut! Nope, don't get the situation wrong here, Chambers can make our lives miserable. He's got guns and helicopters, we know that. He can also have us stopped as much as he wants, anytime he wants without a warrant."

"The conscription thing you mean?" Greg asked.

"Naaah. You can't conscript anythin' unless war is declared by Congress. Last time that happened was World War Two. 'Course, that was the last time there was a real war declared … tell that to the guys who went to Korea and 'Nam! Anyway, like I said, Chambers thinks we're all stupid … and that's good. But … he can make our lives a living hell, and do it legally, too."

Mack looked puzzled. "How? Isn't this still America?"

"Yup, but they've got the power to stop us for safety checks forty times a day if they want. They can stop us, hold us at gunpoint and search the boat for drugs ... all day, every day, without a warrant, if they want. He's still got that memo from the State Department, too, and I guess he had another one when we were in Edgartown. The State Police back-pedaled really easy, too, right? When's the last time you saw a Statey eat crow?"

"Roger that, Cap. So what's on the agenda?" Mack pressed.

"Look here at how these hangs and wrecks plot out. See the pattern?"

"Looks like a body of a headless woman," Greg said. "Nice figure, too."

"Correct-a-mundo, Maine-iac. The old man called this place the 'seawitch' tow. See how there's a clear line up through here, and it turns to go over here?"

"Looks tricky," Mack said.

"That's the whole idea. I'm pretty sure I can get us through here, but it's gonna be damned difficult for the skipper of a Soviet rig to follow us through without towin' up that coal barge ... or that old Liberty ship ... or that pile of rocks ... or ... And take the dividers and check where this is!" he pointed to the chart with his fingers making a drummed 'thump'!

Greg took the dividers and checked how far off the shore of the Cape the "seawitch" was. It varied, but some was inside of twelve miles. "They can't come inside of twelve miles!" Greg blurted out. "You got'em, Cap!"

"I got a couple more tricks up my sleeve. too," Ricky revealed. "First, we've gotta get down through the Sound and out the other end. Mack, you and Greg take her to inside Gay Head, just follow the chart, then get Oz up. We've got some gear work to do while we're steamin' through the Sound. Make sure you watch how the tide sets us towards the Vineyard, too. You guys from up north are used to the tide goin' up and down in big steps, but down this way, the tide goes back and forth in big steps."

The Lizgale steamed along towards Vineyard Sound. Mack had served a short watch getting the boat along the first leg to the eastward, then Greg stayed on until she was half-way between

Devil's Bridge, off Gay Head, and Quick's Hole, the shortcut the New Bedford boats use coming to and from Buzzards Bay.

Ozzie took over at 6:00 A.M., while Greg and Mack made breakfast. After breakfast mug-up, Oz brought her up through Vineyard Sound, past Lucas Shoal, past Wood's Hole where the Oceanography Institute is, past the West Chop and East Chop that make up the two jutting arms of Vineyard Haven Harbor. Meanwhile, Ricky, Greg and Mack changed over to the coarse twine net and made adjustments in the gear to accommodate the type of bottom they would be fishing in.

Ricky took over on the wheel when they were a mile to the westward of Cross Rip Shoal. He laid-to when they were a couple miles beyond Tuckernuck Shoal after they waved to Capt. Bill Coughlin, who was making his morning run on the Nantucket steamer *Siasconset*. The skipper then called for Mack and Greg to join him and Ozzie in the wheelhouse.

"I'm gonna slow things up a little bit. We don't want to beat our way through Pollock Rip with the wind against the tide, if we can help it. That place is nasty enough without going through with this nor'west beatin' against the tide and choppin' it up steep. It's quicker to wait, then go through there, than to steam for Great Round and have to backtrack to the north'ard. In the meantime, I want you guys to take down the anchor from the forepeak, check it out, then add a lot of chain to it. We've got some old chain back in the turtleback ... wrap it up so's she's nice and heavy. Then I need you guys to unshackle the forward door and shackle the anchor up to the forward wire. Lash it down good after you're through so she won't go nuts on us, just in case we hit some weather. I'll just jog along slow and eat up a little time. Should make it easier for you guys to work, too."

After the crew was through readying the anchor to the skipper's orders, as puzzling as they were, Ricky pushed the throttle up to steaming speed and headed for Pollock Rip. They passed Handkerchief Shoal, skirted south of Monomoy Island, steamed through Butler's Hole, then had a relatively smooth departure from Nantucket Sound via Pollock Rip channel, thanks to the fair tide and the lee afforded by Monomoy Island. It was now late morning and the sun shone bright on the breaking water on both sides of them as they went through the Rip. The wind was still out of the nor'west, blowing about thirty knots, with some gusts here and there. The temperature was about thirty-five degrees.

Once clear of the Rip's channel, the Lizgale turned to the northeast, then Ricky put her on a course to head for the bearings that Chambers had given him for the rendezvous with the Soviets. Seven-and-a-half miles before they got to the Soviets, at 3540 and 1090, in eighty-odd fathoms of water inside the 99 hump, Ricky stopped the boat and let her roll in the trough set up by the northwest chop. On the horizon, in the clear air of the late afternoon, he could see the iron curtain fleet working outside of them in the deeper water.

Ricky blew the horn. The crew set the trading packages they were making aside, dressed, then assembled on deck in the cold breeze of the pre-dusk. "Okay, boys." he yelled from the wheelhouse. We're at the 'witch'. Put the anchor overboard!"

With Ozzie on the tackle and Mack and Greg using the roll of the boat, the anchor was hoisted up then swung over the side. "I'm comin' around slow, Oz … set out a hunnerd seventy-five of wire, then put her in the block."

The deck crew did as ordered and soon the Lizgale was towing … not its net, but its anchor! The boat lunged, jerked and bounced between the actions of the waves and the constant fetching-up and letting go of the anchor flukes on the bottom. Ricky piloted the boat in a pattern that looked like a drunk might steer … up this way, a quick turn, over to the westward for a bit, another quick turn, back to the eastward. Ozzie knew all along what was going on, of course, but he delighted in watching Greg and Mack's faces. They were in total shock but didn't want to ask why Ricky was doing such an unorthodox maneuver.

Finally, Greg sidled up to Ozzie who was standing by at the PTO handle and asked, "Wouldn't we catch more if we put the net in the water?"

Ozzie laughed. He knew the surprise was worth the wait so he just shrugged and held his hands up in an 'I don't know' pose. "F … F … fol … foll … follow or … ord … ord … orders!" he said, but when he had a chance, he turned and winked at Ricky who was watching the same show out of the starboard wheelhouse window.

After a half-hour, Ricky slowed the boat and ordered the anchor brought aboard and lashed to the foremast, with the extra chain left installed. When that was accomplished, he turned the boat and steamed for the Soviets. "Get your care packages together, boys," he yelled from the wheelhouse. "Let's go see if your little flower is still blooming, Mack!"

Going beside the *Zvezda Rybaka* was getting to be a regular occurrence. The Soviets saw the Lizgale coming, slowed down to half throttle, the packages were hurled, Mack got to exchange bundles and see his sweetheart, then both vessels parted company. It was just as if the Russians planned for them to show up. Ricky steamed the Lizgale back to the bearings of the "witch," then ordered the gear to be readied for set-out, but not yet put in the water.

"Let's lay-to and grab a bite," he said. "No sense being in a hurry … we've got an hour or so. You got a mug-up for us, Greg?"

Greg was dumbfounded, as was his roommate/shipmate. *Lay-to?* he thought. "Lay-to and eat before we set in? He's lost his marbles!" he said to himself.

"Sure, Cap. We'll get the vegetables on and I'll have it out in fifteen minutes, how's that?" Greg answered. "Whatd'ya say, Mack?"

Mack and Greg put the finishing touches on the evening mug-up. Greg had cooked one of his specialties: roast lamb with mint jelly, assorted vegetables, and an impressive yorkshire pudding for each plate, no small feat from a diesel-fired cookstove. After the meal was savored to its last bite, the crew sat around the foc'sle table and complimented Greg on his mastery of the galley. Mack said it was one of the "best meals he'd ever had." Ozzie, after a minute, stuttered out that it was "f … f … f … f … fi … finestkind" … Ricky, in his own inimitable fashion, paid the highest compliment he'd ever paid to a cook when he nonchalantly said, "It'll make a turd."

Before long, the deck lights went on, the throttle went up, the wind sprayed the deck, the boat eased off to the starboard, and the Lizgale once again became a fishing machine.

Back in Newport, around the time that the trawldoors of the Lizgale hit the bottom with the net trailing close behind, Lee Chambers was about to call it quits for the night when he was phoned by the office of the Commander of Naval Intelligence in Washington:

"Chambers here, at your service, Sir."

"Admiral Rowe here. Chambers, I'll get right to it. Aerial surveillance indicates a window of opportunity for the deployment of the package from Groton to sea. Weathercom has also indicated that a window of fair wind conditions will prevail for forty-eight hours. Can you be ready to implement phase three in twenty-four hours time?"

Chambers checked off the flowchart of the operation in his head before answering: *The foreign fleets are split between Cape Cod and New Jersey looking for a flight test of two bombers that don't exist, and the weather's a go! Hah! The only shoreside detail left is to confirm that the old radar from the* Aurora *was installed on Navy oceangoing tug YS-166. It should be easy beans to steam her to a position to intercept the submarine over where the AT&T cable runs south of Block Island. Then all they had to do is jog along behind the sub and escort her off the Continental shelf, following the path of the phone cable below. The Russkies'll just think it's the* Aurora *patrolling the cable if they signature the signal, after all, it's the* Aurora's *radar, right? Still, why the rush, and should there be one, in the first place?*

"Admiral ... with all due respect, sir ... is there sufficient time to outfit the package for a vacation trip?" Chambers asked.

"Belay that, Chief. The package can be tied up with a pink bow in Scotland. TAC-COM-MEG wants it on its way to Europe A-S-A-P! Are we go?"

Chambers thought quickly, *They're going to move the sub to Scotland and finish outfitting it there? Well, it won't be the first time, I guess. But! The sooner I get it out of here, the sooner I get my new bars and the gold braid they promised me ... and ... retirement, and ... a fat increase in my pension! Oh! One more thing! I'll have to tell Marty to get a hold of his Russky contact and feed them a bunch of bull about the test of the bombers being moved up to tomorrow afternoon. That should be no problem seeing how they're already in position anyways. No sweat. I can have the YS-166 in position for the rendezvous at dusk tomorrow ...*

Chief Lee Chambers felt a certain twinge of majesty when he spoke. Essentially, he was giving orders to an Admiral, instead of receiving them. "Tomorrow. Eighteen hundred hours ... Go!"

"Marty, Chambers here. We're on for phase three at eighteen hundred tomorrow."

"They moved it up?"

"That's affirmative. Can you arrange intelligence cover for tomorrow afternoon?"

"Sure … I guess so, Lee. I'll let 'em know. How are you goin' to get word to the fishin' boats at sea? Won't they be vulnerable when the Soviets find out they've been had?"

"Doesn't matter to me. It's on a need to know basis. They didn't need to know anything up until now and they don't need to know … ever! If we change things before tomorrow night, it'll just compromise the mission."

"Are you sure they won't be sitting ducks for some kind of retaliation? Seems like a lot of funny business going on lately, and …"

"… And nuthin! The mission is the sub, period. We're not gonna have a repeat of the *Suzy and Anne* incident … not on my watch! You understand?"

"Sure, Chief Chambers, sure. Believe me, I sure do understand. Yes, sir," Marty Farmagano barked into the phone angrily. "The tug will be at the designated point south of Block Island at eighteen hundred hours tomorrow. Sir!"

Marty hung up the phone, his head shaking in disbelief. "It's his call…... he's the boss of this operation," he said. "Damn … I hope those guys are okay …"

26

THE SEA WITCH

LAT. 41 DEG. 51.5 MIN. N.
LONG. 69 DEG. 40.0 MIN. W.

After the dishes were washed and put away, Mack made two cups of coffee and sprinted for the wheelhouse between deluges of northwest-driven spray. Ricky's surprising change of face and his unothodox methodology had Mack's curiosity piqued, but the main reason he went to the wheelhouse was that he'd made his mind up that he was going to own and skipper his own dragger someday and observing Ricky Helliott in the wheelhouse was like taking a doctorate-level course in commercial fishing operations. Capt. Helliott had never successfully steered beyond his third year of high school, but he was at the top of his form, and his class, when he had the spokes of the Lizgale's wheel in his hands. *They just don't teach that stuff in books,* Mack thought.

"Coffee, Cap?"

Ricky took the mug and set it next to the compass without looking up. His eyes were glued to the recording paper of the depth sounder, his hands white-knuckled onto the wheel's spokes, his body tense and ready to react.

"Gotta pay attention here," the skipper said. "We've only got about three-quarters of an hour to get through the witch on slack tide. The stuff's here, though ... take a look."

Mack looked over towards the depth sounder and saw large "haystacks" of fish settling down and bunching up near the bottom as they towed along. "What are we on?" he asked.

"Codfish, pollock and haddock, college Cousteau. Should be some flat stuff in here, too. Wanna see somethin'? Watch the double echo come up in a couple of seconds."

Mack maintained a careful gaze on the double echo. The "double echo" is a line drawn across the lower end of the recording paper that mimics the actual readout of the depth readout. When the double echo shows a faint line, the sounder is determining a softer bottom. When the double echo looks heavy and thick, the bottom is harder, or some hard obstruction is underneath. Fish only show up above the top line, not the double echo, therefore they won't be confused for an underwater ledge, hang, wreck, whatever. The sounder actually records the presence of the fish's air bladder, the tiny bubble of air contained within their bodies that keeps them floating upright.

"Ricky, I've got to ask. What was the deal with the anchor?"

The skipper shook his head as he studied the bottom. "Why do you s'pose those fish are so interested in settling down to feed right here in-between all these hangs and wrecks, smart-boy?"

Suddenly Mack realized what Ricky's strategy was. He plowed up the bottom to release the worms and shellfish that would act as bait and attract other baitfish. Slack tide enabled the shoals of fish to settle down in the safe haven provided by the underwater wrecks and hangs. Having one small corner of the ocean where they could gorge themselves, the concentration of fish was remarkably heavy.

Ricky took a quick glance and noticed the enlightened look on his shipmate's face.

"Ever wonder why a farmer plows his field?" he asked. "Gotta loosen things up don't'cha think?"

Mack was impressed. "Ricky, you're all class," he muttered.

"Yup, all class ... all low," the skipper countered. "Now pay attention to that double echo ... you're about to see a Liberty ship, or what's left of one."

Sure enough, the top line of the sounder showed a steep rise. The double echo rose also and changed from a faint line to a very heavy black, showing the steel of the ship below in contrast to the mud around it. Mack was enjoying the show when he had a sudden shocking realization ... if that was a ship below them, and they were towing their net right for it, then ...

Ricky watched with grim determination, then, as if he were following an internal countdown, spun the wheel hard to starboard. Mack smiled and watched in awe as the sounder showed they were moving back off the wreck. The Lizgale went over the hulk of the Liberty Ship, but the net, streaming along behind, missed it when Ricky turned.

In a few more minutes, Ricky pulled the same maneuver ... this time a turn to port away from a sunken coal barge. Next was with a rockpile ... the next with a hang that he didn't quite know what it was, other than that it would rimrack the net if they got too close. When all was said and done, the Lizgale had towed for an hour and five minutes before the tide began to run really hard again. The horn blew for haulback when they were just inside of the twelve mile territorial sea limit at the place where the sea witch's severed head, if she had one, would be.

Down below, as Ozzie pulled his boots on, he began singing a parody of Willie Nelson's "On the Road Again."

On the tow again!
... catchin' codfish on the tow again!
Hope the seawitch will be good to you and me ....
I just can't wait to be on the tow again!

Laying in the northwest chop, the Lizgale's hoister alternately strained and groaned, then ran free as the haulback brought the gear from the bottom. When the doors were raised above the bottom and the net's weight became apparent, the crew knew they were in for a large bag. The tow wires snapped and popped on the winch drums. Silently the crew went through the haulback motions they had, by now, honed to a fine art.

After the doors were swinging from the gallus frames and the ground cables and legs of the net were wound on the hoister drums, it became apparent that this was no mundane hauling of the gear. All of a sudden, the decklights shone on large breaking bubbles that were rising next to the Lizgale's rail. Ricky and Ozzie exchanged knowing eye contact as a look of fear filled Greg and Mack's faces.

When the two younger crewmen noticed the bubbling alongside, they both dove for the deck in anticipation of another impending disaster. All of a sudden, the cod-end of the net shot up and broke the surface, floating like a huge, fish-filled balloon. Ozzie and Ricky let out whoops of cheer, but Mack and Greg interpreted the cheers as warnings and stayed prone on the rolling deck.

Ricky laughed out loud from the starboard wheelhouse window. "If I tied you two up with larchwood and stuffed your pockets full of rocks, you still wouldn't make a decent killick for a fish trap! Get up off that deck and see what we've got!" he yelled, hardly restraining his exuberance. "The old man didn't let us down on this tow, boys!"

Mack and Greg raised their heads slowly, crept to the rail on all fours and peered overboard. They stood up and cheered when they realized what was floating alongside of them ... a full cod-end of groundfish! There were so many cod, haddock and pollock in the bag that the bloated air bladders of the fish made the cod-end float! The mother lode of the sea witch herself lay right next to them, riding in the northwest trough.

"Whatd'ya think, Oz?" The skipper yelled from the wheelhouse.

"T ... t ... tw ... twen ... twent ... twenty ... th ... thou ... thous ... thousand e ... eee ... e ... eas ... easy!"

"Yup, that's my guess, too! Not bad, huh?"

"F ... f ... fi ... fine ... fine ... finest ... k ... k ... ki ... ki ... kind!"

There were too many fish in the bag to take over the rail in one shot, but after they had split the bag and got everything aboard in two lifts, Mack and Greg were too numb to speak. They stood almost waist-deep in a pile of shining, flipping fish that covered the deck from rail to rail.

"Leave the bag aboard, boys," Ricky commanded. "We'll steam out a ways then fish around the Russky guys for the next couple of tows. Wait'll they get a peek at this deckload!"

Once again, Greg and Mack were confused, but decided that Ricky definitely knew what he was doing, even if it was another mystery why they weren't setting the net back in the same place. As they steamed to their new set-in bearings, Ozzie did his best to explain:

"C ... c ... can ... can't g ... g ... get thr ... th ... thr ... through ... un ... un ... un ... unless ... sssss it ... it ... it's ... s ... s ... sl ... sla ... slack t ... t ... t ... ti ... ti ... tide! N ... n ... no ... no s ... s ... sl ... sl ... slee ... ee ... eep t ... t ... to ... to ... tonight!"

Greg and Mack understood. The only way that Ricky could successfully tow the net through such a horrible piece of bottom was to wait for the tide to go slack for maneuverability. That, and the need for the fish to settle down to feed, after the clever anchor trick.

Soon, the Lizgale had her gear back on the bottom; this time it was blue colored mud, close to one-hundred fathoms below the surface. The Soviet fleet was towing to the westward, about three miles outside of them. Ricky smiled mischievously, lit a cigarette and steered the Lizgale right for the center of the oncoming fleet. The decklights and seagulls following advertised their catch as they lunged eastward, towing with the wind on their stern.

The three crewmen started the herculean task of sorting, gutting and icing down the mountain of fish that lay before them. Cleaning up a deckload that big wasn't labor, though ... it was pure joy.

As they towed past some of the Soviet catcher boats, all hands stopped their deckwork to see what the Americans were doing. It wasn't long before the word was passed through the iron curtain fleet ... the Americans were rail-to-rail in fish! Ricky made sure he worked the Lizgale around as many Soviet catcher boats as he could to show off their bounty. With his yellow hat cocked jauntily on the back of his red hair, he chuckled to himself with grievous intent, "C'mon, boys ... you ain't seen nuthin' yet. I'm gonna introduce you to the witch when it's the right time!"

For most of the night, the Lizgale worked with the Soviets, catching greysole, pollock and cod, but the tows were nothing like the first tow through the witch. The deck was never cleared of fish before the next tow was dumped, however. In fact, it took through the second and third tows just to clean up the deck from the first. When the midnight tow was lifted aboard, Ricky ordered that the gear be left onboard and they steamed back to the original set-out bearings for the witch. The next slack tide was one-thirty in the morning and Captain Helliott had another surprise up his sleeve.

It wasn't long after they had set in again and began the tedious job of maneuvering through the sea witch tow that Ricky's plan reached phase two. He laughed to himself when he checked the radar and saw that three Soviet boats had altered their course and were attempting to tow their nets up to the Lizgale's favored haven.

Ricky lit a cigarette and checked the ship's clock. "They should be here just about the time when the tide starts running again," he muttered as he turned away from the sunken hulk of the Liberty ship that met its fate so long ago when a German submarine torpedoed it. "C'mon, boys, just keep-a-comin'!" he laughed. "Steady as she goes!"

Just as the Lizgale finally cleared the witch's head, and were in clear ground inside of twelve miles, the three Soviet boats were just beginning to reach the outboard point of the witch where the bottom was filled with obstructions. Only someone with time and knowledge invested could tow through there ... and ... only someone who understood that this was only possible on slack tide.

As the Lizgale turned and towed to the northward, the tide let loose again. Ricky called out to his shipmates on deck, "Take a break, boys! Look off to starboard and watch the show!"

Ricky switched off the decklights to enhance their night vision as the crew watched across two miles of ocean to see one ... two ... three sets of Soviet running lights come to a grinding, bow-diving halt! Ricky flung open the starboard wheelhouse door and stepped out on the steps like Caesar in victorious glory. How'd'ya like that?" he yelled across the water through cupped hands. "Whatsa matter? Can't tow through a Liberty ship? Hope you've got plenty of coal from that barge! Buildin' a stone wall? Need some rocks, Russky boys?"

In one fell swoop, three Soviet catcher boats had their nets hung-up on some of the most unmerciful, unforgiving, net-rimracking items that the ocean can dish up ... a ship, a barge and a rockpile! Ricky laughed, lit a cigarette, turned on the decklights, and stepped back into the wheelhouse as he yelled to his deck-weary crew, "Five more hours and we hit slack tide again! Attack with vigor, men!"

Onboard the *Zvezda Rybaka*, the third mate had left the bridge after receiving a disturbing radio call. He hurried through the companionways, arrived at the quarters of the chief mate, then gave a bare-knuckled rap on the door.

"*Starpom!*"

"*Da.*"

"I'm very sorry, Comrade *Starpom*. We have three boats ... the twenty-eight, fifty-six and sixteen out of commission!"

"Three boats! Three?"

"*Da!* All three report it is just like they are glued to the bottom. They cannot budge their gear! They were following the Americans, and ..."

"Do you have any idea how the *nachalnik* will take this report … three at the same time, in the same place … and all following the Americans? I told them not to do that!"

"This is true, *Starpom*, but you saw the deckload of fish they had! They had as much in an hour as we have for the whole day. We had to try!"

"Do you need me on the bridge?"

"*Nyet, Starpom*. The *spasatel* will go to assist if they cannot get free."

"*Tak derzhat!* But! … Stay where you know the ground is clear. This is an order! Do you understand why, now?"

The 2:15 A.M. haul-back aboard the Lizgale went smoothly and productively. Fourteen thousand pounds of mixed groundfish were on deck, waiting for a berth in the hold below. After the tow, Ricky steamed the boat back amongst the iron curtain fleet and set in with them again. The various skippers of the catcher boats and the officers on the bridge of the *Zvezda Rybaka* were once again treated to the view of an American boat that was rail-to-rail in fish and … rubbing their noses in it.

Ricky kept working around the Soviets for the remainder of the morning. At the 7:30 A.M. slack water, he couldn't make another set through the sea witch anyway; the three Soviet catcher boats that were hung-up on various "romantic spots" effectively blocked the passage through the tow. Ten o'clock in the morning and two boats still couldn't get their gear free; the one that did managed only to retrieve their set of doors and the parted, severed remains of their ground cables. The old wooden coal barge sunk in World War One by a German U-boat had claimed another net for its decorative adornment.

Once the Lizgale's deck was cleared from the night deckload and the fishing was producing manageable haul-backs, Ricky broke the crew into semi-watches and began to rotate one man off deck for each tow, trying to gain each crewman a little rest. The morning fishing was steady … cod, pollock, greysole and a handful of haddock, but it only took forty-five minutes to clear the deck, leaving a small amount of time to re-coup.

The northwest breeze finally abated about noontime, leaving only a small white-capped chop. When Ricky came back to the wheel after catching a kink, he rubbed his eyes in disbelief. The Soviet fleet was building up, even though the fishing was steadily decreasing.

"Ever'thin' go okay?" the skipper asked in a gravelly voice as he lit a cigarette.

"Yeah, no problem," Mack answered. "They've still given us a clear line and so far are still friendly. I just stayed right on the line like you said. The other two guys finally got off the sea witch hangs about an hour ago. The support tug was helping one of them. You're some kind of pirate, Cap!"

"There's some more folks who just learned you can't catch someone else's fish! The only reason we got through was because the old man found all that stuff the hard way, ya know. There's no free lunches out here … doesn't matter who ya are. When I was a kid, I can remember getting hung-up on that old coal barge. How do you suppose I knew it was a coal barge, book-brain? We spent a good day gettin' offa that thing and were lucky to get the gear back, even though we were rimracked to shreds. There was coal stuffed into some of the meshes that did come up and we got a huge bulkhead timber … I'm guessin' it was forty feet long. That's some bad stuff over there, but we've already got a good trip goin' from it."

"What do you make of these guys? I've counted six more boats coming into the fleet in the past hour. The whole of Georges Bank is outside of us and they want to fish this close? I don't get it." Mack observed.

"Who knows. Maybe they think that the fish we got will be around for them, but I'm not even gonna go back to the witch until we come back from Boston. Those fish have gone inside, probably laying along the outside edge of the beach where the fifty fathom drop-off is. When we come back, we'll snuff 'em out again with the old man's anchor trick. I think we'll just grind away here for today, unless it gets too crowded."

"Then what, Cap?"

"I looked at the bluesheet again before I caught a kink. All the big Boston boats landed about six days ago. They should be headed back off now and our load of fish should look pretty good sittin' in Boston. They won't be home again for awhile, so I think we'll play the market a little bit. We'll steam for Beantown tonight and catch the price tomorrow, then pound the witch again, ya know … make a couple short trips, then head back home through the Cape Cod canal and re-group."

Ricky took the binoculars and scanned the horizon. "Sure is funny that they'd bring this whole fleet in here when they've got this place about mopped up. Fifteen knots of wind and they're headin' in here? We'll be outta here at sundown, so they can have it anyways. They should be long gone by the time we get back."

"What are we going to do about what the Coast Guard guy said?" Mack asked. He wanted to know for three reasons: his paycheck, his safety and … his sweetheart.

"I dunno," Ricky answered as he exhaled smoke out the port window. "I don't understand ever'thin' I know about that mess, either. You can't get too far ahead of yourself in this business, but I'll tell ya one thing, mister … I'm still skipper here. I don't believe him as far as I could throw him, and judging by the fender-belly he's wearin', I couldn't throw him far."

27

RESERVED CHANNEL

LAT. 41 DEG. 54.1 MIN. N.
LONG. 69 DEG. 31.2 MIN. W.

LAT. 42 DEG. 21.27 MIN. N.
LONG. 71 DEG. 2.0 MIN. W.

By three o'clock in the afternoon, the *Elizabeth Gale* was surrounded by Soviet boats, but the situation was definitely different than earlier. Their support tug and their research vessel were rafted alongside the *Zvezda Rybaka*, which had been laying-to since a little after noontime. The three catcher boats that got hung-up on the sea witch were laying-to also, presumably doing gear work trying to get themselves work-wise again. The fleet wasn't working in its usual grid pattern; they were spread out in uncharacteristic disarray.

Back in Newport, Navy tug *YS-166* left her berth to take up her rendezvous position southeast of Block Island, directly over the phone cable laid twenty-two fathoms below. Over in Long Island Sound, a surrounding cover of Navy vessels was well underway from Groton, escorting a nuclear submarine that was keeping moderate speed at periscope depth.

On board the *Zvezda Rybaka*, the *nachalnik* and members of the intelligence corps from the research vessel were spread out along the bridge wings and rails, waiting to catch the first glimpse of the new composite-framed American bomber taking off from Otis Air Force base. Similarly, far to the westward, other factory ships and their *nachalnik* and intelligence crews were in the same stance, waiting for the other bomber's flight from Andrews Air Force Base. Soviet anticipation was high as the weather was excellent for picture taking and intelligence gathering. The Soviet crews stood by patiently, cameras ready, waiting for the golden moment.

The fishing crews were confined below decks. The afternoon was declared a *banya* day, the showers and steam baths were open to everyone, not just the officers. The crew wasn't sure why they were given the afternoon off, but were glad nonetheless; time off at sea usually came from a hurricane or some mechanical breakdown. There was almost a party atmosphere aboard the Soviet vessels.

And the men on the Lizgale and the other boats to the westward were unknowing pawns of the "spice trade," oblivious to the situation they were an unwitting part of.

No one knew that there was no flight test of a new bomber, that, in fact, there was no such plane.

At five o'clock, as it was getting close to sundown, the Soviets began getting edgy about the empty sky. Just as they were about to contact their agent on shore, the radar officer came to make an announcement to the intelligence crew gathered on the wings and deck:

"Comrades, we have a faint sighting of an aircraft coming from shore! A very faint blip, like almost nothing."

"Good!" *Nachalnik* Sokhorov said. "Where is it?"

"It is hard to distinguish, but they are headed directly towards us," the third mate answered. "About four miles to the west."

Sokhorov addressed the members of the intelligence crew who were nearby. "This is it, my fellow comrades! The absence of a hard blip on the radar must be the new composite-framed aircraft! The Americans were trying to build a bomber that was nearly invisible on radar. It would seem that perhaps they have succeeded. Prepare your photography equipment!"

The intelligence corps trained their cameras on the horizon. The Powerful lenses on these cameras would clearly show a person's eye color at a half-mile. They were ready. The aircraft became visible and the cameras followed the plane's trajectory as those aboard the *Zvezda Rybaka* grew more eager in anticipation.

"Follow them closely!" Sokhorov ordered. "Document every move! The Kremlin will surely decorate us for providing the information on such an important event!"

But soon the photographers looked puzzled, then almost frightened.

"*Nachalnik* Sokhorov!" one camera operator exclaimed. "Respectfully, Comrade, please cast your eyes on the aircraft! It looks like the face of our fallen leader, Nikita Kruschev!"

Sokhorov focused through the camera as the aircraft flew up to the *Zvezda Rybaka* at an altitude of fifty feet. The plane circled the bridge of the ship three times and dipped its wings.

The Soviet crew was stunned. Shocked. Speechless.

What would the ramifications be in the Kremlin after they reviewed the pictures and videotapes of a single-engine Piper Cub flying overhead with Chambers' jack-o-lantern face in the passenger seat window, and ... Chambers showing the universally understood signal of the upward thrust middle finger?

Nachalnik Sokhorov was livid. He hoisted the camera over his head and hurled it into the sea as he shouted a barrage of Russian expletives and futilely shook his fists at the plane. His eyes went to the three stricken catcher vessels, still attempting to fix their gear. He looked towards the horizon and saw the other vessels of his floating *sovkhoz*, displaced for many, many miles off the good fishing by the promise of this farcical espionage coup. He looked to the eastward and saw ... the Lizgale, still working on her last tow of the trip.

"The Americans!" Sokhorov seethed. He turned to the captain of the research ship and barked, "Contact our comrades, the East Germans. Make sure your research ship can carpet the bottom with explosives. The Americans will surely return, but will never leave!" Then he turned to Captain Minolin and *Starpom* Fedorovich: "Have Kochen bring me the *ofitsiantki.*"

"But, Comrade Sokhorov ..." the captain protested, "Kochen is secured below. We ..."

"I issued an order, Captain Minolin! Kochen is the leader of the *Komsomol*, his father is third in line at the Kremlin. He should be the one to address what acts of treason against the party mean when committed by a crewmember. Trading with the Americans!

Stupid *dizbuks!* Now move, before you two are answering your own charges of treason!"

Onboard the Lizgale, it was almost time to haul back, put the gear aboard and steam for Boston. The crew was passing the remaining time of the tow huddled in the wheelhouse, "shootin' th' breeze" before sundown.

"That was strange, huh?" Mack said to Greg as they watched a small plane circle the *Zvezda Rybaka*, then fly off again.

"Weird, that's for sure. Almost like he was lost and circled to ask directions," Greg replied. Ozzie's nod concurred.

"Hey … look over there!" Ricky said. "Isn't that one of those research boats that the Russkies have?" He laughed and lit a cigarette. "They prob'bly sent them over to figure out where all the fish we got came from … fat chance on locatin' 'em now."

The haulback was uneventful but that was just fine with the crew of the Lizgale. The net spilled out a few bushels of mixed fish; nothing big, but not too bad, considering the pounding that the grounds had taken from the large fleet of iron curtain boats nearby. Ricky ordered the doors brought aboard and secured, then the net was picked over and flaked down into its storage place along the starboard rail. The crew began sorting and storing the catch as the skipper turned and set a course past Peaked Hill Buoy to clear the northern tip of the Cape and head for Boston. The sun's last rays were down below the westward horizon; just a faint glimmer remained. The ocean lit into a pink colored reflection as the northwest breeze abated to leave the sea perfectly calm at sundown. Spirits were high again … another nice trip caught in a short amount of time.

Meanwhile, Navy tug *YS-166* was laying-to at her appointed position eight and-a-half miles southeast of Block Island, just outside of the old wreck that was rumored to have sulphuric acid onboard when she went down. Twenty-two fathoms below them was the west leg of the trans-Atlantic phone cable that was laid to the southeast and eventually went off the continental shelf. The skipper watched the escort flotilla approach through the sundown glow as they steamed towards him from the westward. The *Aurora*'s old radar was working a-ok and clearly showed the Navy boats coming. The rendezvous went off without a hitch; the support craft went back to Long Island Sound and the *YS-166* followed the course of the cable at eight knots with the sub just below the surface ahead of them, headed out, undetected by the Soviets.

Onboard the *Zvezda Rybaka*, *Starpom* Fedorovich hurried down two decks then threaded his way along the companionways that were filled with reveling, singing, dancing crewmembers. He walked briskly past, looking at the faces quickly. He had to find young Kristiian and big sister Mari and somehow ensure their safety before he was forced to let Kochen free of his handcuffs.

The *starpom* found Kristiian in the company of Yuliya, one of the young *bufetchitsas*. She was taking the afternoon off from her stewardess duties and was teaching Ukrainian folksongs to some of the children aboard. *Starpom* took her aside and ordered her to very quickly and calmly take all the children to his cabin and stay with them there. When he asked if she had seen Mari, the answer Yuliya gave caused him to sprint away: "She was taken topside by Petrovich Kochen, *Starpom* Fedorovich. The *Starshi Master Dobychi* was ordered by the *nachalnik* to release him. Surely, you must have known that ..."

Starpom Fedorovich retraced his steps back along the companionways and ran up the stairs, climbing two to three steps at a time. *I took too long looking for them,* he thought. *I should have gone directly to that murderous bilge rat ... now the bo'sun has released him ... and ... he has her!*

"Ahhh, my Dear, the fresh air smells so good. Did you not miss me while I was confined to the factory lines below?"

"I missed you not, and I will miss you never," Mari spat out as she struggled to get free from Kochen's grip. "Help!" she cried out.

"They are all below decks, partying and drinking their homemade vodka, my *puristaa*," said Kochen, who easily controlled her escape attempts. "They cannot hear you or help you. Please help yourself and cooperate and I'll see that the *nachalnik* won't prosecute you for plotting with the Americans. Surely, you must be wise enough to know where that will lead you!"

Mari stomped on his foot and momentarily shook free of his grasp, then began running down the length of the *shlupochnaya paluba*. The boat deck was long but it was relatively easy for Kochen to sprint and ruthlessly tackle her, slamming her face painfully on the deck. He wrestled her up over his shoulders, saying, "I love it when you kick and scream, my darling. Your fingernails feel like small daggers of love!"

Running onto the deck, *Starpom* Fedorovich saw the horrifying scene as Kochen hoisted Mari over the rail and held her struggling, over the sea. "Kochen!" he yelled. "Bring her back aboard! Now!"

"Save yourself Fedorovich!" Kochen screamed back. He looked at Mari's terrified face, then said, "You could have had it so good, my dear, but now the sharks will have you instead. You wanted to go to America ... here's your chance!"

He released his grip and with a savage smile watched her bruised and bloodied face splash into the sea seconds before *Starpom* Fedorovich could reach him.

The two men grappled around on the deck. Kochen had no mercy for the man who had locked him in handcuffs and was bent on killing the *starpom* with his bare hands. But Fedorovich was still a worthy and cunning fighter and was seething with anger from what he had just witnessed. As the two opponents tried to get the best of one another, the vessel suddenly turned sharply, throwing the fighters into a roll against the rail.

On the bridge, oblivious to the events aft, Captain Minolin was following the orders of the livid *nachalnik*. The *Zvezda Rybaka* and all the other boats of the *sovkhoz* simultaneously turned east at full throttle and began steaming for the Northeast Peak, the farthest reach of Georges Bank.

Ozzie was hunched over, picking the deck, when he momentarily stood up to straighten his back. Out of the corner of his eye he thought he saw something hit the water as they steamed past the *Zvezda Rybaka*, but *naaaah, it was probably nothing. No gulls anyway.* He went back to his deckwork alongside Greg and Mack as the Lizgale sliced on.

A few minutes later, Oz was down below in the hold chopping ice when the thought came back to him, *No gulls ... no gulls.* He retraced what he saw. A splash ... the ship turned and steamed off. No gulls. No birds of any kind ... A splash that wasn't garbage and didn't have any baitfish around ... Oh my God!

Ozzie threw the ice chopper down and yelled over at Mack, who was putting in a penboard to hold in the last of the codfish that Greg was dumping down from the deck. "M ... mmm ... mmma ... ma ... Mack! N ... n ... nnn ... no ... g ... g ... g ... g ... gul ... gul ... gull ... gulls!"

Mack fixed the last penboard in the keeper slot and turned around. "What?"

"N ... nnn ... n ... n ... no ... g ... g ... g ... g ... gggu ... gulls!" Ozzie screamed with his hands waving.

"What?" Mack asked again, puzzled. "I don't follow, Oz, what's up?"

Ozzie waved him off. He didn't have time to explain. He bolted for the ladder, roared out onto the deck then ran for the wheelhouse. The engineer burst through the door, threw Ricky out of the way, grabbed the wheel and spun the boat around. He pushed the throttle handle forward until the Lizgale's engine was on the pin ... eighteen-fifty r.p.m.'s ... full speed!

The skipper picked himself up off the sole at about the same time that Mack and Greg hurried up the steps into the wheelhouse. "What's wrong?" they both asked. "What's goin' on?"

"You lost your marbles or what, Oz?" he demanded. "What the hell's gotten into you anyways?!"

Ozzie was beside himself. He knew exactly what had to be done but couldn't waste precious time to explain first.

"Sp ... spl ... spla ... splash ... sh ... sh ... sh! N ... n ... no ... no ... no ... g ... g ... g ... ggg ... ulls! "

Ozzie pointed towards the eastward sea in large, sweeping arm movements.

"Oz," Ricky said, "let me take the wheel. Now calm down and sing it to us. Take it easy, man and just sing it out!"

Ozzie handed over the wheel as he stood back and took a deep breath. "Get back to where the Russian ship was. Man overboard!" he sang.

It was six-thirty when the Lizgale headed back to the eastward. When they reached the best guess-timate of where the *Zvezda* was located, it was close to seven o'clock. Thankfully, the sea was flat calm and the moon was out, but what or who were they looking for? The decklights of the Soviet fleet were just fading over the eastern horizon as the Point boat idled around in a search pattern, sweeping the sea with the searchlight.

Ricky ordered Greg and Mack to go to the forepeak so they would be in the best place to hear a cry for help as he stayed on the wheel and Ozzie manned the searchlight. They started their search at the bearings they figured for the last position of the *Zvezda*, then circled in an ever-widening radius. Ricky checked the tide vector on the chart and tended to favor the north side of the search, but he still held to a tight circle for the most part … they weren't gone that long.

Up forward, Greg and Mack shaded their eyes from the searchlight and tried to focus on the surface of the sea around them. If they got their eyes in the right place in relation to the moonlight, they could actually see a little bit if they really worked at it.

"Got any idea what we're lookin' for, Mack?" Greg asked as he scanned the port bow.

"Nope," Mack answered, keeping watch off to starboard. "The Soviets are long gone. You'd think if they lost someone, they'd have realized it before we got back. If they put that whole fleet to work searching, probably whoever went over is back aboard by now."

"Let's hope so, for their sake," Greg added.

The Lizgale searched on for another few minutes when Greg thought he saw something. "Mack … do you see something over there?" he asked, pointing off to the port.

Mack came alongside Greg and squinted his eyes. "Where?"

Greg pointed out about a hundred feet off the boat. "Over there. See something kind-of bobbing up and down?"

Mack looked again. "I sure do!" he realized. "Ricky! Ozzie! A hundred feet off the port bow!" they yelled.

Ozzie swung the searchlight over and immediately found the shape of a person's head bobbing above the water. When the light hit the eyes of the victim, there was one wave of an arm, then the head and body slipped underwater. Ricky put the throttle back and turned on the decklights as he brought the starboard side of the boat alongside the stricken person. Greg, Mack and Ozzie converged at the starboard rail and peered overboard.

Ozzie was the first to see the head rise slightly below the surface before it sank again. While he pointed furiously and attempted to jabber out that he saw the victim, Mack took one look, tore off his oilers and boots and dove overboard.

Ricky came running from the wheelhouse. "Damned fool college idjut!" he yelled into the sea. "Are you crazy?"

Mack came up for air, then went back underwater. When someone is underwater, seconds seem like hours. When you're waiting on deck for someone to surface from underwater, it seems even longer. Mack Mackenzie was no free-diver and really wasn't much of a swimmer at all. His lungs were burning as he tried to flap his way down, but he knew why he had to give it his all ... he'd seen that face before and had been in love with it since the first time he'd seen it.

On deck, Greg, Ozzie and Ricky clutched the rail in panic. Mack had been down there way too long ... Greg couldn't wait any longer. He pulled off his oilers and boots and dove in.

Greg was an athlete and a certified scuba diver. He'd also had some training in free-diving. He swam as deep as he could, then reached out and grabbed aimlessly in the water. By a stroke of God, he latched onto someone's hair and began pumping his legs for the surface.

When Greg's head broke clear of the sea, two more heads followed. Mack sputtered and coughed as Greg let go of his hair, then the both of them helped their stricken victim to the rail where Ricky and Ozzie grabbed her shoulders and hoisted her aboard. They laid her on the deck, then retrieved Mack and Greg, shivering with numbing cold but still helping to get the girl into Ricky's bunk back aft. She was breathing, but she was blue and unconscious.

At Otis Air Force base, the phone was ringing.

"Chambers here. State your business and speak quickly. I'm retiring tomorrow."

"Chief Chambers, Group Boston has received a distress call from the *Elizabeth Gale*. They're requesting a helicopter airlift for a man overboard. We need your okay."

"Did they say who the crewman was?"

"Actually, the call was for a woman to be airlifted, Sir. Late teens or early twenties. Facial trauma. Near-drowning victim."

Chambers thought for a moment, his eyes squinted into pencil lines. "Advise Group Boston that the *Elizabeth Gale* is no longer on a confidential mission and this distress call is the cryptic signal that they are clear. Reply with the 'hee-lo' being deployed elsewhere ... that's my signal to them to break off. How on that?"

"Understood, Chief."

Chambers laughed out loud as he opened his briefcase and donned the gold-braided hat of a Lieutenant Commander. "God, I'm gonna miss this job!"

Greg brought two fit-outs of Mack's dry clothes, coffees and a cup of bullion for the patient as the *Lizgale* made safe passage north of Peaked Hill Bar and steamed across Massachusetts Bay for Boston. Soaking wet and freezing, Mack had refused to leave the patient's side. It wasn't long before she was dressed in some of his dry clothes, safe and covered in blankets in Ricky's stateroom bunk. Her color had come back, and her breathing sounded a lot better, but she still wasn't fully conscious. Mack gently brushed the hair away from her cheeks and winced as he saw the extent of her injuries; a black eye, her right cheek cut, her lips swollen and bruised. Her nose looked like it took an awful thud … maybe that was broken, too. Still, in spite of all the trauma she had gone through, her beauty could not be masked or mistaken. It was her! Here she was! It was a miracle, but right now, he was so worried about her …

"What kind of person could do this to you and leave you out there?" he whispered to her closed eyes as he lovingly stroked her hair. "You're safe with me now."

In the wheelhouse, Ricky fumed as he hung up the radio microphone. "How in hell can they say that they can't send the chopper? It's somewheres else? Idjuts!" He turned around and yelled back to Mack, "No chopper's comin' so take good care of her!

Onboard *YS-166*, things went great … "fartin' in satin," they say. The night was clear and calm and there was no boat traffic to speak of. The radio was fairly quiet … no conversations concerning anything in their general area. There were no problems reported from the sub up ahead. The coffee was always on, the cable patrol/sub escort was a cakewalk. On through the night, the same report would apply. A couple hours before dawn when they crossed the one-thousand fathom curve east of Block Canyon, the sub dove deep to traverse the Atlantic and the *YS-166* turned and started the twelve-hour steam back to Newport. Mission accomplished. Easy beans.

Ricky kept the engine on the pin as they steamed to Boston. As Race Point fell away behind them, Mari would alternately regain some conscious moments then drift off again, always mumbling the word "christian." Mack bandaged her cuts and abrasions and held ice on her swollen face to help ease the pain while she was sleeping.

About half-way between Race Point and Minot's Light, she awoke, sat up and took a small amount of the bullion broth that Greg brought. Before she dozed off again, she smiled through her pain, clutched Mack's hand, then whispered the word '*kapteeni*'.

Crossing Massachusetts Bay, the Lizgale passed Minot's Light, steamed for the buoy at Ultonia ledge, went past Point Allerton and skirted past Lovell Island. Ricky cut through the Narrows, hooked up with President Roads, passed the south end of the runways at Logan Airport and at three-thirty in the morning they were tied up at the South Boston Army Base in Reserved Channel. A bushel of lobsters and ten haddock later, an Army staff car was transporting Ozzie, Greg, Mack and Mari through the streets of Boston en route to the Brighton Marine Hospital.

28
BOSTON

LAT. 42 DEG. 21.27 MIN. N.
LONG. 71 DEG. 2.0 MIN. W.

LAT. 41 DEG. 51.5 MIN. N.
LONG. 69 DEG. 40.0 MIN. W.

The folks at Brighton couldn't have been nicer. When the Army vehicle pulled up to the Emergency Room, Mari was immediately brought in and cared for, no questions asked. In the Public Health Service, they were used to caring first and asking questions later. Insurance wasn't a pre-requisite for treatment, especially if you were from a merchant or fishing vessel. When things had calmed down and Mari was sleeping comfortably, a nurse came into the room to finish the admissions paperwork.

"Now, you say she's one of the crew on ... um ... the F.V. *Elizabeth Gale* out of Point Judith. Is that correct?"

Greg, Ozzie and Mack looked nervously at each other. "Yes, that's ... right," Mack eeked out.

"And her name is ...?"

Mack caught eyes with Ozzie, then scrunched his face in silent panic.

"Sh ... sh ... sh ... sh ... she ... she's m ... mmmmmy ... my ... s ... s ... sis ... sist ... sist ... sister," Ozzie stammered out as Greg and Mack looked back at him in wide-eyed shock. "S ... s ... s ... s ... su ... sss ..."

Before Ozzie could finish, a voice came from the door: "Susan Gwendolyn Marsden! Her name's Susan Gwendolyn Marsden." It was April! April? "And she ships out as cook for these ruffians, if you can believe it," she joked, trying to deflect the severity of the situation. "Two-twelve Sainsbury Avenue, Narragansett, Rhode Island," she continued straight faced. "How is she?"

"She's a lucky girl, that's for sure. They got her out of the water in the nick of time." The nurse checked the chart, "She's got a few cuts and bruises, but there's nothing broken and all her vital signs are good. The hypothermia symptoms are gone ... no frostbitten limbs or members. She's had a mild concussion but I'd say she'll be healthy enough to release by tomorrow, barring anything unforeseen."

The nurse pulled April aside and whispered in her ear, "I guess that explains why we couldn't understand her gibberish ... she must have some kind of a speech impediment like he does. Shame, too. What a pretty girl. I think she thought she was near to death. She wanted to make sure we knew she was a Christian; that was the only word we could understand. If need be, the Chaplain comes in at eight, but she'll be fine."

While April and the nurse were carrying on a normal-sounding converstion, Greg, Mack and Ozzie were still trying to pick their chins up off the floor. April! How in heaven's name did she know? Greg hadn't even had time to call her! He shook off his surprise and did the only thing he could do at that moment ...

"Prillie, you never cease to amaze me," he said as he interrupted their conversation and hoisted her into his burly arms, sweeping her off her feet. "How did you ..."

"Before you two get too carried away," the nurse butted in, "can you please tell me what happened to Susan so I can finish my documentation?"

"I'm just a skipper's daughter, that's all," she whispered as she buried her head against his chest. She raised her face, kissed Greg, then winked at him. "So what happened, did she try to work the deck with you guys again?"

"Oh ... oh ... yeah. Yes. We told her not to, but you know, um, Susan. She's always trying to help," Mack joined in. "You know those Marsdens ... can't wait to help ..."

"I remember trying to help my father and brother one day. I went overboard in the twine, too, but I was lucky enough to do it on a summer day and I didn't hit my head on the rail like she did, right? She's still just as beautiful as ever, though, don't you think, Mack?" April asked.

He smiled back and mouthed a silent "thank-you," then looked over at the sight in the hospital bed. The I-V tube running to her wrist ... the monitor screen cycling away showing her pulse ... her beautiful light brown hair falling around her face in curls ... the rythmic rise and fall in her breathing. He shook his head in ardent disbelief as Ozzie crooned from the back of the room:

Fairy tales can come true ... they can happen to you ...
If you're young at heart ...

"C'mon, boys," April said. "I'll take you down to the boat. I'm sure Ricky's got your hail listed on the auction by now. He's probably pacing the deck waiting for help to slide over to the fish pier. Mack, I'll tell him to hire an extra lumper to take your place unloading ... that is, if you want to stay here."

Mack didn't really hear what she had said but waved a good-bye in their direction. He was sitting next to the bed, bent over in the chair so that his head was next to Mari's. She woke slightly, put her hand on his cheek, then went back to sleep muttering the words "*rakastaa kapteeni.*"

"See what I mean? I wonder what that meant," the nurse whispered to April as they went out into the hall.

April looked back into the room and saw their quiet glow before she shut the door. No translation needed.

Late that afternoon, Mari was sitting up in bed and Mack was spoon-feeding her some soup when April burst into the hospital room.

"Mack! You've got to stop them! They're leaving!" she cried.

"Who? What's going on? What's the matter, April?"

"Ricky's leaving the dock! He said he was going to go back where the fish were, make a short trip, take out in the Vineyard, then head back to the Point."

"What about me?" Mack worriedly asked. "Am I fired?"

"Of course not. You're his little brother, for Pete's sake! It's not you, Mack ... Ricky said you were fine right here and could get a ride back to the Point with me tomorrow. It's not that ... it's that damned sea witch place ... he's heading back!"

"April, I've never seen you like this. What's the problem?"

"Mack, I asked, then I pleaded with him not to go back there. I've got an awful feeling about this. We can't let them go!"

"What did he say?"

"He said that he was the skipper and that was that. He's even left the dock with money in his pocket!"

"If he's already gone, what can I do?"

Mack certainly didn't understand everything, but he had gained an acute appreciation for April's intuition. He thought for a second, then snapped his fingers and handed the spoon to her.

"This is April," Mack said. He moved his hands to show Mari that was her name, then repeated, "April. April. Okay?"

"Ah-preel" she said and nodded in understanding. "Ah-preel."

Mack ran from the room and went to the pay phone at the end of the hall. He fed every piece of change he had into it, then dialed the operator and asked to be connected to the Boston Marine Operator. It wasn't long before the call went out on the VHF:

"Fishing vessel *Elizabeth Gale*, fishing vessel *Elizabeth Gale*, this is the Boston Marine Operator, Boston Marine Operator, channel sixteen. Please shift and answer channel twenty-eight for traffic. Boston Marine to the *Elizabeth Gale*. Shift and answer channel twenty-eight for traffic. Over."

The Lizgale was just clearing Point Allerton when Ricky looked up at the VHF and shook his head. "College idjut," he muttered as he grabbed the microphone.

"Boston Marine, the *Elizabeth Gale* on twenty-eight, over."

"Roger, *Elizabeth Gale*, Boston Marine Operator. Stand by for traffic, over."

"Ricky, It's Mack ... um ... where you going, over?"

"I'm gonna take care of my business, and I'd like you to take care of yours, book-boy. I'll meet ya back at the Point, over."

"Cap, are you sure that you want to head back out there? Um ... over."

"I think I can run this boat without a scrod tellin' me what to do, if that's what you're askin', over."

"But, Ricky, you know April better than I do. She's pretty upset, over."

"Sorry, Old Man, but this rig's goin' where I point it. As far as I can see, you've got more to worry about than I do, don'tcha? Over."

Mack had to think quick. How in hell could he get him to turn around? He searched his brain, then threw the only card he had left …

"Cap, April said you left with money in your pocket. You know you can't start a trip like that. You know you can't do that! Over."

"College idjut! I've gotta save every dime I can get, and so do you. When I catch up with you at the Point I wanna talk about throwin' some money together to buy out Doris. We fish hard, pay off this boat, then we get one for you, then two boats pay for one. Besides, I'm thinkin' like I'll need to buy a wedding present. Looks like you'll have a real stupid attack goin' sometime in the future. Look, Mack, I've gotta pay attention. You go take care of the women and I'll see ya back at the Point. *Elizabeth Gale* off and clear with the Boston Marine Operator, and thanks for the assistance, over."

"Boston Marine off and clear with the Fishing Vessel *Elizabeth Gale*. Have a good trip, Captain."

Three days later and all the Point boats were tied up again. There wasn't a sound … or a dry eye … when Ozzie went to the front of the crowd on the state pier and roared out a song, tears pouring down his face, his white-knuckled fists clutched in front of his body. Many years later he said he'd picked this particular song for Ricky's funeral because the Hellion always revered his late grandfather who was a merchant captain as well as a fisherman. He died a hero on some secret mission in World War Two …

They dragged her down dead from Tobermory,
Too cheap to spare her one last head of steam,
Deep in diesel fumes embraced, rust and soot upon the face,
Of the one who was so clean …

They brought me here to watch her in the boneyard.
Just two old wrecks to spend the night alone.
It's dark inside this evil place,
Clouds on the moon hide her disgrace;
This whiskey hides my own.

It's the last watch on the *Midland*.
The last watch alone.

One last night to love her,
The last night she's whole.

My guess is that we were young together.
Like hers, my strength was young and hard as steel.
And like her too, I knew my ground,
I scarcely felt the years go 'round ...
In answer to the wheel.

But then they quenched the fire beneath the boiler,
Gave me a watch and showed me out the door.
At sixty-four, you're still the best;
one year more and then you're less
... than dust upon the floor.

It's the last watch on the *Midland*.
The last watch alone.
One last night to love her.
The last night she's whole.

So here's to useless superannuation.
And us old relics and the days of steam.
In the morning, Lord, I would prefer,
When men with torches come for her,
Let Angels come for me.

It's the last watch on the *Midland*.
The last watch alone.
One last night to love her
The last night she's whole.*

---

*Music and lyrics by Stan Rogers. www.stanrogers.net

29
SEBAGO

Lat. 43 deg. 51.1 min. N.
Long. 70 deg. 30.0 min. W.

Chappy's old Dodge was still rolling along a few miles away from Sebago Lake when Mack finally left the memory of the ordeal and tuned in to the cab's lively conversation.

"Yuh, well, I guess the old general was right, huh?" Chappy asked.

"Who?" Mack butted in.

"Who? General George Patton, who else we been talkin' about? Gawdawlmighty, Spice, ain't you payin' 'tention?"

"I guess I was thinking about something else. Are we almost there?"

"If we're lucky, it'll be a few minutes," Greg answered.

"Hey guys," Mack said, "I think when we get close, we should leave the truck and go the last few hundred yards on foot. If something's going on, we don't want to announce we're there and cause more problems. God only knows if the State Police took us seriously, but I'm not planning on it."

Greg shook his head in agreement and said, "Good idea, but if we can believe the gas guage, we'll be out of gas before we need to ..."

At that moment, Chappy's truck sputtered, bucked and went silent as he steered to the side of the road.

Mack dropped his face into his hands as they coasted to a stop. "Murphy's Law, again!" he moaned.

"See? That's what I was sayin' about Patton," Chappy chimed in. "He said that Murphy's Law didn't apply, 'cause if it was true, then it must have a flaw built into it, too. The General said you couldn't use Murphy's Law for an excuse 'cause Murphy's Law was written by some guy named O'Brien ... that's the mistake, see? And ..."

"Chappy, we've got a life and death situation here!" Mack said, his hands flailing in frustration. "What would Patton do now?"

Chappy got out of the truck and slid under the frame, tinkered around, then got back into the seat and went through his start-up routine. The old Dodge kicked and back-fired as the engine turned, but it eventually came back to life. He pulled back out onto the road and continued on. "That's what Patton woulda done, Spice," he said sternly.

Mack managed a weak smile at the upturn of events and asked, "How'd you do that? I thought we were out of gas!"

"Gawdalmighty, Spice, you don't think I'd head into battle with just one tank of fuel do ya? I was lead driver in the Red Ball Express ya know. One thing I know is how to move fuel. Ole' Betsey here's got two tanks in her, okay? Now, Greggie, you just do the naviguessin' and tell me where to turn, and Spice, just sit back and enjoy the ride, will ya? And don't get so cussed het-up!"

Dr. Grayson parked the van and the passengers got out, glad to stretch their legs. She introduced everyone to Petey, then they started down the path through the tall pine trees to the lakefront.

"April's out on the lake," Petey said as they strolled along. "You know our only time off without students is this afternoon, so she took one of the sailboats and went for a ride around Squaw Island. You know the signal, Dr. G., would you like to let her know you're here?"

"I think Mr. Brown should have the honors," she said. "Will you show him how to display the colors?"

"Sure thing."

Petey, Dr. G., Chris and all the students walked out of the pine trees and went down to the beachfront section of the camp. "It's really a rudimentary system, but it works every time," Petey explained. "Follow me, is it Doctor Brown?"

"Not yet, and it's just Chris," he answered, "I didn't catch what your field of study was, Dr. Lamell. Special education?"

Petey laughed. "No, I'm afraid not, and just Petey works for me, thanks. Nope, I help out here and split the administrative chores, but I mostly work from memory on spec. ed. My doctorate's in mathematics. I poop around over at MIT during the academic season, but I made sure I always have the summers to be here; Occam's Razor and all that aside, of course."

Chris smiled in understanding as they stopped at the bottom of the flagpole. Above them, the stars and stripes waved in the warm late summer breeze. Petey lowered the flag, raised it to the top, lowered it again, then clipped on another red colored flag underneath it. He handed the rope to Chris and motioned for him to raise both flags to the top. As the students and Dr. G. looked on, the American Flag resumed its rightful place at the top of the pole, with a triangular red flag flying beneath it.

"That's the old small-craft advisory flag from Pt. Judith," he explained, pointing to the southward. "April's in the boat way off there just to the east of Squaw island. See the sail?"

Everyone looked, and sure enough, the boat's sail indicated that she had seen the signal and was turning around to head back to the camp.

"She'll be a little while tacking back here. Hey, the dining hall's open for business, buffet style. You folks hungry from your trip?" Petey was answered with a chorus of 'yesses' and he led the way up the hill to the screened-in mess hall that overlooked the beach. "The kitchen's this way," he beckoned. "Everything's right here ... just help yourselves!"

The students dug into the food locker while Petey went back on the porch and sat down between Chris and Dr. G.

"This sure is a beautiful place here, Petey," Chris marveled as he crossed his long legs in front of the adirondack chair he was sitting in. "How long have you people had the camp out here?"

"Oh, a few years now, I guess. I was a student here when I was in my high school years, then I worked here during college. I kind-of let the place grow on me, or with me, or in spite of me, I guess. April's helped a lot of kids, including me, over the years, that's for sure. Hey! Speaking of beautiful places, what's going on out at the island?"

"It's been a great summer," Dr. G. answered. "Not too much fog, a great crew of kids, and we've made a few curriculum changes that went extremely well, thanks in no small part to Chris Brown, here. He's also engaged in some compelling research, wouldn't you say, Chris?"

"Well, it's not math at MIT by any means, but I think it's really important to document what's happened to the fishermen. My point of view is that they are hunter/gatherers, hence, they are an ancient culture trying to fit into modern times."

"Sort of like technology changes, but people don't?" Petey asked.

"Exactly! My words exactly!" Chris exclaimed.

"Well, that's not genius talking," Petey quipped. "Take math, for instance. For the most part, we're just working off of old postulates, equations and principles that were figured out and handed down to us by ancient cultures. Throw the keys to that van to Galileo or da Vinci and they'd be lost on how to start it or drive it, but I bet they could figure out how to build it, and after a couple hours they'd probably know a lot more about it than you and I ever could."

Chris and Petey chatted on for a few more minutes, new acquaintances who sounded like the oldest of friends. Dr. Grayson sat silently and listened as she maintained a constant watch for April's boat. It wasn't long before the fluttering of sails was heard and April's boat rounded the point and slid towards the dock.

"Oh. Here's April now," Petey said as he started to get up. "I'll go help her tie up."

Dr. G. reached out and held him in his chair with her hand. "Petey, why don't you let Chris go help her ... he's an old sea dog," she said with enough force in her voice and hands to make her wishes clear.

Petey was puzzled, but answered, "Sure. Okay Dr. G.," as he sat down.

Dr. G. and Petey watched from the porch as Chris strode down the hill and went out on the pier, waved hello, then bent down to grab the docklines. April was back-to him, trying to gather up the flapping sail and secure it before she drifted away from the pier.

"This is where *my* research comes in," Dr. Grayson said to Petey as she shaded her eyes for a better view of the dock. She sat forward in her chair, then whispered, "It's time to sink or swim, Chris Brown."

"The entrance road to the camp is right around the corner, Chappy," Greg said. "I think we can leave the truck on the old logging road just beyond there and walk through the woods. That'll put us on top of the rise and we'll be able to see the whole layout of the place."

"Sounds good," Mack said, tensely. "I just hope we're not too late!"

Chappy followed Greg's directions and turned off the main road about fifty yards beyond the camp's sign. They bumped in off the street a little ways, then Greg gave the slashed-throat sign to kill the engine.

"Okay. I say we head for the top of the hill and see what's goin' on," Greg said. Mack was already jogging down the old dirt road. Greg caught up and they hustled along together, as Chappy shook his head and walked along behind, still keeping an enviable pace for a man of his age.

"Kids," Chappy muttered in disgust as he watched them run away. "Buy 'em books and they'll tear out the pages. I s'pose there's no reasonin' with 'em, so just let 'em go!"

Mack and Greg reached the top of the hill, laid prone and peered over the top of the rise. Their worst fears were already coming true; the school's van was in the parking lot and the whole camp was silent. No one was down by the log cabins, no one at the rec hall, no one walking on any path. No movement except for a sailboat coming north through Camp Cove. Wait! The sailboat! It was a camp sailboat, and … the long brown hair of the skipper!

"Oh my God, it's April!" Greg whispered in fright. They rose to run down the hill and warn her, but a car was heard rumbling along the road and stopping in the parking lot. They froze and crouched back down, then looked down the slope to the left.

"Dear God, we've gone from worse to worser," Mack groaned. "Here's Mari, Liz and Gale!"

Greg snapped his fingers. "You go back and tell Chappy to get to them and get 'em outta here. I'm gonna head down to the point and try to intercept April before she sails into this trap!"

Greg quickly went down the side of the rise and rapidly made his way along the shoreside path, staying out of sight of the camp. Mack ran back and convinced Chappy to cut through the woods to the parking lot and tell his family to get to safety by way of the local police station.

As April sailed by Greg's position, he tried furiously to get her attention, but she was tacking the sails back and forth and had her head behind the fluttering canvas when he tried to raise her. Oblivious, she sailed right on by, went up the cove and headed for the dock. He ran back to his original outpost on top of the hill and was joined there once again by his old shipmate.

"I told Chappy to tell them to get to the police station and bring some help," Mack said, out of breath. "At least they're safe for the time being."

"Good. I haven't seen a sign of anybody ... Dr. G., the students ... Chris Brown!" Greg squeaked out between breaths. "What do you s'pose is goin' on?"

"You got me, Cap," Mack said as he rolled over to look beyond the top of the hill and survey the scene again. "Uh-oh! Greg! Look!" he fearfully exclaimed.

"It's ...

Chris Brown reached over, took hold of the bow line and secured it to the cleat on the pier. He walked aft, knelt down and repeated the same moves on the sternline. As April finished tying the sail around the boom, she said, "Thanks for the help. I'm April Gregory. Pleased to meet ..."

She turned around in mid-sentence and was face to face with Chris when she stopped, gasped and put her face in her hands. Tears began to flow uncontrollably. She was crying and laughing, in waves of alternating emotion as she jumped from the boat and fell over him, sprawling both of them on the dock.

"It's ... you!" she shrieked. "It's you! We always knew you were alive! It's you!"

From the porch, Dr. Grayson and Petey could hear — and see — the shrieks of joy coming from the waterfront.

Petey stood, looked over at Dr. G. and asked, "Is she all right?"

Doctor Grayson, wise sage, mother to none but mom to all, stern taskmaster and brilliant academician was letting her own tears flow in torrents. She couldn't answer. All she could do was stand, hug Petey and sob away.

"He's got her! He's got April! Let's go!"

Mack and Greg bounded over the top of the hill and ran to the beachfront like a scene out of D-Day. They ran with all their might as Greg yelled, "I'm comin', Prillie! I'm comin'!"

"Let her go!" screamed Mack as he and Greg raced down the dock and muckled Chris Brown around the neck and arms as April's grasp on him was torn free. The three rolled into the water with flailing limbs as Greg and Mack tried to gain supremacy over the dumbfounded but athletic and instinctively self-defending Chris.

When Chris's face broke water, he gasped for breath and yelled, "What the ..." just as Mack hauled off and swung a punch at him, doing more harm to his own knuckles than Chris's face.

"What the hell's going on?" Chris yelled again just before his head was drawn underwater by Greg's mighty grasp and Mack's fisticuffs.

"Stop! Stop!" April screamed at the top of her lungs. "Stop!" she cried, as she bent over the water and yelled down below. "Greggie, Mack! Stop! Let him go!"

Chris got the upper hand and surfaced, flipping Greg away. He reached down and grabbed Mack's collar, bringing Mack's sputtering, coughing face above water.

"Listen, you two," he said sternly, keeping a firm grip on Mack, "Fun's fun, but would someone mind telling me what in hell you guys are doing?"

Before April could speak, a voice came from behind her. A wavering, incredulous, disbelieving voice.

"Kristiian?"

Mari jumped from the dock and into Chris's arms. They clutched each other in an embrace that had been pent up for twenty years. There were enough tears flowing to fill the whole of Sebago Lake another foot higher.

Greg swam over and draped his arm around Mack's shoulder, their eyes bulging and their mouths agape.

"Lord luvvaduck," they gasped.

EPILOGUE

The watchtower at Dam'iscove, two days later …

"Quite a sight, isn't it, Mack?"

"Hard to believe, that's for sure. I guess it's proof that miracles still happen. 'Course, you had it figured before all of us."

Dr. Grayson shrugged. "The power of faith, that's all."

Jim Mackenzie and Felicia Grayson sipped their tea as they watched Chris and Mari laughing at the end of the wharf. Chris was trying to teach his sister how to pilot his kayak without tipping over as she was struggling with the paddle, making more splashing than headway.

"They haven't stopped talking for two days, they've got a lot of time to catch up on," Mack said, still shaking his head in disbelief. "All this time I thought he was long gone for dead. I mean there was no trace of him anywhere — none! A miracle! Truly, a miracle."

"All he had to do was get under your nose, that meant you'd never find him," Dr. G. laughed.

Changing the subject, she asked, "Have you given any thought to the research you two were collaborating on? Things got a little out of hand, but he's still the best chance we all have for getting some objective information out on fishing. That was your hope out of all of this, right?"

Mack took a deep breath, exhaled, then turned away from the water view and caught Dr. G.'s eye. "It doesn't matter now. It was a last-ditch effort on my part, trying to educate the public through him. But it's too far gone. You know, Felicia, it's gone. It's done. Finished," he said.

"Whatever are you talking about?"

"Fishing. It's done. It's all over. His study will be a landmark piece for what happened historically, but it's too far gone to fix now. Close the casket after I jump in."

"Is that what your final report to Chris Brown's Ph.D. committee will say?"

"Well, all the stuff that's happened in the last few days kind-of forced me into living all those memories over again. I wanted to help save the fishing industry, sure, but more importantly, I really wanted to save that way of life, I guess. All the times we spent fishing out of the Point, all the things that have happened ... it's gone."

Dr. G. shook her head in puzzlement. "Mack, I've never heard you like this ... what in blazes are you talking about?"

"Well, I've been thinking about all the times we spent out there. Buddy, Ricky and Ozzie taking us in like we were family and all. Felicia, the first time I stood in the wheelhouse of that boat," he motioned his head northward to indicate the Lizgale, "the first time Buddy gave me the wheel I knew. The first time I had those spokes in my hand, I knew I was home. I knew exactly where I was and that was exactly where I was supposed to be. I knew what I wanted to do, period.

That's gone, not only for me, but for eternity. Nobody can ever feel that ... ever again."

"There's still plenty of people going out on boats, Mack, I don't ..."

"It's gone, Felicia! Gone!" he angrily snapped back. "When Greg and I got aboard those boats, we were going to do whatever we had to so that we could get our own boats. I spent every spare second up in that wheelhouse so that I could learn to be a dragger skipper. I went without what little sleep there was to get, and dammit, I saved every dime. All I wanted to do was work my ass off and be left alone. Hell, we were producing food, whoever heard of putting food producers out of business? This is America, dammit! You're supposed to be able to work as hard as you want! It doesn't matter now ..." his voice trailed off. He took off his hat and flung it into the air, then sat down.

After a lengthy silence, Dr. G. ventured, "It doesn't matter?"

"Nope. You know, they're talking about cutting the days-at-sea down again. They want to cut the days-at-sea from eighty-eight to fifty-nine days or some such foolishness. All because some bunch of flatlanders got together, hired a lawyer and took the thing to court, and all because they don't understand that every time you put in a conservation measure, just like this, the boats will land less fish. I can see it now ... 'they're catching less fish in fifty-nine days, so we need another drastic cut-back.' All from another bunch of people who've never set foot on a boat or even owned a pair of boots. It's not going to end until it's all gone. Hell, it's been more than twenty years of this madness ... they've killed it!" he said angrily. "I got to thinking as we were coming back to the island ... ahhh, it's stupid ..." He stared out at the ocean in silence, shaking his head in disgust. "I just wish ..."

"Go ahead, Mack, you know you're only going to tell me anyway," Felicia Grayson encouraged. "What were you going to say?"

"Back when I was a kid, Felicia, there was this cartoon that I always got a kick out of. There was this dog called Mr. Peabody and he had a pet kid named ..."

"Sherman!"

"Yup. Sherman. And they'd go back in time, see ..."

"For Pete's sake, Mack, I'm not that old! The way-back machine. They'd go back in time in the way-back machine, right?"

"Yup. Well, I'd like Sherman to set the way-back machine for the fall of 1975 and leave it right there. Set it up in the Smithsonian or something and leave it right there so that anyone who really wanted to see what freedom was like could look in and see it. Free! Free to go where you wanted, free to work as hard as you wanted. Free! ...

"... You know, right now you can't even take a boat out dragging without having a satellite transponder aboard and calling an eight hundred number before you leave the dock," he continued. "Every move you make is watched. Go over the line and you lose it all ... boat, family, house, everything. Every week, there's a new set of rules and regulations. Every time you open up the mail there's a new chart in there that makes the ocean look like a jigsaw puzzle ... 'you can go here, but not here, and only on every third Tuesday,' or some such crap," he ranted.

He swept his hand at the sea, then continued, "A buddy of mine just lost his boat because he was a few yards over the Canadian Line. Busted by the United States for being in Canadian water. Back when we were all starting out, we all fished alongside each other. There wasn't any line out there, and everyone got along for the most part. Now, it's craziness ...

"... And how about the guys today? Is there any guy out there who can put the spokes of a wheel in his hand and know he's going to own his own boat someday? Nope. The licenses are frozen by limited entry and the cost of a boat is ridiculous, plus no bank will ever go for it. There isn't a living soul who can stand in a wheelhouse and know he's home … he only knows he's in a nice place to visit. How do you spend your life just visiting, Felicia? How do you know what you want to do but all you can do is just visit? How? You tell me!"

"I don't know, Mack, I really don't," she answered sadly. She thought for a second, then asked, "So what would the scene in the way-back machine look like?"

"Me. Have Sherman zero the thing in on me. Me. I'm standing there in the Lizgale's wheelhouse with Buddy explaining things, Greg's down below cooking, Ricky's mending the net and Ozzie's singing to the engines. We're steaming off for wherever we damn well want to go … to do damn well what we want to … and not bother a soul! Just freeze that picture for all eternity.

"Sure, Mack. Sure. And what do we call it?"

"The last really free man in America. Just call it that."

About the Author

Capt. Kevin McCormick has, in his own words, "done everything there is that can be done in a boat ... that's legal." Starting out as a youngster lobstering and clamming from an outboard powered skiff, it was a short jump to shipping out as crew on gillnetters, draggers and lobster boats. After graduating from the University of Rhode Island, Magna Cum Laude, with two degrees in marine science, he worked his way up through the inshore fleets of northern New England and the offshore fleet of Point Judith, Rhode Island, eventually spending twenty-three years as owner/captain of two New England fishing vessels and a research vessel.

In succeeding years, Capt. McCormick has performed grant work and research for the National Marine Fisheries Service, generating technical reports in advocacy of fishermen cooperating with scientists on fisheries issues. He used his research vessel to create pilot coastal ecology school programs for middle schoolers, and even ran a whale watch tour ... complete with ocean kayaks. He also donated his expertise and labor to his hometown, helping to create a municipal aquaculture entity there.

Capt. McCormick now divides his time between the marine construction industry of Boston, writing fiction, building skiffs and performing music in his church and the surrounding community. He lives with his wife and two daughters on the North Shore of Massachusetts.